Mistress Oriku

Mistress Oriku

STORIES FROM A TOKYO TEAHOUSE

Kawaguchi Matsutaro

TRANSLATED BY ROYALL TYLER

TUTTLE PUBLISHING

Tokyo · Rutland, Vermont · Singapore

Published by Tuttle Publishing, an imprint of Periplus Editions (HK) Ltd.,
with editorial offices at 364 Innovation Drive, North Clarendon, Vermont 05759 U.S.A.

This book has been selected by the Japanese Literature Publishing Project (JLPP),
which is run by the Japanese Literature Publishing and Promotion Center (J-Lit Center)
on behalf of the Agency for Cultural Affairs of Japan.

Original title: *Shigurejaya Oriku* by Matsutaro Kawaguchi
Copyright © Atsushi Kawaguchi 1969
Originally published in Japan by Kodansha, Tokyo
English translation © Royall Tyler 2005

Library of Congress Cataloging-in-Publication Data

Kawaguchi, Matsutaro, 1899-
[Shigurejaya Oriku. English]
Mistress Oriku : stories from a Tokyo teahouse / Kawaguchi Matsutaro ;
translated by Royall Tyler.
p. cm.
ISBN 0-8048-3842-9 (hardcover)   ISBN 4-8053-0886-9 (pbk.)
I. Tyler, Royall. II. Title.
PL832.A92S513 2007
895.6'35—dc22   2006025198

ISBN-10: Hardcover, 0-8048-3842-9; Paperback, 4-8053-0886-9
ISBN-13: Hardcover, 978-0-8048-3842-9; Paperback, 978-4-8053-0886-8

DISTRIBUTED BY

North America, Latin America & Europe
Tuttle Publishing, 364 Innovation Drive, North Clarendon, VT 05759-9436 U.S.A.
Tel: 1 (802) 773-8930 Fax: 1 (802) 773-6993
info@tuttlepublishing.com www.tuttlepublishing.com

Japan
Tuttle Publishing, Yaekari Building, 3rd Floor, 5-4-12 Osaki, Shinagawa-ku, Tokyo 141 0032
Tel: (81) 03 5437-0171 Fax: (81) 03 5437-0755
tuttle-sales@gol.com

Asia Pacific
Berkeley Books Pte. Ltd., 130 Joo Seng Road #06-01, Singapore 368357
Tel: (65) 6280-1330 Fax: (65) 6280-6290
inquiries@periplus.com.sg www.periplus.com

FIRST EDITION
10 09 08 07 06   10 9 8 7 6 5 4 3 2 1

Printed in the United States of America

TUTTLE PUBLISHING® is a registered trademark of Tuttle Publishing,
a division of Periplus Editions (HK) Ltd.

CONTENTS

CHAPTER ONE

Life on the Sumida River

"Tokyo was so nice in those days!" Oriku narrowed her eyes as she spoke. It was early Showa, the late 1920s. She was in her early sixties, Shinkichi in his late twenties. She was talking about the city as it had been back in the Meiji period, some forty years earlier.

"You know, you could drop a line in the river from the garden of my place and catch a sea bass. The tide brought them all the way up here. In summer you could jump in from the jetty—people didn't swim so much as just cool off in it. That shows you how clean the Sumida River was back then."

She heaved a sigh and lamented the ever-grubbier landscape of Tokyo. Shinkichi, too, was born in Asakusa, and he knew how pretty the Sumida River had been in Meiji. When summer came, water sports took over the whole river, from the Ushijima Shrine to Kototoi, and there were children everywhere, learning to swim.

"When I think of Tokyo in those days, what makes me saddest of all is seeing the river so dirty now. I don't care how much the world has changed, or civilization has progressed—couldn't they at least do something about the river? If it *has* to be like this, they might as well just fill it in and turn it into a park." Flushed with indignation, she really thought they could do it.

"And then, at night the tanuki badgers would come out, and they would give the old caretaker such a fright that young girls wouldn't work here. There were no modern conveniences in those days—no automobiles or the like—and when you went out at night, you'd go four or five together, hand in hand, swinging lanterns, along the bank. It was quite something! Rickshaws wouldn't come late at night, and after nine o'clock there wouldn't be a soul along the Mukōjima embankment."

Oriku's Shigure Teahouse stood beside the river, among the reeds, on land within the Terajima village boundary. The Mukōjima embankment followed the river straight from Makurabashi to Kototoi, but at the Kototoi dango shop it turned right, then left at the Chōmeiji Temple corner and continued on between peaceful rice fields on the right and, on the left, a marshy expanse of reeds. In those days the embankment was made of high-mounded earth, with a row of sturdy cherry trees on either side. These were of course beautiful in blossom time, but they were lovely, too, when covered with leaves. In fact they had a special charm in every season. When the blossoms were at their height, people came in animated droves to see them, and on one side of the embankment teashops with reed blinds sprang up all along the river, from Makura Bridge to Kototoi. Over the entrance to each shop hung a festive curtain that fluttered in the breeze to invite customers in.

These were no simple wayside teashops, either, but the outposts of famous Tokyo restaurants, serving sushi, light dishes to go with saké, or hearty soups for teetotalers. Inside, drunken revelers would be singing and dancing, or having the geisha with them sing songs amid bursts of happy laughter. It was all a colorful flower-viewing paradise.

However, this noise and bustle went no farther than Kototoi. The teashops disappeared once the embankment split off from the river and turned away from the Chōmeiji Temple corner toward Shirahige Shrine. There the visitors were people of taste, come to enjoy the blossoms in peace. With paddies on the right, and on the left that long, marshy stretch of reeds, the gay flower-viewing pandemonium faded away.

The Shigure Teahouse, an elegant inn and restaurant, had been built there among the reeds. The inn-restaurant combination was still unfamiliar in those days, although no one was likely to complain if a restaurant guest somewhere spent the night. A sign to the left of the embankment announced, "This way to Shigure Teahouse." If you went down there, you came to a tasteful, wattled gate with the name "Shigure Teahouse" written in white letters on natural wood, hanging above it in a formal frame. From there a winding path cut through the reeds led you to the teahouse itself, with its thick, thatched roof.

From the outside the place looked like a farmhouse, but the inside was done in a luxurious sukiya style of restrained elegance. There were eight tatami-floored rooms, large and small. Behind the main building stood four smart annexes. No meat figured on the menu, nor sea fish; only loach, carp, whitebait, and other small fish caught in the Sumida River itself. The closing dish to every meal was chazuke, green tea over rice, served here with clams brought in from Kuwana on the Ise coast, and prepared in the shigure style, boiled down in tamari soy sauce and flavored with ginger and pepper. Those clams were Oriku's pride. She had them sent once a month from Kuwana, and she made sure they were of a quality unavailable anywhere else in Tokyo.

Shinkichi had tasted them, too. The shigure clams, as big as your thumb, were served on freshly cooked rice, sprinkled with flaked nori seaweed. You could eat them just like that, or you could pour tea over them and turn the dish into a rich, clean-tasting chazuke.

Shinsuke had eaten that sort of chazuke at Kuwana as well, but the clams there kept getting smaller with the years, until overharvesting made them harder and harder to find. The clams at Oriku's Shigure Teahouse, however, were famous among all those who came from afar to enjoy the pleasures of Mukōjima, and her extraordinary success in so isolated a spot shows just how delicious they were.

"People nowadays don't even know what good food is anymore. They have saké with some tuna sashimi, then some shrimp tempura with their rice, and they think they've eaten well. I don't care how good all that may be, you can't eat sashimi and tempura three days in a row. At my place, though," she declared proudly, "you can eat clam chazuke three hundred and sixty-six days of the year and never get tired of it." It was just like the irrepressible Oriku to add an extra day to the year's regular three hundred and sixty-five.

"And that," she went on, "is why people come from everywhere to enjoy it. Statesmen, industrialists, kabuki actors, samisen masters— they all used to come. Everyone who'd had their fill of fancy cuisine."

Her pride swelled visibly as she spoke. The wealthy, the powerful, the idly elegant: her Shigure Teahouse attracted the cream of them all. When you poured hot tea over those big, beautiful clams—still sizeable despite the boiling-down process they had been through—resting on their bed of warm, cooked rice, they would plump up again, delicate, succulent, bursting with flavor, color, and fragrance.

"Eating shigure clams at Kuwana is what got me into this business. I was amazed. I could never have started up this restaurant if I hadn't known that taste. There are more than enough restaurants in this world already, and you get nowhere if you don't try something different. At the time I'd decided not to make my move until I'd found a signature dish, something people would talk about. So those clams that time in Kuwana were, as they say, like the Buddha turning up in hell—they were a friend in need." She was extremely grateful to those clams.

Until Oriku set up her restaurant she had run a Yoshiwara establishment named the Silver Flower. In short, she had been a brothel madam. This is what she had to say about that.

"I was on my way to becoming a courtesan, you know. I was born a long way from here. I may look like a native of Edo, but actually I'm from the country, from Kōzuke Province. I was sold to the Silver Flower when I was eighteen. I'm an old woman now, as you see, but in those days I was just too pretty to be a farmer's daughter. Don't laugh! It's true, it's true!"

"You still are, you know."

"Oh no, I'm not! People can flatter me all they like, but when I sit in front of the mirror, the truth is there to see. That's all there is to it. In my late teens, though, I had a small, neat figure, with bright eyes and a cute nose. My family was so poor they sold me off to the Yoshiwara, and when I got there I was as naive as you can imagine. They couldn't just set me on my own, entertaining customers, so the owner and his wife had me stay in their own room at first and do the chores, to learn a bit of the business."

Soon enough the owner took a liking to Oriku and more or less raped her; and since the rules strictly forbade a brothel owner to carry on with one of the women of the house, she never became a prostitute at all. Instead she ended up as the owner's mistress.

"His wife was jealous, you know. I myself had no idea what to do, but he was slick, and he managed to talk her around. 'At my age I can't really see anything wrong with a man keeping *one* mistress, anyway. This place takes up your time,' he'd tell her without a qualm, 'and I don't see why you should complain if I amuse myself a little elsewhere. Oriku is just a girl, as innocent as she could possibly be—surely that's a lot better than some woman or other from who knows where!' And he just set me up as his mistress in a house at Hashiba. He was over fifty, and his wife was about the same age, so four or five years after I arrived she died, and he moved me straight from Hashiba to the Silver Flower. That's how I came to help run a brothel. Not long after that he died, too, and I became the proprietor. They had no children of their own, and their adopted daughter, Oito, became quite attached to me."

That was how she spent the next fifteen years. Then, when she turned forty, she found Oito a husband, let the couple have the business, and started the Shigure Teahouse on her own, right here at Mukōjima.

"The land was practically free, but the area was more or less a marsh, and whenever it rained for a while, water seeped up from everywhere. What a mess! I had to have earth brought in and the whole property built up higher, and that *did* cost a bit! It might look a little lower when you come down to it from the embankment, but actually it's at nearly the same height. If it wasn't, it would be waterlogged all year round." There was pride in her voice, too, when she described all the trouble she'd had when she built the place.

"Oito was dead set against it, you know, and she tried to talk me out of it. 'What's the point of setting up a restaurant in a solitary spot like that?' she'd say. 'You'll never get anyone to come! Stay with us here, instead, please!' She'd be almost in tears. But at the time I was fed up with the world. I'd been a man's mistress at eighteen, I'd worked like mad as a madam till I was forty, and the thought of doing that for the rest of my life made everything seem completely pointless. All I wanted was a quiet life, you see, somewhere away from people. I couldn't afford just to amuse myself as I pleased, though. So I set up this place. In the beginning, no one thought it would last. The times weren't what they are now. I knew nothing about publicity, I just went around to everyone I knew, giving away hand towels printed with the name and location, and asking them to give the place a try. I knew a lot of people, thanks to my job all those years, and other tea-house owners—the ones who'd send clients on to the Silver Flower—might bring their customers out, but the place was just too isolated, and they felt as if they'd come to some distant province. There wasn't much transportation in those days, and once you crossed the river you felt that you'd arrived at the back of beyond. That sounds crazy now, doesn't it, when it takes less than ten minutes by car!"

She laughed a man's full-throated laugh. The world was so different now from what it had been back then, she could hardly believe it.

"I'd had to ignore everyone's opinion to go ahead, and I was really worried about whether there would be any customers. The place started out less than half the size it is now. I'd managed somehow to get it going, but I was afraid no one would actually come all the way out there. The first one who did was actually the kabuki actor Danshirō, of the Omodaka House. The Omodaka House was another Yoshiwara brothel, practically next door to the Silver Flower. I'd known him for a long time. When he heard I'd opened my restaurant he became my very first customer. I can't tell you how happy I was. And he didn't come alone, you know. He brought his friend Yaozō with him, as well as five well-known kabuki actors. Nearly ten of them came crowding in, and threw us into a panic!"

The memory of how the minute her place opened she had had to look after almost ten customers, meanwhile scolding her inexperienced waitresses, had become her very favorite story, one that she proudly repeated to Shinkichi whenever she saw him. The shigure clam chazuke she had been so nervous about was a surprise hit. She felt big tears running down her cheeks, she said, when they told her they'd never eaten anything so delicious.

That was when it all began. Kind Danshirō spread the word to everyone at the Kabuki-za, and a procession of the greatest stars—Utaemon, Uzaemon, Ichizō, the real pillars of the stage at the time—turned up there. They in turn told others, until the fame of the Shigure Teahouse spread far and wide.

"They say actors are coldhearted, but it's not true. If Danshirō hadn't come then, the place wouldn't have become famous anything like that quickly. 'If you're tired of fancy dishes, try the Shigure Teahouse at Mukōjima,' he'd tell everyone, so the name of my place really got around. That makes him the Shigure Teahouse's great benefactor. That's why I still take special care of guests from the entertainment world."

"Doesn't taking care of them *too* well sometimes get you into trouble, though?"

"Why no, not at all. Why should it? I'm too old by now to lose my head over a man, but on the other hand, I'd hate just to dry up and wither away, and besides, I denied myself so much, for so long, while I was running that brothel, I won't have anyone criticize me for indulging myself a little."

"No one's particularly criticizing you, but I was just wondering whether you don't carry it a bit far."

"Nonsense! There's no such thing as going too far in playing around with men. Isn't keeping each fling to one night, then moving on to the next, a lot safer than losing your head over one man? What's dangerous is going on and on with the same one. You get stuck on him, you drag him home, you sit him down across the brazier from you—why, by that time, even you would never come back!"

In short, Oriku kept her little affairs tidy and clean. She had felt until she turned forty as though life was over for her. Then unlooked-for success had found her. She had enjoyed her flings, and she had been fond of younger men, but she had never gotten in too deep. In principle, each man had one night only, but she never left unpleasant feelings between herself and any man she had spent even a day with. Instead, she remained his friend and did all she could for him.

An actor by the name of Ichikawa Monnosuke was the one who started her off on this second life. Monnosuke, an onnagata, played the role of the wife for great actors like Danjūrō or Kikugorō. He lacked any particular looks, but he had a clear voice and a well-modulated delivery, and his acting, while not showy, conveyed great skill.

He would play the wife to Danjūrō's Chōbei in the great Bathhouse Scene; if the play was *Ōmori Hikoshichi*, he would do Lady Chihaya;

and Osono in the Saké Shop Scene was his greatest success of all. As much at home in historical as in domestic dramas, and a special stand-out in plays adapted from the puppet theater, he really was extremely good. He never won any great popularity because his performances, however expert, offered little beauty, but Oriku liked him very much.

"Did you make love with every man who appealed to you, no matter who?"

"What a dumb question! If you made love with every man you liked, you would wear yourself out and head straight for an early grave. Connecting like that is a matter of rhythm and timing—it just happens. That's how it was with even Monnosuke. He came to the tea-house by himself two or three times. Coming out all this way alone suggests a certain naïveté, but at the time I myself had no experience of this sort of thing, so Monnosuke became my first man."

"You mean you were a virgin?"

"You *do* say awful things, don't you! No, of course I wasn't."

"Well, but I suppose you'd been alone those ten years since the man who'd brought you to the Silver Flower died."

"Right, I was the madam, so I sat in the back room all day long and couldn't take my eye off the business for a moment. The last thing I could do was to get involved in some fuss with a man!"

"Since you thought life was over for you, Monnosuke must have been a second youth, so to speak."

"Yes, I suppose you could put it that way. I might not have had any affairs at all if I hadn't had that one with him, so I wouldn't have known anything about love—what I did with the proprietor of the Silver Flower was just duty, after all. My heart would never have known those moments of anguish. Monnosuke was a seasoned warrior who'd already been through a hundred such wars, and he had me, at forty, in the palm of his hand."

"I see. So your first real experience of a man came after you turned forty."

"Come to think of it, they say the pleasures you taste first in middle age are like rain that starts late in the day—they just go on and on; and it's true, for a while I was really swept away. Basically, though, I'm no fool, and I knew that if the rumor of what was going on ever got about, it would do the business I'd worked so hard to set up no good at all. That thought really shook me awake. So I backed away from him and put out the fire before it got out of control."

"I have to hand it to you there."

"Well, you know, it's the business that was at stake."

She lost her head over Monnosuke, yes, but that was the last time. Never again did she so forget herself. If a man showed signs of becoming overattentive, she would withdraw from him, put on a show of being terribly busy, and wait till he came to his senses. However, she never failed to do the right thing over the years by every man she had had that sort of bond with, be he an actor or some other kind of entertainer.

"Monnosuke is the only one I fell in love with. When we split up, I heard he was complaining that Oriku had abandoned him, but really, he was too old for that."

"But didn't Monnosuke keep coming to the restaurant, even afterwards?"

"Yes, he kept coming till he died. He was two or three years older than me, but in personal matters he treated me as a sort of elder sister and would always come to talk them over with me. I made him a lot of fans, too; and two years after we parted he turned up with a very unusual problem."

Oriku was in her fifth year of business, the economy was prospering, and the Shigure Teahouse was doing very well. Every day was a whirl of activity. She left the cooking to the chef, but she looked after the chazuke herself, kept a sharp eye on the size and quality of the clams, and personally made sure the tea was exactly as it should be. As she worked she was dripping with perspiration, the trailing length of her kimono sleeves tied up out of the way so she could get on with the job. Then, one day, in came Monnosuke, looking glum. Normally, whenever he turned up he was taken straight to the Paulownia annex.

"I wish you hadn't come just now," she told him, without even untying her sleeves. "I'm too busy. I have no time to talk to you."

"I'm glad you're busy, but surely you needn't be so greedy as to take it this far. You're making yourself a nice enough living already."

"What are you talking about? If the restaurant didn't do well I wouldn't make a living at all!"

"Now, don't talk nonsense. You have the Yoshiwara behind you. They wouldn't want you to suffer." He spoke with the gentleness of an onnagata.

Monnosuke, like everyone else, assumed that even after signing over the Silver Flower to the former owner's daughter and her husband, Oriku still received support from them, so that the Shigure Teahouse was just an amusement for her, and whether or not it did well was beside the point. Such talk enraged Oriku.

"That's enough of your wild guesses! You've no idea what you're talking about! Once I left I was just like anyone else to them—I would never look to *them* for any help! No, if this place lost its popularity, there'd be nothing for me to do but hang myself." As so often with him, she flared up and gave him a good piece of her mind.

"I see. So you get no support from the Silver Flower?"

"Of course not! I wouldn't take it even if it were offered. Instead the Silver Flower built me this place. I worked fifteen years there, after all. That was fair enough."

"Well, I don't see why you have to get so angry about it."

"Angry? Of course I'm angry! Here I am, working my head off, and people imagine the Yoshiwara is supporting me! I can't stand it!"

"Sorry. I should watch my tongue."

"Well, look out—you might do it again."

Between the two of them, it was impossible to tell just from their manner which was the woman and which the man. In fact, it was always like that. That's how it was with the gentle, feminine Monnosuke and the quick-tempered Oriku, every time they were together.

"I came today, you see," Monnosuke said timidly, "because there's something I simply have to ask you."

"Something outlandish, I'm sure. Well, I still have two parties of guests to look after. You can wait till I'm done with them."

Back she went to the kitchen, and untied her sleeves only after the two parties were properly taken care of. The kitchen was of a gener-ous size, since the building was a remodeled farmhouse, and its polished wood floor shone. The hearth was set into the floor at the base of the main pillar. Oriku sat and gave directions from there, and also personally made the tea.

Once the last two parties were gone and her sleeves were untied, Oriku washed her face and returned to the Paulownia. Monnosuke was drinking gloomily by himself.

"You look terribly depressed. Has something happened?" She sat down. Their affair might be over, but they understood each other and could talk about anything.

"I just don't know what to do. I can't tell anyone else, so I thought I might at least get you to listen to the story." He had none of his usual cheerfulness.

"If it's that bad, I don't want to hear about it."

"You're right, I'd much prefer not to trouble you with it, but you see, it concerns Mr. Matsushima of Kayabachō."

"Mr. Matsushima? He's your benefactor, isn't he?"

"Yes, he's been my benefactor for ages. When I took my present name, he's the one who provided the curtain for the event. I can't tell you how much he's done for me. When *he* wants something of me, I simply can't refuse."

"What *does* he want of you, then? Surely a man like that wouldn't be unreasonable."

"I'm afraid he's asking a lot, though. You see, he has this maid named Ohisa. You probably don't know her—she hasn't been with him that long."

"No, I don't know him well enough to know his maids. Are you saying you've gotten this Ohisa pregnant, or something?"

"Goodness no! And if I had, do you really think I'd come to you about it? No, the one who's gotten her pregnant is Mr. Matsushima himself."

"Oh dear, that's poor, knocking up one of his own maids. It isn't like him."

"It certainly isn't. It seems his wife gets after him about everything. She doesn't know yet, so apparently so far, so good; but he'll really be in for it if she ever finds out. On top of all that, Ohisa is getting big, and she's left the shop to go back to her parents."

"Why are you carrying on to me this way about somebody else's love troubles? I'm busy, and you could spare me this nonsense."

"No, no, I haven't even gotten to the real problem yet."

"What? You're impossible! For pity's sake, then, just get on with it! What *is* this all about?"

"Mr. Matsushima wants *me* to marry Ohisa."

"He *what*? Just like that? Big belly and all?"

"Yes. He wants me to marry her and treat the child as mine."

"Well, that's a good one."

"I think so too."

"That's what you get for messing about so long as a bachelor."

"Yes, and that's exactly why I asked you to marry me. But you wouldn't, would you!"

"Of course I wouldn't. Me, at my age, an actor's wife! The idea!"

"Yes, that's why you said you didn't want me. So it's your fault, too."

"It's not that I didn't want you. It's just that, to me, the business comes first."

"Right, so I've given up. In exchange, you might at least help me out. What in the world should I do?"

"That's entirely up to you. I can see you taking a wife, after tasting the pleasures of life as you've already done, but not then having your own child. You might as well just go ahead and say yes. People will accept it readily enough, if you let it be known there was something between the two of you from before. Mr. Matsushima's a very presentable man, and the child's bound to have looks. You don't, and that does you no good despite your skill. Mr. Matsushima's son would make you a good successor. Marry Ohisa, and everyone will be happy. Don't you agree?"

Eager as Oriku always was to be helpful, these words slipped out of her mouth before she even knew what she was saying. Monnosuke seemed to have been expecting just that tone of voice.

"Then I'll do as you suggest. I hope I may avail myself of your good offices."

"Good offices? What do you mean? This has nothing to do with *me*."

"But this isn't the sort of thing a man can look after all by himself. Won't you please talk to Mr. Matsushima for me?"

"Why in the world should *I* have to do that?"

"There isn't anyone else I can ask, and it isn't as though I was just adopting a kitten or something, you know. This woman is going to be my *wife*. There's my teacher to think about, and I'll have to introduce her to my other benefactors, too."

"Mr. Matsushima will take care of all that for you. You won't have to say a word."

"But I'm sure everything will go much better—much more smoothly, you know—if you step in as go-between. Nothing you'd say would ever strike a false note."

This was just what Monnosuke had had in mind. If he was going to marry someone's pregnant maid, he wanted everything done properly, or as much as possible under the circumstances, but he could not very well say so himself, so he had been planning to use Oriku all along.

"All right, I'll talk to Mr. Matsushima."

"I'll be very grateful."

"I've never known a man to go on and on making such a nuisance of himself as you do!" She looked angry, but she was not displeased. It was her way always to do anything she possibly could for someone she had had that sort of connection with, even once.

"Matsushima" was a well-established restaurant at the Yakushi corner of Kayabachō. Oriku had known the owner ever since her Silver Flower days. In his mid-fifties, with a pale, slender face, he looked good in his kimono of lustrous, striped cotton, and you could see at a glance that women would find him attractive.

Oriku put in a phone call to Matsushima's place and got him on the line. He willingly came out to Mukōjima. The streetcar ran as far as the Kaminari Gate, and from Azuma Bridge a penny steamer would then bring you to Kototoi. After that, it was just a matter of strolling along the embankment. That was the way most people came if they were in no hurry, but Matsushima was impatient, and at Azuma Bridge he hired a rickshaw.

It was late autumn. The cherry leaves were yellowing, and there were few people about. Still, the Asakusa Kannon main hall and pagoda, the Shōden temple grove, and so on, seen from the embankment, looked the part of famous sights of Edo. In fact, the whole view could have been a Hiroshige print.

"It's always so beautiful out here!" Matsushima did not go straight in, but instead stood a while in the entrance and gazed around him. When he came down from the embankment, the reeds were so thick that he felt as if he were dropping down into a marsh. The gate was almost hidden by the reeds. Once he actually reached it, though, they turned out not really to be that tall. The winding little path quickly rose until suddenly the full, tranquil sweep of the Sumida River opened out before him, from Hashiba on the far bank to the torii of Masaki Shrine. To someone from Kayabachō the place seemed like a country villa. Out on the river the red-footed gulls were gathering in flocks, and sailboats were drifting lazily by. The autumn stream was especially clear.

"You could live forever in a place like this."

"Not me, I'm afraid. I can't just take it easy, the way you do."

"The way *I* do? What gave you *that* idea? It's not like the old days anymore. There's a lot of competition. I'm off to the market at three every morning. It gets hard, when you're as old as I am."

"You're still doing that?"

"Still? How do you think my place would keep going if I didn't? For Japanese food, everything depends on the raw materials. I can't serve my customers anything I haven't inspected myself."

"I'm impressed. That's what makes your restaurant the place it is."

"And you—they say you go in person twice a year to Kuwana, which is why your clam chazuke is always so good. The quality goes down right away when you leave the marketing to other people."

They headed for the annexes, chatting about cooking. She took him to the Paulownia, where she and Monnosuke had talked. An original Hokusai painting hung in the tokonoma.

"All right, auntie, what was it you wanted to discuss?" Matsushima had hardly sat down before he got right to business.

"What do you mean, 'auntie'? You're being rude!"

"When a woman's over fifty, you know, auntie's what she's called."

"Well, not me. I'm only forty-five. If I'm 'auntie,' you're 'unk.'"

"Ha, ha, ha! Wicked repartee, as ever!"

He slipped out his tobacco pouch, while a maid brought in a tray of saké and two small dishes of wild greens. Matsushima was sufficiently fond of saké that it sometimes caused him problems. Apparently one of these problems was the maid Ohisa.

"What I wanted to talk to you about, you see..." said Oriku, pouring for him, "is this business of Ohisa."

Dead silence. Matsushima put down his cup.

"Monnosuke told me the whole story. It was a sudden shock for him, and he needed *someone* to talk it over with, so for one reason or another he came straight to me."

"He's completely lost his mind!"

"I don't see the problem. You needn't worry that *I'll* let this go any further, but it certainly might have if he'd told someone less reliable."

"Well, I suppose you're right, but I don't see why he had to tell you."

"I didn't want to hear about it, either, but now that I have, I'm concerned. You're not just anybody to me, and Monnosuke knows that. That's why he came to me."

"Does he know about you and me?"

"He wouldn't have come to me if he didn't. He came because he knew that *here* he could safely wash your dirty linen in private."

"So he knows, does he, about you and me."

He gave the cup back to Ohisa. "I'm a sloppy drunk, you know. Even with Ohisa, it isn't as if I had planned to get involved with her that way. Oh, I had my eye on her, it's true, but she's a good worker, and all I actually meant to do was be nice to her. It's drink that got me into this mess."

"You're always getting into trouble that way, aren't you. I suppose I'm one of your little lapses, too."

"That was a long time ago. I've forgotten all about it."

"Not *that* long—it was just three years ago, you know, and now you're asking me to dispose of a pregnant girl. Men are awful, they really are."

"You're right. I'm sorry."

He slipped off his cushion, put both hands to the floor, and bowed his balding his head low before her. "Please," he said, "I will be grateful for anything you can do to help."

For Oriku, Monnosuke and Matsushima were both partners in pleasure, and she had a bond with both. She could not very well abandon either.

"Get Monnosuke and Ohisa together before anyone finds out about the baby, give them just enough of a wedding reception to keep up appearances, and buy them a little house—anything will do. Then, in exchange for Monnosuke's taking on your child, look after him for the rest of his life." Oriku laid down the conditions she had worked out beforehand.

Matsushima accepted them as a matter of course. "I understand all that without your telling me. Obviously I'll look after him, considering the burden involved. He'll have a monthly allowance, too. You needn't worry about that."

"Forgive me. I was sure you'd say that, knowing you as well as I do. Obviously, an actor works only half the year. His wallet's thin, however brilliant a show he may make. To him, marriage means debt."

"I know, I know. Stop harping on it."

"Fine, I will. I gather Monnosuke would be glad to have the child, since it's yours, even if he had to ask for it himself."

"Anyway, I'll appreciate whatever you can do. It will be a relief to have you step in. I feel as though a great weight is off my shoulders."

"A woman from your past comes in handy at a time like this, doesn't she. This isn't the sort of thing you can discuss with family."

"You're absolutely right about that."

"This is why it's important to stay friends, so you can talk things over calmly, even after you split up. It's no good for either the man or the woman to end up glaring at each other in silence. I'm the living proof of that. I'm sure it's only because we were together once that we can talk this way."

She was repeating herself, but on this subject that was her way. She was always telling young people, too, how essential it was that if they had to part, they do so on friendly terms.

For a man and a woman to cross the last barrier and sleep together, their bodies merged, creates a bond beyond the reach of any calculation, a bond achieved under the guidance of natural affection. Once that depth of relationship is reached, honor it forever! Such was the philosophy of love that Oriku had defined and upheld ever since the days when she managed the Silver Flower.

Matsushima laughed. "All this heartwarming talk of yours just makes me want to get in bed with you again!"

"You must be joking! There's nothing more pathetic than relighting an old flame."

"As things are now, though, I'll never be able to look you in the eye for the rest of my life. I just won't feel right until I've gotten you where I want you again, in bed."

"And you think I'll go along with that, to make you feel better?"

Matsushima roared with laughter.

So their talk ended in merriment on both sides, and it got things moving in the right direction. Ohisa became Monnosuke's bride, and no one was the wiser. The reception was a small, private affair, and in due course she had a son. Monnosuke was overjoyed.

When an actor had a son the event was celebrated with red rice, but there was no joy for a daughter, since she could not become his heir. In other lines of business, the young man who joined the family by marrying a daughter could be officially as a son, to assure succession, but in the world of kabuki this was not possible. Sometimes an actor could perpetuate his name by adopting a fellow actor's son, and this worked well enough if he actually knew a suitable boy; but if he did not, that was that. Monnosuke and Ohisa had both been praying that it would be a boy, so they were very happy indeed. As for Mr. Matsushima, he gave them a formally wrapped present of a hundred yen—the equivalent of a million yen these days. For an actor's family a son was a golden egg, while a daughter made just another mouth to feed and was treated as a nuisance.

So Monnosuke was delighted, and when the boy was a month old Monnosuke brought him in his arms to Mukōjima, to show Oriku. He was a pretty, pale-skinned baby, with a distinct resemblance to Matsushima.

"You'll have to take proper care of your wife, now that she's laid you a golden egg," Oriku reminded him. That had been her greatest concern. Ohisa had already been pregnant with Matsushima's child when Monnosuke married her, and Monnosuke might sometimes say cruel things to her. The thought made Oriku feel sorry for Ohisa.

"Oh no," Monnosuke assured her, "I'm very happy, really. She looks after everything so beautifully I feel like telling her she should be a restaurant maid, and she's a marvelous cook too. That's not surprising, I suppose, since she spent all that time in a restaurant, but even so, she misses nothing, and on top of that she's brought me this lovely little boy! I can only thank both you and Mr. Matsushima." His joy was unrestrained.

"Mr. Matsushima will be so relieved to hear you say all this! Ohisa will be wanting to do her very best for you, considering the condition she was in when you accepted her, so make sure you're always good to her, since you are so pleased with her."

In short, it was a fine case of "all's well that ends well." Still, the whole thing made Oriku want to laugh. Monnosuke and Matsushima, both men with whom she had no trivial bond, had apparently been destined to become entangled with each other in this way.

"It couldn't have worked out better, and let's hope that it keeps going well from here," she would say to herself with a wry smile. "My little flings turned out to mean something after all!"

Thereafter, Matsushima and Monnosuke continued their visits to Mukōjima, making the long trip out there whenever they tired of fancy food and felt like some clam chazuke instead. From spring through autumn the place was full, but the stream of customers dried up when the cold set in. The menu on offer was hardly dazzling enough to bring people all the way from Azuma Bridge through the freezing river wind, and the sleepy faces of patrons crossing on the Hashiba ferry, homeward-bound from the Yoshiwara, disappeared when winter came. Silence settled over the place during the winter months. Nonetheless, mornings when it snowed were special. Quite a few fanciers of fine scenery would come out to view the snow at Mukōjima.

Oriku had this to say on the subject. "Nowadays the snow doesn't stay even when it falls, so there's nothing to talk about. The cars keep driving by and messing it up, so there's no time for it to accumulate. You can't enjoy a snowy scene if the road isn't thickly covered with snow. Maybe there are just too many people now, or the sun's hotter, or something, but anyway, what snow does fall melts right away, and it just doesn't feel like the old days. And it isn't just snow either. The way the view changes with the seasons is losing its charm too. Speaking of how pretty the snow was—people would come from far and wide to enjoy it, and of course, there's still that haiku of Bashō's, engraved on a standing stone at Chōmeiji Temple:

> *Come on, everyone,*
> *snow-viewing, slip and slide,*
> *till we all fall down!*

That just shows how beautiful the snow at Mukōjima used to be. I admit, though, it was quite a job, keeping the path that led down from the embankment clear. Snow would cover the whole expanse of dead reeds, till from the veranda it looked as though the houses on the other side would soon be buried. Not a single ferry crossed the river, and everything was so quiet that you felt you had been washed clean through and through. It was pretty lonely by yourself, so you'd invite someone to join you, and you'd have a drink together. Young people these days have no idea how delicious saké can be, when you drink it like that with a friend, gazing out at the snow. You'd make it good and hot, and with it of course you'd have a hot stew. Monkfish is especially good when it's snowing. Saké drunk like that with a man you like, over monkfish stew—why, it used to be heaven on earth! People in the old days enjoyed good food even more when the setting was a pleasure too. 'Food just tastes better there, the rooms are so pretty,' people used to say, but no one talks like that anymore. Everything's crude and obvious now. The tonkatsu breaded pork is thick, tender, and cheap everywhere, and everyone's happy with deep-fried pork, so it's no wonder they don't really understand food at all. Obviously, I have nothing against tonkatsu itself. Young working people are welcome to eat it instead of a bentō box lunch, but I wish they'd make some distinction between bentō meals and real food. The kind of bars where you just sit down and grab a bite are fine if you live in town, but don't people ever feel like drinking somewhere with a really nice garden? Even at my place—I built it in the Meiji period, after all, so there's plenty of land around it—you can enjoy clam chazuke in a handsome, elegant room. These days you could never make a profit from setting up a place like this, and once I'm gone, there'll be no one to carry it on. The days of pleasure in saké and snow will never come again."

Whenever she got talking like this, Oriku would lose herself in memories of how beautiful Mukōjima had been back in earlier years, and how many fine sights it had offered. And as she talked, she would become intoxicated with the sound of her own voice, until she no longer even saw the person with her and would begin to resemble some mad old woman chasing ghosts from the past. Like the mother of Umewakamaru, who wandered the banks of the Sumida River in search of her son, Oriku would talk on and on as she called to mind visions of the good old days.

She talked well too, and she had a fine voice. Back when she was a kept woman, living at Hashiba, she had worked hard to learn itchū-bushi samisen and voice under Miyako Itchū himself; so that her voice still swept her listener along with her, when she got going on old times. From age nineteen to twenty-five she had been someone's mistress, then till forty a brothel madam. Thereafter, for all her hard work, she had had not a care in the world, and it showed: despite her years she had nothing about her of the old woman. She had just turned sixty when Shinkichi first met her, but her face was as fresh as ever, her back was unbent, and although she never used makeup, she cut a very presentable figure.

Monnosuke's son grew up strong and healthy. He first appeared onstage at age six, and at sixteen he took the name Monjirō. His real father, Matsushima, soon passed away, and another of his sons—Monjirō's half-brother—took over the business. The restaurant continued to do well, and Monjirō, as much in favor with the son as he had been with the father, went there often.

There had been no talk when Ohisa became Monnosuke's wife, but word that Matsushima was Monjirō's real father got out in the end and became something of an open secret.

Whenever the offering changed at the theater, Monjirō brought the new program out to Mukōjima and spent a leisurely day there. An actor's son matures fast, drinks, and amuses himself with women; his is not the strict upbringing imposed on the son of a townsman. Still, Monjirō was relatively sober in his behavior. Even at the Shigure Teahouse he drank no more than a glass of beer, and he always addressed Oriku with boyish affection as "auntie." This naturally endeared him to her. She would take him to her own room, where they would eat their chazuke together. Then they might go out and fish from the dock, stroll off to Chōmeiji Temple for some delicately flavored sweets, and wander on to Hagi no Sono, the Bush Clover Garden, or Hyakkaen, the Garden of a Hundred Flowers. For Oriku, Monjirō was a handy amusement, and when he got back she would give him a bit of pocket money. The more she did for him, the more he played up to her, and he would keep her engaged in conversation until late in the evening. Sometimes he would even spend the night.

Since there was a lot of traffic in the main building, and people started clattering around there early in the morning, Oriku had taken over the Paulownia annex for herself. Even if the others were occupied, the Paulownia was hers. When Monjirō stayed over, he and Oriku would sleep side by side in the annex's main room, on separate futon, but in summer the mosquitoes were so bad that they slept within the same mosquito net. He even turned up suddenly late at night, drunk. He had taken a rickshaw from Azuma Bridge, and he plopped himself down on the kitchen floor, mumbling, "Please pay the rickshaw man." This was not the first time this kind of thing had happened. By no means a sturdy drinker, he suffered for it if he was made to drink too much.

"There's nothing worse for you than drinking more than you can take!" Oriku scolded him.

"I'm angry tonight, so please don't *you* be angry with me!" he said. Nice young man that he was, he made up to her just as though she had been his real mother. She had the rickshaw man paid and half-carried him to her private room in the Paulownia. It was early August. She put him to bed in the mosquito net, since the houses along the river were buzzing with mosquitoes, and being so drunk he immediately began snoring loudly. Ten o'clock had come and gone, the other guests spending the night were quiet, and the even the kitchen fire had sunk low. Oriku had changed into her nightclothes and was just about to have a nightcap.

"Give me some, too!" Still sleepy-eyed, he began to get up and move toward her.

"I will not! Basically, drinking isn't a good idea anyway, and I'm certainly not going to let you drink more than you already have. Just be a good boy and go to sleep."

"But I can't sleep when I'm angry! Tonight my friends made a fool of me."

"In what way?"

Oriku sat there in her nightclothes. It was chilly near the river, toward dawn, and she was wearing a thin silk slip with a pink sash. She may have been in her mid-fifties, but she still had considerable allure.

"A lot of us got together tonight in a bar behind the Kabuki-za, to brag about our conquests." He still looked sleepy.

"Young men do that, you know. You should have done your bit of bragging too."

"But I have no conquests to brag about! So they all made fun of me. 'That moron hasn't had a woman yet!' they kept saying. They treated me like an idiot. It made me so angry, I just couldn't take it anymore."

"Well, you weren't very smart. Why get angry over something like that? All you had to do was pretend!"

"But I'd *told* them I haven't!"

"Talk about being naive! What a baby!"

"Yes, I'm a baby, I know. Even if I'd faked it, though, it's still true, I've never experienced a woman. I've fallen for women, women have fallen for me, but it's just that I've never gone all the way, and it's driving me crazy! If I could just once experience the real thing, after that I could tell whatever lies I need."

He was hanging his head, looking sweet, comical, and pathetic all at once. She readily believed it *was* driving him crazy.

"You've never been to the Yoshiwara?"

"No. The women in places like that turn me off."

"Don't be cheeky. You'll find the most popular of them is just like any other girl. Well, tomorrow, go to the Silver Flower. Everyone there knows you, and you can have as good a time as you like. That should do, shouldn't it?"

"I don't want to. It's not that buying a girl worries me. I just don't like the idea. If a woman can feel strongly about being a virgin, then a man can, too. I want my first woman to be someone I can remember forever after. I'm damned if she's going to be some tart!"

His face was bright red. Come to think of it, there was something to what he was saying. There could be nothing wrong with a man cherishing his first time, just the way a girl is likely to do. Oriku had had her first experience with the owner of the Silver Flower, and even now the memory of that first night was clear in her mind. She understood how he felt. Still—

"If that's what you really insist on, you'll never find anyone. If you won't have a woman who's for sale, you'll just have to keep waiting for the right chance."

"Your talking that way just convinces me I'll end up with some woman who means nothing to me after all, and it makes me afraid."

"Well then, I see no way out. You're a man, not a woman. Why not just let things take their course?"

"Dammit, no! I won't have it!"

Red-faced, he glared at Oriku.

"Auntie, won't *you* show me?"

"What? *Me*?"

"Yes, you. You're always so sweet to me, and I really love you too. It'd be a memory I'd always cherish. Besides, in time I'm bound to be appointed principal actor."

"Wait a minute! I can't do *that*!"

Oriku straightened up. This was just too unexpected. Flustered, she was also overcome with confusion that the sixteen-year-old Monjirō should feel that way about her. Naturally, she had not yet given up her taste for men, and she fully intended to have a good time with the right partner, if she found one. Anyone other than Monnosuke's son might well have put the age difference out of her mind. Kabuki people customarily subjected a colleague's first sexual partner to minute scrutiny. They called the experience "fude oroshi," or "testing the brush." Oriku herself had been through it before. So far she had pampered him like a child, and she had no particular reason to say no, but the thought of Monnosuke's past with her convinced her it was out of the question.

"I won't have you talking like that. Please. I just can't."

She meant this to be her final word, but she simply could not mention Monnosuke. Needless to say, Monjirō fought back.

"I can't accept that. I've had the courage to be frank with you, haven't I? I'm asking you straight out: please, show me what it's like. I'm sure you've done this 'testing the brush' before. Everyone at the theater says you have. Please, Auntie, please."

As he spoke, he threw himself tight against her. The full impact of his strong young body toppled her over, and he clung to her leechlike, with all his strength. Struggling to push him away got her nowhere, and every word she tried to say came out too loud. The Paulownia was a separate building, it is true, but it was high summer, and every room, everywhere, was wide open. Any cry from her would be heard. For a while she resisted, but in the end she gave up and let Monjirō do as he pleased.

As soon as she woke up the next morning, she went straight to the bathhouse. It was behind the main building, and when there were overnight guests the water was heated early. Despite luxurious soaking, she felt as though the events of the night had soiled her in some way. She thought of the Monnosuke of old. Yes, now she had that bond with the son too, as well as with the father. An indescribable sort of shame seemed to flow through her, like black blood. She scrubbed her arms and legs, and dashed water over herself to wash away any reminder of what had happened.

She did not return to the Paulownia after her bath. Instead she went to a room facing the river and had a cold beer.

Monjirō got up and came to join her. His expression was happy and peaceful. At first he betrayed a touch of embarrassment, but he looked full of life. He was completely different from the night before.

"I'm sorry," he softly, his own beer glass in hand. "I'm confident now. I could have made up stories, but I'd never have felt confident until I'd known the real thing. I apologize."

For all his expressions of contrition, he looked distinctly happy.

"It's going to feel wonderful, later on, knowing you were my first. I'm just so happy, when I think I could fall in love with a woman even better than you." His words conveyed real joy.

"You're not to tell anyone, you know."

"No, I won't. But when anyone asks me who I 'tested the brush' with, I'll be proud that it was with the mistress of the Shigure Tea-house!"

And off he went to the Kabuki-za, still looking light and cheerful. Oriku's early feelings of revulsion largely melted away at the sight of his joy. Better me, she told herself, than just any woman. By evening she had forgotten all about it.

It was not Oriku's way to dwell on what was over and done with, and if anything somewhat unpleasant happened, she would usually have forgotten it in a few days. By the next day that business with Monjirō had healed over like a scratch, and she no longer gave it a thought.

Two years later, Monjirō was promoted and took a new name. Monnosuke, his father, succeeded to his own teacher's name and became Ichikawa Mon'emon, while Monjirō assumed his father's and became the third Monnosuke. Mon'emon then paid another visit to Mukōjima.

"I would very much appreciate your backing on this occasion," he said politely. "I will not ask for it again."

Oriku was of course resolved to do whatever she could, and she gladly agreed. Mon'emon never normally brought her theater tickets unless she particularly requested them. He faithfully sent her a summer yukata every year during the gift-giving season, but that was all. He never displayed the slightest trace of cupidity. Knowing his character as she did, she replied, "I was thinking about this, too. Knowing as I do what sort of man you are, I'll approach the Silver Flower about it too."

She went on, "Your acting success can rise no higher, now that you're Ichikawa Mon'emon. Let's drink to that before you go." She ordered a festive meal and served the saké in the great room of the main building.

"No congratulations could give me greater pleasure than yours," said Mon'emon, for all his years ever the gentle onnagata. Then, later, when a few drinks had given him the courage:

"I understand Monjirō made himself a bit of a nuisance to you."

"Yes, when he was drunk he'd come bursting in and say whatever he felt like."

"He *did*?" He stopped himself. "I gather you taught him how to make love," he said with perfect equanimity, as though it were the most natural thing in the world. "You shouldn't have gone to such trouble."

Oriku felt herself blush.

"He was so happy to have been initiated by the right person. I'm very grateful." He expressed his thanks without a trace of irony or innuendo.

"Initiated"—he had stressed that word with particular appreciation.

Ah, yes, teaching and learning . . . For Monjirō it had been an education. There had been nothing shameful, nothing uncomfortable about it. She had simply acted as his teacher. For Mon'emon's lover of all those years ago to spend the night with his son had simply been a matter of education, an experience a man needed. Mon'emon's gratitude came from the bottom of his heart. Some people might leer and snigger, but no, to him it was just education. Oriku was impressed.

Any lingering aftertaste was gone now. Oriku could experience the satisfaction of knowing she had done a good deed.

"For the ceremony, let's give you a proper stage curtain with both your names on it: Mon'emon and Monnosuke. 'From the Shigure Teahouse,' it'll say."

"Goodness! Thank you! I hadn't dared hope for so much."

Mon'emon bowed happily to her and left in an elated mood.

"That's what makes a man a man," Oriku reflected. Of her regrets at having been susceptible enough to let young Monjirō to get the better of her, she could only think, "I wasn't yet a true child of Edo."

That autumn at the Kabuki-za the promised stage curtain, bearing the names Mon'emon and Monnosuke, and inscribed "From the Shigure Teahouse," brilliantly captured the audience's attention. Oriku was there too. She looked radiant.

CHAPTER TWO

Tempura Soba

All the Shigure Teahouse customers, from the greatest man to the humblest, fancied Oriku. This was partly because Oriku did her best to make them want to keep coming.

"Look what a long way it is to get here! Wouldn't it be wrong of me not to flirt with them a little?"

That was her policy, and she left no guest entirely to the care of a maid. Celebrity or nonentity, it made no difference to her. She would step forward to greet each one; when the meal was served she would fill his cup in person; and, if requested, she would bring out her samisen to sing kouta or hauta songs, or even sometimes a kiyomoto ballad.

In her Hashiba days she had worked hard and acquired the requisite skill. She played the samisen well; her voice had strength and character; and when she sang, with a tipsy flush around her eyes, "Oh, to be with you, / oh, to see you, / I could grow wings and fly to you! / Poor little caged bird, / it's hard, too hard!" the guest would get all shaken up. "I do believe she's in love with me!" he would think, quite pleased with himself. All this made her a hit with the customers. These alluring performances of hers were never perfunctory, but when it was time to bring on the clam chazuke she would rush back to the kitchen, sit herself down by the hearth, check the hot water, and prepare it in person.

"The Shigure Teahouse's reputation would suffer if the clam chazuke was off," she would explain to the maids.

"Let someone else do it, for once!" one of her regulars might say.

"Oh no, I can't do that!" she would reply. "Why, this restaurant is my whole life!" When it came to the clam chazuke, she would allow no one else to touch it.

"If that's how you feel, Oriku, then you'll never be able to get away for a while. Isn't that right?"

"Never mind. I don't care to, anyway. I go to the theater or the music hall only during the day."

"And suppose you found yourself a lover. What would you do then?"

"Thank you for your kind concern," she would laugh, "but you needn't worry about *me*!"

She had so many customers that she did sometimes come across one she liked, but she amused herself only with artists from the entertainment world. She stayed away from respectable pillars of the community.

The artists in question included not only actors, but also kiyomoto or tokiwazu samisen masters, the heads of the Fujima or Hanayanagi schools of Japanese dance—whoever it was had to be at the top of his profession, or she would have nothing to do with him.

This policy of hers began when Monnosuke told her, "Never get involved with anyone conventionally respectable. Amuse yourself only with a man who lives by his art. A respectable man is gauche and susceptible," he went on to tell her, "and if you let him, he'll cling to you forever, which will make things hard for you. Once you're trapped that way you'll neglect your business, and the reputation of this place you're so proud of will suffer. An artist understands these things better. He knows what he's doing, and he'll give you no trouble, regardless of how things work out between you. An artist may very well have a romantic streak, but he doesn't get in over his head—he's able to keep things light and to part lightly. And another thing: always choose an artist of the first rank. A man like that values his reputation, and that makes him discreet. If he's an actor, go for someone like me or higher. If he's in Japanese music, he should be the head of his school. As for music-hall artists, if I may say so, you should have nothing to do with them. They can be fun, but your clientele here is first-class— you manage to attract even statesmen, people like Itō Hirobumi. The Shigure Teahouse would start to lose its luster if it got about that you were involved with some storyteller." To a degree Monnosuke was pleading his own cause, but his advice was perfectly sound. A first-rank artist undoubtedly had a first-class grasp of these things.

Monnosuke was the second man in Oriku's life.

Having been warned that actors were fine, but storytellers were not, Oriku stayed away from music-hall artists. However, she still enjoyed the atmosphere of music halls. The Silver Flower's former owner had been an ardent fan of the great Enchō I, and many artists visited his place. Enchō and his students would perform short comic and sentimental pieces there when the girls took their day off.

At the time, Enchō I was already old and had lost the vocal power of his youth, but his art itself continued to gain in refinement, and his sentimental pieces had something so special about them that he never failed to move his audience to tears. Particularly in the highlight section of his own *Shiobara Tasuke*, he gave a quiet, convincing intensity to the long scene—almost half an hour—between Tasuke and his beloved steed. Menaced by his entire family, Tasuke is about to leave his home forever when he bids farewell to the faithful horse that has long served him so well. The horse, Ao, sadly seizes Tasuke's sleeve in his mouth and will not let him go. Tasuke, overcome, embraces Ao's muzzle. "You're the only one who wants me to stay!" he cries; at which the Silver Flower girls all burst into tears, and Oriku too.

"Talk about mastery, that's the real thing!" the Silver Flower proprietor exclaimed after the performance. "Kikugorō V was so impressed by Enchō's *Shiobara* that he adapted it for the stage, but even *his* rendition of it didn't come up to Enchō's. Genuine mastery has frightening power." He simply could not get over it.

Oriku was swept along too. "What happens to Tasuke after he says goodbye to Ao?" she asked.

"I'm not sure, but he eventually finds himself a position in Edo, serves out his apprenticeship, and becomes a successful shop owner. That's how the piece ends, but a lot goes on in between."

"I'd love to hear the whole thing."

"Then you'll have to go to the theater where Enchō performs. I'll put in a word with him and have him do *Shiobara*, if you like."

"Where is Enchō's theater?"

"I hear next month he'll be at the Hakubai in Kanda."

"Oh no! It's quite a way from here to Kanda."

"It is not! By rickshaw you can be there in an hour, and if you go seven days in a row, you can hear the whole thing."

"But I can't do *that*, just to suit myself! I can't be away for a whole seven days!"

"Of course you can. It's all right. You work so well, you deserve a rest. Enchō's sentimental stories aren't just fun; they can teach you something, too. You've been with me since your teens, and there's a lot about the world you don't know. You'll learn all sorts of things."

So, at the proprietor's insistence, Oriku traveled daily, for seven days, from the Yoshiwara to Renjakuchō in Kanda to hear Enchō do *Shiobara Tasuke*.

The star of the Hakubai Theater was then Enchō's disciple, Enshō, and Enchō appeared there as a guest artist. This was about 1896. Kanda was indeed a long way from the Yoshiwara, but Oriku refused to give up. It meant something to Enchō, too, to be doing *Shiobara* by special request from a fan, and he put his heart into it more than ever. Each day's performance was a masterpiece. Oriku assumed at first that three days would do her, but once she began, she could not bear to miss the rest. Enchō's heyday was past, and physically he had visibly weakened. The beautiful voice that had once filled the hall was uncertain now, and sometimes difficult to make out. However, its defects only deepened its appeal, and it communicated poor Tasuke's suffering directly to the heart. Evening after evening Oriku forgot herself under its spell.

When Oriku was in her late twenties, having not long before become the mistress of the Silver Flower, Renjakuchō was Kanda's liveliest quarter and boasted no fewer than three music halls. The Tachibana Theater, near Sudachō, offered performances by such masters of the Yanagi school as Ryūshi, Kosan, Bunji, Bunraku, Tamasuke, and Shinshō; while at the rival Hakubai Theater you could hear Enchō and other San'yū-school stars like Enshō, Enkyō, Enkitsu, Enba, En'u, or Ensa. The competition was intense. However, the Yanagi artists eschewed any instrumental accompaniment, while the San'yū side offered, in addition to Enchō and his disciples, the colorful En'yū, who started the suteteko dance craze, the belly-laughing Mankitsu, Entarō with his horse cart, and other such madcap players, with the result that the Hakubai Theater was always far ahead. The ever-serious Ryūshi, who was the mainstay of the Yanagi side, clove to the straight-and-narrow in his art and accepted no one who deviated from it. The Tachibana Theater performances were as a result quite somber, and despite all this loyalty to the highest principles of the storyteller's art they could not compare in popularity with those at the bustling Hakubai. On top of that, the fact that Enchō was appearing at the Hakubai as guest artist meant that the theater was sold out every day, with the audience overflowing into the lobby and even a row of people standing all the way at the back.

Oriku had her seat reserved, of course, complete with a cushion and an ashtray, just to the right of the storyteller's dais. She entered through the greenroom before Enchō came on. All the San'yū artists knew who she was, and those who had warmed up the audience for the master would greet her politely. She tipped all the attendants and artists and was honored accordingly. Leaving the Yoshiwara at sunset, she reached Kanda about seven. Enchō mounted the dais only at eight, and after a bumpy hour in the rickshaw she was hungry. Except for one vegetable market, behind the Hakubai it was all restaurants: Kinsei, Miyoshi, Iroha, Hinode—one after another, offering everything from sea bream to chicken stew at Botan, or soba at Yabu. Soba being a favorite of hers, Oriku alighted daily just before the theater and went straight around the corner to the Yabu soba restaurant. She had filled out since coming to the Yoshiwara, and in her striped kimono and black haori jacket she looked older than her years. All heads turned her way when she came in alone. A flagstone path led straight in from the entrance, with a long, narrow tatami-floored space on either side for the patrons—the effect was quite elegant. Since she was by herself she sat down in a corner, and almost every day she ordered tempura soba. In flavor, the Yabu soba was a cut above that served elsewhere, and it was correspondingly expensive. Around town, plain soba generally cost two sen, but at the Yabu it cost three, and the tempura soba eight. The bowl of soba was served with a great big kuruma prawn, and the dish left a pleasant aftertaste. Once you had finished, you poured the hot liquid from the soba pot into your bowl and drank that too. Oriku was doing just that when two boys came in and sat down beside her. One was about ten, the other perhaps thirteen. They had on striped cotton with simple Kokura obi, and they had taken off their aprons, to carry them instead. With their pale, youthful faces they did not look like shop boys from some merchant establishment. Side by side they sat, right next to Oriku. Oriku still had plenty of time, so she took out her tobacco pouch and had a smoke.

"I'll have one tempura and one plain." The elder of the two placed his order. Oriku thought it quite extravagant, for a boy.

"Just plain for me," the younger added in a low voice, hunching his shoulders forlornly. The two might have come in together, but they did not order in at all the same way. The bigger called for two whole servings; the smaller for just one. The bigger boy spoke confidently; the smaller boy with embarrassment.

Smiling, Oriku continued to enjoy her smoke. Her pipe was fine bamboo from Laos, with silver fittings, and her tobacco pouch was gilded Dutch leather.

The place was crowded, and the soba the boys had ordered never seemed to come. They did not talk. The small one sat there in gloomy silence, while the big one looked sharply around him. At last their orders arrived. The big one ate his tempura soba with gusto, while the small one picked forlornly at his plain soba.

Oriku began to feel quite sorry for him. Clearly, his pocket money would not cover tempura soba; plain was the best he could do. She could bear it no longer.

"Young fellow!" she abruptly addressed him. He looked at her in surprise.

"I see your friend is eating tempura soba. What's the matter, then? Don't you have the money for it? I'll treat you if you don't. You must have some, too." She called the waitress over and ordered him tempura soba before he could regain his composure, then paid for his and hers together.

Eyes wide with astonishment at receiving so unexpected a treat from a lady he had never met, the boy placed his hands on his knees and artlessly bowed his head. "Thank you very much," he said. "You are very kind."

The bigger boy looked the other way and kept eating, ignoring the whole thing. The way he had ordered tempura soba just for himself, without a thought for his younger friend, despite their both coming in together, had made Oriku angry. That was why she did it.

"Who can those two be?" she wondered as she left. Respectable shop boys would not have been going out to eat soba at that time, and besides, there was something a little too casual about their dress. An odd pair! However, she soon forgot all about them. Enchō had already mounted the dais when she entered the theater, through the back. *Shiobara Tasuke* ended that night. The master's daughter fell in love with Tasuke, the two were married, and the scene in which she cut off a long, trailing sleeve to demonstrate the depth of her feeling provoked merry laughter. It all ended very happily. Oriku, who had come from the Yoshiwara seven days in a row to hear the great Enchō in his declining years, felt glad and fully satisfied.

"Now I have at last reached my sixtieth milestone," Enchō said after concluding the piece. "This is the year when I must bid farewell to the Tasuke you have loved so long. I am extremely grateful to all of you for coming to hear me, and particularly to a certain lady who has come from afar every day for seven days. To her, from the storyteller's dais, I offer my special thanks."

He bowed in the direction of Oriku, and the audience, who had no idea who she was, applauded. Blushing, Oriku left her seat and expressed her heartfelt thanks to Enchō. That was the last time she heard the master. He passed away two years later, in 1899. He was sixty-two.

So Enchō was gone; but Enshō, his star pupil, was very good indeed, and people said he even surpassed his teacher at *The Peony Lantern*, which he had inherited directly from him. Oriku's trips to the music hall, which had begin with *Shiobara Tasuke*, continued. She became a fan not only of Enshō, but after him of Ensa, En'u, and Enkyō, and, on the Yanagi side, of Bunji and Tamasuke. When the Namiki Theater was built on Hirokōji, near the Kaminari Gate, she went there three days a month or so, to hear her favorite artists. Then she left the

Yoshiwara and opened her Shigure Teahouse, and those same artists turned up there, one after the other. Enshō had died, but Enkyō, Enkitsu, and Ryūshi IV came; so did, more assiduously than any of the others, the young Kosanji and Bafū. They frequented the Silver Flower, and when they took the ferry across the river, on their way home in the morning, they would stop by for chazuke. Both loved their saké, and they drank plenty of it there, too.

"We're both broke today, so we're each going to perform for your guests instead—that'll get us off, I hope." The words were slurred.

"Fine, but you can't possibly perform this drunk. So forget today. Just go home. You can do it some other time."

"Come on, be serious. I don't care how drunk I am, I'm sober when I perform. Get all your people together in the main room. Tell your annex guests, too, if you have any. Tell them Kosanji and Bafū are each going to do a turn—oh, some of them will come, I know they will." The speech was still slurred.

Kosanji and Bafū were both popular young storytellers, and both were certainly good. Kosanji was fine-featured and slender, Bafū red-faced and roly-poly. The two together would make an amusing pair.

Every one of the restaurant staff gathered in the big main room, and the guests staying in the annexes gladly joined them when they heard what was going on. Among them were some handsome, elegant couples who pleased the two especially. Kosanji decided on *Five in a Night*, his special favorite, while Bafū chose *Old Bones*. Their quintessentially Edo art perfectly suited their audience. Drunk or not, when the time came, each sat up straight and sounded exactly as he did in the theater. They gave a wonderful show, and the delighted audience took up a collection for them.

"Oriku, this is all yours. Now we're even, I trust." They held out the bag with the money in it.

"Nonsense! A bill's a bill; a gift's a gift. You promised to pay your bill by performing. Whatever the audience wants to give you is something else. Take it! All right, I won't contribute myself, but *Five in a Night* and *Old Bones* certainly cover the bill!"

"I just knew you'd say that!" said one.

"You're a real child of Edo, you are!" said the other.

"Now, now," said Oriku, laughing, "calm down! Have a good time, by all means, but in moderation! You're the current Yanagi stars. The whole line depends on you. Your art's important, but so is your health. Please don't ruin it with drink!"

She put her opinion bluntly enough, but they were hardly the men to heed it meekly, and they kept stopping by. Kosanji seemed to have a crush on Oriku, but that was about the time when Monnosuke warned her against involvement with music-hall artists, and she had no desire to oblige Kosanji. Still, Yanagi and San'yū artists kept coming as before, crowding into the Shigure Teahouse for parties to celebrate promotion to principal artist, assumption of a new name, or succession to a great name from the past. The Namiki Theater was just on the other side of the river, across the Azuma Bridge, and that was where Oriku went whenever duty required her to attend an artist's performance.

The performers' names were written on lanterns hung in a row near the entrance to the narrow street, on the main avenue from the Kaminari Gate to Komagata. The ground nearby was paved with flagstones always kept gleaming wet. "Welcome!" the attendant who took charge of the customers' footwear would call out as you entered the door. It was a very comfortable theater.

Whatever other obligations she might have, Oriku always put her business first, and she went to hear a music-hall storyteller only during the day. The Shigure Teahouse had been going for three years when there was a special performance to celebrate the promotion of a young man named San'yūtei Shinkyō to principal artist. Oriku had never even heard of him, but he nonetheless took the trouble to come in person to Mukōjima in order to deliver the illustrated, block-printed invitation.

He left the following message: "I gather that Mistress Oriku goes to the theater only during the day. Three of us among the young principal artists have therefore organized a daytime performance at the Namiki Theater, and we would be most grateful if she were kind enough to come."

This happened while Oriku was away at the Yoshiwara, on a visit to the Silver Flower. She supposed she might recognize Shinkyō, since the invitation identified him as a disciple of Enshō IV—after all, Enshō had visited the Silver Flower often, to perform in Enchō's place. She felt sorry for the young man, reflecting that things could hardly have been easy for him after his teacher's death, and she looked forward to seeing whether he had inherited Enshō's skill, or whether anything at all of Enchō lived on in him. So, on the appointed Sunday, at one o'clock, she entered the narrow street leading to the Namiki Theater. Her face was well known, and everyone there knew how many artists frequented her place.

"Good afternoon, and welcome," the attendant greeted her. "I'll put your footwear in a separate place." He did not give her the chit that others received so as to be able to reclaim their geta later on. Not to get that chit at a music hall meant that you were an honored habitué. Oriku's generous tips had put her in good standing. She liked that. Asakusa did not generally favor daytime performances, and the theater was only about two-thirds full, many of those present being in any case invited guests. Cushions, each provided with tea and an ashtray, were placed before the pillar to the left of the dais for the three young performers: Enju, Kinraku, and Shinkyō. Not that they were really all that young, each being thirty or so and thoroughly skilled. Enju did *Mind's Eye* and *Flattery*, and Kinraku *A Tight Game* and *Pale Blue Cotton*. They were very good. At last it was Shinkyō's turn. The program announced *Blossom-Viewing Broke*. Oriku could not really place him, even after he mounted the dais. Small, round-faced, and nice-looking, he inspired little confidence, but he obviously felt at home on the dais and seemed indeed to belong there.

"I realize it was presumptuous of me to arrange this three-man performance, and that I may have earned your displeasure," he began, "but I want you to know how grateful I am for the stature you have given me." He spoke sincerely, without a trace of affectation.

"*Blossom-Viewing Broke* is of course a specialty of mine, but for a particular reason I am taking the liberty to change the program in order to do instead the "Farewell to Ao" scene from *Shiobara Tasuke*, which I learned from the great Enchō. My teacher, Enshō, was very good at it, too, and he kindly made me rehearse it intensively. However, he warned me not to try performing a sentimental drama of this kind while I was still young. 'You will not have the power really to touch people's hearts until you are past forty,' he said. 'I will teach it to you, but I will not have you mount the dais and perform it.' And that is why, until today, I have never done so. If my performance conveys anything of the great Enchō's and of my teacher Enshō's skill, I hope you will be able to forgive my forwardness in attempting it."

Far from being a perfunctory little speech for the occasion, Shinkyō's words sounded utterly genuine. Oriku was all ears. She wondered what that "particular reason" could possibly be, and his talk of having learned the piece from Enchō and Enshō filled her with nostalgia for days gone by. Shinkyō never once looked at her, but she nonetheless sensed he was aware of her. She also suspected he had suddenly changed his plan when he learned she was there. His voice was firm and settled; unlike those of so many young performers, there was nothing unstable about it. His delivery was warm, too, and brimming with feeling. Oriku could still hear Enchō's voice in that same great scene, the one in which Tasuke, under threat from his entire family, bids farewell to his beloved horse, Ao, before leaving home forever. She knew the story intimately, having heard it twice—once at her old home in the Yoshiwara and once at the Hakubai Theater in Kanda— and those experiences were not ones she would ever forget. Shinkyō's *Shiobara*, today, certainly offered a good deal to remind her of the master. At first she listened somewhat distractedly, but his polished excellence gradually drew her in until, sure enough, when the farewell came, she wept.

"Be brave, oh, be brave, Ao! Let my sleeve go! I must leave!"

His sobbing voice sounded very like Enchō's. Oriku was deeply impressed. Enchō had said when he performed *Shiobara* at the Hakubai that it was for the last time, and indeed it had been. He had never recovered the strength to do it again. Shinkyō's *Shiobara* today brought back Enchō in person, displaying a precocious grasp of the sentimental repertoire's subtle appeal. Not that he did not have some way to go yet—he had mastered the piece, yes, but it was not yet entirely his own. Still, he had brought tears to every eye, and the audience was very pleased.

"After bidding farewell to Ao and putting his home behind him,"

Shinkyō explained at the end, "Tasuke goes into service in Edo with a firewood and charcoal wholesaler, and little by little he makes a success of himself. That will have to wait for another time, though. The farewell to Ao is as far as I can go today."

The rather small Namiki Theater shook with thunderous applause, which went on and on while Shinkyō continued to bow in acknowledgment. Oriku applauded too.

"You'll be as good as the best!" an old man cried from just below the dais. "Keep at it!" The audience burst into renewed applause.

On her way out, Oriku found her footwear ready for her at the exit. The theater owner appeared, to thank her.

"I'd never heard Shinkyō before," she said, "but he's good, isn't he?" She gave him the bag containing a gift she had brought, with the request that he pass it on to Shinkyō. The wind along the river felt good in the rickshaw on the journey home. Brimming with the satisfaction she always felt after a fine performance, she had a good mind to become one of the young man's regular patrons. When she got back, she was informed that Mr. Tamura, from the Ichimura Theater, was there with a whole crowd of actors. The staff was frantic. Oriku slipped off her haori jacket and rushed to the main room, to find Tamura Nariyoshi, a giant of the theater world, there together with his son Hisajirō and over a dozen young actors like Kichiemon, Mitsugorō, and Yonekichi.

"Where were you?" Tamura teasingly demanded to know. "You said we could come anytime, you'd always be here! You must be taking it easy lately!"

"By no means! I certainly am not! The young storyteller San'yūtei Shinkyō had a special performance today, to celebrate his promotion to principal artist, and I felt it was my duty to go. If I had known you were coming, you would have had no occasion to reprove me. I may go to the theater during the day, but I am always back in the evening."

"I see, I see. Well, if it's duty to an artist, go right ahead. You're forgiven."

Great man that he was, he smiled at the mention of "duty."

"Shinkyō is pretty good for his age, isn't he?" Hisajirō remarked. He seemed to have heard him before.

"I was extremely impressed," Oriku replied. "He seems very solid."

"What did he do today?"

"'Farewell to Ao,' from *Shiobara Tasuke*."

"He *did*? He really had the nerve to perform *that*?"

"I know what you mean, but I heard Enchō's *Shiobara*, and Shinkyō certainly learned his lesson well. He got plenty of tears out of me, I can tell you that."

"Really? I'd like to hear him do it myself."

Hisajirō seemed to be quite a fan. Oriku gathered that next month they would all be performing a new set of plays at Mukōjima, so they had come to see what the place was like and, incidentally, to try some of that chazuke. The saké had been served, each actor had his sure-to-satisfy dinner of river fish before him, and all were chattering merrily. Kichiemon sat quietly in morose silence, but Mitsugorō was engaged in lively conversation with the others about all the trouble they had had with the new play.

"Oriku," the great Tamura asked, "do you think *Shiobara Tasuke* would work as a stage play?" Kichiemon gave Oriku a thoroughly actorlike glance.

"Hmm, I wonder." Oriku paused to think. "The late proprietor of the Silver Flower had heard Enchō do it, and he also saw the kabuki version by Kikugorō V. He used to say that Enchō, just with his fan, got closer to the heart of the matter than Kikugorō ever did, with all his props. That's my feeling, too." She said exactly what she thought.

"Perhaps you're right," Kichiemon nodded. "I never heard Enchō's *Shiobara*, but I thought the same thing when I heard Enshō's. Even 'Farewell to Ao' has greater truth to it when heard from the storyteller's dais. The sorrow of a stage-prop horse just doesn't quite do it, somehow." He watched the expression on Tamura's face.

"Could be, could be. If the horse should fall over, there goes the play." Tamura nodded in turn. Having just come from hearing the scene, though, Oriku could not help being impressed by all this earnest interest in whether or not it would work on stage.

At last the chazuke had been served and eaten, and the actors had departed in a procession of rickshaws. Oriku thought it was still early, but actually it was past ten o'clock. Time had flown in such pleasant company.

"Mistress Oriku, you have a visitor waiting for you!" Ofune, the head maid, brought her the news. "I didn't tell you because Mr. Tamura was here, but he's been waiting for nearly an hour."

"Who is it? Do I know him?"

"No, I don't think so. It's San'yūtei Shinkyō, the storyteller."

"Really? Shinkyō? Is he here alone?"

"Yes. He says he wants to thank you."

"That's a bit much in the way of manners. He has quite a job ahead of him if he's going to thank every member of his audience in person!"

"I don't know what it's about, but anyway, I took him to the Camellia annex. It was the only one available."

"Well, business is certainly good when I'm not around!" Smiling, Oriku set off for the Camellia. Each annex was named after the characteristic flower in its garden. The Camellia featured big, red and white variegated camellias that bloomed there magnificently, to the right of the path, from mid-February through March. The annexes themselves were modest in size, but each had its own spacious garden. In the Camellia, Shinkyō was sitting alone, a small earthenware jar of saké before him. He slipped off his cushion as soon as Oriku came in and humbly introduced himself, just as an artist does.

"I am Shinkyō. Please forgive me for imposing on your time. I am most grateful to you for receiving me. If I have presumed to trouble you this way, it is because I am so anxious to give my thanks." He kept his head bowed low, with both hands on the tatami floor. Presumably he had changed after the performance and come straight here, dressed with severe discretion in a dark, warm-toned grey cotton haori jacket over a very quiet cotton kimono.

"Such ceremony! Goodness, please sit up! I'm no good at bowing myself, so do please straighten up! I was a guest at the theater, but now you're *my* guest, and you mustn't be formal. Now that I'm here, please allow me to pour you a cup."

She picked up the saké jar and was about to do so when Shinkyō stopped her. "No, no," he protested, "I did not come for that. I am here to thank you, you see."

"There's no need for you to thank me. It's a storyteller's job to earn a living from telling stories, just as it's my job to earn a living from selling chazuke. As long as I go to hear you, and you come to eat here, we're even, if you see what I mean. Please don't make such a big thing of it."

"No, no, Mistress Oriku, you do not understand. I am not here to thank you for coming today. I am here to express my thanks for sixteen years ago."

Shinkyō's face changed. The blood drained from it, and he suddenly turned pale.

"Sixteen years ago? What *do* you mean? I have no idea what you're talking about."

"You don't? Mistress Oriku, have you forgotten? I have not, and I never will as long as I live." He placed his hands very properly on his knees.

"Sixteen years ago, Mistress Oriku, you went every day to the Hakubai Theater in Kanda to hear the great master Enchō perform *Shiobara Tasuke.* You must remember that."

"I certainly do. That was when I was still in the Yoshiwara, and Kanda was a long way off. But how do you happen to know that?"

"On the last day, you went to the Yabu soba restaurant behind the theater and had tempura soba. Do you remember?"

"Mm, perhaps I did. I always liked that soba place in Renjakuchō, and I still go there now and again. The tempura soba there is so good."

"Yes, you had it that time too. I was sitting next to you, and I watched."

"Why on earth do you still remember a little thing like that?"

"Well, you see, I was just eleven then, and working at the theater as an errand boy. Sometimes I'd get a tip from one of the artists, and being a boy I was always hungry, so I'd rush straight out to the Yabu. It was expensive for a child like me, but I had no time to look further. Expensive or not, in I'd go. But that day I was with Enji, a budding artist and a close disciple of Master Enkyō. He brazenly ate tempura soba, but that was beyond my means and I had to make do with plain. So there I was, just longing to grow up fast and be a success, so that I too could afford tempura soba, when the lady sitting next to me—

you—apparently saw how I felt. 'Young fellow,' you suddenly said, 'I'll treat you to tempura soba.' You called the waitress over and placed the order. I was flabbergasted and just sat there like a stump. Then you paid for yours and mine together, and left. It all happened so quickly, I completely forgot to thank you properly. Then the soba arrived, steaming hot and delicious. You know what it's like there. They don't deep-fry the big, juicy prawn till the dish is actually ordered, which makes the tempura soba there completely different from anywhere else. I was just a boy then, but even so, I didn't feel like picking up my chopsticks right away. I just sat there, staring at the soba you'd bought me."

What he remembered from sixteen years ago seemed still to be as real to him as though it had happened yesterday. And now Oriku remembered, too. The two boys had come in together, and the big one had ordered tempura soba, while the little one had sadly ordered plain.

"I see," she said. "That boy was you."

"Yes. It was the happiest moment of my life. At first I simply could not believe it, and even when the soba came, I was still in a daze. 'What are you gawking at? Go ahead, eat!' Enji said, so I finally did. 'Do you know who that was?' he asked. 'That was the mistress of the Silver Flower, in the Yoshiwara. She's been coming every evening to hear Master Enchō's *Shiobara Tasuke*.'"

"My goodness, that's amazing, the connection between you and me."

"Yes, it's an amazing connection. At the time I must have been looking jealously at Enji's tempura soba. You saw all that, I'm sure. You were so wonderfully kind to a boy of whom you knew nothing, either who he was or where he was from! When I had finished, I raced back to the theater and peered through a crack at the back of the stage. I saw you sitting there, next to the dais, and I stared at you hard enough to bore a hole in the wood. Even at that age, I wanted somehow to do well enough to be worthy of thanking you. I know the whole thing sounds like one of Master Enchō's sentimental dramas, but still, it is perfectly true. For someone like you, Mistress Oriku, it was nothing, but for me, what you did was beyond price. I have never eaten tempura since, not once. I decided it would be taboo for me until the day

I was worthy to thank you. That is when I asked Master Enshō to take me on as a disciple and began to learn his art."

Shinkyō fell silent and wiped his eyes. Childhood memories had filled them with tears.

"After my teacher had died, and I finally became a principal artist, my first thought was to pay you a visit. You knew nothing about this, Mistress Oriku, but I owe you an enormous debt of gratitude. So I planned today's three-man performance accordingly, and when you were kind enough to come, I was so happy, I was just so happy. . ."

"But I really did nothing to make such a fuss about, you know. It was just a bowl of tempura soba. You mustn't exaggerate."

"No, no, you still do not see. For you it was just a bowl of tempura soba, but what I shall never forget is the warmth of your kindness. I worried about whether you would actually come and hear me perform as a principal artist, but you did, and that old memory then convinced me on the spur of the moment to do *Shiobara Tasuke*."

"It's quite embarrassing, to imagine you thinking of me that way. But you did *Tasuke* very well. You certainly mastered the lessons you were taught. I assume it's true then, that, as you said before you began, you were told not to perform it until you were forty."

"Yes, it is true. I thought it was a bit soon myself, but Master Enchō's *Shiobara* returned to me when I stopped to remember that day. I did not feel that way until I actually seated myself on the dais, but as soon as I saw your face, that performance at the Hakubai Theater sixteen years ago came back to me. It was the last night, and I will never forget how Master Enchō looked. He himself said it was his very last performance of *Shiobara*, and he turned out to be right, so that was my final memory of him. When I saw him there at the theater today, from the dais, I felt he was telling me to go ahead, it was all right, I could do *Shiobara*; so then and there I made up my mind, and I did. That warning against doing it till I was forty had made me want to try it so much, I could hardly stand it—and then, there you were. I could not help myself. I know I should not have, but I was carried away."

Perhaps his tears had dried by now; at any rate, he moved to pour himself some saké.

"Now, now, I'm a woman, this is what I'm here for." Oriku picked up the jar. The saké was cold.

"Dear me, it's icy!" She plunged the jar straight into the kettle on the hibachi.

"Well, I'm very pleased, I must say. To think that seeing my face made you want to do *Shiobara*! I really appreciate that. You *are* a bit young for it, and it really isn't completely yours yet, but you gave it wonderful energy and style. The obvious pleasure it gave the audience proves that. That was truly heartfelt applause, not just some hand-clapping to be polite. They were simply delighted."

"I hope so."

"Of course they were. A sentimental piece has real flavor, unlike a funny one with a punch line. Anyone can just go ahead and tell what happens in the story, but to make the audience actually *feel* the loneliness of the great world out there, beyond the village, or Tasuke's sorrow as he prepares to leave home—that's really hard, I'm sure."

"It is indeed. Today I felt like a student dragged before an examiner. At first I was shaking. Stop it, stop this right now, I kept telling myself, but it didn't help. I clearly remembered the way the great Enchō did it, and Master Enshō, too, but I still couldn't do it exactly like that. It's strange. Art is really frightening. In the end it all turned out to be a remarkable, quite unexpected lesson. Even so, the tempura soba I had at that soba place. . ."

"Now, that's enough. You're embarrassing me."

She lifted the jar from the kettle. "Let me pour you one."

"But first, Mistress Oriku, won't you let me pour for *you*?"

"With pleasure. It really makes me very happy when I think you never forgot a little thing like that, but took it instead as an encouragement that spurred you on."

She lifted her cup as Shinkyō poured. When she brought it to her lips, she experienced a sort of rush of feeling. It was not desire, but Shinkyō did look very attractive.

"How old are you now?" she went on.

"Please don't ask."

"Well, you were eleven at the time, and it's been sixteen years, so I suppose you must be twenty-seven."

"That's right, I'm a chick hardly out of the shell."

"Young indeed—just my age when I heard Enchō."

"In other words, you're now the other side of forty."

"Yes. I was just forty when I set up this place."

"But you look so young!"

"Don't flatter me. A woman has no age."

"Indeed, indeed. An artist, either."

"I'd ask you to come again, but you probably won't have much of a chance. Still, do come by, if you think of it."

"Thank you very much. I certainly would like to. Would it matter if it was late in the evening?"

"No, not at all. Just give me a ring, and I'll get things ready."

"I'll really appreciate it. I owe you so much, I'd like to keep coming the year round."

"On the other hand, if you're *too* late there won't be any more rickshaws, and the ferry will have stopped, too. You won't be able to get back."

"That will suit me perfectly, if I may be allowed to spend the night here."

"What? This is only a chazuke restaurant, you know."

"So they say. I hear you don't find shigure clams like yours anywhere else in Tokyo."

"Would you like some?"

"Yes, please."

Oriku went back to the main house and sat down by the kitchen hearth, but the way she picked out the clams was new. Usually she went about it just as a man would, but for once she was back to being a woman. Shinkyō was far below her in age, but all the same, deep down she was excited. That a single bowl of tempura soba should have given him such pleasure, for so long, and served to spur him on toward mastering his art—there was something so sweet about that, an appeal beyond simple desire. She had them bring a tray laden with chazuke and two or three jars of saké. Midnight had come and gone already, and the whole place was quiet.

"Stay away from music-hall artists," Monnosuke had said.

"Well," Oriku told herself, feeling contrary, "it all depends."

Shinkyō, tonight, certainly yielded nothing to Monnosuke in the way of dedication to his art. In that sense, you felt, he really was solid gold.

Oriku, who knew everything she needed to know about amusing herself with men, never let herself just get carried away. She chose her man herself. If she did not like a fellow, she kept away from him. If she got on with someone, she did not hesitate to get close to him physically as well. Letting one thing lead to another, making mistakes, becoming involved against her better judgment—she avoided all that; but if she liked a man, she went right ahead, with no regrets.

That night, she finally lay down with the young Shinkyō in her arms. That feeling of sweetness had been desire. Shinkyō clung to her, weeping. All night long he kept his arms around her and never let her go.

He left at dawn, while everyone was still asleep. Then it was over; he never came to Mukōjima again. He had spent the night the very first time he came, and that night was to be all. He did not return. Oriku was sorry, but for Shinkyō that was that. She had been planning to feed him tempura the next time he came, but she never had a chance to do so, and she shrank from the thought of chasing after him. Meanwhile, five years went by, and she heard from afar that he had become famous.

Then, in the autumn of the fifth year, he came strolling down from the embankment with a fan of his. There was an entirely new weightiness to his presence, now that he was a major star. He said he was the featured performer at the Hakubai Theater, which they remembered so well, and so had the honor of going on last.

"How about it, Shinkyō? Shall we go to the Yabu and have some tempura soba?" Oriku said teasingly.

Shinkyō frowned. "Mistress Oriku," he said, "I still do not eat tempura. I mean not to eat it ever again."

"Now, don't be impertinent. You may not like tempura, but you seem to have quite a taste for clam." The quip, which was just like her, contained not a trace of pique. Shinkyō remained unmoved.

"Mistress Oriku," he declared gravely, looking her straight in the eye, "the good name of the Shigure Teahouse would have suffered if I had presumed further on your kindness."

"That's just an excuse. You ran away from me, didn't you. Coward!"

"Say whatever you like. I have no intention of remaining an entertainer forever. No, I keep working for the day when I can become your lover openly. Then I will be back, I promise."

"What a talker! You'd better hurry—I'll be a sixty-year-old biddy pretty soon."

"A woman has no age. Please wait for me, Mistress Oriku, until the day when I can enjoy tempura soba with you before all the world."

Shinkyō's eyes were clear and calm. Oriku found them overpowering. She had seen, she felt, into the heart of a single-minded man.

Not long afterwards, she heard he had opened a restaurant and inn on Uguisuzaka, at Ueno. However, no word came from him to say he felt like tempura soba. Had those clear eyes been telling the truth, or not? Even if they were not necessarily to be believed, they had seemed to say that, somewhere in his heart, he was waiting.

As an artist he had achieved early success, and he had retired early too. He was clever. That one night they had had together was over, but she felt as though the story itself was not over yet.

CHAPTER THREE

The Kannon of Asakusa

The Asakusa Kannon temple is home, so to speak, to all those who inhabit downtown Tokyo. An Asakusa native need only step onto the temple grounds to feel he is treading his native soil. When he returns after years away—when he comes up the stone-paved Nakamise Avenue, goes in through the Niō Gate, and catches his first sight of that great roof—tears spring to his eyes. The denizens of downtown Tokyo are all deeply religious. Their faiths vary, but whatever else they may believe, every single one reveres the Kannon of Asakusa.

Formally, the temple's name is Kinryūzan Sensōji. In its branch of Tendai Buddhism it comes under Kan'eiji, the "Eastern Mount Hiei" at Ueno. Being a Tendai temple, it belongs to the wrong sect for many of those who make the pilgrimage to it, but none of them cares. No one would think of quibbling over a divine presence that extends its protection to all of Asakusa. (In recent years the temple has wisely relieved its pilgrims of the last shred of doubt by dropping its Tendai affiliation and establishing its own Kannon sect.)

Although country-born in the old province of Kazusa, Oriku had been making the Asakusa pilgrimage ever since she first went there with the Silver Flower's proprietor, after she was sold to the Yoshiwara and settled into Hashiba as his mistress. Over time Kannon had become the object of her personal prayers, and she visited the temple often. Whenever the press of business kept her away for too long she felt apologetic, and she would then hurry there as soon as she could. No neglect of hers ever made Kannon angry. Oriku always felt as though the deity greeted her with a smile. Although not especially devout, she never passed a shrine or temple without bowing toward it. Most such places are a bit gloomy, being set among thick groves or deep forests, and so solemn a mood pervades their grounds that you can hardly stand before them without straightening your collar, but that kind of formality is unknown at the Asakusa Kannon temple. The main hall stands alone and unadorned in its corner of the flat, parklike grounds. No forest stands behind it, nor does any other contrivance serve to enhance its dignity. It has a Niō Gate and a Five-Story Pagoda, but for the people of Asakusa these too are friends. No one scolds the children who amuse themselves by swinging from the enormous straw sandals—the ones belonging to the great Niō guardians— hung on either side of the gate. Behind the hall a famous ginkgo tree towers skyward, the only real tree to be seen. The broad, open space that contains the Enma, Jizō, and Nenbutsu halls attracts street performers of all kinds, while, behind it, a clamor of women's voices from a row of tea stalls invites passersby in for a cup. Popular pleasures constitute the temple's only ornaments. Far from being solemn, it is wide open to the sky and as unpretentious as it could possibly be.

Oriku liked that. The sight of naughty little boys sliding down the main hall's stairway balustrades always gave her the sense that Kannon, who loves children, must be smiling at their antics. The hall, one hundred eight feet square, has on each side a flight of steps that you are welcome to climb without taking off your shoes, and no one objects either if you run all the way around the hall on the veranda that surrounds it. Inside, it is light and airy, and pilgrims feel almost as if they were off on a picnic. Many come as much for pleasure as for prayer. A few more serious adherents may have made the traditional vow not to leave the temple grounds before coming to pray before Kannon a hundred times in a row, but most are simply people dressed in their finery, and, of these many—for such is the character of Asakusa itself—are from the entertainment world. All the visitors to the temple together make a very colorful picture, and so do the rows of votive lanterns, each inscribed with an evocative name, that hang from the ceiling of the hall.

The inhabitants of the Yoshiwara were all, without exception, Kannon devotees. When an employee there returned a little late from an errand, saying that he had gone to pray to Kannon before starting back was enough to avert a scolding.

"I'll go by the temple on my way home, if I'm done before dark." That was what Oriku always said when she went out. Every route she might take back to Mukōjima led through the Kaminari Gate. This remained true whether she crossed Azuma Bridge by rickshaw, walked through Shōtenchō and took the ferry from Imado Bridge, or boarded the steamboat from Azuma Bridge to Kototoi. As a result she was in a position to visit the temple as often as she liked. And yet her visits were surprisingly infrequent.

"I can't believe it! I haven't been for three months!" Whenever a thought like this struck her she would rush off, sometimes arriving after sunset, when they closed the great doors of the main hall. Packed though it always was as long as the doors remained open, the hall grew quiet once they were shut and twilight had set in. The women who sell pigeon food packed up their things and left, the daytime noise and bustle abruptly ceased, and dusk came on. The building itself was lacquered in brilliant red-orange, but the doors were black, and the area before the hall grew suddenly dark once they were closed.

"Oh no, I'm too late! The doors are shut!" Oriku more than once clicked her tongue in disappointment as she came through the Niō Gate, but, closed or not, she did not turn back. Instead she ran up the steps and saluted Kannon anyway. Even after sundown people went on tossing ringing coins into the great big offering box. Oriku had nothing in particular to ask for, so she just prayed in a general way for the soul of the Silver Flower's late proprietor, the success of her Shigure Teahouse, and the prosperity of the Silver Flower. Her usual offering was a five-sen coin. In those days most people offered just five rin. Few tossed in a silvery coin like that, but Oriku was one of them.

That night—not late, but around seven, just after sunset—Oriku was on her way home from the Ichimura Theater. It was late March, and the cherry buds had just begun to open. The area was dark enough to make her nervous, thieves not being unknown in the vicinity, and she was therefore making sure her wooden geta clattered loudly on the stone pavement. Beggars lay on the foundation stones under the main hall, and youths sat hunched up, their arms around their knees, beside the great offering box. They pretended to be asleep, but really they were waiting for a coin to bounce off the bars across the top of the box and fall to the ground.

"Mistress Oriku!" Oriku was about to leave again, after praying a moment to Kannon, when a young man's voice hailed her from the far side of the offering box. "Can't you spare some change?" She could only see his outline.

"Who are you?" Oriku asked, glancing back. She had just started down the steps.

"I know it's you, Mistress Oriku. I saw you throw in that shiner."

He had not missed it. Copper coins were called "clinkers," and silvery nickel-copper coins worth five sen and up were "shiners." He would hardly come running after her once she reached the bottom of the steps, what with all the other pilgrims to distract him, and if she said nothing to him now, that would be that. However, it worried her that this street urchin knew her name.

"How do you know who I am?" She peered at him in the dim light, but he stuck close to the offering box and refused to show his face.

"How do you know my name?" she repeated. "Just tell me, and you'll have an offering too."

"We all know you, Mistress Oriku."

"Now, now, don't try to put me off! It makes no sense, your recognizing me this way."

She took out two silver ten-sen coins.

"Well, anyway, you do, so you've got me." She placed the coins on the edge of the offering box.

The boy stretched out both hands toward them, but apparently he could not actually reach that far, because when he bent forward he lost his balance and began to fall.

"Goodness, look out!" Oriku said, rushing to him to catch him as he fell. "What's the matter?" she asked, helping him up. His whole body was shaking. "There's something the matter with you, isn't there?"

He looked as though he would fall over again, right there on the steps, if she let go.

"Hold on, now!" She carried him down one or two steps.

"Is anyone out there?" she called. "Could you help me, please? This boy is sick!"

Shadowy forms came running up the steps toward her—apparently other street urchins like him, from underneath the hall.

"Sorry!" With this apology, one of them put his arms around the boy to get him to his feet.

"*Now* look at you! We *told* you, didn't we?"

"We *told* you you shouldn't come tonight, but you just wouldn't listen!"

They were going to half-carry him away. His eyes were closed. Oriku had a feeling she had seen that innocent, grubby face before.

"Wait a minute! Isn't he Bandō's son?" She came down the steps after them. "I'm sure you're Bandō's son, aren't you."

"Yes, I'm Shūsaku." The boy opened his eyes and answered her himself. Apparently these ragamuffins did not know one another's first names.

"Look, I'm sorry, but I know him, so I want you to leave him to *me*."

"Fine, fine. He's all yours. Take him anywhere you like."

"But he's ill!"

"You've got *that* right! We told him to stay in bed, but no, he ignored us, and *now* look what's happened to him!"

"Will you take him for me to the Niō Gate and put him in a rickshaw?"

"Carry him, you mean, like porters?"

There were four of them. They picked up the limp Shūsaku and got him to the gate, where the four together managed to get him up into a rickshaw. Oriku gave them a silver fifty-sen coin, and they watched the two rickshaws leave. She took the easy way, around by Azuma Bridge. Her arrival home with a grubby boy had the whole place in an uproar. Everyone violently disapproved of her picking up some beggar boy from Asakusa, but Oriku gave no one, not even Ofune, a word of explanation. Instead she carried Shūsaku straight to the bath, washed him off everywhere, dressed him in a yukata and a padded jacket, put him to bed in her own Paulownia room, and called the doctor. The doctor said it wasn't serious; the boy just had a bad cold. She fed him rice gruel and medicine, and kept him there for the night.

"Where on earth did you find him?" Ofune asked, frowning. "Everything he had on stank. All we could do was throw it away."

"Fine."

"But where's he from?"

"He's Mitsunojō's son."

"Beg pardon?"

"Bandō Mitsunojō, in Kanda. This boy's his son."

"You mean, the boy they say ran away from home?"

"That's right, Shūsaku. He's Shūsaku."

"Well, this *is* a surprise!"

"For me too. I was just starting home after going by the temple when someone called me by name from beside the offering box. At first I didn't know who it was, but then I recognized him. He called 'Mistress Oriku!' and collapsed right at my feet. I couldn't get over it."

"He certainly knew who you were, didn't he?"

"Yes, he probably remembered me from when he was here."

"Mitsunojō must be terribly worried about him. Shall I call Kanda right away?"

"Just a minute. Things are a bit complicated over there, and we can't afford to make a wrong move."

"Complicated or not, he's Mitsugorō's heir. Mitsugorō's bound to be concerned."

"Well, there's no great hurry. After Shūsaku's mother died, a mistress moved in, and they say things aren't going well—the household is in turmoil."

"I see. They say she has a son too."

"Yes. I suppose that's why Shūsaku left home."

"Poor thing!"

"Yes, just look at that face—he's a child. Isn't he sweet?"

The hastily washed face was innocently asleep. His father, Bandō Mitsunojō, was a dance teacher of the Bandō school. His forebears had held the hereditary title of Dancing Master and received a stipend from the Tokugawa government for teaching dance to the women of the shogun's palace. Then the Tokugawa regime had crumbled, and they had set themselves up as dance teachers for the people of the town. The present Mitsunojō had a practice stage near the Kanda

Myōjin Shrine, and he was very good indeed; his hand and arm movements had a special refinement. He had little following in the entertainment world itself, since he did so many pieces derived from Noh,
but he had many students from the best families. The Bandō line of
kabuki dancers remained in principle a single house, and since Bandō
Mitsugorō III had taught Mitsunojō I back in the early 1800s, the present Mitsunojō continued to acknowledge the present Mitsugorō as his
master. Shūsaku, Mitsunojō's eldest son, was said to show promise,
but family difficulties had driven him to leave home and join the street
urchins on the grounds of the Asakusa Kannon temple.

"Master Bandō is on the line." Ofune had rung Mitsunojō the next
morning.

"Shūsaku's at your place, you say?" Mitsunojō's voice resounded
imperiously.

"Yes. I was so surprised! He seemed unwell, so I brought him home
with me."

"What made you do *that*?" The voice sounded displeased.

"Well, I just didn't like the idea of him wandering around forever
in a place like that."

"You should've left him there."

"But he was ill!"

"That's his problem. He's the one who decided to bolt, and now
he's making himself a burden on other people. I won't have it! Just get
rid of him, any way you like." The tone was cold and peremptory.

"Get rid of him—you mean, you don't care what happens to him?"
Oriku was offended.

"If he wants to do as he pleases, it's up to him. One of these days
he'll see the light and come back to say he's sorry. Until then, you're
to ignore him. I can only apologize for the trouble he's caused you."

Mitsunojō said no more. With heartless cruelty, he hung up. Oriku
was furious. What kind of father would not care what happened to a
sweet boy like that? Perhaps his mistress had him bewitched, or perhaps he had always been like that, but at any rate, the kindhearted
Oriku could hardly believe it. Ever since opening her place she had
thought him a polite, considerate guest, a fine-looking man, and an
admirable teacher. How wrong she had been!

"Master Bandō must have been surprised," Ofune remarked from behind her.

"No, he wasn't, not at all. He told me to get rid of his son."

"Is *that* what he said? After you've been so kind to him?"

"Well, I don't know what else to do. He's the boy's father, after all."

"He has no love for him, does he."

"So it seems. If he really has no use for him, I'll take him on and bring him up myself."

Oriku's anger refused to abate, but Shūsaku was soon up and about again. He was still a child, and he got over such things quickly.

"I'm very sorry to have caused you all this worry," he said apologetically.

"What can have happened? You have such a fine home—what in the world made you do it?" Oriku's reply sounded severe.

"A fine home? You have no idea what you're talking about, Auntie." He pursed his lips.

"Your father's mistress moved in after your mother died—I'm sure it must be difficult for you."

"It certainly is. I can't even begin to tell you."

"Very well, but what are you going to do now? You can't just go on this way. You'll end up a tramp on the streets."

"I know that."

"Well then, stop. I gather you have promise, and now of all times is the time to learn. Right? Tell your father you're sorry and go home."

"Go home? I'd rather drown myself in the river." The tone of his voice changed. Home was obviously a subject he preferred not to discuss.

"Auntie?" He was looking Oriku straight in the eye. "Will you listen if I tell you what I really want?"

"As much as you like."

"Then please do. I want to learn to be a dancer."

"But not from your father?"

"No, of course not. My father isn't the only teacher around. There are lots of others, and I can learn anywhere, as long as I really want to. That's what I think, anyway." He looked resolute. Judging from Mitsunojō's voice on the phone, and Shūsaku's obvious resolve, there was no longer any affection between father and son.

"So what do you have in mind?" Oriku sat up straighter. "You mean you want to learn some other school of dancing, not Bandō?"

"That's right."

"And you absolutely refuse to go back to Kanda."

Shūsaku nodded in silence. "It wouldn't be any use, your telling me to go home. You don't know this Omura woman. She's really something."

"I hear she's quite a lady."

"Quite a horrible lady, yes. She moved right in with her son, and she practically told me to get out."

No doubt he was prejudiced, but he really hated his father and stepmother.

"I wish you'd talk about me to someone you know, Auntie. Could you possibly do that?"

"I suppose I could, but I wouldn't want to embarrass your father."

"*He* won't care! He doesn't want me around—it'll be a relief for him," he said, giving her a pleading look.

"I'll do *anything*!" he went on. "I'll polish the floors, or whatever else anyone wants me to do. Just the thought of going back to Kanda makes me capable of anything. Please think about it. You understand—this other woman is now sitting on the cushion that used to be my mother's." His speech had dropped to a whisper. The faintness of his voice spoke volumes: the more deeply he loved his mother, the more he detested his father. Oriku could see why.

"All right, stay a few days. You can help with the garden, and meanwhile I'll think it over."

With that, she kept him at Mukōjima. Once properly bathed and dressed in the clothing Oriku happened to have on hand, he made a very fine young fellow. Sleeping under the temple's main hall had accustomed him to a frugal life, and he never just sat around indoors. Sweeping and tidying the garden, helping the maids with the heavy chores—it was a big place, and there was always plenty of work. The maids were glad to have him. "Shū-chan," they called him, and they looked after him very nicely.

"If Mr. Bandō doesn't want him, Mistress Oriku, why don't you adopt him?" This was Ofune's suggestion.

"He wants to be a better dancer than his father, so I'm thinking about who might take him on." A teacher for Shūsaku: that was the one thing on her mind.

"I found you at Kannon's temple, so you should probably have an Asakusa teacher."

"I'll leave it up to you," Shūsaku replied. He seemed in no particular hurry. Instead he went around looking quite relaxed. Everybody liked him. There were no other men at the Shigure Teahouse, so he was everyone's darling, and he never acted as if any task was beneath him.

The place suddenly became very busy, as it did every year when the cherries started coming into bloom and an avalanche of blossom-viewers filled every room. With the women working at a frantic pace, Shūsaku was caught up in the same whirlwind. No dance study for him! He became the restaurant's general servant. He never complained, though.

"We can't ask Shū-chan to do *that*!" Oriku would say about some task or other that he then did gladly anyway. "I'm here to help till the blossom-viewing season is over," he would say.

"I've never known such a nice boy!" Ofune could hardly get over it. "What can Mr. Bandō possibly have against him? He's wonderful!"

"It's because this Omura, his mistress, has a son of her own. Shū-chan has a stubborn streak, and it seems he refuses to call her 'Mother.'"

"Why should he? He can hardly start calling her 'Mother' at his age."

"You're quite partial to him, aren't you? You didn't like him much at first, though."

"When he first came he wasn't well, and you couldn't tell just what he was like, but now it's Shū-chan this and Shū-chan that—everyone thinks the world of him. Just yesterday the ceramic drainage pipe was blocked. He dug three feet down to it, got himself covered in mud, and fixed it."

"You really mustn't have him do things like that! He's not a common laborer, you know."

"That's why everybody is so happy to let him have his bath and bring him fresh clothes."

"It's just not right, though, when he's the natural successor to the

position of head of the Bandō house. You really mustn't do it anymore."

Oriku spoke severely, but all this meant nothing to Shūsaku himself. Easygoing by nature, and rendered confident by an excellent
upbringing, he had what it takes to remain cheerful through adversity.
Oriku knew she should not go on putting him to work this way, but
she had no idea whom to approach. His being Mitsunojō's son made
it unlikely that any of her countless acquaintances would take him
on, and the old title of Dancing Master that had honored his forebears now worked against him. As a result, no school of Japanese
dance bore him any goodwill.

When the cherry blossoms had fallen and the crowds were gone,
Oriku made an early morning pilgrimage to the Kannon of Asakusa.
She had no idea what to do about finding a teacher for Shūsaku. She
felt things might work out if she brought the matter to Kannon in person, since it was at the temple's main hall that she had first found him.
And so, late in April she climbed the temple steps. It was still too early
for there to be many visitors, and the air inside the hall felt cool and
fresh. There was a desk to solicit contributions for redoing the roof.
Oriku made her contribution and then went to stand before Kannon's
main altar. The great chest containing Kannon's image was imposing,
and many candles were burning before it.

Oriku clapped her hands, as always, and prayed, "Please bless
Bandō Shūsaku with a good teacher." That was her only prayer. She
felt certain Kannon would help the boy, since he had slept for some
time in the darkness of Kannon's main hall, and she repeated her peti-
tion over and over, till she at last felt she had done all she could. Then
she pressed her palms together in salutation, made a low bow, and
left. Of course, a suitable teacher was hardly likely to fall into her lap
just because she had prayed to Kannon, but nonetheless she felt a bit
better as she started back down the steps.

Just then someone called out to her. "Mistress Oriku!" It was a
man's voice. She did not even have to stop; he descended the steps
beside her.

"You seemed quite absorbed," he said. "Was there some special
urgency to your prayer?" His dignified voice sounded kind.

"Goodness, it's *you*!" Oriku cried out in astonishment. "You were here too?"

She halted right there. The man on the steps with her was the kabuki actor Ichikawa Danshirō, whom she had known since her Yoshiwara days. She owed him a debt of gratitude for having brought a large number of guests with him to the opening of her Shigure Teahouse. At present he was living in Senzokuchō, Asakusa.

"What a surprise to run into you this way! You're quite right. I was asking Kannon for something."

"I thought so. You looked ever so serious. Is some lover of yours ill?"

"No, no, nothing like that. I've ended up looking after a boy, and I'm worried about him."

She paused on the flagstones below the steps. She had had a sudden idea. Danshirō was especially famous among kabuki actors for his dancing. No, he was not the head of a school, but in pieces like *Kisen*, *Utsubozaru*, or *Tsurionna* he displayed a lightness and grace quite out of keeping with his clumsy build. It was just a fleeting inspiration, but if she asked Danshirō to take on Shūsaku, would he really say no? Surely Kannon had brought her to Danshirō for just this. Such were the thoughts flitting through her head.

"Actually, I was just thinking about calling on you with a request," she said. "Are you off to work now?"

"No, I'm just back from Osaka. The show at Dōtonbori is over, and I took the night train back to Tokyo. I've just arrived, and I came to greet Kannon before going home."

"I see. You didn't go straight home, but came by the temple instead?"

"Well, you know, I just don't feel right if I don't make a little pilgrimage here whenever I get back to town."

He was still smiling. Typical Asakusa man that he was, visits to Kannon were just a normal part of his life.

"Then I'm sure you have a lot to do today. I'll call on you another time."

"Rubbish! It's no problem at all. I'm off next month, you know. By all means come, if you have something to talk about. I've brought plenty of good things from Osaka—let's eat them together."

Danshirō, too, had been formed by the Yoshiwara, and they understood each other so well that he eagerly urged her to come home with him. His wife, however, who had the respect of everyone in the acting profession, would not stand for any nonsense, and Oriku could only wonder what trouble she might get herself into if she nonchalantly turned up with him when he returned from Osaka.

"All right, but I have somewhere else to go first. I'll just get my little errand done, and I'll be over after that."

"I see. Don't disappoint me, though! I'll be expecting you. We'll have lunch together. I'm sure Okoto will be glad to see you, too."

On that light, friendly note Danshirō set off down the path behind Kannon's main hall, surrounded by his manager and disciples.

Okoto, Danshirō's wife, was a Yoshiwara brothel owner's daughter. She declared when she married him, "When an actor's short of money he goes downhill. I'll go into business just to make sure you can take time off whenever you feel like it." So this sage wife, more than a match for any man, borrowed money from her parents, set up a brothel, and gave Danshirō the freedom to master his art fully.

Danshirō might be endlessly good-natured, but his eagle-eyed wife was a different matter. Oriku first returned to Mukōjima and had Shūsaku get things ready. Then she set out again, carrying a gift of shigure clams.

"Where are you going?" Shūsaku asked suspiciously.

"I'm off to have a talk with Ichikawa Danshirō." Oriku was frank about it. "Whatever happens to you, your father is the head of a school. Rather than attach yourself to some half-baked teacher somewhere, I think you'd be far better off as the disciple of a real master like Danshirō. It could get quite tricky if you were to approach either Fujima or Hanayanagi."

"That's true enough, but would Danshirō teach me?"

"We'll just have to see. If he won't, I'll have to think about it some more."

"I wouldn't mind becoming an actor, if he wanted me to."

Oriku shook her head. "No, I'm afraid you're too old for that." Childhood training was essential for actors, and by the time he was sixteen or seventeen an untrained boy was seen as having no possible future.

"I want you to walk to Senzokuchō, Shūsaku. I'll take a rickshaw. Try to reach the door of the house about the time Danshirō and I have finished talking it over. You know the place, don't you?"

"Yes—it's right there at the corner of Ennosuke Lane."

Ennosuke, Danshirō's former professional name, had come to identify the lane on which he lived. Even today a memorial stone stands there to mark the spot.

Danshirō and Okoto were both expecting Oriku when she arrived.

"Why didn't you come straight here with my husband?" Okoto asked. "Lunch is ready. We've been waiting for you."

In the best of moods, she had lunch served in the room next to the kitchen, just as though Oriku had been one of the family. Hers was the warmth of an old denizen of the Yoshiwara.

"Before we eat," Oriku said, sitting up very straight, "I have a request."

"My husband is a great fan of yours, Oriku, and I'm sure he'll happily do whatever you ask." Okoto was all smiles.

Having no intention in any case of keeping anything from her, Oriku touched on the situation in Mitsunojō's family and went straight to her request that Danshirō teach dancing to the now-homeless Shūsaku.

"But I'm an actor, not a dance teacher," Danshirō replied gravely.

"So there would be nothing wrong with your accepting him as a student of acting. He would of course run errands for you, and I hope you would take him with you and teach him when you perform."

"If he's to be an actor I don't mind, but if he's going to be a dance teacher, then it's out of the question."

"Isn't that up to him, though? As long as he keeps his mind on learning, it will be far better for him if he stays with you, instead of going off to some half-baked dance teacher."

"She's right, you know," Okoto put in. "There are hardly any teachers left who really teach. You could at least meet him. Mistress Oriku does so much to keep us going, you could for once do as she asks."

"All right, I'll have a look at him. Bring him around sometime."
Danshirō still looked bothered.

"I've asked him to wait at the gate. I'll have him come in right away."

"Dear me, you leave nothing to chance, do you?" He smiled wryly.

Oriku brought Shūsaku in. Sitting there in his most formal posture,
he looked very sweet.

"What a nice boy!" Okoto exclaimed.

Her husband said, "I can't take you on as a dance student, but as
an acting student, all right. You can go onstage and learn by watching the masters dance. It's important for a dance teacher, too, to have
the experience of actually appearing onstage. So try it and see how
far you can go."

Danshirō spoke gently while Shūsaku listened, his head bowed.
There were tears in Shūsaku's eyes. It was so rare for Danshirō to take
on a disciple that, now that he had accepted Shūsaku, Shūsaku knew
he could expect a great deal of demanding practice. There would be
nothing indulgent about his daily training. None of that mattered,
though. He was absolutely determined to go through with it and show
his father a thing or two.

Danshirō's house in Senzokuchō was equipped with a first-class
practice stage, one so splendid that people said no other actor had
anything like it. Okoto's business talent provided for the household
so well that the bath facilities, too, were beyond reproach.

Shūsaku was a very nice boy, and Okoto thought the world of him.
"He'd be well worth adopting, if we didn't already have sons of our
own," she would say. She had every confidence in him.

Ennosuke, their eldest, was married and had his own home. In the
Senzokuchō house itself lived Matsuo (the present Ichikawa Chūsha),
Kōmori (the present Ichikawa Kodayū), and various daughters, all of
whom made the household only too lively. At first Shūsaku went there
every day from Mukōjima, but in the end he moved in and hardly ever
visited Mukōjima at all.

"The place feels empty without Shū-chan!" Ofune or one of the
other maids would often remark sadly.

"It's good for *him*, though. Why, he's a disciple of the famous
Danshirō!"

"Yes, of course, it's wonderful, but he's bound to be well looked after wherever he goes, and Senzokuchō is so close, you'd really think he could go back and forth from here!"

Alas, Shūsaku did not come back. At the theater he sat just below the curtain, in a kabuki stagehand's black garb and hood, to study what was happening onstage. Someone with his natural aptitude, watching the same play twenty-five days in a row, would remember every gesture and movement.

Now and again he would be given a bit part, and when a dance piece was on he would always be there as a stagehand. The experience of appearing onstage gave him confidence. He was nice-looking enough always to leave a good impression, and he moved so well that Sarunosuke and his brothers liked to keep their eye on him. Knowing he was Mitsunojō's son, people did not treat him quite the same as the rest of Danshirō's other disciples, but set him a little apart. This could feel like a mixed blessing at times, but his skill certainly improved rapidly. Soon he was appearing in every jōruri-derived dance piece, and he often took the kind of minor role designed to show off the star.

When Danshirō's whole troupe went off on tour, Shūsaku's name was on the list of actors. He might be assigned to dance in a lively finale scene, or to perform the major role of the woman boatman in *The Omnibus Boat*. He got better every time he performed, until he began to win the praises of Danshirō himself. He spent three years at Senzokuchō, his assurance and confidence growing the entire time.

In April of that third year there was a ceremony for the inauguration of the Nihonbashi Bridge, and Danshirō's entire troupe was charged with providing the entertainment. They were to dance on a temporary stage at one end of the bridge. Danshirō did the Priest Kisen, Sarunosuke did the Tea Woman, and the disciples, including Shūsaku, all appeared as priests.

"I'm going to be in the show for the opening of the bridge at Nihonbashi!" he announced happily when he turned up at Mukōjima. In the last three years he had changed completely. Now he was a fine-looking young man. Oriku was delighted, and the whole household was as excited as when a boy sent off somewhere into service comes home.

"My teacher's wife wants you to come and watch me practice, Mistress Oriku, if you wish. Will you do that?" He spoke like a grownup too.

"I'd like nothing better, and besides, I've been thinking I really must call on your teacher and thank him."

"My teacher says he's looking forward to seeing you too."

"He is, is he? I won't be going there for a scolding, will I?"

"Oh no. I think you'll be going there to hear him sing your praises."

"You certainly believe in yourself, don't you!"

"Yes. I don't know whether I'm really any good or not, but I know I've tried as hard as I possibly could."

"That's wonderful. The most important thing in life is really to put your heart into things. It would have been nice if putting your heart into it had worked with your father in Kanda, but I suppose that would not have been enough."

"That's something else altogether. Putting my heart into it or not had nothing to do with it." His voice was the same, but the progress he had made showed in his expression and demeanor.

The next afternoon Oriku went to Senzokuchō, to find such a clutter of footwear in the entry that she could hardly get in. The house was in chaos. It was the twenty-ninth of April, 1911, the day before the opening of the Nihonbashi Bridge, and the day also for the general rehearsal of *Kisen*. All the musicians were there, too; the stage was overflowing with them. To the accompaniment of the orchestra the kiyomoto and nagauta musicians were singing their alternating parts, while the hallway and the greenroom fairly burst with the press of stage managers and other such people involved with the production. The rehearsal was already under way. Danshirō and Sarunosuke were onstage, while Okoto kept a sharp eye on everything from in front of the stage. The Takanawa school provided the kiyomoto musicians, the nagauta musicians were Ijūrō's, and the instrumentalists were from the Umeya school. Apparently they were not working together very well on their alternating responses, because they were going over the same part again and again.

"That's just not it, you nagauta people, you're coming in late!" Okoto barked her orders, and the artists sweated away. In matters of theater nothing escaped the perfectionist Okoto, who, as they knew all too well, was herself highly accomplished at dance, at the samisen, and at everything else. They were not alone, either, in feeling nervous. Even Danshirō kept an eye on how she reacted.

"Was that bit all right?" he might ask. Another time he might ask for help with a part that had slipped his mind. Up, then, she would come, onto the stage.

"We can't have *you* forgetting, can we!" And to the kiyomoto musicians, "All right, the 'Beauty at the Window' scene again please, from the top!" Then she herself danced the problem passage.

Danshirō watched her attentively, and the part he had forgotten seemed to come back to him. In silence he admired the grace of his wife's hands and arms, while Oriku looked on too, entranced. Okoto's mere presence had the whole troupe keyed up; every one of them was in a state of finely tuned nervous tension. There was no sign of Shūsaku. The piece came to an end after the dance of the host priests, with everyone still in place, but although the rehearsal was over, no one got to his feet. All eyes were on Okoto. She seemed to have a few words for Sarunosuke, the Tea Woman, too. By now Sarunosuke was a popular actor in his own right, but in his mother's presence he listened respectfully. Oriku envied her. Once the discussion of the rehearsal was over, they all clapped their hands together, and the gathering was over. It was a moment unique to the kabuki world.

People began to disperse. Danshirō wiped his face with a towel, while Okoto fanned him with a large fan. It was only late April, but his yukata was soaked.

"You must be exhausted!" From her corner of the room, Oriku bowed to him in greeting.

"Oh!" Okoto exclaimed. "You were here, watching?"

"Yes, I was. I was impressed. I felt acutely how demanding true skill really is. Also, I came to thank you for being kind enough to look after Shūsaku."

"No, no, there's no need to thank us," Danshirō replied. "He's such a nice boy, I'm delighted to have been entrusted with him. I don't take many students, but he's well worth it." There was sincerity in his voice.

"As a matter of fact," Danshirō continued, "I have something to show you today. Have a look at this!" He took a letter out of a drawer. "Go ahead, read it."

"All right."

Oriku examined the envelope. It was from Bandō Mitsunojō. The letter was a brush-written scroll, in formal epistolary style. The gist of it was as follows. "I am grateful for your taking the trouble to look after Shūsaku. He ran away from home three years ago and has not been back since. It will give me the greatest possible pleasure if, thanks to you, he is able to grow up in a worthy manner after all. In this matter I leave everything to you. Please do whatever you think best."

On finishing it Oriku looked up at Danshirō and Okoto. "I'd been meaning to tell you," Danshirō explained, "but, you see, next month I'm scheduled to dance at the Kabuki-za, under Mitsunojō's direction. Since I have his son with me, I can't just pretend I know nothing, so I wrote to him. This is the reply he sent me."

"I apologize again for causing you all this trouble."

"His letter is nicely phrased and all, but underneath he seems to be telling me I can do with the boy whatever I like. Wouldn't you say so?" He did not look pleased. "Mitsunojō never made any approach to me, and I only wrote him because I didn't want to feel uncomfortable when the time came. To be honest, his answer put me in a bad mood."

"I'm very sorry."

"So—I know I should have talked it over with you, but I didn't— I went to ask Fujima to accept Shūsaku as his disciple."

"My!"

"If he wants to be an actor, then I'll gladly keep him here indefinitely, but if he's really to become a dance teacher, he has to go elsewhere. That was the way I saw it. Fujima is the senior master of dance, so I thought the best thing to do was to approach *him*."

By "Fujima," Danshirō meant Matsumoto Komazō (who just that year had assumed the new name Kōshirō), the son of Fujima Kan'emon. Komazō was younger than Danshirō, but they had both studied under Danjūrō.

"Did Fujima agree?"

"Not at first, no. He seemed very reluctant when he found out Shūsaku was Mitsunojō's son. So I took Shūsaku to his house and had him dance for Fujima's father."

"Goodness me!"

"Being the kind of man he is, Fujima immediately liked what he saw, and he accepted Shūsaku on the spot."

Speechless, Oriku lowered her gaze, with tears in her eyes. Suddenly, there was Shūsaku himself, bowing in thanks to Danshirō and Okoto.

"My husband hates putting himself out, but on his own he went all the way to Fujima's house for you," Okoto put in. "You should be very happy about that!"

Oriku looked at Shūsaku. "You're the luckiest fellow in the world," she said.

"I know," Shūsaku replied. "No one has ever had luck like mine." His posture was still very formal.

"You must never forget how much you owe your teacher."

"I never will."

"Now, Mistress Oriku!" Danshirō clapped his hands. Three young nagauta musicians entered from the next room and lined up on the stage.

"I had him do *His Master's Man* for Fujima's father, so I thought you should see it too. I wasn't sure it would go over well, but the old man's approval left no doubt about the matter. You must see for yourself."

"It will be a pleasure."

Shūsaku mounted the stage. In a low voice Okoto ordered the three musicians to begin. He started *His Master's Man* right from the hanamichi entrance, stamped the expected strong beat, kept his posture admirably low, and gave just the quality required to every movement and gesture. The piece conveys in dance the amusing antics of a servant who slips away from his master and wanders off on his own. Nothing about Shūsaku's performance of it suggested immaturity. He even managed to give a perfect imitation of Danshirō's particular mannerisms. The part where the hero dallies with the young lady was delightfully naughty:

> *All this makes me feel quite shy,*
> *but I get the drift*
> *you with all your tricky words*
> *keep on hinting at,*
> *and I wouldn't mind a bit*
> *your undoing my sash—*

There was wit, elegance, and real beauty in his:

> *Now that we've been together,*
> *you've opened my eyes . . .*

And the stamps that punctuated the dance had impressive power. His closing lines were light and fun.

> *Look how the lively music*
> *carried me away,*
> *till my most honored master*
> *just gave up and left—*

The final pose he struck, lantern in hand, had a fine, manly vigor. His audience was all on his side, of course, but even so, his rendition of the piece clearly left nothing to be desired.

"Well done, well done!" Okoto exclaimed, applauding. Oriku had no words, only tears. Embarrassed or not, she could only weep.

"He's good, isn't he?" Danshirō observed with satisfaction. "Two or three years with Fujima, and he'll be quite a dancer."

"Thank you, thank you, thank you!" Oriku's tears simply would not stop.

"All right, now I've done my bit. At first I felt as though you were asking a little too much, and I wanted to refuse, but you got me with your remark about Kannon having brought us together. Meeting you like that at the temple left me no choice. Otherwise I'd have said no."

"I see."

"Tomorrow is Shūsaku's twenty-first birthday. It's a pleasure to think I'm the one who's made a man of him. Anyway, my part is over.

You can take him home with you now." Such clear-cut decisiveness was typical of him.

He turned to Shūsaku. "I said everything I had to say to you yesterday. Now all you have to do is keep it in mind. And be sure not to forget how much you owe Okoto."

Shūsaku could hardly speak, either. All he could do was to show by his humble posture all his gratitude toward Danshirō and Okoto.

Oriku's tears flowed, but they were happy tears. All that Danshirō and his wife had done filled her with joy, and Shūsaku's extraordinary progress at *His Master's Man* made her confident of his future. When they left the Senzokuchō house, after endlessly repeated thanks, the sky was a leaden gray, but Oriku's mood was set to the fairest of weather. The surge of emotion carried her unconsciously, and all but in silence, to Kannon's main hall. Kannon's mediation on her behalf had made it impossible for Danshirō to refuse. That was what he had said. Her own prayers to her beloved protector had allowed Shūsaku to become a man. With their hearts too full to speak, the two went up to the main hall and bowed their heads before the great chest containing the image of Kannon. It was here that Shūsaku had slept beneath the steps, and here too that Oriku had run into Danshirō. Her debt of gratitude to Kannon was manifold. After a long moment of prayer they descended the stairs side by side and started toward the great gate.

"I was so nervous that I had completely forgotten," Oriku said, "but you must be hungry."

"I should be, but what with everything else, I'm not really hungry at all."

"You don't want to eat anything?"

"I'd rather go straight back to Mukōjima. I'm looking forward to thanking Ofune and the others."

For Shūsaku, the restaurant at Mukōjima was home. Now he was a proper man, he felt like showing himself to all the people there who would sincerely share his joy.

At the Shigure Teahouse everyone crowded eagerly around him, some exclaiming over his fine figure, others praising his good looks.

"Congratulate him, everyone!" Oriku called out to them all. "Danshirō approached Fujima Kan'emon, and soon Shūsaku will begin training toward taking a professional name! On top of that, tomorrow is his twenty-first birthday, so we can all celebrate it together. Then he'll go on to the opening of the Nihonbashi Bridge, and the day after tomorrow he'll call at the Fujima house in Hamachō. Today we'll be getting him in the mood!"

They were all in the great kitchen. Shūsaku was practically blushing. His once-childish face was now a man's, and a bluish hint of beard showed on his chin. Oriku sat him down in the main room, where he happily partook of the specialties of the house. Ofune and the others all danced attendance upon him, and the place was very lively indeed.

Shūsaku never lost his dignified composure, despite downing one cup of saké after another. "This is the happiest day of my whole life!" he exclaimed, sinking with profound gratitude into blissful intoxication. Oriku was so happy, and Shūsaku was so sweet, that she kept her cup by her as the afternoon wore on. Since customers would be arriving after sunset they moved him to the Paulownia annex, and left him and Oriku alone there. The maids no longer came to look after them once the restaurant picked up. The late spring breeze brought them salty air from the rising tide.

"I won't thank you, Auntie," Shūsaku began. "I may well need your help again in the future, and besides, now that my father's abandoned me, you're the only parent I have."

His warm, tipsy gaze embraced Oriku.

"You did well, you know. Danshirō took good care of you, I'm sure, but there must have been difficult times. You did very well."

"I think I'd rather go to Fujima's daily than actually live there. Would it be all right if I went from here?"

"Of course it would. This is my room, so for the time being you can stay here. I'll have a room prepared for you."

"I can't imagine when I'll ever be able to repay you."

"You repaid me in full just now, for everything you owed me up to today, with that *His Master's Man*. I had no idea you could dance like that. Frankly, I was amazed."

"It makes me very happy to hear you say that."

"If you want to reward me, just keep making progress in your art. That's all I need."

"You really love art, don't you, Auntie."

"Art and men: those are my pleasures." She kept a perfectly straight face. Embarrassed, Shūsaku finally laughed too.

"I helped you out this way because Kannon brought us together, but when I saw you dance today, I fell in love with you. I assume you're familiar with girls?"

Shūsaku tried to laugh off the question.

"Have you ever been in love?"

"Well, no, I haven't. For one thing, I've never had time."

"You've never had an adventure?"

"No, of course not."

"So you've never had a woman?"

"Um, no."

"We can't have that. Now that you're a man, it's not right for you never to have experienced a woman. You won't have the right kind of courage when you need it, and anyway, the art of a man who's never known a woman just isn't complete."

"Really?"

"Yes, really. When he takes a female role he isn't able to give his dancing the proper seductiveness."

"I suppose not."

"Shall I teach you, then?"

"What? *You*?"

"Do you mind?"

"Why, no, but somehow it doesn't seem right."

"It's fine. It's just something you need to learn—what a woman's like."

"I see what you mean."

"You're bound to learn somewhere, sometime, but wouldn't it be just the thing for you to first know a woman on the very evening of the day when you've fully become a man?"

Shūsaku blushed and gazed at the floor in silence. He was thanking her for the lesson he was about to receive.

"It's not time yet, though. You won't fully be a man till after midnight, so till then just drink up."

"All right."

"I'm so happy that tonight I'll sing, too. I hardly ever play the samisen anymore."

She took out her samisen and restrung it, looking remarkably youthful. Once the strings were in place she tuned them and sang the itchū-bushi song "Koharu Puts Up Her Hair":

> *That's the way it goes, this life,*
> *twisted like coiled hair*
> *into an unhappy knot—*
> *all-consuming love*
> *you knew from the very first*
> *would lead you astray.*
> *So you set your boxwood comb,*
> *silent, in your hair,*
> *and hold the mirror up to look,*
> *while helpless tears*
> *down your cheeks run in a stream*
> *to give your sidelocks gloss—*
> *all, alas, for fleeting joys . . .*

Had the idea of sleeping with Shūsaku only just entered Oriku's head? Had she been thinking about it for some time? There is no way to know. Perhaps she had been looking at him as a woman looks at a man ever since she half-carried him home from Kannon's temple. She could have been helping him all along with this day in mind. There certainly was pleasure to be derived from imagining touching his pristine body.

"Yes. I'll teach you all you need to know."

So ran Oriku's tipsy thoughts. When eleven o'clock came she put her saké cup away and headed for the bath. She wanted to be clean for the unsullied Shūsaku. While she soaked, she contemplated the heightened color of her skin. Her lower belly was a bit more rounded than it might be, but she had some way yet to go before she reached fifty, and she was still sound in every part. She pinched her upper arm: the taut skin colored a healthy red. Cupping her flushed breasts, she stepped out of the bath.

CHAPTER FOUR

The Yushima Koto

"Younger men are attracted to me for some reason. I don't know why, but I don't feel at all right about it when the age difference is too great. Here I am, at my age, and boys in their early twenties fall in love with me. When a youngster makes an overture, somehow I just can't turn him away, and I end up getting into the mood. I shouldn't do it, should I? Sometimes a young fellow from the kabuki world asks me to guide him through his first experience, and I don't want to be unkind and shame him. Still, it's embarrassing, and often I don't know quite what to do. On the other hand, his being so much younger prevents complications later on. Strangely enough, once you're used to young men like that, the older ones seem too much trouble. Young ones are clean and fresh, and they give you a nice feeling. An older one can be quite a nuisance. If you don't look out he'll try to hang onto you, and the fine principle of 'one man, one night' easily breaks down. So when youngsters come around, I may say to myself, 'Oh no, not again!' but I end up going along with them."

Now and again Oriku would justify herself this way. She felt a bit shy before Ofune and the others, since they knew all about her various younger lovers, but no amount of embarrassment could make her want to hide her actions.

"My husband died when I was in my twenties, and all I did after that was work, work, work. I ignored my own desires completely. Really, though, I'm neither stock nor stone—there are times when I want a man, and at my age I see no reason not to indulge myself. If I like someone well enough I'll have fun with him, all in good measure. So I'd appreciate it if you could look the other way. It's simply too boring without some diversions, and I don't want to go sneaking around out of sight just because there's some man I'm fond of. This is my place, and I'll take him to my own room. Please grant me that too. I have no intention of compromising my business, or losing my head over someone and worrying all of you. I'll look after what's mine very nicely, thank you, and I hope you'll understand." Such was Oriku's bold, frank way of going about having a good time.

Not just in matters of love, but in every aspect of daily life Oriku was open and straightforward. She was never timid, and she hated it when people acted secretive and sneaky.

"That's exactly the kind of boy I like," she would say to Ofune. "What do you think of him?"

Ofune would give her a wry smile. "I don't know who'd bother to ask *me* about men!" she would reply. She liked Oriku's way of doing such things. When it came to running the business, too, management decisions were made more or less in common with the whole staff, and although the nominal pay was low, everyone got a bonus according to profit. Oriku was never out to make money just for herself. Her aim was always that the business should thrive for the good of everyone who worked there.

"You can't run a business all on your own," she would say. "It won't do well unless the people who work for you feel that it's theirs too." To tell the truth, she drew a monthly salary herself. She employed an old accountant, and she made sure everyone knew the balance each month.

In those days progressive management was quite the thing, and so too was an open management style. The statesman Itō Hirobumi praised her style more warmly than anyone. "We are now entering an age," he said, "when it behooves managers to earn money not for personal gain, but for the benefit of all the workers. You are an extraordinary woman! The way you manage your business here should serve as a model for the future." A great man like Itō favored Oriku's chazuke restaurant because he loved the character of Oriku herself. Oriku mourned when she heard that he had died in Harbin. "This is a sadder blow than when my own husband died!" she wailed. Thanks to him, an impressive array of politicians and government officials frequented her place.

The army general Count Tanabe Mitsumasa even joked, "How about it, Oriku? Won't you have me as your lover?"

"A man of power makes me feel caged. I don't like it. And a Minister of the Imperial Household, to boot? No thank you!" Such was Oriku's reaction, and she flatly refused. Count Tanabe really was Imperial Household Minister at the time.

"I hear you go only for younger men." He grinned. "Men in their twenties." Loving younger men was all right, though. She didn't remember ever approaching one herself, only being approached. That was how she had gained this reputation of hers.

"Well, I can see you're never going to go for *me*," he continued, "but a young man, then—would you be nice to him?" He was still smiling. Oriku smiled back.

"No, no, I mean it. There's a young man I'd like you to look after." He was serious now. With a man like that you never knew whether he meant what he was saying, or whether he was joking. From Kōchi in Tosa Province, he had joined the imperial side in the lead-up to the Restoration and held several important posts in the Meiji government, and he was now Imperial Household Minister.

"What are you talking about?" Oriku had grown more serious, in response to the count's earnest manner.

Once the maids had gone and the two were alone, the Count began, "You'll probably laugh at me for bringing this up, but I have a friend whose only son, nearly thirty now, insists he doesn't want a wife and refuses to marry. Not only that, but he's never once slept with a woman."

"Are there really still people like that?"

"Yes, I know, the whole thing is mad, but in this regard he seems completely impossible."

"Whose son is he?"

"I'll tell you later. I'd like to ask you to take him in hand."

"But what do you want me to do?"

The Count's eyes sparkled again with merriment.

"I want to bring him together with a woman of experience and have him find out what a woman is like. I'd like to impress on him how wonderful a woman is."

"And you are asking *me* to do that?"

"Now, don't be angry! They say you always have young men around, falling in love with you, and that in the entertainment world it's seen as an honor to be given your sexual initiation by Oriku."

"That's nonsense!"

"No, no, I looked into it thoroughly. The talk is that you're a wizard at teaching the art of love."

"You're embarrassing me, Count Tanabe, talking this way!"

"It's not *me* talking this way, it's everyone. I hope you'll add one more young man to your list of experiences. He's very handsome, you know. Won't you at least meet him?"

"Very well, Count Tanabe, I suppose I will, if you say so."

"Please do. I'd really appreciate it. I'll bring him around tomorrow." His tone was more earnest than ever. If this was what the Imperial Household Minister wanted, Oriku was in no position to refuse. In response to her vague answer, neither assenting nor dissenting, the Minister's secretary turned up at Mukōjima the next day in the company of a young gentleman. He was indeed handsome, tall, and very slender, and his features conveyed genuine distinction. Whether or not the secretary was familiar with the circumstances, he soon left the young man there and went away. The young man fidgeted about, unsure what to do with himself.

The cherry blossoms had fallen, and the trees on the embankment were putting forth fresh new leaves. Amid all these signs that spring was here in full force, Oriku was not displeased to find herself seated face to face with a youth.

"Do you know why you are here?" she asked. They had stepped down into the garden, and she was showing him around the establishment. It was about two in the afternoon. There were guests in one of the annexes, but all the other rooms were empty. No maids were about. On the riverbank, a boat equipped with fishing poles and a bait box was moored at the dock for the pleasure of daytime guests.

"What about trying some fishing?" Oriku led him into the boat and dropped two baited lines into the water. It was a windless, sleepy day, just the kind when the fish are likely to bite. Uncertain what to do next, Oriku tried striking up a conversation, but she got back only brief, perfunctory replies. She did not even know yet what he was called. It was just as though he were an abandoned orphan.

"What is your name?"

"Kawahara," he answered simply. "Kawahara Yasuo. What am I here for?"

"That's my question to *you*. Why have you come?"

"Don't you know?"

"No, I don't," Oriku said. "Count Tanabe told me there was a young man he'd like me to look after. He didn't say anything else."

"Then I'll be going. I don't want to put you to any trouble."

"No, no, you're no trouble at all. Considering what my place is like, you couldn't possibly get in the way, all by yourself like this. You needn't worry. Just enjoy yourself."

The young man hooked a small carp. Silently, he took it off the hook and tossed it back in. There was nothing fussy or hurried about his movements. They were poised, leisurely. He put down his pole and took out a cigarette case. It was silver, and it had the chrysanthemum crest on it. Oriku jumped. Who *was* this Kawahara Yasuo, with his cigarette case engraved with the imperial crest?

"That's a nice case you have there."

"Yes, it's a gift from the Imperial Household."

"A gift to you personally?"

"I'm not sure. I don't really know who I got it from."

"Is it really all right to use things with the imperial crest on them like that, every day?"

To Oriku, the sight of the chrysanthemum crest was positively frightening. The Emperor meant absolute power, and the mere idea of having his crest, to say nothing of actually approaching him, inspired her with awe. Fine though the case might be, it held only Golden Bat cigarettes, a very inexpensive brand at five sen for a package of ten. The disparity between the silver case with the imperial crest and the cheap cigarettes inside it seemed to sum up young Yasuo himself.

Does this fellow know what he's doing here? Oriku wondered as she watched him smoke his Golden Bat. He seemed to, yet seemed not to. Meanwhile, he lazily enjoyed his smoke.

"Do people actually come all the way out here?"

"Yes, surprisingly enough, they do. Ever since the old Edo days, fanciers of fine scenery have come to Mukōjima for blossoms, moon, and snow."

"You must mean only old people, though. Not young ones, surely."

"Oh yes, they come too. It's perfect for lovers who want to enjoy themselves unobserved."

"You've built yourself such a big place. Is the business doing well?"

"For the moment we're popular. You never know about the future, though."

"The Sumida River really makes the place, doesn't it—being able to look out over the river this way from the restaurant."

"That's right. You'd think the Shigure Teahouse owned the river. That's its special attraction."

"It's a good thing the river doesn't charge you a user fee."

"It certainly is. Why, we couldn't have that!"

At last the young man laughed. His beautifully white teeth gave him a fetching smile. There in the boat they chatted for a while about what a user fee for the Sumida River might do to Oriku's business. He had on a simple ikat-weave hakama over a splash-pattern kimono. Nothing about his clothing or his appearance gave any clue to his background.

"What was here before you came?"

"Nothing. It was just a reedy marsh. The land was practically free."

"No doubt, but raising the level this way must have cost a fortune."

So he knew about things like that.

"Yasuo-san, what sort of work have you been doing?"

"I've been working in a bank."

"Ah, now I see why you know about user fees, land prices, and other boring things like that."

"When you work in a bank, you get into the habit of evaluating people's wealth. Even visiting someone else's place, you immediately start wondering how much the person paid for the land, and so forth. They aren't very nice people, bank workers."

His response was so mature that Oriku could hardly believe he had never known a woman. Although shy at first, he seemed thoroughly grown-up once they started talking.

"What is your relationship with Count Tanabe?"

"He's supposed to be my uncle. He's a nice man, though I wish he weren't always quite so eager to be helpful."

"If he's your uncle, then you're from a great family yourself."

The young man chuckled as though making a little fun of her.

After sunset the young man settled into the Paulownia annex, took a bath, and had some saké. He was a good drinker, and he enjoyed the regular dinner menu, too.

"That is *good*! I stay away from meat, so this is just the kind of food I like." He cleaned up every dish. When the evening guests began arriving and Oriku went off to the kitchen, he remained behind, drinking by himself. The cooking fire was put out at eleven, and late-night arrivals got only the ever-ready stew.

"Let's spend the night drinking." In a mood to relax now that her work was done, Oriku could be frank. The news that the young man in question had reached nearly thirty without ever knowing a woman had convinced her he must be a lumpish boor, but as it turned out, he was not at all. He understood things well, knew the ways of the world, told jokes, and was articulate. That he should never have known a woman seemed impossible.

"Yasuo-san, I've heard that you've never known a woman, but that can't be true."

"It is, though." He blushed.

"Really and truly?"

"Really and truly."

"I can't understand it. How could a man like you still be so innocent?"

No matter what she said, all he did was blush.

"What Count Tanabe asked me to do was to teach you the way of women. Do you mind?"

In response she got a questioning silence.

"I'm over forty, you know. Is that all right?"

"It's all right." He nodded slightly, in clear assent.

They went on drinking till past one o'clock, then she lay down in the same room with him, as though too drunk to know what she was doing. There was nothing wrong with his body, and he had no trouble performing as a man. They enjoyed the available pleasures and slept till ten o'clock the next morning.

When they awoke he kept his gaze lowered, sure enough, and would not look her in the eye. Seemingly dazzled, he spent the entire day in the Paulownia.

"Count Tanabe will be worried about you. Please go home." But he just kept his eyes to the floor and said nothing about complying. That night, too, he stayed in the Paulownia. Having him there night after night made things difficult for Oriku, but she could hardly just order him to go. Again they slept together. Perhaps he really had never known a woman, but he had nothing against women. In body he was sound, and he certainly had a man's desires.

"Are you sure it's true that you'd never known a woman?"

"Yes, it's true," he murmured.

"You've never had a chance to be with one?

"No."

"You've never been to the Yoshiwara, or somewhere like that?"

"Places like that get on my nerves. I don't like them, and I don't feel like going there."

"That's probably because you have no friends. Is that it?"

"Perhaps."

"You understand now, I'm sure. You mustn't worry your uncle any more. Go ahead and get married."

"I don't want to."

"I won't have you saying that. I promised Count Tanabe I'd teach you what it's like to be with a woman. That was my job, and I've done it. Now you know, that's the end of it."

"It was a job, was it."

"Yes. My job was to get your fire started."

"I don't like it."

"I don't, either. If you stay on here, you'll get in the way of the business."

"Yesterday you said having me here was no trouble at all. So were you making that up?"

Oriku said nothing.

"I'm staying. I can pay. Think of me as a guest."

"No, Count Tanabe entrusted you to me. I won't have you here as a guest. In the first place, I'm more than ten years older than you."

"I have no age. It's stupid to choose someone according to age. I want to marry you."

"Nonsense."

"It's not nonsense. I mean it."

His expression was indeed serious. He was going to marry her, and nothing she could do in the way of reproving or consoling him could make him change his mind. He made no move to leave. During the day he went to the riverbank to fish, but he threw back anything he caught. Only fishing itself absorbed him, or at least helped him pass the time.

Oriku's anger had no effect. He calmly stayed on a full week in the Paulownia. Ofune complained. "Just how long do you plan to keep that man here?" she demanded to know. "Everyone's watching—you'd better not go too far!" Her tone was vehement.

"He's a nuisance for me, too, but he just won't leave."

"Well, if *you* can't tell him to go, *I* will."

"All right, all right, I'll get him to leave today."

For once Oriku was at a disadvantage. Normally she had little trouble sending a man off, even if he needed a bit of a talking-to, and her failure this time was weighing on her mind. Things were just not as they should be.

Yasuo turned out to be surprisingly brazen. He behaved almost as if he owned the place.

"I don't know what you have in mind," Oriku began, "but this is where I work. I wonder what you'd do if a woman came to visit you at your bank and then refused to leave. It's the same thing. Count Tanabe asked me to teach you, and I did. That's all. My job is done. Please go today."

"No. I don't want to."

"That won't do. You're making things difficult for the restaurant."

"If I go, I won't be able to see you anymore, will I. I'll go if you promise to see me again."

"For now, just go. We'll talk about that later."

"No, I say. I'm not going anywhere unless you promise me that."

"What a problem you are!"

"I don't care. I know I can make you happy, and I'm not leaving."

To Oriku's distress he would not be moved until she promised. Then at last he left. Oriku felt utterly drained. Most men had a good time and left again without a fuss. She had never had one just move in and refuse to budge. Once he was gone, and she had recovered a little, she suddenly felt lost. It was as though another self, not her usual one, were sitting there, blankly, in the Paulownia annex. When the kitchen had been busy she had kept her mind on other things, but now that the fire was out, she felt unbearably lonely.

The strangeness of drinking and sleeping alone made her unexpectedly sad. Never having been seriously in love, she felt particularly confused. First the proprietor of the Silver Flower had made her his mistress, then his wife had died and he had moved her to the Yoshiwara itself. None of this had been under her control, and life had given her no chance to become acquainted with love. That is why all this was now so especially upsetting. The room where she had once lived alone so cheerfully now seemed desolate, and once the night had wrapped her establishment in silence, the loneliness became unbearable. She could phone him, if only she knew where he lived. Never before had she felt the urge to do such a thing, and she wondered what had come over her. However, she had no idea of his address, or even of who he really was. If he did not come looking for her, she had no way of contacting him. Ten days later she had a phone call from Count Tanabe, or at least from Sasaki, his secretary. "The Count wishes to have lunch with you," he said. "Since he does not have the time to go to Mukōjima, he hopes you will be good enough to join him at Kagetsu, in the Konparu district of the Ginza. Will that be satisfactory?"

Of course she agreed. Count Tanabe obviously wanted to talk about Yasuo. She arrived early, to find the Kagetsu owner expecting her.

"Every restaurant in Tokyo is amazed by what you've done. The talk was that you could open a chazuke restaurant out there all you liked, and no one would ever go. It's just stunning. You have quite a touch." Oriku's success in as unlikely a place as Mukōjima had the big Tokyo restaurants all agog.

Count Tanabe arrived at the appointed time. He wore a dark suit, which he never did on his visits to Mukōjima, and he sat there looking somewhat constrained.

"I'm hungry," he said. "Let's eat while we talk."

He had the food brought right away and ordered beer.

"I apologize for making you come all the way here, but I want to talk to you about Yasuo."

Oriku had been right.

"I should never have asked you to do it, but anyway, it seems the medicine worked only too well, and now he's in love with you. I can't imagine you welcoming that outcome."

"It's no joke, no. Just think how much older I am!" Oriku's anger conveyed her feelings, in reverse.

"That's what I thought too, at first, but he doesn't care about age. He's absolutely serious about wanting to marry you."

"What nonsense! Please don't encourage him." So she said, although what she felt was quite different.

"He's such a serious fellow, I don't know what to do with him. He keeps thanking me for having brought him together with his ideal woman, and he means it. But, Oriku, how old *are* you, actually?"

"Over sixty."

"Rubbish! I'm being serious, and I'd appreciate a serious answer. So, what do you say? Won't you go ahead and marry him?"

"This is no joke, I tell you! Can I possibly, as I am now, turn myself into a wife? The very idea!" She made herself angrier than ever.

"You absolutely refuse?"

"There's nothing even to consider. I simply don't understand, Count Tanabe, how you can seriously even suggest such a thing!"

"So it's no use my asking you further?"

"No indeed, I should say *not!*" She turned away from him as she said it. It was a big lie, but she could not have said anything else.

The Count reflected for a while in silence. "I was wondering whether or not to tell you," he said, "but I think I will. Actually, I'm at my wits' end too."

"Surely *you* have nothing to worry about, do you?"

"You see, the truth is that Yasuo is an illegitimate son of one of the Princes." He kept his voice low. Oriku gasped.

"No one is supposed to know about him, and I've been bringing him up myself."

"Does *he* know?"

"Of course."

"Does the Prince?"

"Privately, yes."

"What sort of person is his mother?"

"This is an imperial family secret. I trust you will bear that in mind when I tell you." His tone was insistent.

The imperial family employed women officials, and sometimes one of its members becomes involved with one, so that she has a child. The emperor's sons are called Princes, and they are treated accordingly. However it appears that the Princes' sons were not identified publicly and were disposed of in various, suitable ways. Yasuo's mother withdrew from the palace pregnant, gave birth, and passed away without seeing her son grow up. Count Tanabe took the now parentless Yasuo under his wing. After graduating from college, Yasuo went to work at the Daiichi Bank. The name Kawahara was his mother's. All his support expenses came from the imperial family, through Count Tanabe.

"So that's who he is. What about it, then? Won't you marry him?"

"Why on earth should I want to do that? Knowing he's a Prince's son just confirms that I couldn't. One day he'll obviously find a far more impressive bride than me."

"That's where he's different. You're his first woman, and he's fallen desperately in love with you. He wants to be with *you*, he says. Well, there's no need to marry him—won't you please just share your life with him? You rent him a house somewhere and go there from time to time. That would do."

"And what about *him* in the meantime, living there all by himself? Would he just be waiting for me to come?"

"No, no, he's qualified to teach Tsukushi-school koto."

"What? What did you say?" Oriku stared yet again.

"He's good at the koto. Didn't he tell you?"

"No, he didn't. He said nothing at all about playing the koto."

"He's like that. He doesn't talk about himself."

"I suppose he might let the Prince's name slip if he ever did. Anyway, being good at the koto certainly gives him something to do."

"Exactly. Buy him a house where he can hang out his shingle as a koto teacher, and he'll be fine. He doesn't have to earn his living at it. It needn't be more than a pastime."

"Now that *does* sound like a nice life!"

"So you'll do it?"

Oriku simply could not say any longer that she objected. She found it hard to believe that so young a man could be a koto teacher, but his father's princely lineage gave him the privilege of conferring the most senior titles in that school, and koto music was a hereditary accomplishment in his line. Teaching the koto would hardly make him rich in the modern world, but it would be thoroughly honorable. Besides, Oriku, too, felt confident of her own ability at the koto.

"Don't you think it would be just right for a Prince's illegitimate son to be a koto teacher?"

Despite his wry smile the Count, normally so quick with a joke, was completely in earnest.

"Yes, it would. I myself love music and the theater. Thank you for explaining the situation. I suppose I could think the matter over." She left the Count with this vague reply.

At Mukōjima, Ofune could not get over it. "A Prince's illegitimate son? Well, that's that, I suppose. You'll have to do what you can for him!" Her eyes were spinning. The news astonished everyone, and they all came to see Yasuo quite differently.

Only Oriku herself did not change. "I hear you're very good at the koto," she started in on him as soon as he turned up. "Why did you keep that from me? It's important!"

"You must have heard that from Count Tanabe."

"Yes, I did. I've never met anyone as vague about himself as you! Why didn't you tell me you play the koto?"

"It's a woman's instrument. I was embarrassed."

"Why? All the great koto masters are men. The Count asked me to set you up as a Tsukushi-school koto teacher, and he gave me money for the purpose. Shall I do it?"

"Please do." For the first time ever he bowed his head to her.

"I want you to show me how well you play. You're too young to attract much in the way of students."

"I'd prefer none at all."

"No, no, that won't do. If you're going to teach, you have to be serious about it. I don't want Count Tanabe to have to keep on worrying about you."

The koto that Ofune had prepared was brought in, and Yasuo sat down before it, looking as if he wished he were anywhere else.

Once he was seated his expression changed. Despite disliking having to play, with the koto before him he drew himself up into an alert, dignified posture. The way he fitted the plectra to his fingers and adjusted the bridges was precisely correct, and his training on the instrument was obvious.

Oriku felt another surge of happiness. She had always been certain she could not love anyone who had not mastered one of the arts, and in this case too she had been quite right.

"This is an Ikuta-school koto," he said. "The Tsukushi-school koto, like the Yamada koto, is a little shorter." His expression was now intent. Once he had the instrument tuned to his satisfaction he bowed. Oriku returned the bow and sat up straight, out of respect for a princely lineage entitled to bestow the highest ranks in music.

Yasuo began simply. The piece was *Crane and Tortoise*, a felicitous, thoroughly familiar work to which he gave a beautifully clear tone. All the maids gathered in the corridor outside to listen. No one had ever played a koto at the Shigure Teahouse before.

The sound was indeed lovely. When he had finished, Ofune sat down in a corner of the room. The maids lined up in the corridor, seeking another glimpse of Yasuo's face.

"Thank you. We rarely have a chance to hear such music. It was wonderful." Ofune was delighted. The Yasuo who refused to leave had been to her no more than a nuisance, but she thought quite differently of him now. The koto master who was a Prince's son moved her deeply.

Oriku's mood changed somewhat, too. If he was *this* good, she needn't blush to take him as a lover.

Yasuo, who wanted to live at the border between the more urbane and the more traditional parts of the city, moved into a house in Yushima's Umezono district. For a geisha neighborhood, it was surprisingly quiet. Immediately behind it stretched an up-market quarter inhabited by the residents of Hongōdai. No, he was unlikely to attract students, nor would he remain there forever. This was just a temporary refuge for someone reluctant to go out in the world. Yasuo would not always be a local koto teacher. He was biding his time.

Once the house was rented, Ofune got his things together. He carried his koto.

"Can we be together every day?" he asked Oriku. Only that concerned him.

"I'll come every ten days." Oriku still refused to indulge him.

"Ten days is too long. *Please* make it once a week!" He was like a child begging something from his mother.

So he set up shop as a koto teacher, with a pretty maid named Oyuki to do the chores around the house. At first the maids from Mukōjima took turns coming for lessons, but really he was a teacher only in name; no music came from his place, since he had practically no students. For this reason, Oriku decided to come for a weekly lesson herself. Afterward, she would spend the night. In this way she came gradually to understand Yasuo's loneliness. His attachment to her involved longing for his mother. At first she had indeed been his lover, but in time he became a spoiled child who seemed to want a lover less than he wanted a mother.

Three months after moving in he had four or five students. Some were young geisha; apparently, news of the handsome young koto teacher had gone through the geisha quarter. However, he took no more notice of his students than he did of the lovely Oyuki beside him. All he did was to wait for that bittersweet lover's visit once a week.

Oriku herself came to feel similarly constrained. She would set out for Yushima at about ten in the evening, after the day's business was more or less over. By that time Yasuo was finished with his lessons and had set out the saké. This was the only time he became really human again. He did not drink that much. Instead he sat across from her, holding her hand and never letting it go, just like a boy clinging to his mother.

"This is a problem!" Oriku cried, from a mixture of happiness and bewilderment, every time she came to see him. She had never been loved this much before, nor had any of her affairs gone on so long.

"A problem? Why? You don't have to come if you don't want to. If you do want to, though, we should get married."

That was his only subject. "If you don't come I'll resign myself to losing you, but if you feel like coming, then I want you to marry me." He kept saying the same thing over and over again.

"Then I won't come anymore. Count Tanabe asked me to look after you, and I've done that. Today's the last time."

So she would say, but a week later she could not bear to stay away. Her route to Yushima was straightforward enough: she would take a rickshaw along the embankment to Azumabashi, then a tram, changing at Umayabashi. When she got off, she would pass through the torii of the Yushima Tenjin Shrine, turn right, and the house was on the second cross street. She knew she could not go on forever like this with so young a man; no, she would simply have cut it off sooner or later. Soon enough a year had gone by and she was no closer to making up her mind.

That May, Count Tanabe turned up at Mukōjima.

"I have another request today," he said. "The Konoe Division will be marching out here at noon the day after tomorrow. The route goes from Takebashi to Kanegafuchi, and Prince Hachijō will lead the parade. He will have lunch at the Shigure Teahouse."

"Really?"

"You've had no notification yet from the Division?"

"Not a word."

"Well, it will probably come tomorrow. You will need to provide lunch for the Prince and his entourage. Prince Hachijō is Yasuo's father." Count Tanabe's expression was stern.

"The Prince will not drink, since the parade will not be over, but I want you to have Yasuo there."

"Very well."

"However, the whole thing is to be secret. After lunch the Prince will take a walk in the garden. I want you to arrange for him to encounter Yasuo there in a completely natural manner."

"Does the Prince know what Yasuo looks like?"

"Of course he does."

"Won't the Prince's entourage object, if the two talk together?"

"You are to let things take their natural course. If the Prince shows signs of avoiding him, then let him do so. The best thing is for you not to concern yourself with whatever happens."

"I'm worried, though. Just hearing that the Prince is coming makes me nervous."

"The lighter you keep things, the better. The Prince dislikes formality."

"Will you be there too?"

"No, I can't be there. The event the day after tomorrow is military, which means that the Imperial Household Ministry is not involved with it at all. Please see that everything goes well."

Once the Count was gone, Oriku asked Yasuo over from Yushima. The news about the Prince had immediately gotten her keyed up.

"It's been a year since I was invited to the restaurant!" Yasuo walked all around the place, looking fondly at everything.

That same day, an officer of the Konoe Division came to make an inspection, and chaos reigned because of work on the garden, but Yasuo took it easy in the Paulownia annex.

Trumpets announced the arrival of the party from the division a little before noon, whereupon the local people all gathered on the embankment to watch. The Prince was on horseback. He took lunch in the main room, together with his aides and his duty officers. The menu served was the usual one, and as always Oriku personally prepared the concluding chazuke. She felt proud when the Prince took a second helping.

The Prince was in his mid-fifties. He sported a fine beard, and in his perfectly tailored uniform he presented an imposingly manly figure. When the meal was over Yasuo wandered out into the garden. The Prince then went for a stroll himself, as planned. Oriku accompanied Yasuo, while two aides attended the Prince. Upon noticing Yasuo the Prince put on a show of surprise. His aides withdrew to a distance, while Oriku hastily turned back and watched from behind a cherry tree. Yasuo saluted the Prince politely. The Prince considered him attentively, then approached and spoke to him, although his words remained inaudible. The two talked together quite naturally, without visible constraint, for about ten minutes. The Prince's aides then rejoined him, and Yasuo saluted him once more with a bow. The Prince's lunch break had taken fifty minutes. As he was leaving, he personally congratulated Oriku on the excellence of the meal and apologized for having put her to so much trouble. Oriku only bowed her head. Once the Prince was gone, everyone crowded around Yasuo, begging to know what the two had talked about, but Yasuo only smiled. He told Oriku nothing, either. Oriku felt quite satisified— satisfied with the figure cut by the Prince, who had known he was speaking with his son.

A month later, Yasuo mentioned that Count Tanabe had resigned as Minister of the Imperial Household.

"I'm not surprised," Oriku replied. "He kept on talking about wanting to do that."

"They say it's all over the papers."

"He must feel relieved. It must be a trying business, working with the palace."

"He's already received his next assignment, though. He's going to Taiwan, as Governor General."

"That will be quite a job too, won't it, and so far away!"

"I'm going with him as a member of his staff."

"What? You *are*?"

"I'll be gone about two years. You don't stay long in a place like that. At first I said no, but what with one thing and another I couldn't refuse." His tone of voice had changed.

"I don't suppose you could, no. I didn't expect you to go on doing what you've been doing forever. No doubt the Prince is looking after you."

Yasuo, who fell silent whenever the Prince was mentioned, said nothing at all. His life at Yushima had lasted a year, and so too had Oriku's quandary.

"You won't be playing the koto anymore, will you."

"Hmm, I wonder."

"The Prince has no heir, does he? You're the only one."

"I'm his son, I know, but I'm really not. I have nothing to do with him."

"Anyway, now you have your chance to make your way in the world."

"I'm happy enough as I am, but I'll have to follow Count Tanabe's orders."

"This should have happened long ago. It's all a bit late."

"Apparently it takes a word from the Prince."

"I'm sure it does. That's why your meeting at Mukōjima was important. When are you leaving, by the way?"

"I don't know, but I'm supposed to move to Count Tanabe's house in Azabu by tomorrow morning."

"Are you looking forward to it?"

"No. All I want is still to marry you, but it can't be helped. I give up. I'll follow my own path."

"That's right. Everyone has to do that."

"I'm not so sure. Sometimes you follow a path you don't like. As far as I'm concerned, my greatest happiness would be to spend the rest of my life in this house as a koto teacher."

"No, no, that's no way to be happy."

"At any rate, I'll just take what comes. I'm resigned to whatever the future may bring. The dream of the house at Yushima is gone."

"No it isn't, not until tomorrow morning."

"Now I'm finished with playing the koto, I think I'll donate one of my instruments to the Yushima Tenjin Shrine and leave the other at Mukōjima. What do you think?"

"I'd be delighted to have one, but I don't know about the shrine."

"It should be fine, as long as I donate some money with it."

"Do you give money, too, when you donate a koto?"

"Certainly. You always donate money."

It was evening already, but he took the koto to the shrine himself, to proceed with the formal donation. The plum trees were in full spring leaf, but the Shrine had no visitors. The grounds were empty. It is Izumi Kyōka, in his novel *A Woman's Lineage*, who made the Yushima Shrine grounds famous, thanks to the love affair between Otsuta and Hayase. During Yasuo's time in Yushima the only thing there was a restaurant called Uojū. The shrine itself was not widely known. A knoll behind the main sanctuary afforded a fine view of Shinobazu Pond and gave the children a nice place to play.

"I told the priest that when you donate a koto to a shrine, you first play it for the god; but I just didn't feel like doing that." He sounded dispirited.

"You should, you know. That will be the last time, after all."

"I've already donated it."

"You don't mean ever to play again?"

"I'll be glad to, if I can, but I don't know what's going to happen."

"You're going to go to Taiwan and make a success of yourself, and perhaps you'll become the Prince's heir."

"No, if worse comes to worst I may have to succeed to Count Tanabe."

"Doesn't he have any children?"

"Just two daughters, both of them older than me."

"That should be all right, since you like older women."

"If *you* were his daughter I'd have no complaints."

"Rubbish! If *I* were in the picture I'd be his wife, not his daughter."

"It must be hot in Taiwan." He changed the subject. The thoughts in his head were tumbling over each other.

"I feel sorry for you, when I think about it, being a Prince's son but unable to claim that recognition. Who taught you the koto?"

"At first there was talk of my being taken into the Prince's family, but for that I had to be able to play the koto. I didn't like it—I was made to study the koto even before I went to school. Now things are different, and I have nothing to do with the koto anymore. Instead, I'm off to Taiwan, where I risk being turned into a soldier."

"Well, that's no great surprise. After all, Count Tanabe is a general."

"From waif to koto teacher to soldier. What a life!"

"Just keep on rising in the world. However you may change, the Shigure Teahouse will always be the same."

"I hope so. To me, it's my real home."

"That's wonderful. It will always be there for you, whenever you come back."

"I only hope I'll be able to."

"Of course you will. I'll always be the same, too."

"But of course you'll take another lover."

"Does that matter? You'll have a wife too. You'll be with Count Tanabe's daughter and become his heir. That's the natural way for things to go."

"If they do, will you still let Mukōjima be my home?"

"Certainly. No matter what happens to either of us, the Paulownia will always be available for you. You may come whenever you miss me."

"Can you really promise that?"

"It's not a promise. That's just the way it is between you and me."

"I see. The way it is between me and you. It's the only such refuge I have. Fishing in the river, drinking saké in the Paulownia, I forget all the troubles of life. Fame and fortune no longer mean anything to me, and I think how nice it would be if I'd never been born."

"There you go again!"

"And I'll say it again and again. Being a Prince's son is no fun at all. Count Tanabe is the only one who cares about me."

"Surely that makes a good reason to marry his daughter."

"I will if I have to. She's no beauty, I assure you, with her dark skin and her protruding teeth. The older one's married, but no one wants the younger."

"Looks don't matter. It's the heart that counts—the person."

"Talk about person—there *is* none, Oriku, apart from you."

"And that's why I'm here. I'll always be your woman, you know."

They sat down on the rocks of the knoll and, as they talked, looked down on the roofs below them. The roof tiles undulated on and on like the waves of the sea. Beyond them, to the left, stretched the dark expanse of the Ueno woods.

"Would you like something to eat somewhere? There's the Rengyoku noodle place, or eel at Izu-ei."

"No, let's eat at home.

"Then let's go."

"Let's. The best place of all is the one where I can be alone with you."

They went back the way they had come, entered the Umezono-chō lane, and drank goodbye to each other in the house where the "Koto Lessons" sign no longer hung. It was nearly dawn when they finally fell asleep, the thought of parting having sustained them through the night. Yasuo clung to her till day came, weeping that he would never snuggle close to his mother again.

The next morning she saw him as far as the Count's gate, behind Keiō Academy. He carried only a small suitcase. Beside the imposing, Western-style iron gate there was a small door, and beyond it an expanse of gravel. As he passed through the door, suitcase in hand, Yasuo looked like a poor orphan being taken in by a forbidding family.

Two years later he returned, wearing the uniform of a lieutenant. "It's good to be home!" he said, sprawling out in the Paulownia annex. His face was exactly as it had been two years before.

A year later he was back again. This time he was a captain. Again he stretched out in the Paulownia annex and clung to Oriku. His rank had gone up each time he came. Oriku asked no questions, and he said nothing. He married Count Tanabe's daughter, as expected, and when he appeared at Mukōjima he did so, as before, like a child seeking his mother.

No doubt Yasuo would keep coming as long as the Shigure Teahouse lasted. Up and up he would go, each time he returned, from lieutenant general to general. He would probably become a count, too. But however high he rose, he would take his ease here as he had always done, and, as always, Oriku would hold him in her arms.

Oriku was just that kind of woman.

CHAPTER FIVE

A Master Craftsman

This began while Oriku was still living in the Yoshiwara.

Among the craftsmen regularly employed by the Silver Flower was a cabinetmaker named Tetsunosuke. Oriku's late husband had thought so highly of him that he accepted no desk, display shelf, brazier frame, tobacco tray, or other such personal item made by anyone else. The young women's rooms, too, were invariably equipped with Tetsu's braziers and storage chests. The house contained so many of his things that he was there every day, like a regular employee; even so, he had more work there than he could easily handle.

When a girl went home at the end of the year, it was customary to present her with a mirror stand, a sewing box, or some other accessory of the kind a woman requires. Tetsu's workshop at the Silver Flower was downstairs. He was in his early thirties, and there was such a distinction to his looks that you could hardly believe he was a craftsman. The girls fussed over him, but he ignored them. He lived with two apprentices in a house in Ryūsenjichō. He had been married once, but then his wife had died, and he had remained a widower ever since. He was over thirty and yet he had never inspired any racy gossip, nor did he indulge himself in any way. With him it was work, work, work. At the same time, though, he was stubborn and taciturn. Once he was on the job there was no point in talking to him. He would not answer.

"It's the mark of a master to be like that. He's skilled, he's eccentric, and his work is his only pleasure. Once he's past forty he'll be a magnificent craftsman." Oriku's late husband heaped praise on Tetsu and singled him out for favor.

Even after Oriku started up her Shigure Teahouse, everything in her room, including the lampshades, was Tetsu's work. A cabinetmaker must also know how to paint and to apply lacquer, and it is particularly in that regard that he differs from a carpenter or a maker of sliding panels and doors. She still kept beside her the elegant tobacco tray her husband had used until his death, with its pattern of dew-spangled grasses—the grasses painted with the slenderest of brushes, and the dewdrops inlaid silver. Being so finely, so thoughtfully done, his work lasted well and gave pleasure in use year after year.

When Oriku's husband died—she was twenty-six at the time—the unmarried Tetsu came to collect his tools and take them back to his Ryūsenjichō house. "Your husband ordered so many things from me that I needed to have the workshop here," he said, "but now it will be just a matter of the occasional repair. Please get in touch if you need me. I will come immediately, anytime."

Tetsu bowed low to Oriku before he left. He no longer had full-time work there, now that Oriku's husband was gone, and the workshop disappeared. He still turned up, though, four or five days a month, to look after this or that.

It was not clear that Oriku would be up to running a high-class brothel, and Otsune, her husband's elder sister, was the most worried of all. Otsune had married into a restaurant called Katayama. "You're still so young, Oriku," she said, "you must be lonely all by yourself. Don't you think you should get married?" The ceremony to mark the third anniversary of her husband's death was over, and Oriku felt that running the place was a burden too heavy for her. Her adopted daughter, Oito, had only just started elementary school—the thought of the long life that stretched ahead made her feel helpless. At Suzaki, in Fukagawa, there was a similar establishment named the Fan Breeze, and the second son there, a man of thirty, let it be know he would not mind marrying into the Silver Flower. Otsune conveyed the message. It was not as though Oriku had shared her husband's life because she loved him, and she had happened to end up as she had done only because he had saved her from becoming a woman of pleasure; so the idea of marrying again did not worry her. She realized that the job required perhaps more of her than a woman could do alone, and that the best thing might be to take a suitable husband. She therefore decided she would make up her mind by the day of her formal introduction to the man from the Fan Breeze.

Just then Tetsu arrived. "It is the anniversary of your husband's death," he said. "I hope you will allow me to make an offering." He was carrying a water-pail-shaped flower vase he had made, containing bellflowers. It was very handsome, and he had brought out all the beauty of the grain of the wood. When he set it down before the Buddhist altar, the flowers looked wonderfully fresh and bright.

"What a pretty vase! I'm sure my husband is very pleased with it." Oriku was looking at the flowers. Tetsu had made the altar, too. Her fastidious husband had requested many special details, and the project had taken a long time. Now Tetsu himself had placed an offering before it.

He prayed before it too, then sat down with an air of awkward constraint. "Will you be taking a husband now, Mistress Oriku?" he asked almost inaudibly, gazing down at his knees. He did not look at her face.

"So you've heard, have you?"

"Yes, I have."

"I'm not sure I like the idea, though. It's just that with Otsune so worried about me, I can't really say no."

Tetsu arched his back and looked up at her. "You say you don't like the idea, Mistress Oriku?"

"I'd be fine just as I am, if only I could get by alone, but this is difficult work, as you know, and a woman can't manage all by herself. So for the sake of the business I've resigned myself to getting married."

"I see." He looked very depressed. "Well then, I must be leaving."

"Just a moment! Now you're here, I hope you'll have a drink before you go."

"No, thank you, I'm afraid I have too much work to do." He was already getting to his feet. He did not seem at all his usual self.

"Surely you're not in that great a hurry. You've brought such a beautiful vase!"

She called into the next room, "Bring Tetsu some lunch. And put some saké with it!"

"Yes, ma'am!" a maid answered in her drawling voice, and a tray appeared before Tetsu. Something was always kept ready for private visitors, and saké and a light meal could be provided at any time.

"Thank you. You are very kind." He no longer insisted on leaving.

"My husband would feel abandoned if I let you leave again, after you came all this way, without offering you something." She tried to pass it off with a playful smile.

"No," he shot back, lifting his cup, "he already feels abandoned."

Oriku felt his words pierce her heart. She had put her confused feelings into words and so had come under fire. She could not answer.

Tetsu said no more and drank his wine in lonely silence. From out in the street came the lazily whistled call of a pipe-mender who was passing by, looking for customers.

"Mistress Oriku!"

"What is it?"

"Are you sure you can't handle the business by yourself?"

"I doubt it. So far I've managed somehow to get by, but the future worries me. At the moment things are fine because the girls are all very nice, but I'm so young, you know. Any slip of mine could damage the place's reputation, and that would make my husband extremely sad indeed. That's what bothers me."

"It shouldn't. It wasn't like him to brood over something like that." The tone of his voice was different. He did not normally talk this way, and although his eyes seemed to question her, he caught himself in the end and said, "My, I hope you will forgive me. I should not have spoken as I did. Please excuse me. Thank you very much for your hospitality." He tidied himself and rose to his feet.

The prospect of Oriku's remarriage did not please him. On the contrary, he found it distressing. Among all the craftsmen employed by the Silver Flower, only Tetsu shed tears when her husband died. Oriku remembered him quietly weeping at the bedside. Her husband's favorite for years, he seemed to have loved her husband in return, for there he was, this ever-silent man, sobbing under his breath. It had been a touching sight. Now the news that she would remarry had drawn sharp words from him before he left. In truth, however, Oriku herself still hardly knew what to do, and Tetsu's words extinguished any wish of her own to take a second husband. She decided that if she could manage by herself after all, she would, and in that spirit she put off giving Otsune any answer at all. Otsune began sending messages demanding one. The party in question seemed to know Oriku, and the urgency apparently came from him. Lodged as they were in her heart, Tetsu's words had inspired her to delay setting a date for the meeting, but she could not go on putting it off forever. Should she simply refuse? Should she meet him after all and see what he was like? He would be shamed if she turned him down *after* meeting him.

Oriku wanted to see Tetsu again and talk the matter over. Since she could not very well do so at the Silver Flower itself, she went instead to his Ryūsenjichō workshop. Her husband's grave was at Yanaka, so she could go there and drop by Tetsu's on the way back. That would do as an excuse.

Tetsu was working at his cabinetmaker's bench, shaping the tongue of a joint with his chisel. At the sight of Oriku he blinked, rose in haste, and began tidying up. His workshop was the front room; behind it, one six-mat room and another three-mat room constituted the rest of a proper craftsman's dwelling. Oriku sat down in the larger room and looked the place over. For a man's, it was neat and pretty. The small brazier frame was one he had made himself.

"I would have come to you, if only you had sent for me! It is really too good of you to have troubled yourself this way." His expression was sternly formal.

"I'm just stopping by on my way back from Yanaka." Oriku's explanation sounded a little pat. She was worried about calling on a man this way.

"So what can I do for you?"

"It's not about work. Thank you so much for the flower vase the other day."

"You are very welcome."

"My husband must be very happy."

"You are too kind."

Having expressed her thanks, Oriku fell silent for a moment.

"You didn't much like that talk of my marrying again, did you, Tetsu?"

"No, no, I hope you will forget all that. I am sorry I spoke as I did."

"I didn't mind in the least. Actually, I just don't know what to do, so I felt like talking it over with you."

"You did?" Tetsu looked up at her gravely.

"If you feel unsure which way to go, I suggest you give up the idea." He made no bones about it. His distaste for Oriku's remarriage was audible in his voice.

"But I just don't know whether a woman can do it alone. That's what worries me so."

"Does it really matter if you can't?"

"Of course it does. It's my responsibility to look after the business my husband left me."

"I disagree. I think looking after the business matters much less than looking after yourself." His tone, as serious as ever, made his words sound almost like a threat. "It's fine if the business falters, I would guess. Your husband won't like your remarrying, Mistress Oriku. That's how fond he was of you."

"Do you really think so?"

"Yes, I do."

"He'd rather I remained unmarried, even if running the business turns out to be too much for me?"

"That's what I think. You are still young, though, Mistress Oriku."

"Age has nothing to do with it. Young or not, I can do it if I really make up my mind to."

"That's right. After all, you're managing right now, aren't you?"

"That's only because I still have my husband behind me. When I'm really on my own, though . . ."

That is what troubled her. She had no objection to living alone, but the idea of the business failing terrified her.

"I gather from what you say that you would be remarrying for the sake of the business."

"Exactly. Just for the business."

"You would be making a mistake. Marriage is not that simple a matter. If you mean to marry, Mistress Oriku, you should find some-one you like. Never mind what the Katayama lady thinks. If you marry someone you don't really like, just for the sake of the business, you'll be doing him no kindness either, will you?"

As usual, he spoke without looking her in the face. He was trying to convey to her his disapproval of her marrying someone she did not love, just for the sake of the business.

"The way you talk, I'll never find anyone I like well enough!"

"If you can't, then what's wrong with your getting on with the job by yourself?"

"My husband wouldn't mind my finding someone I liked?"

"I think he would be pleased."

"I don't understand. Won't he be upset if I'm no longer alone, whether I like the man I'm with or not?"

"For you to remain single would be the best of all, but he'll be pleased as long as you're happy."

"As you see it, then, it's my liking the man or not that makes all the difference."

"That's right. I'll be happy, too, if you get together with someone you like."

His eyes as he spoke were young, and his face had the innocence of a child's. His tone was less an experienced craftsman's than a student's. Go ahead, as long as you like the fellow, but I'm dead against it if you don't: that is the message Oriku got. She smiled. Tetsu seemed so much younger than she.

"Perhaps I should just give up the idea, Tetsu, if you're that opposed to it." She could afford to be generous, for she now felt growing confidence that she could indeed run the business, even on her own. "But I'm still so young. It will be hard spending the rest of my life alone."

"I understand. I'm sure you'll find someone in the end, though."

"What would you do, then, if I fell in love with *you*?" she was going to say, but could not.

Tetsu was looking down at the floor, blushing, when his apprentices returned, wet bath towels in hand, humming a tune. At the sight of Oriku they saluted her in haste and fled to the workshop. Oriku took the opportunity to get to her feet.

"I'll be back to talk things over some more."

"No, I'll come to you."

"We can't talk like this at the Silver Flower, though, can we?"

"No, I suppose not."

"Thank you. I'm very grateful."

"For what? All I did was talk out of turn."

Oriku stepped through the workshop and got into a waiting rickshaw. As it began to move, Tetsu appeared at the front of his shop to see her off. Their remarkably good talk had left her with many strong impressions.

The next day Oriku visited Otsune and declined to proceed with the marriage negotiations. Otsune did not reproach her. She seemed to have seen it coming.

"Is there someone you're in love with?" she asked frankly, like a true daughter of Asakusa. Katayama was doing very well in those days as a popular restaurant, serving everything from favorite main dishes like chicken and egg on rice to small dishes to go with saké. It was full whenever you went there, and Otsune bustled about the year round. Being so busy, she had little time for idle talk.

"I suspected you didn't like the idea when you didn't answer about meeting him." Otsune wiped the perspiration from her forehead.

"I thought it over very carefully, but I got worried about accepting someone I don't know, just for the sake of the business."

"I understand. It's one thing when you're just a girl, but it's natural to be more cautious when you're approaching thirty."

"Thank goodness!" A sigh of relief escaped Oriku's lips. She had been sure she would be chided for refusing Otsune's good offices, but not at all. Far from being annoyed, Otsune was actually sympathetic.

"Not even Heitarō liked the idea of your remarrying." The patrons kept coming in as Otsune spoke, and she gave each a warm greeting, meanwhile signaling the staff to look after this and that. Koyama Heitarō was her husband.

"Goodness, Otsune, I just don't know how you do it!" Oriku could not help exclaiming over the whirl of activity.

"I'm just used to it, that's all. Won't you have something to eat before you go? Our chazuke lunch is a big hit these days. Do try it. It's very nice."

Without waiting for an answer she had a waitress bring one. A vast list of everything the restaurant offered was posted on the wall, to-gether with the price of each item. The lunch tray brought to their table turned out to include rolled egg with dried mackerel and kin-pira-style burdock root, miso soup with tofu, and pickled vegetables heaped into a generously sized bowl. The egg and burdock root went with the pickles, which were the main dish. They consisted of nicely colored eggplant, white melon, and giant radish—all put up in miso, with a little red ginger sprinkled over, Asakusa-style. All the pickles were freshly made and thoroughly appetizing.

"We're especially proud of our pickles. While you eat, just think of everything else as a side dish. The whole thing is only twenty-five sen, and rice comes with it, too." Otsune's face wore an expression of pride. Oriku gladly took up her chopsticks and found everything indeed very good. The egg and dried mackerel were commonplace enough, but the pickles were delicious and salted just right.

"Who makes these pickles?" Oriku asked.

"I do. I won't let anyone else touch them. I do the pickling myself."

"No wonder they're so good! They're absolutely perfect."

"They're not nearly as good when I let anyone else do them. I'm practically never able to be away."

"I can imagine. Pickling this much must take almost all your time. Twenty-five sen is very cheap."

"That's why the lunch is so popular. Lately it's been selling so well that I've been making the pickles in advance. If I don't get a batch done early in the morning we run out during the day."

Everywhere in the restaurant, people were busy with their chazuke lunch.

"To tell the truth, this is just the kind of business I'd like to be in. Wouldn't you and your husband like to take over the Silver Flower, Otsune? We could trade."

"Now, now, don't talk nonsense!" Otsune would have none of it and practically told Oriku so outright.

Years of keeping women and selling love in so grand a manner had somewhat inured Oriku to the nature of her business, but this visit to the Katayama restaurant made her envy Otsune her more honest trade. When Oito grew up and married, she would leave the Silver Flower to her and open a restaurant just like this one. Oriku kept that wish in mind ever after her chazuke lunch that day.

Once the deed was done, and Oriku was home again in the Yoshiwara, she had an entirely new outlook. She would work as hard as she possibly could, wait for Oito to grow up, give her the business, and start a new one. That was her aim now.

Tetsu came to the Silver Flower two or three times a month. Something was wrong with a shōji panel, something had happened to a sliding door—this sort of thing was not really in a cabinetmaker's line, but Tetsu did it without complaint. However, he never spoke more than necessary to get on with the job. He and Oriku never talked as they had done at Ryūsenjichō, but maintained instead a mutually respectful silence. They kept their words to a minimum.

Many years went by.

And indeed, in the year of Oito's marriage, Oriku gave the newlyweds the Silver Flower and started her long-dreamed-of Shigure Teahouse. The Katayama restaurant, where a simple chazuke cost twenty-five sen, had inspired it, but at her place a meal cost two whole yen, with chazuke as the concluding dish. Both food and setting were high-class, but there had been doubts about whether anyone would really come to a place like that for expensive chazuke. Tetsu took charge of the furnishings and accessories for the opening.

Oriku tried to draw a line between items he would make personally and items he would entrust to lesser craftsmen. "This isn't the Yoshiwara anymore, Tetsu," she said decisively, "and there's no need for you to make the things for everyday restaurant use."

"Please don't be so formal. I owe your late husband the chance to become a real craftsman. Money has nothing to do with it. I would prefer to make everything myself."

"That's all very well, but surely it's too much work for just one man."

"Yes, so I'll draw up the plans and have most of the work executed by other reliable craftsmen. I'll personally make only the things for your own use, Mistress Oriku."

"But the date of the opening is already set. I can't afford not to have everything ready in time."

"It will be. The wood is already seasoned. You don't need to worry."

Tetsu took full responsibility for the entire order. He made the tables and braziers for each room, and the other items he had made by fellow craftsmen, according to his own specifications. For the shōji and fusuma panels, too, he chose workmen of whom he approved, and in a month everything was already half done—sufficiently, at last, that Oriku's business could get under way. To make that much progress that quickly, Tetsu and the others had in the end to work all through the night.

"Only you could have accomplished this much, Tetsu, I'm very grateful." On the last night, Oriku brought out saké to thank him.

"No, no, it was nothing." He looked happy, but his eyes were drooping.

"You must be exhausted. I don't suppose you got any sleep either yesterday or the day before."

"It's not at times like this that a craftsman feels tired—it's when he has no work and doesn't know what to do with himself."

"I see. That's how it is?"

"He loves what he does, so when he's working he forgets everything else. That's why I have no wife."

"I made it on my own too."

"Yes, you did."

"It's half your fault, you know."

Blinking uncomfortably, Tetsu drank the saké she had poured him. The fragrance of new wood filled the just-finished room, and the tatami mats were pristine. The furnishings Tetsu had made with such care suited the room perfectly. All were beautiful.

"Won't you have some too, Mistress Oriku?"

"Why, perhaps I will. We're celebrating, after all."

Oriku picked up her cup. The burden of this project had been on her shoulders a long, long time, and at last she felt relieved. The Silver Flower she so disliked running had passed to Oito, and henceforth she could return to being her real self. No matter how she rationalized it, she had never been able to escape the sense that the work of managing a brothel was unclean. Now she was free of it, and although new labors lay ahead, her human dignity was safe.

"You still have a lot of work ahead of you," Tetsu remarked.

"Oh, I know. I don't mind. I just didn't like the business I was in."

"You know, though, Mistress Oriku, I still regret having said perhaps too much that time. I think what I said may be the reason you never remarried and remained a widow at your age."

"Oh it is, it is. If you hadn't been against my remarrying then, I'd undoubtedly have accepted that young man from the Fan Breeze."

"I can't tell you how sorry I am." He pressed his palms to his knees and hung his head. "Why did I ever say those things then?"

"I still remember it. My husband would prefer me to remain unmarried, even if the business failed."

"Please don't say it again! It just makes me feel worse than ever!"

"Come to think of it, you're still single, too, aren't you?" She gave the words an unintended emphasis. It was perfectly true, though: Tetsu had never married, either. "In all this time you've never met anyone you liked?"

"No, I haven't."

"I don't understand how that's possible for a good, skilled man like you."

"I'm eccentric, as you know, and there just hasn't been anyone. I've had offers now and again, but I can't help it, I just don't like the idea, and by now, at my age, people don't even try anymore."

"How old are you?"

"Forty-three."

"You're three years older than me."

"That's right." He knew Oriku's age. After all these years they understood each other well, but for Oriku to marry a craftsman was out of the question.

"You can't possibly not have a woman, though, by your age, even if you don't openly call her your wife."

Tetsu put his hand to his head. "Please don't, Mistress Oriku! You never miss anything."

"What could be more natural, though? At your age, it would be strange for you not to have a woman. Why not get together with her?"

"Mistress Oriku!" He slapped his hand against the back of his head. "Please stop this! I don't want to talk about it!"

"I see. All right, I won't ask you any more. If you remain single forever, though, you'll be lonely when you're old. Think about that."

"This is the only wife I need." He pointed to his favorite chisels, which he had placed behind him. A cabinetmaker's chisels are his life, since for fine work he uses little else. He has a special holder for them, and when you spread it out, you find over a dozen of them inside— large and small, each in its individual pocket. The holder is rolled up like a scroll and tied with a cord, and the cabinetmaker always carries it with him to an outside job. The saws and hammers go in his toolbox, but he never lets anyone else carry his chisels, which he always keeps with him.

By this time, even Tetsu's colleagues referred to him as Master Tetsu and knew him as a dedicated worker. He thought of nothing but his work, to which he gave every moment of his time, and seemed to have no need for a wife. Oriku liked his devotion to his profession, as well as his straightforward, honest character, and although she could not marry him, she felt she would not mind meeting him in secret. The discovery that he had a mistress was therefore at once a disappointment, a relief, and a bittersweet pleasure.

They did not drink that much, and once the second flask was well and truly empty, Tetsu brought their conversation to a close. "Thank you very much for your hospitality," he said politely, and went away. With the beauty lent by the furnishings he had made, the entire room had suddenly gained new splendor. Everything of his, down to the most minor accessory, gave lasting pleasure. The wood was always firm and strong, though planed astonishingly thin. The wooden fastening pins he made only hardened with the years, and never moved.

As Ofune often said, "When you're accustomed to Tetsu's things, you just can't use anyone else's." Devoted to his work, kindhearted, and profoundly discreet, Tetsu was a craftsman of a kind that had become rare.

"He does good work, doesn't he," Ofune remarked after he left, running her hand over the brazier frame and the table.

"He said that for the time being he's made only the things I can't do without and he hopes I'll be patient a little longer for the rest. He hasn't started the chests, cabinets, mirror stands, and so on yet."

"That's just like him." Ofune was not surprised, either. They discussed Tetsu a while longer and then tidied up the room.

Oriku was just about to take a bath when she heard Ofune's piercing cry, "Something terrible has happened, Mistress Oriku, something awful!"

"Something terrible has happened to Tetsu! Come, please, quickly, quickly!" It was the girl who had accompanied Tetsu from the Yoshiwara. She all but seized Oriku's hand and dragged her off by force.

Oriku followed her, to find Tetsu lying on the kitchen's wooden floor, pressing his hands to his side. She went up to him, assuming at first that he had been seized by a cramp.

"Ahh!" She uttered a cry of distress. There was blood on the beautiful new wooden floor. His face was deathly pale, and he groaned softly, lacking the strength to speak.

Unfortunately, the telephone was not yet connected. Oriku had the girl run to fetch the doctor and tried, but failed, to move Tetsu into the main room. She scolded the trembling maids and had them halfremove Tetsu's clothing. He was bleeding cruelly from a spot above his hip.

"One of you," she shouted, "get some dry cloth—I don't care what it is—and keep it pressed right here! We have to make sure he doesn't lose any more blood."

She applied layers of towels to the wound and kept one hand pressed down hard in order to stop the bleeding. Apparently the incident, whatever it was, had happened not ten minutes after he left, and he had stumbled in, ashen-faced, to collapse on the kitchen floor.

The doctor came immediately, from nearby in the town. He calmly inspected the wound, disinfected it, applied a generous quantity of styptic, and wrapped Tetsu's hips in layers of double-thickness cotton bandage. It took four or five people to lift him up, despite his pain, so that the doctor could do it. When at last the bleeding stopped, Tetsu said, "I'm sorry, I'm so sorry!" to everyone and made as though to leave straightaway. Oriku rebuked him, had bedding laid out for him in the room next to the kitchen, and made him lie down. She still had not had a chance to ask him how he had gotten the wound.

"How on earth did he come to receive a large wound like that?" the doctor asked Oriku. Neither Ofune nor anyone else had any idea.

"He was here till just a short while ago. He had a little to drink, then he left. He was gone only twenty minutes or so. Can you tell what happened to him?"

"It's a knife wound. Fortunately, it's not that deep. The knife struck the hipbone and didn't reach the internal organs. If it had, he wouldn't have made it."

"Someone stabbed him, then?"

"Yes, obviously. No one would stab himself there."

"He isn't the kind of man anyone could hate. What *can* all this be about?"

"There's another thing," the doctor said with a grave expression. "I'm required by law to report a wound like this to the police. Please understand that I have no choice in the matter."

"You can't just keep it quiet?"

"No. I *must* report any patient with a suspicious wound. I can't cover it up."

The doctor wrote down Tetsu's name, address, and age. He could not actually question a man who was lying there gritting his teeth and pressing his hands to his wound. Oriku and the maids were quite bewildered. They washed the bloody floor with soap but could not remove the stain. Tetsu had lost so much blood that his face lacked any color of life.

"We'll just leave him quiet like this for tonight. Someone will have to watch him. The rest of you, go to bed."

Oriku had given her orders and returned to her room when two policemen from the Mukōjima police station arrived, one in uniform and the other in plain clothes. With glaring eyes they spoke threateningly to the maids.

"There's someone here with an injury, isn't there? Don't hide him. You won't help him by doing so." They were presumably looking into the doctor's report, but if so they certainly were acting fast.

A maid took them to the room where Tetsu lay. He seemed to be in great pain, but his face had better color than earlier.

"I am very sorry," he apologized to the plainclothesman.

"Was it the woman they call Ōsaki Tama who stabbed you?" The plainclothesman had gotten out his notepad. The Shigure Teahouse people knew nothing of all this, but the policemen did.

"It happened somewhere out in front of this restaurant?"

"Yes, down below the embankment." At last Tetsu's voice had regained a little strength.

"And the weapon was a carpenter's chisel?" They seemed to have questioned the culprit. Tetsu nodded unhappily.

"Could we have a look at the wound?" They turned to Oriku.

"I don't think that would be a good idea."

"Is it serious?"

"Not terribly. Apparently, the blade hit bone and didn't go in far."

"Do any of you know Ōsaki Tama?"

"No, none of us knows her. He finished some work for me today, and he had just left."

"Did you hear anything? A quarrel, or something?"

"No," Ofune put in, "no one here heard anything. The embankment is some way off, as you know."

"So he came back here after he was stabbed?"

"Yes. He collapsed in the kitchen and just lay there. He didn't say anything. We were very surprised to find him there bleeding, and we called the doctor."

"What doctor? What's his name?"

"Dr. Minami, from just over there by the embankment."

"Ah, Minami, is it?"

"He said he would be reporting the incident."

"How do you know about Ōsaki?" Tetsu asked the policemen.

"None of your business. Just answer my questions. The police know everything." The man's tone was peremptory and contemptuous. "That's what you get for two-timing a woman, you creep."

Oriku glanced at Ofune. Two-timing a woman? What on earth was going on? The quiet Tetsu apparently had dark secrets.

"Come to the Mukōjima police station when you can walk. You understand? You'll be arrested if you don't."

The detective looked disgusted, but the uniformed policeman, being a patrolman in the area, spoke more gently. "We're sorry to have troubled you," he said politely as they left.

Once they were gone the women broke into excited chatter.

"Mistress Oriku, what is going on?"

"Something must have happened!"

Well disposed as they were toward Tetsu, they were all in a flutter.

"I just don't understand!" Oriku exclaimed. She felt betrayed, after having trusted Tetsu as she did.

"Did Tetsu have a mistress, then?" Ofune had followed Oriku to her room.

"I have no idea."

"Could the woman actually have meant to kill him?"

"The only way to find out is to ask the man himself. At any rate, it's a bad business. The restaurant isn't even going yet, and already we've had blood on the floor."

"It's horrid."

"It certainly is. It just isn't like him. Tomorrow we'll have an apprentice come from Ryūsenjichō and take him home."

Lacking anyone on whom to vent her irritation, Oriku took a quick bath, had a beer, and went to bed. Angry or not, the preparations for the opening had tired her out, and she slept well.

Tetsu was already gone when she awoke the next morning. Apparently the apprentice had come for him by rickshaw at dawn.

"I hope he's all right. It was a nasty wound." Naturally Oriku was still worried about him.

"He was surprisingly energetic. 'Please thank Mistress Oriku for me,' he said. He was still pale, though." Ofune looked sleepy. She seemed to have been up late the night before.

"He confessed," Ofune continued.

"Oh?"

"Not in detail, but he apologized to you for having caused you such trouble by making a mess of things with a worthless woman. He was crying."

"It's nothing for him to cry about. Some woman fell for him, and he nearly got himself killed."

"He says he won't be back."

"He could be a bit braver." Oriku smiled wanly and asked no more. Ofune seemed to have more to say, but Oriku ignored her and went to look at the kitchen. All trace of the blood was gone.

"You got the stain off?"

"Tetsu's apprentice planed it off," the young girl explained. The place hardly showed, since the floorboards were new. There was plenty of work left to do, but Tetsu never came back to apologize.

Ten days later, Oriku was called to the police station, where she was questioned on the relationship between her and Tetsu. Having nothing to hide, she answered fully and truthfully. "Tetsu has said nothing since, and I haven't asked him anything, so at my place we know nothing at all about his private life." Such was her reply before she left.

"It *was* a woman, wasn't it?" Ofune and the others asked when she returned. They were breathlessly eager to hear the details.

"I don't know anything." Oriku was still in a bad mood. She did not at all like having been called in by the police.

"I misjudged him," she said. "I would never have thought it of him."

"What can you expect, though, when he's still single at his age?"

"Well then, why doesn't he marry her? He kept talking as though he had no one in the world, and all the time he was secretly carrying on with that woman. What a fake!" Oriku was furious. After that show of purity and innocence, he had turned out to be corrupt after all. He did excellent work, yes, but as a man he was no good at all. Oriku did not want even to see his face, and she sent him not a word. The work that remained undone need not affect her opening.

Her success following the opening has already been described. Her acquaintances from her Yoshiwara days came as custom required, and there was never any need to worry that the place might fall idle. Once the opening was over, everything went fine.

Two months later, Oriku was summoned to court. The document said she was to appear as a witness in the trial of Ōsaki Tama.

Once again Oriku was angry. After all the trouble Tetsu had caused her, she had on top of everything else been called to court!

"Just have a look at this!" She was so upset that she showed Ofune the summons.

"What do they want you for? You know absolutely nothing about this business!"

"You're going to come with me."

"What use could I possibly be? You should take someone else."

"No excuses. I want *you*."

Oriku scolded Ofune roundly, then set off with her to the Marunouchi courthouse. Never having been in such a situation before, she sat timidly, as requested, in the waiting room, but even then she remained anxious. She had done nothing wrong, and there was nothing for her to feel guilty or sheepish about, but somehow she was nervous anyway. The thought that she had been called to court because of *him* made him even more hateful. She had been waiting nearly an hour when a bailiff led her into the courtroom itself— another new experience for her. It was smaller than she had expected, and she noticed that a small woman sitting at the front glared at her when she entered. Some distance away was Tetsu, hanging his head. Dr. Minami had said at the time that the incident would not end with a police interview, and sure enough, the matter had been forwarded to the public prosecutor. Tetsu's position was that of the injured party, while Oriku seated herself as a witness. There was a scattering of spectators, and someone in legal robes, apparently a lawyer, stood near the woman. Soon everyone rose to their feet while the judge entered, and silence fell over the room. On the dais was a row of five magistrates. Oriku had no idea who they were.

The judge sat down, and the questioning began. Apparently Ōsaki Tama was thirty-four and ran a small oden restaurant in Ryūsenjichō. The area was just north of the Yoshiwara, and if you strolled down the embankment there you came to a row of half a dozen drinking spots. They attracted customers who stopped in for a drink on their way to the Yoshiwara, and in each there were women who knew their way around.

The entrance to the Yoshiwara was through the main gate. There were seven other gates as well, but normally they were all closed, and passage through them was forbidden. In the past, people had been allowed to pass through them freely, but then seven of them were shut, in order to preserve the distinction between the gay quarter and the town, and only the main gate remained open. Those coming from Asakusa therefore followed the embankment from the south and turned left at a landmark willow tree. But to reach the main gate, people arriving from Shitaya and Ueno went through Ryūsenjichō and turned right at the same willow. On the way, those from Asakusa drank enough to get slightly tipsy at the shops on the embankment, while the people from Ueno did the same at the oden place below it. The shops therefore all did very well.

It seemed that Ōsaki Tama had been running the oden shop below the Ryūsenji embankment for the last five years. Oriku gathered from the exchanges between the judge, Tama, and Tetsu that the relationship between Tama and Tetsu had begun three years earlier.

"Why did you cool toward her, after three years of relations?" The judge pressed on with his interrogation. Tetsu hung his head, mortally embarrassed by Oriku's presence, and answered in a voice too low to be heard.

"Did you promise to marry her?"

"No, Your Honor, I did not." Tetsu was quite definite.

"It's a lie! He's lying!" the woman screamed. "The man tells nothing but lies!" A bailiff rushed up to rebuke her, and the judge gave her a stern warning.

"I will not have such outbursts in my court!" He then called for the witness Okamoto Oriku.

"Present, your honor," Oriku replied.

When she rose to her feet, the woman again shrieked like a lunatic, "That's her! She's an evil woman! She's the one who stole Tetsu from me!" The bailiff forced her back to her chair, whereupon she broke into unrestrained sobbing. The judge said not a word, perhaps because he was utterly fed up with her, and instead swore Oriku in.

"Explain your relationship with Koyama Tetsunosuke," he said softly.

"It is not a 'relationship' at all, really. He is a cabinetmaker, one so skilled that people call him a master, and I have known him in that capacity for years. My late husband favored him a great deal, so my association with him goes back more than twenty years. When I decided to open the Shigure Teahouse, I entrusted him with all the work in his line, and on the evening that it was more or less finished I treated him and his fellow workmen to some saké. He did not drink that much."

"It's a lie! Tetsu goes through a half-gallon at a time! That woman is lying!" This new outburst was too much for the judge, who ordered the woman removed. A bailiff half-dragged her out through a door to the right. Oriku, looking on, was aghast. Never before had she been the object of such filthy insults, nor had she ever felt so utterly miserable.

"Please continue," the judge said once the woman was gone. However, Oriku had lost track of where she was, and she had to think before she went on.

"The other workmen left first, then Tetsu a while afterward. Not ten minutes later he was back, holding his side, covered in blood, and deathly pale; he had collapsed on the kitchen floor." She gave a fair account of what had transpired. The judge seemed to know the rest.

"You did not have intimate relations with Koyama Tetsunosuke?"

"Certainly not! I kept urging him to get busy and find himself a wife, since it's not good for a man to be over forty and still single, but, quiet and uncommunicative as he is, he rarely says anything to any of us, and we never really talked about it. He works in silence, and he is very good at what he does."

"You're quite sure of what you're saying? Anything but the truth will put you in contempt of court."

"I am quite sure. I swear it." With these emphatic words she looked up at the judge severely.

The court was then adjourned for the day, and Oriku stepped with dignity into the corridor. Ofune appeared from among the spectators, pulled at Oriku's sleeve, and burst into tears. Neither could speak in the presence of the bailiffs, but Oriku roundly reproved Ofune for sobbing as they left. She ignored Tetsu, who seemed to be on his way out as well. They boarded the first streetcar that came along and rode it in silence to Azuma Bridge. Once they had alighted, Oriku paid no attention to the ferries and rickshaws. Instead she crossed the bridge and set out to walk home from there.

The cherry trees along the embankment were covered with swelling buds that would soon blossom if the fine weather held. Their branches swayed in the spring breeze. The teashops along one side of the path were ready to receive blossom-viewers, and makeshift shelters for customers were beginning to appear in front of them. Everything had to be ready in advance, since it would be too late by the time the flowers opened and the hordes of visitors quickly arrived. The tide of people rose and ebbed swiftly, the cherry blossom season being so short. All the business was done in barely ten days, and a teashop with its rush mat–covered benches could be put up in a day.

They strolled along at a leisurely pace, looking up at the branches. Ofune had wanted to take a steam ferry, but Oriku had preferred to walk. Not wishing to return home in her present state of mind, she hoped to dispel her dark mood beneath the trees. Although still seething with anger when she started out, she had calmed down by the time they reached Mimeguri Shrine.

"Would you like some sakura cakes?"

"No, now that we're here I don't feel like anything. I'll send for some, though, if you like." Ofune was extremely anxious to get home.

"Well then, let's just rest a little."

They dusted off a rock placed there for the purpose and sat down. Oriku took out her tobacco pouch, and Ofune held out a match to light her mistress's pipe. Oriku had a leisurely smoke. Across the river, the Shōten Temple grove was dark against the late afternoon sun. Seagulls rode the river on the rising tide. As always, it was a peaceful scene.

"Ofune?"

"Yes?"

"What did you think of that woman today? That woman with the oden shop, Ōsaki Tama."

"She's crazy. I can't imagine what Tetsu was doing carrying on with her."

"I felt sorry for him."

"Not me! It makes me so angry, the thought of him being with a lunatic like that!" Ofune was still furious. Oriku, meanwhile, was feeling better. The woman had been so awful that she now pitied Tetsu.

At last she understood why he had always kept his gaze lowered and looked glum when the subject of women came up.

"Surely there's nothing wrong, though, with Tetsu having had a woman."

"That's not what I mean. When I think what a miserable woman he chose, the whole thing seems so stupid, it really gets to me."

"Men aren't like women. They have urges. When they follow them, one thing leads to another, and afterward they regret the entire thing. He probably made a mistake when he was drunk."

"But haven't you said before that men do nothing but bad things?"

"It depends on who you're talking about. Tetsu is a very proper man. You trusted him too, you know."

"I did, yes, but not so much anymore."

"You shouldn't talk that way. His only pleasure is his work, and he has no other amusements. Forgive him his lapse with Tama."

"You're too indulgent with him, Mistress Oriku, after all he's put you through."

"Well, I *was* angry back there. You were crying, you were so sorry about the whole thing, and I was just furious—not with Tetsu, though. I was so furious with that woman—Tetsu seemed to have shrunk to half his normal size, and I couldn't be angry with him anymore when I saw that. You could tell from his face how sorry he was to have been involved with that worthless creature and to have acted so foolishly."

"Well, all right, but I just can't stomach his having fallen in with a woman like that."

"I trust you won't go on talking that way. I've started to feel sorry for him, actually. I can tell you now, I suppose: once upon a time I even considered marrying him."

"Really?"

"Oh yes, really. His skill is first-class, and he's a good, quiet man. Of course I couldn't marry a craftsman, but I did think about it."

"You *did*?"

"What can I say? Even I get lonely sometimes. Still, I really wanted to find him a good wife, you know, and at one time I got to the point of suggesting that I might arrange for him to be with *you*."

"Be serious! I'm already forty!"

"Exactly. The ages didn't seem right, so I gave up the whole idea. It's really sad to see him the way he is, though. He must be bitterly regretting having gotten in so deep with a woman like that, just because of some passing urge. I don't suppose he'll be back here. It's a shame for him to have wrecked his life over such a woman. Now there's only one way to set him right again. Do you know what I mean?"

"No, I don't."

"I'll give him a little fling."

Ofune was speechless. Her jaw dropped.

"You're surprised?" Oriku asked.

"I certainly am! It's ridiculous!"

"But there's no other way to make a real man of him again. He'll fall to pieces if I leave him alone. His being such a nice person makes him fundamentally weak."

"But you can't do a thing like that, you just can't!"

"He'll get his courage back if he spends a night with me. He thinks he can't come here anymore, and I'm sure he wouldn't even if I asked him to."

"You may be right about that."

"I can't marry him, but I don't dislike him, and that's what I plan to do, so he can come back here with his head held high, as before."

"If that's all you want, you don't have to go that far."

"No, I want to do that much for him. Does it matter if I like him? I've felt like doing it before, but then I was in the Yoshiwara, and I couldn't. Now I have a bit more freedom, so indulge me. I'll pay no attention even if you do try to stop me, so don't."

That was that. Oriku stood up. She was cold from sitting so long on the rock. Ofune seemed unconvinced, but Oriku's mind was made up. The decision had made itself, so to speak, the moment her glance took in both Tetsu and that madwoman.

Her resolution never wavered with the passage of time, but Tetsu did not return to Mukōjima. The trial ended with the woman being sentenced to a year in prison for inflicting bodily harm, but she was put on probation because she had voluntarily given herself up to the police. Tetsu stayed away even after the sentencing. Oriku did not feel like initiating the approach, but if he came she fully intended to sacrifice herself for the sake of his peace of mind and so make a man of him again. He did not come, however. Perhaps he felt awkward or ashamed, but at any rate, he did not show his face again, and the work he had left remained undone. But he was bound to turn up sooner or later. Oriku silently awaited that day.

CHAPTER SIX

Two Sons of Edo

The Shigure Teahouse closed only one day a year, in late April, after the cherry blossoms were gone. When the trees were in bloom, the place was more crowded than Oriku had ever imagined it could be, since so many people strolled down the embankment to stop there on their way home from blossom-viewing. The restaurant had just enough room and utensils for forty. When the number reached fifty, the cups, bowls, and so on began to give out, the service deteriorated, and the space became uncomfortably cramped. With thirty guests or so everything remained nicely relaxed, but when over a hundred insisted on cramming themselves in, the whole staff could only throw up their hands in dismay.

The place was known to attract great men of all kinds, and an endless procession of blossom-viewers wandered down there for a look at the customers. Oriku had not the heart simply to turn them away, but at the same time she was not equipped to serve them all. As a last resort she therefore devised the Cherry Blossom Bentō.

She put up a stall on the embankment, where the path led down to the Shigure Teahouse; hung a blossom-decorated shop curtain at the entrance, with some colorful lanterns; and dressed the maids in suitable kimono, with red cords to tie up their sleeves, and set them all to work selling two-layered bentō lunches. These were no ordinary bentō, either. The double cypress boxes, four inches square, contained, in the bottom layer, a generous serving of cooked mountain greens accompanied either by freshwater fish of the season poached in sweetened soy sauce and saké, or by small funa carp prepared in the sweet kanro style (such dishes being a specialty of the Shigure Teahouse, which avoided saltwater fish); and, on the top layer, an inviting array of shigure clams, rice, and two different types of pickles. A splendid bentō it was indeed, and at one yen it came with a two-gō bottle of saké, nearly a pint. Bentō sold to the blossom-viewers generally cost fifty sen, but the double price Oriku charged made it possible to provide high-quality fare. The idea was that those who purchased the Cherry Blossom Bentō would be able to use the restaurant proper.

"Those who wish to take the bentō away with them are welcome to do so," the maids with the red sleeve-cords would announce gaily, "while those who wish to eat it immediately are invited by all means to use the Shigure Teahouse. We can heat your saké for you, and bowls are available for making chazuke.

"In cherry-blossom time we serve only bentō—one yen for a double bentō box and a bottle of saké—and the restaurant is available for your use!" The maids repeated the message over and over, and the idea that for just one yen you could get all that and step into the Shigure Teahouse, too, made the bentō a great success. On the very first day, their hundred bentō sold out in the morning, throwing the kitchen staff into a panic. For the next day they struggled to add forty more, but those, too, were gone just after two o'clock, and to their loud distress they had nothing to give those who came later.

With the partitions between the restaurant's three main rooms removed, the place could accommodate fifty people with their Cherry Blossom Bentō lunches. Habitués were taken to one of the annexes in the rear, but they got bentō too, since it was impossible for the staff to prepare anything else. They were delighted.

Oriku's brainchild was a smash hit. In two weeks the restaurant had sold three thousand Cherry Blossom Bentō. Extra maids and kitchen help had to be hired. No one in the place, including Oriku, ever had time to sit down to a meal. Day after day they had nothing for lunch but musubi—rice balls wrapped in nori seaweed—and nishime vegetables boiled in soy sauce; while in the evening it was all they could do to prepare the bentō for the next day. They could not possibly prepare a regular meal for any guest who happened to turn up, so even the regular customers got Cherry Blossom Bentō, which was such a success that some people even came there specially to get it.

Oriku, who never did things by halves, scorned the idea of just getting on with making and selling whatever sort of bentō seemed a good idea at the time. No, she brought in someone with a take-out kitchen in the Yoshiwara, studied the preparation of bentō food, and ordered the most expensive bentō available from the fish market, for her cooks to examine. The process took a month. The Yoshiwara itinerant food stalls were affiliated with a restaurant specialized in delivering orders around the quarter, especially the sort of fare known as kuchitori—simmered meat or fish dishes in a sweetened sauce. Oriku adapted the kuchitori style from the itinerant stalls into something pleasing to both drinkers and lovers of sweeter food, and her bentō did very well. Some felt that one yen was a bit high, but Oriku was adamant. "A perfectly ordinary bentō, neither good nor bad, would do nothing for the Shigure Teahouse's reputation. It would be less work to make something cheaper, but considering that we're known for high-class chazuke, I have no intention of selling anything for less than one yen." She tested the product herself, over and over again, and the bottle of saké added to the final version perfectly matched the customers' taste. The food itself was generous in quantity, and for an elderly couple one bentō and one bottle were generally more than enough. Once the fame of the Shigure Teahouse's Cherry Blossom Bentō began to spread, the inhabitants of Tokyo, insatiable in the pursuit of novelty, gathered from afar to sample it, and the rush continued unabated even after the flowers had passed. There was always an endless stream of visitors to the whole Mukōjima area, whether elegant fanciers of cherry trees in leaf, or pilgrims to the temples of the Seven Gods of Good Fortune or the Six Amida Buddhas.

"Isn't it a bit odd to be selling Cherry Blossom Bentō out of blossom season?" a customer would remark now and again. The name was therefore changed to "Shigure bentō," and the stall out on the embankment stayed up until about the twentieth of May. There were not as many customers as in blossom time, but even so they would sell fifty or sixty bentō a day. Even guests coming to stay in one of the annexes might say, "Just bentō will do. They're cheap and good." Still, it just did not feel right to be carrying bentō boxes out to an annex. Oriku therefore had a special version of the bentō made, to be served in a larger, more impressive lacquered box, and containing additional dishes such as chilled carp sashimi and a bowl of soup. The chazuke was served afterward. All this cost one and a half yen, not including saké. It, too, was a great success, more so even than the restaurant's regular fare, and for a long time it continued to be a signature offering of the Shigure Teahouse.

In this way, the bentō that had originally been intended to serve only during the blossom-viewing season remained available until the twentieth of May. Total sales reached six thousand, for a monthly turnover four times higher than usual.

"I can't believe it, Ofune, I just can't believe it!" Oriku was both delighted and amazed. "We really didn't have to make *that* much!"

"It wasn't just for profit, though! You have to remember that we felt we simply couldn't handle being swamped by guests that way in blossom time. Even you, Mistress Oriku, can never have imagined this degree of success."

"I certainly didn't. You must all be exhausted."

"'Exhausted' is hardly the word for it. Shige-san can hardly move his arms any more, and he has to call in a masseuse every evening. Why, we went through ten thousand eggs!"

"We did? *Ten thousand?*"

Only someone of the Meiji period could appreciate how huge the figure "ten thousand" sounded then. The times were such that a thousand yen in savings made you quite comfortable, and with ten thousand you could live off the interest. The mention of ten thousand eggs made Oriku's eyes pop.

"It certainly sounds as though we're making money hand over fist, but I hope the accounting is right. With ten thousand eggs for six thousand bentō, a quick flick of the abacus might well show we made no profit at all. I don't like to think that we did all that work for nothing."

"No, that's not right, but it's true that we overdid it with the two-gō bottles of saké. One gō would have been plenty. A real drinker wants more than that, while for people who drink little, one gō is too much. We wasted a lot there."

They had miscalculated somewhat with the saké, but they *had* made a considerable profit. Once the bentō-making stopped, Shigezō, the chef, spent the entire day sleeping and never got up at all.

"I don't blame him. I thought we might take turns resting, but let's just close up shop for the day and all go somewhere together."

Ofune was all for that, of course.

The cooks, the maids, the helpers, Tomé-san the watchman—all twenty-six of them were keen to go somewhere. But where? When asked for suggestions, some favored a theatrical performance of some kind, some a picnic, some a boat trip to Shinagawa to do some sea-fishing. The discussion was endless.

"We'll never get anywhere like this," Shigezō declared, "since everyone wants to go somewhere different. Let's just have Mistress Oriku make the choice for us." Ofune supported him, and they all agreed to abide by Oriku's decision.

Oriku's response was quick and definite. "There's nothing unusual about going to the theater," she said, "and besides, you all have different tastes in the matter. The idea of fishing off Shinagawa isn't bad, but those with no interest in fishing wouldn't have any fun, and it would be too bad if anyone got seasick. The best, I think, would be a stroll across the fields to Horikiri. Don't you agree? Someone should go on ahead to prepare the way, and the rest of us will walk to the Odaka Garden or the Musashi Garden. From there we can head off to Yotsugi and have lunch at the Yoshino Garden. It's too early for irises, and it doesn't much matter what flowers are in bloom. While we stroll along, the men can drink saké, the women can peel hard-boiled eggs, and we can all talk all the nonsense we want. It'll be fun."

No one disagreed with Oriku's choice, so Tomé was sent ahead to arrange the saké and the food, while the rest set off at a leisurely pace along the embankment.

"If it rains, we'll just put our holiday off and wait for better weather," Oriku had declared. "I'd hate to turn away any guests who might take the trouble to come all the way out here, though, so I'd like to leave three of us behind—we'll draw straws to see who stays. The evening before, the kitchen will prepare twenty bentō, and the guests who are satisfied with bentō are welcome to them." Oriku, who thought of everything, made sure that unexpected guests should be properly looked after, and also that those who remained behind should be generously rewarded.

On the morning of the twenty-second of May, the sun was hot already in a limpid sky. No smoke rose from any factory chimneys, nor were there any cars to raise clouds of dust. Under the deep blue heavens, the rustic paths that stretched before them were breathtakingly beautiful. The way to Horikiri led along the Mukōjima embankment, through Kanegafuchi, to the Ayase River. Although not wide, the river was deep, and its swiftly flowing water was so clear that you could see the schools of little funa carp at the bottom. Almost all the funa served as sashimi at the Shigure Teahouse came from the Ayase River; the local farmers caught them and brought them around to sell. Funa taken from a bad river just taste of mud, but ones from a river like the Ayase have pure white flesh, taut and firm when sliced into sashimi, and very good when eaten with vinegar and miso with a little mustard.

As Shigezō, the chef, walked along, he tossed shelled, short-necked clams into the river from baskets he had brought with him. "The funa have been my livelihood for years now, so today I'm thanking them," he explained. He would pick up the shelled clams and scatter them in a wide arc over the river. The funa seemed to love them and clustered around avidly—some, to everyone's delight, even leaping from the water. Shigezō tossed the clams to them, little by little, as he went, and the school of fish followed him.

"Are they all funa?" Oriku asked, fascinated.

"No, not all of them. Some are other kinds, but the funa are the only ones you can eat." He had the clams in two small baskets, chopped fine to make them easier for the fish to swallow.

"Let me give them some, too." Oriku took a handful and tossed it in, but instead of spreading out, it sank in a lump to the bottom.

"The river is deep here, and if you don't do it right the clams just sink into the mud. You have to scatter them lightly, over a wide area, so the fish can get them before they sink."

Having done this before, he was used to tossing the clam meat out in the most effective way. Oriku had never seen little fish dart so quickly after food. The maids followed Shigezō, uttering cries of astonishment. The ordinary way to Horikiri involved turning left at Ayase Bridge, but they had followed the embankment along the river, scattering food to the fish, and by the time the food was all gone they had come quite a long way.

The farmers were hard at work, tilling the rice fields before the rainy season. To each one, Oriku called out as they passed, "Thank you for all your hard work!" One of the last things her late husband had enjoined upon her was respect for farmers. "We have the farmers to thank for being able to eat our food in peace," he had said. "Covered in mud they plant the seedlings, keep them watered, drive off pests, always fearing of rain and wind, and in so doing keep the price of rice remarkably low. That it should be so low is a great help to all, for the poor could only die of starvation if it were high. When you follow a path through the rice fields, you must always thank the farmers." Oriku did as her husband had said, and as they walked along, she taught the maid to do the same.

Their path led them away from Horikiri and toward Yotsugi. "We *could* go to Horikiri," Oriku announced, "but the irises there aren't out yet. The Yoshino Garden at Yotsugi, on the other hand has a garden restaurant where all kinds of flowers are in bloom. So let's not go back to Horikiri, but instead let's go straight on to Yotsugi."

They left the Ayase River and took a slender path through the rice fields. Expanses of nameless wild flowers and clumps of seri parsley were everywhere, and each time they came to another one, the men would stop to drink some cold saké and the women would chatter excitedly. Their gay laughter was like the twittering of birds. Everyone, from Oriku herself down to the lowest kitchen helper, was on the best of terms. This was a rare thing for a restaurant staff in Meiji days, and it was the key to the Shigure Teahouse's success. Oriku, the cooks, the maids, everyone, formed a close-knit fellowship. If the place made a profit, all had their share, in accordance with rank and age. The whole staff got on well together, and the lineup of faces remained exactly the same as when the restaurant had opened.

"You aren't getting any younger, you know, and a woman ages quickly," Oriku might remind the maids. "If you find someone you like, you should marry him."

"Are you trying to get rid of us, Mistress Oriku?" they would retort. Not a single one had left since the opening. Even those hired temporarily as extra help had moved in and stayed.

"Is the Yoshino Garden really this far?" This expression of discontent came from Ofune.

"What's the matter? We're out for a walk, after all. We spend so much of our time sitting down that I feel we need a walk from time to time."

"*You* may sit a lot, Mistress Oriku, but not us. We spend the entire year on our feet, walking back and forth to the kitchen."

"That kind of walking doesn't count. What's actually good for you is walking along paths like this, through the fields."

"Perhaps so, but it's still too far."

"It's not even lunchtime yet!"

"I've been starving for ages, and my tummy is complaining!"

"Look at all the eggs you've eaten, and you're *still* hungry?"

Ofune and Oriku often had such little spats, and the others just grinned. They all were so unaccustomed to walking that by the time they reached the Yoshino Garden the men were dragging themselves along and the women were quite short of breath.

The news that the mistress of the Shigure Teahouse was on her way brought the owner of the Yoshino Garden out to the gate to greet them. Tomé had everything ready and was waiting to greet them. The famished horde never gave the flowers or the scenery a glance. Instead they sat themselves down in a pavilion on a little knoll and started right in on the saké.

"The cooks went to great trouble when I told them the mistress of the Shigure Teahouse was coming," Tomé explained excitedly. "I don't know whether what they serve will be to your taste, but I hope you can make do!"

"There's no need to worry. We didn't come here for the food. We're out for a walk, that's all, and it doesn't matter what we have for lunch."

Still, the food was not bad at all. It was country-style fare—lotus root, taro, and burdock root cooked together, fresh fava beans, and loach-and-egg stew—and tasted very good. The tipsy men showed off their performing talents as though celebrating the New Year, and the drinkers among the women joined them to sing popular songs and turn them into improvised dances. In short, the party was very lively indeed, and no one gave the surrounding scenery a thought.

Oriku picked a good moment to remove herself from the gathering. "The villa of flowers," people called the place, and indeed, its twelve acres boasted streams, knolls, and a lake divided into several parts, one being devoted to irises that were indescribably beautiful when in bloom. Oriku felt refreshed whenever she walked the grounds, and so she abandoned the drunken revelers in order to stroll round the garden. The path around the lake branched off occasionally toward a hillock thick with camellias, an expanse of azaleas, or an arbor of pale violet, late-blooming wisteria. There was no end to the different places you could go. When you let the scenery draw you on to the furthest depths of the garden, the path eventually led you right out between the rice fields. At the Yoshino Garden there was no line between inside and outside—no hedge, no fence—and the path went straight out into the fields. Flustered, Oriku had just turned back and set off down the flower-lined path when she heard someone most unexpectedly call out to her.

"Hello, hello! You from the Shigure Teahouse!" The voice was clear and penetrating. "Aren't you Mistress Oriku from Mukōjima? You are, aren't you! You're Mistress Oriku!" The voice came from a little pavilion on a knoll to her right. Stretching to peer up in that direction, she saw a slender, handsome man standing there on the veranda.

"Yes, I am Oriku from the Shigure Teahouse. May I ask with whom I am speaking?"

"With whom?" he retorted, in a voice redolent with sarcasm. "What do you mean? It's me! Ichimura! Ichimura Uzaemon, for goodness' sake, the actor!"

Oriku was flabbergasted. "Mr. Ichimura!" she gasped, otherwise speechless.

"Mr. Ichimura? What *is* this? Who are you here with, anyway? Who's your friend? I won't let you off if you try to hide it!" Sounding like a true son of Edo, he hastily slipped on his zōri sandals and came down the path to her right. He was dressed in a lined jacket worn casually and secured with a tied-dyed, silk crepe sash. He looked thoroughly alluring.

"No, no, it's not just one or two people I'm here with. Everyone from the teahouse is here today on an excursion."

"Really?"

"I swear it. Just look at that pavilion over there." She pointed to a pavilion, half-hidden among the trees, where male voices could be heard singing and laughing.

"I see, I see. That's quite a party you have there!" He came up to her with an affable expression. "You never come to see my shows, do you!"

"Yes, I do. I can't stay for the second piece, but just the other day I saw you do Sanemori."

"Why didn't you come backstage, then?"

"Well, if I did that, I couldn't just look in and then leave right away. I'd have to go around and greet everyone, and I end up feeling it would just be too much trouble."

"I see your point. I'm sure that kind of thing is a real nuisance when you're in business."

"Yes, it is. You can't just go and say hello to a particular favorite."

"Who *is* your favorite these days?"

"I have no favorites, past or present, except for one Ichimura Uzaemon."

"Don't flatter me! You probably don't mean it, though."

"Who cares? It wouldn't mean anything even if I did. I just enjoy watching the play."

"Goodness, you're very clever now with your tongue!"

"I'm serious! What does my liking you have to do with it? We're too far apart in age."

Bantering this way, between truth and make-believe, they set out together along the path, which twisted and turned till they came out beside the lake, in the middle of a bed of flowers. Natural log seats were scattered about here and there under the trees. The afternoon sun was hazy, and mist rose from the edges of the lake.

"Is this all right?" Oriku asked. "Aren't you with someone?"

"Goodness, no! Just my students, my chief aide, and the theater's prop master—no one else. I don't drink, so they're better off without me."

"It's strange, though, that there's no sign of a woman anywhere around you."

"The thing is, you see, next month we're doing a play that involves the garden here at Yotsugi, so I brought my prop master along to have a look at the place."

"Really? The irises here are in a play?"

"Yes. The garden has been here since the old days of the shogunate. It started with a restaurant, called the Yoshinoya, at Hikibune. The owner sold flowers on the side."

"What's the play about?"

"It's an amusing one. In the first act the Shogun visits the garden and falls in love with a farmer's daughter."

"You're doing the role of the Shogun, I suppose?"

"I expect so, yes. I plan to, anyway, since the play is good fun."

"The Shogun you play—I suppose he forcibly possesses the farmer's daughter?"

"Don't jump to conclusions. You're not the playwright, after all."

"It's obvious, regardless of who the playwright may be! Your Shogun then takes her back to Edo Castle, and since she now belongs to him, she presumably has a child."

"For pity's sake! You should give up your restaurant and write for the theater!"

"If I were a playwright, I'd make you play the part of a very unattractive man every time you had an affair."

"You're awful!"

He slapped her lightly on the back and burst into laughter. Uzaemon being so naturally merry a fellow, they had this kind of good-humored fun whenever and wherever they met. When he carried on with a woman he did so boldly and freely. "Let's spend the night together," he might say with unabashed exuberance, and if he got back, "I can't tonight, I'm afraid," he would reply without a trace of rancor, "I see—well then, some other time!" And that would be that. In his later years, when summoned as a witness in a case brought by a Shinbashi geisha named Hidematsu, he behaved in court with impressive self-assurance, never betraying even a flicker of nervousness. The news of Uzaemon's appearance at the trial figured prominently in the newspapers, and in the course of his testimony he astonished everyone—officers of the court and audience alike—by speaking for Hidematsu and frankly admitting that, "Yes, I had relations with her." Wherever he went he remained in full command of himself, and he made no distinction between those above him and those below. He was a model son of Edo.

"I hear business is good at Mukōjima."

"Thank you. Yes, we're getting by."

"Excellent! A faltering business isn't much to talk about."

"I hope you'll come and see for yourself." Talk of business made Oriku a little tense.

"Is your day finished now? Have you done what you needed to do?"

"Yes, I think so. They can have more fun without me."

"That's right. At a time like this the boss does well to disappear. How about it, then? It's still early. Shall we go somewhere together?"

"You have people with you, too, though."

"As with you, they're better off without me. I might as well leave them to their own devices."

"So where shall we go?"

"Anywhere—it doesn't matter. Let's just get on our way and take whatever we find."

Uzaemon's carefree tone of voice was characteristic. Oriku felt perfectly at ease with him. She prided herself on enjoying her affairs before all the world, but one time only; she never went with the same man a second time, no matter who he might be. Uzaemon therefore made an ideal partner for her.

Once the decision was made, Oriku asked Ofune to keep an eye on things thereafter, while Uzaemon made the same request of his own retinue. Then they left the Yoshino Garden together, side by side, in two rickshaws. The way back to Mukōjima would have made a long walk, but by rickshaw it was hardly any distance at all. The slender path through the reeds led them to the Tōbu Line tracks with their locomotives puffing lazily along; beyond the tracks stretched the outskirts of Mukōjima. This was where the avenue of cherry trees began.

The rickshaws suddenly sped downhill when they reached the Suijin embankment, leaving Oriku wondering where they were going; then, at the bottom of the slope, the edge of the Suijin grove came into view. "Oh dear!" she said to herself. They were obviously headed for an inn and restaurant named Yaomatsu, the Shigure Teahouse's main competitor at Mukōjima and a far older place, Oriku's being a mere upstart in comparison. The idea of turning up at Yaomatsu, alone with Uzaemon, was thoroughly embarrassing, but by this time there was nothing she could do about it. They descended the embankment and took a path through the fields, to find the Yaomatsu's famous chief maid waiting to greet them. You could see a rickshaw coming down the embankment from the front of the restaurant.

"Welcome, welcome, Mr. Ichimura!"

She greeted Uzaemon with obvious pleasure as he alighted, but her color changed when she saw he had a woman with him. Uzaemon was a keen patron of the Yaomatsu, so much so that later on he even built a room there, named "Tachibana no Ma"; and for that reason his arrival always caused a great stir. The sun was still high, and Oriku was too embarrassed to get out of her rickshaw. She herself was over forty, while Uzaemon was at most only thirty-three or thirty-four—a far younger man. The rickshaw man had put down the shafts, but Oriku remained hunched forward inside. Uzaemon had not gone in, either; instead, the chief maid was whispering to him. They seemed to be arguing animatedly about something, though Oriku could not hear what they were saying. Suddenly, geta clattered on the stones of the path.

"What's the matter? Why aren't you coming in? Do you have someone with you?" It was a young woman's piercing voice. Oriku stiffened. She heard Uzaemon softly trying to smooth the matter over;

then all at once a woman's arm, slender and white, reached right into the rickshaw.

"Stop it, do you hear me?" It was Uzaemon's voice. Oriku could just imagine the chief maid's agitated figure. The hand seized Oriku's sleeve, and she panicked. Whoever the woman was, it was outrageously rude of her to thrust her arm straight in this way, and Oriku automatically slapped it hard with the flat of her hand.

"Ah!" There was a low cry, and the arm was withdrawn.

"Pardon me, young rickshaw man, but please take me away again."

Oriku felt better. The rickshaw turned back toward the embankment, but no one seemed to be coming after her. Perhaps Uzaemon had been dragged inside; at any rate, she could no longer hear his voice. The rickshaw man seemed to understand, for he mounted the embankment at a good pace. Had it been pure chance? Had Uzaemon forgotten a promise? Had a woman friend happened to be there, seen him arrive, and rushed out to him? Whatever the case might be, this sort of thing was likely enough to happen to a popular young actor. It had been a mistake for her, a woman in her forties, to follow a star ten years younger all the way there, and the outcome had been a good lesson, though she also held it against him. She was furious with herself for having been so thoughtless.

She should have put him off tactfully when he first invited her to go somewhere with him, but instead she cheerfully followed him, and this was what her foolishness had earned her. Nonetheless, she was angry. If he had been at all sincere, he could have acknowledged her arrival with him, even if that meant sending the other woman packing. Oriku felt sick as she reached the gate to her own place. The sun, sunk low at last, lit up the leaves. She tipped the rickshaw man generously and descended the embankment. The tall reeds rustled in the evening breeze.

"Oshin! Oshin!" she called as she came in through the kitchen and plopped down on the floor.

"Goodness, Mistress Oriku, welcome home! You're very early, aren't you?"

"Fill me a teacup—never mind if it's cold."

"What? With saké, you mean?"

"Of course I do. 'Cold' obviously refers to cold saké."

"Right away!" Oshin's voice, too, had a cool ring.

Oriku emptied the large, nearly full teacup in one breath.

"Did something happen?"

"Why?"

"Well, you never normally have a drink of cold saké the moment you come home."

"And is there something wrong with having one?"

"No, there's nothing wrong with it. I'm just surprised." Oshin was watching Oriku's face curiously. She had come back from accompanying the others on their outing.

"Did something unpleasant occur?"

"I'm done in, that's all. I so seldom walk anywhere, I'm just exhausted." Still, she remained thoroughly upset. It had not been *her* idea for the two of them to go somewhere together. The invitation had been *his*, and look what he had gotten her into! The foul aftertaste of it—of having been made to look like a fool, of having been shamed—simply would not go away.

Toc, toc, toc, toc, toc. There was a noise somewhere. It sounded like light blows with a small hammer, not driving a nail, but perhaps knocking out a shelf. On and on it went.

"What's that sound?" Oriku sat before the kitchen hearth. The saké she had just swallowed was still sloshing around in her stomach.

"We have a rare visitor. Tetsunosuke brought a tea chest and a storage chest today, and he's been tapping away like that in your room since this morning." Oshin cocked her ear in that direction too.

"He *has*? So Tetsu's here, is he?" They both listened. There was something familiar about the sound. The turmoil in Oriku's heart seemed to melt away.

"Those pieces certainly took him a long time, didn't they?"

"Yes, but he probably found it difficult to come, after all the trouble he caused you."

"How does he look?"

"Not very comfortable. He seemed relieved when I told him you weren't here."

"He's amusing himself at my expense. Properly, he should have come long ago to offer me an apology."

"Well, yes, but that's the kind of man he is—he just can't get out the right words." She shot a conciliatory glance toward the interior of the building.

Oriku could hardly just stand up and go straight to him. It was two years since he had been stabbed by a woman and hauled into court. She had managed to get by without those two chests, despite her need for them. Apparently they were now ready.

She set off toward the Paulownia annex, meanwhile feeling a tipsy flush rise to her face. She found the whole place, from the veranda on in, covered by protective matting, upon which Tetsu was tapping at the corners of the chests. He did not want the stress and strain of transport to have loosened any of the joints. The tea chest was made of mulberry, and the storage chest of fine-grained paulownia. The fittings were antiqued silver.

Tetsu sat up straight when he saw Oriku, blushed scarlet, and bowed, both palms to the floor. Speech was beyond him.

"The tea chest took two years, didn't it."

"I am very sorry." His eyes remained downcast, whether because he had been so slow to finish the work, or because he felt guilty over the trouble he had caused. Finally he said, "Actually, I was afraid when I came that you might have hired somebody else."

"Yes, I thought about doing that, but unfortunately I don't care for anyone else's work."

Tetsu's face showed gratified surprise.

"You've made everything I've ever used. It's fate, I suppose."

The look of surprise remained, but nothing she said could embolden him to look up at her.

"Is it all done, then?"

"I still don't like the lampshade I made, but yes, once that's fixed, there are just two or three little accessories left. The lacquer has to dry before I can paint on the designs and bring them to you."

At last he lifted his gaze, perhaps encouraged by her remark that she liked no one's work but his, and grateful also for her confidence in him. "I cannot apologize enough for what happened," he said. "I never imagined I might make things so difficult for you."

"It's all right, it's all right. Let's not talk about it. I'll just get angry again if we do."

"I didn't think I would ever be able to show my face here again."

"I learned a lot, though. If it hadn't been for all that, I would never have seen the inside of a courtroom."

"I only wish the earth would swallow me whenever I think about it."

"What happened to her, anyway?"

"She was sentenced to a year in prison, but the sentence was suspended because she had turned herself in."

"What did she do then?"

"She felt too ashamed to go back where she had been before, so she sold her shop, and I gather she returned to her home."

"Without seeing you again?"

"I hadn't seen her for a long time, and when she suddenly turned up like that, demanding that I marry her, I refused to talk to her. I suppose that's what got her back up and made her do it." His voice was so low that Oriku could hardly hear him. It was as though he were whispering to the floor.

"So you no longer have any relationship with her, of any kind?"

"I can't imagine her coming around again, after doing to me what she did."

"And because of what she did, you're still as single as ever?"

"Yes." He said no more, then glanced at the furniture fittings. "Is this where you would like this piece?" he asked. It had been so inconvenient to warm saké or make tea in her room without a tea chest that she had also ordered a cabinet with drawers. He seemed to have finished what he was doing, for he quickly tidied up and rolled up the drop cloths.

"I'm done for the time being. Thank you very much. I shall return soon."

"Surely, though, you'll have a drink before you go."

"But, well, I'll be back again."

"Is there something you have to do?"

"No, not especially."

"Then wait a little while. It's sunset now, and the place is closed because everyone went on an outing today."

"So I hear. Oshin told me about it."

"We went to the garden at Yotsugi, but no one had eyes for flowers or scenery. They started in on the saké as soon as we arrived, and what with the singing and dancing, it was quite a party."

"They must have had a wonderful time. I don't know anywhere else where the whole staff gets on so well together."

"I barely managed to sneak away . . . and now I'm hungry. It's been such a long time—I hope you'll have something to eat with me."

"Are you sure it's all right?"

"Of course it is. With *you* there's no need to worry. However drunk you may be when you leave, you needn't be afraid anyone may stab you on the way out."

"You're awful, Mistress Oriku!" Tetsunosuke's wry smile was accusing.

Now that they were relaxing, the teasing started. "You said not to talk about it, and yet right away . . ."

"A little remark like that, I just couldn't help it! Besides, you'd just been having a good time."

"I'd say there wasn't much good about it." His frowning face wore the same boyish look as always.

Just then Oshin came in with some saké and leftover bentō. Only two couples were staying in the annexes. Apparently even longtime customers had been turned away on the grounds that the place was closed, and just six people had come during the day, so that half the bentō they had prepared remained unsold.

"There's nothing wrong with having some left over. After all, we made them so as not to disappoint our best customers."

"They may still go, though. The sun's only just setting, and more people are bound to come." Oshin left a large bottle of saké beside the brazier.

They had some right away. The bad taste left by that Yaomatsu incident made Tetsunosuke an ideal drinking companion, and her pleasure at the expression on his face as she teased him gave the saké a special quality. Tetsu, too, gradually grew more relaxed.

"Make yourself more comfortable! Don't you feel awkward sitting there so formally in your work trousers?"

"Very well then, if you insist," he replied as though on cue. He sat cross-legged instead and began to fill his own cup, instead of waiting for Oriku to pour for him. He had come only reluctantly, hardly knowing what to expect, but she was in a remarkably good mood, and they joked back and forth as they drank, till in no time they had emptied two or three bottles. Oriku, too, felt fine. She put a kettle on the brazier that Tetsu had made and warmed the saké herself. The table was a bit crowded with those two bentō on it.

"I wish it were a little bigger."

"You're right. I sized it in proportion to the room, but I'll make a bigger one."

"That's easy to say, but it won't be free, I'm sure. No doubt it'll cost a lot."

"No, I'm not doing this for the money. It's my pleasure to make these things for you, and the new table won't cost you anything if you like it."

"What? You *know* I can't agree to that!"

"No, no, I don't want any money, really I don't. I wouldn't take a penny from you, Mistress Oriku. Order anything you like, and I'll make it for you. Really, I'm happy to make you whatever you wish."

He gazed at Oriku, his eyes flushed with drink. Something in his expression suggested what lurked in the depths of those eyes. Oriku was drunk, too, and she felt like doing something to wash away that aftertaste of the Yaomatsu. . .

Oriku had not forgotten her talk with Ofune there on the Mukōjima embankment, that day two years ago on their way back from the trial. The only way to restore Tetsunosuke to full humanity was for her to sleep with him: those words still rang in her ears. Two whole years later, that same shadow still clouded his face, and this was just the night to clear it away. Everyone would undoubtedly be back late, the men having stolen off somewhere together, while the women had presumably gone on to Asakusa to enjoy the show at the Miyako-za.

"You look pretty cheerful."

"Yes. I was afraid when I came that all I'd get was a piece of your mind. I never imagined being entertained this way. It's like a dream!"

"I'm not going to lecture you. You looked like a fool at the time, but I wasn't angry. I did think you an idiot, though, for having involved yourself with a hopeless woman like that."

"A proper idiot, yes, I certainly was. Some demon must have gotten into me."

"No doubt it did. That demon eventually gets in whenever a man or a woman is alone. I imagine fear of it made her want a husband, but you told her no."

"I didn't mean it like *that*, though! But what about you—does that demon get into even you sometimes?"

"Of course it does. I'm only flesh and blood, after all."

"I suppose so." His eyes filmed over, and he sadly lowered his gaze. Talk of marriage, or of this demon, seemed to make him gloomy.

"I'm very fond of you, though! Look how I turned down that man from Suzaki, just because you didn't want me to marry him."

Oriku had showed her hand. Tetsunosuke blushed scarlet, and tears sprang to his eyes.

"I'm very fond of you, too, Mistress Oriku, very fond indeed. That's why. . . That's exactly why. . ." Unable to continue, he instead took up his cup.

The saké affected him even more, once their talk reached this intimate level, and he brought the cup to his lips at every pause. Oriku, too, was in an exalted mood. She plainly discerned Tetsu's hope that she would save him. After that incident he had had nothing further to do with women and had plunged himself in despair into his work, simply drinking himself to sleep when he was tired. Such had been his daily routine, but now at last he sensed the warmth of human flesh.

Both shared the same sentiment, and they forgot the lateness of the hour to lose themselves in saké. Little by little, as their feelings merged, they became profoundly intoxicated.

◆　◆　◆

In the autumn of that year, all of Mukōjima was flooded. Without fail, in early fall the Sumida River would overflow its banks and invade the low-lying areas around it. Since the Shigure Teahouse stood in marshland, its garden was submerged every year, but the house site itself was built up to the level of the embankment and had never yet been flooded. This year, however, the water was very nearly up to the veranda, and the whole area of Terajima Village looked like an ocean.

The fire brigade had issued a warning the evening before, to the effect that the high tide that night would be especially dangerous. When it rained for days on end in early autumn, the water flowing down from high in the mountains swelled the Sumida River to the very top of its banks, and when this coincided with a high tide, low-lying downtown areas disappeared beneath the waves. In Oriku's own neighborhood, houses built below the embankment stood in water up to their eaves, and their inhabitants had to seek refuge on the embankment itself. Beyond the embankment, the whole territory of the villages of Terajima and Koume would be underwater, and across the river, the entire area from Hashiba and Imado to Sanyachō and Yoshinochō would be a muddy lake.

At the Shigure Teahouse they took up the tatami mats and put all the furniture and accessories in the attic, up over the ceiling. If the water rose above the floor, the idea was that everyone should get up in the attic too. The place had no proper second floor, but the attic was high and sturdy enough to serve equally well as a refuge.

"If the water rises any higher it will overflow the embankment, and people will die. I'm sure it won't, though." Tomé-san, a native of Mukōjima itself, had long experience of these floods, and he knew how far the water would go. Looking out from the veranda, all you could see was a vast expanse of flowing, muddy water. The path down from the embankment had vanished, and only a small boat allowed any communication with the outside world.

"I think it might be time for you to seek safety, Mistress Oriku," Tomé observed. "Follow the embankment to Azuma Bridge, and you'll be fine after that."

"Going to Azuma Bridge would be all very well, but there's no one anywhere to take me in. I haven't a single relative in Tokyo."

"What about the Silver Flower?"

"If it's this bad here, the Yoshiwara must be flooded, too. Besides, I don't like going to someone else for help. I can't imagine it rising all the way to the roof."

Oriku had not the slightest intention of fleeing. The water level remained roughly the same, as Tomé-san had said it would, neither rising nor falling. During the day it dropped a little, then rose again toward evening. High tide came about six o'clock, and after that the worst seemed to be over. The problem, though, was that they were short of food. There was plenty of rice, but with the kitchen under water they could not cook it. On receiving the initial warning they had prepared a quantity of rice against future need, but there were too many of them, and the cooked rice had soon run out.

"I don't know what to do, Mistress Oriku. Rice we have, but I can't cook it." Shigezō, the chef, was pale.

"Not one of us has left, despite the flood, and with thirty people here it's no wonder we're short of food."

"Perhaps we should all chip in to go and buy some."

"That's all we can do. I want all the men to go and buy us some provisions."

"Very well. I'll have someone I know cook the rice, then we'll bring it back here."

The men were about to set off when Tomé called out, "Mistress Oriku, someone's here in a boat!" Tomé went splashing down to the service entrance and looked out from the veranda. Sure enough, it was a boat from the local fire brigade. A young man plied the oars, and the three passengers were all earnestly attired in firemen's garb.

"Hello! Is everyone safe there? Is Oriku all right?" A familiar voice echoed over the water.

"It's Mr. Ichimura!" The realization brought Oriku instant relief. Ready by now to accept anyone's help, she awaited the boat's arrival. Sure enough, it was Uzaemon. In his work trousers, cloth leggings, straw sandals, and embroidered jacket he cut as elegant a figure as a fireman of old in a play.

"Goodness, Mr. Ichimura, have you really been kind enough to come all the way out here?" Oriku felt a rush of joy.

"Well, I was worried about you. I thought it would be bad in this area, but it's even worse than I'd imagined." As he spoke, Uzaemon leapt from the boat to the veranda—which was easy enough, since the boat could pull right up to it.

"What a flood!" He stepped across the floor beams, bare now that the tatami had been taken up, into the main room, where he gazed out over the river. The river little resembled the Sumida River they normally knew. Down the middle, the swift current rushed past, laden with tangled debris from upstream.

"I'm very impressed by the way you're managing to get through this!"

"Well, we don't have much choice, do we? There's nowhere else to go."

"Things should be all right now, though. I thought you might be short of food, so I've brought you plenty. I had rice cooked in a great big pot and made into rice balls, and I put in lots of takuan pickles too. There, look!"

He turned round and pointed back to the kitchen. Tears sprang to Oriku's eyes. In a time when no one else had come to ask after her, the great star Ichimura Uzaemon had had his disciples bring her rice balls!

In the kitchen rested a mountain of salted rice balls, accompanied by appetizing takuan pickles.

"I hear Mr. Ichimura brought us all this wonderful food!" Ofune, too, sounded close to tears. The men of Shigezō's party looked thoroughly relieved. Tonight would be the last of it; the next day the water would drop, and they could cook rice. If they could just get through tonight . . . Oriku's heart missed a beat, and at last she wept. Her gratitude was beyond words.

"I'll never forget what you've done for us, never!" That was all she could say.

"What are you talking about? Don't exaggerate! All I did was bring you some rice balls. I thought you might need them—that's why I came."

"I don't deserve such kindness. Everyone here is so grateful to you!" She lowered her gaze to hide her tears. Just then, the unpleasant memory of that moment at the Yaomatsu flickered across her mind. Perhaps this gesture of his was meant as an apology, one that he could not express in words, but one that was better than any words.

"Mistress Oriku, Tetsu came on the same boat!" Ofune was looking down at a corner of the kitchen. And there he was, sitting discreetly in formal posture, likewise in work trousers and straw sandals, and wearing a jacket emblazoned with the name "Shigure Teahouse." Before him lay a basket heaped high with hard-boiled eggs.

"Tetsu, you brought us hard-boiled eggs?"

"Yes. I'm sorry it took me so long to get here. Ryūsenjichō is even worse than this, and last night I had to sleep on the roof."

"But, Tetsu, surely you should be looking after yourself instead!"

"There's nothing more I can do. I left my apprentices to look after things."

"It's at times like this that you find out who your real friends are." Oriku did not actually say this, but she certainly thought it. Uzaemon and Tetsunosuke, both true sons of Edo, understood human feelings. How lucky she was to know them! Swallowing her tears, she glanced from one to the other.

One was a brilliant, popular actor, the other an unknown cabinetmaker. Although utterly different in livelihood and outlook, both had the same blood in their veins.

"I imagine this is about as high as the water will get," Uzaemon remarked in his charming voice. "I'm impressed that not a single one of your people sought refuge elsewhere. It shows how much they think of you, Oriku."

"Yes, well, it was quite a challenge, cooking rice for them all, and your rice balls are like the Buddha turning up in Hell—a godsend."

"Hardly an expensive Buddha! Anyway, it certainly was worth coming if they've made you happy. I'll be on my way, then. Make sure you clean up properly, once the water is gone. Nasty illnesses can get around at times like this. Wash out the kitchen with particular care."

Having delivered these detailed instructions, he leapt lightly into the waiting fire-brigade boat. Everything about him—his figure, his voice—was enchanting, and Oriku greatly regretted that nothing had happened that day. With such reflections as these in mind, she watched the boat pull away from the veranda, meanwhile bowing her head again and again. Once he was gone, everyone began praising his kind ways, his dashing figure, his profound thoughtfulness, and so on.

"Mr. Ichimura isn't the only thoughtful one, though!" Oriku interjected loudly. "Just look at Tetsunosuke! With the water up to his own roof, he still managed to bring us all this!" She purposely countered exclusive praise for Uzaemon. Uzaemon's gesture included an apology for the Yaomatsu incident, but Tetsu's sprang from pure love.

A servant put water to boil on a charcoal burner, while everyone gathered round to eat rice balls with their fingers, and Oriku peeled a hard-boiled egg.

The sun sank low, all the lanterns were lit, and they heard the members of the fire brigade uttering constant warning cries. Once night came, Tetsu would be unable to leave.

Saké was heated in a large kettle, and everyone, including Oriku and Tetsu, got a teacupful.

"You won't be able to leave, you know, once it's dark. Is that all right?"

"Yes indeed. I plan to spend the night helping you here."

"Really? That's so kind of you." She truly meant it.

Her rule was to spend one night only with a man, never more, but Tetsunosuke might turn out to be a special case. Once the water was down, once everything was back to normal and the business was going again, it could do no harm to invite him back for a night in the Paulownia annex.

Holding her cup of saké, she looked at Tetsunosuke as he sat there under a lantern. He had his teacup too, and he was watching her. A flush of warmth touched both their faces.

CHAPTER SEVEN

"Bitter Spring" (Part 1)

"Mistress Oriku, Mistress Oriku!" Ofune's piercing voice resounded as she ran. Always excitable, she came rushing in, raising great cries, whenever something unusual happened. Even from the kitchen you could hear her shouting agitatedly in the distance. Oriku scolded her every time she did it, but she never mended her ways.

"I keep telling you not to shout so loud. You never seem to listen."

"But I just can't believe it! It's impossible not to be amazed!"

"Nobody's going to be amazed, with you bellowing like that. Has a lizard gotten into the ceiling, or something?"

"No, no, nothing like that." Ofune came right up to her and practically whispered in her ear, "Hagiwara-sensei's wife is in the annex!"

"You don't have to get that close! Stop breathing down my neck!" Oriku frowned and leaned away. "By 'Hagiwara-sensei' you mean Shunpō-sensei?"

"Yes, Shunpō-sensei's second wife!"

"I'd be much obliged if you'd drop the 'second'!" Oriku retorted. "I'm always warning you not to gossip about the guests, and I just can't have you spreading such talk!"

"But she's in there alone with a young man!"

"It must be her son, then, Shuntai-sensei!"

"It's not, though! Even I would know Shuntai-sensei, and besides, this one is younger."

"Whoever he may be, you are to ignore the whole thing. Talking about guests behind their backs is unacceptable. An innkeeper must never reveal a guest's identity. It's a rule of the trade."

Oriku's severe reproof left Ofune apparently unconvinced, and for that matter, Oriku did not much like the news either. Hagiwara Shunpō was a new arrival in the world of koto music, although in truth he was over seventy. An acknowledged master originally of the Ikuta school, at the age of about thirty he had abandoned the old repertoire in order to perform only new compositions of his own. He was a revolutionary who had caused a profound stir in the tradition-bound koto world.

His vision had always been weak, and after thirty or so he lost his sight entirely. His present wife, Takako, had started out as a live-in disciple who assisted him in his daily life until he got his hands on her, and, although she was young enough to be his daughter, made her his wife.

Oriku herself liked Shunpō's music, and in her Hashiba days she had taken lessons from him. She had kept the koto she played then, although she rarely touched it now. Back then she had still been the mistress of the proprietor of the Silver Flower, and while awaiting his visits she led a tedious life enlivened only by the usual lessons in tea, flower-arranging, and other such accomplishments. Hardly knowing what else to do with herself, she had studied every art she could think of, with emphasis on itchū-bushi, but including also kiyomoto, toki-wazu, and utazawa. The only ones she left out were nagauta and gidayū. In the end, she even resorted to singing Noh. The proprietor being so much older than she, she felt she needed these skills for the time when she would be alone again; however, he disliked both nagauta and gidayū, and would never let her study them. His Yoshiwara upbringing had given him fastidious tastes, and he enjoyed kiyomoto, tokiwazu, and utazawa; but he made a wry face even at itchū-bushi. It therefore took her three months to obtain his permission when she approached him about studying koto with Hagiwara Shunpō. Being blind, Shunpō did not always come in person, but was represented instead by his son, the junior master Shuntai, or sometimes by Shuntai's younger sister, Yamato.

Shunpō, then about fifty, had young, live-in disciples guide him wherever he went. He shaved his head like a Buddhist priest, wore the dark, plain garb of an artist-recluse, affected the senior teacher's cloth cap, and carried a long cane. This getup made him look older than he actually was, but it suited him, and it conveyed the great master's fierce dedication to his art. His two or three live-in disciples took turns accompanying him, so that the same one never came twice in a row.

Shuntai, the junior master, was still thirty or so, and a very presentable man. Unlike his father he dressed poorly and casually, looking like a student in his Kurume-cloth kimono and Kokura-weave trousers. In fact the figure he cut was the exact opposite of his fastidious, blind father's. When he came by himself, Oriku, being so young, always had a maid sit behind her, lest anyone entertain any suspicions; but the maid's presence did not constrain him in the least, and he showed no sign of caring whether she was there or not. Shunpō's teaching method was to play the piece once himself, then to talk as Oriku played it back to him, listening with his blind eyes turned to the ceiling, meanwhile voicing the rhythm. In contrast, Shuntai had a koto placed before each of them, sitting face to face, and played as he taught. That made his lessons the easier of the two to remember.

However, Shuntai by no means came every time. Oriku got Shunpō about once every three months, Shuntai three times in the same period, and Yamato four or five times. At the rate of three lessons a month, the total for three months came to nine. The female students got Yamato more often than not. Oriku was still in her early twenties, and a woman teacher was certainly safer, but Shuntai's lessons were the only ones she actually wanted.

Although undoubtedly beautiful, in character Yamato was sullen and obstinate. She said very little; she played briskly, like a man; and she was the strictest of the three.

"You haven't got it yet? I'm serious about teaching you, and I'd appreciate your being serious about learning." Oriku found this sort of dressing-down thoroughly intimidating. At first she was glad to have such a good teacher, but the succeeding lessons became increasingly painful, until Oriku even let Shunpō know that his daughter's lessons, although well taught, were simply too strict. Shunpō ignored her complaint, on the grounds that "No art can be mastered unless it inspires fear and awe." However, the problem was not Yamato's severity alone, but also the icy meanness she conveyed. Perhaps she despised a brothel-keeper's kept woman; at any rate, her attitude made it quite plain that she could do without going to such a place to teach. She touched neither the tea offered her, nor the sweets, and she left with no more than the chilliest farewell glance.

In all these things Shuntai was utterly different. On entering the gate he did not step straight into the entrance, but instead took a turn along the garden's flagstone walk and down to the river. Though not wide, the garden was fairly long, as was the house. The houses along the Sumida River were all alike in that respect, broad river-front lots being unavailable.

Oriku's house was like that too. When you came through the gate, the entrance, with its lattice door, was on your left, and on your right was a brushwood door into a garden thick with hagi bush clover that in summer grew as tall as a man. Camellia, mokkoku evergreens, and many other shrubs had been planted tastefully here and there, and grew as their natures dictated. In contrast, the Silver Flower had a conventional garden with stone lanterns, a big, twisty pine, and a pond inhabited by colored carp. Since the view of the Silver Flower's garden was so familiar to him, Oriku's patron kept the one at her house looking quite natural. Shuntai seemed to like the path through the tall hagi fronds, for he almost always approached the house by way of the garden. He would make his way through the hagi down to the bank, gaze at the river scenery, and sit there on a stool to enjoy a cup of tea.

The view of Mukōjima, as seen from Oriku's Hashiba garden, centered on the location of the future Shigure Teahouse. Upstream you could see as far as Kanegafuchi and, downstream, almost all the way to Makura Bridge. The opposite bank was an unbroken expanse of reeds, where in winter hundreds of wild ducks made their nests. To the left was the Hashiba ferry landing, with the little ferryboat going lazily in and out. Sailboats glided down the middle of the river. Once the big bridge was built, all the boats became motor-driven, but in those days the freight craft all had sails, and when one hove into view, you had plenty of time to gaze after it till it disappeared. Sometimes peddlers came by, too, selling things from boats. The small farmers of the Senju area would come to sell the produce from their fields. Their stock was small, but it was fresh and cheap, and every house gladly bought from them. A perfunctory rinse had left mud still clinging to the fresh-picked cucumbers, eggplants, giant radishes, and rape blossoms, but all these vegetables and greens tasted so good that once you had tried them, you could never go back to the ones sold in grocery stores.

It was late autumn when Shuntai first came, and little remained in the fields. To fill out their wares the farmers were selling various dried goods or types of mochi they made on the side, like azuki beans, broad beans, or bota-mochi sweets filled with azuki-bean paste.

"Here, my good woman, I'll take some of that bota-mochi." Shuntai stepped down from the jetty to buy some from the boat and had a piece immediately, right where he stood. This being their first meeting with him, Oriku and her maids were shocked and wondered what kind of boor he might be; but his studentlike informality made him easy to approach, and a maid hastily brought him some tea.

"I'm so sorry, I've been very rude. The bota-mochi this good woman brought to sell looked so tempting that on my very first visit here I'm afraid I've committed a breach of manners. It was delicious. I can't eat all this by myself, though, so, all of you, please have some, too. I'll have just one more." He picked up another and gave the rest to the maids. The package, wrapped in the sheath of a bamboo shoot, was so full that it was hard to tell how many he had actually bought. He gazed at the scenery, eating his bota-mochi and sipping tea. Only after enjoying the view to his heart's content did he finally enter the house.

"That bota-mochi must have been awfully good!" Oriku could not stifle her merriment.

"Dear me, I'm terribly sorry to have indulged in such behavior on my very first visit. I hope you'll forgive me." So he said, at least, but as he seated himself before the koto his expression remained unruffled. Oriku, who had not been taking lessons long, had so far mastered only three easy pieces, and she therefore required more work than the other students. Shunpō gave her four lessons, Yamato a total of six, and the eleventh lesson was Shuntai's. He came when she was just about to give up on the impossible Yamato, and his youthful informality was such a relief that his lessons went beautifully.

Shuntai came three times in a row, but then it was back to the mean-spirited Yamato, whose every lesson was a trial. The maids stayed well away from her when she came, whereas when Shuntai came the maids and the old women all made a great fuss over him.

"Couldn't I possibly have you every time now, Shuntai-sensei?" she asked in a pleading tone after continuing for half a year.

Shuntai laughed. "So you don't get along with her, is that it?" He sounded as though he had expected her question.

"Umm, that's not exactly what I mean . . . It's just that she makes me feel so small and stupid."

"I understand. To tell the truth, I can't stand her, either. Woman or not, I've never known anyone so impossibly narrow-minded."

"And I have the impression that Yamato-sensei doesn't like me, either."

"That's not so. You're not the only one to dislike Yamato. Even I can't stand her. I can't imagine that anyone in the world actually likes her."

"It's not so much that I dislike her—it's more that I'm afraid of her."

"Exactly. So am I."

"But aren't you her older brother?"

"Yes, and her older brother is afraid of her, you see. The woman never forgives a slip. Everyone makes mistakes, but she has no mercy for any error, not even the smallest. That's why she inspires fear in a fellow like me, with all my faults."

"But she's a master of her instrument, isn't she?"

"Yes—my technique's not up to hers. Art is more than technique, though. Since we in my father's line have nothing to do with the old repertoire, we constantly have to compose new pieces. Performing one of them may be a matter simply of technique, but composing one takes talent and personal quality. They say character shows quite plainly in a new koto composition, and it's true that audiences don't respond to the ones my father composed at times when he was troubled. You can't come up with anything good unless your heart is serene—that's the difference between a composer and a performer. Yamato performs well, but she's not much of a composer. A work of art reveals its creator's best and worst: that's the problem we face."

There was passion in Shuntai's voice, which conveyed feeling so strong that he seemed intoxicated with his own words. Oriku listened respectfully. Despite his casual, studentlike manner, his face took on a thoroughly serious expression when he talked of art.

"Do you compose new pieces yourself, Shuntai-sensei?" Oriku asked gravely.

"Yes, I do. I'd have nothing to perform if I didn't, since I don't do anything old. I have fifteen or sixteen pieces of my own—not that they're any good."

"Won't you teach me one of them—one you're satisfied with?"

"Heavens no! I don't have anything worth teaching to someone else. I'm nowhere near good enough yet."

"Don't be so modest! Just teach me one, please."

Shuntai grew even more serious. "Actually, I'm working on a piece evoking the flow of the Sumida River as seen from the garden of your house. It isn't finished yet, but I hope you'll learn it if it comes out well." He glanced toward the river, visible beyond the veranda.

"I see. That's why you go down to the river as soon as you arrive."

"That's right. It's so peaceful, I feel the mystery of the river's flow would go well into koto music."

"Can you work the bota-mochi into the piece too?"

"Touché!"

Shuntai's seriousness dissolved. He slapped his head with one hand and burst into laughter.

Oriku began feeling attracted by the innocent genuineness of everything Shuntai said and did. Usually quite casual in his manner, he changed completely whenever the conversation turned to art, becoming then almost a different person. His professionalism was impeccable. He was thoroughly refreshing.

"I'll gladly come if you want me to. My sister has better technique and tone, though, and besides, you're still a young woman yourself."

"And, being a woman, I enjoy learning from a man. I mean nothing bad by that, though. It's just an impression, but I don't believe Yamato-sensei likes coming to my house. I'm a kept woman, my patron runs a brothel, and Yamato-sensei is too proud to be pleased about teaching anyone associated with so low a profession. That's the way it seems to me, anyway."

She had said what she thought. She also disliked taking lessons from someone who felt that way. Shuntai listened but said nothing. On the subject of his sister's faults he did not like to agree, but he himself was engaged in a struggle against her pride. He did not reply, but he came more often after that. The two were close in age, after all, their personalities matched, and they enjoyed each other's company. Shuntai's arrival brightened the whole day, and they all gossiped about him after he left.

"Mistress Oriku, you must have a crush on Shintai-sensei," the maids would tease her.

Needless to say, however, Oriku herself never said a word about entertaining such feelings, nor was Shuntai ever guilty in word or deed of the slightest indiscretion. They pursued their professional association in a mood of profound, mutual respect and communed with each other on that level alone. Never did they physically betray anything resembling what the maids suspected. Nonetheless, Oriku looked forward to his lessons, and both were aware that the feeling between them went beyond the common one between teacher and student.

Summer was heaven in a house beside the river. There was something especially wonderful about the coolness of the nearby water. As autumn approached, the river became still clearer, and you began to see children emerging from the reeds on the other side, to take a swim. You had only to drop in a line to catch any number of fish, and the view on a beautifully moonlit night was just like a painting. On nights when the moon was full, it rose just as the lesson ended, and Oriku sometimes then invited him to stay for dinner. Her hospitality included saké, but it took very little to get him drunk.

"Your name, Oriku, is unusual," he once remarked. "Where does it comes from?"

Oriku was proud of bearing an uncommon name. "My grandfather gave it to me," she replied. "I was born in Kōzuke Province. He'd been a village headman in the old Bakufu days. He was also a tea master, which is rare in the countryside. Since he worshiped Sen no Rikyū, he bent Rikyū's name a little and called me Oriku."

"I see. So Oriku comes from Rikyū. That's a nice idea. Only a tea devotee would think of that. He must have been a remarkable man."

"He had some learning, despite being a farmer, and he left a diary in old-style Japanese, written entirely in Chinese characters. I can't read it at all. Apparently he learned tea by having a master come from Edo to stay with him. He received authorization to transmit the highest teachings of the art, and I was told that he gave lessons to anyone wishing to learn."

"I don't suppose he's alive now."

"No, he died at eighty-six, back in the late 1880s. I was ten at the time."

"Guidance from a grandfather like that, at so young an age, must have had a great influence on you."

"Yes, I doubt I would have ended up like this if my grandfather had lived longer."

"Forgive me for saying so, but it's a shame that someone like you has ended up with the life you lead."

"Oh no, I'm grateful to my patron for allowing a farmer's daughter to live as I do. Actually, I was sold off to be a prostitute, but he saved me from that and installed me here instead. I owe him a great deal."

"Do you plan to go on this way indefinitely?" Shuntai peered narrowly at her, but she did not answer. The question was one she had never considered before, having accepted her fate without complaint and feeling, if anything, only gratitude for the comfort she enjoyed.

Oriku's silence made Shuntai uneasy. "I apologize for my indiscretion," he said. "I assure you that I had no intention of asking anything too personal."

He dropped the subject, put down his saké cup, and hastened away. Nonetheless, she knew perfectly well what he meant. Behind his question she had glimpsed something of his own feelings, and she wondered what he might have said next, if she had denied wishing to continue as she was. Perhaps he would have confessed to being in love with her. She might have been happy to hear that, but she was also glad she had not.

There were times when Oriku herself wondered how long her life as a kept woman was to go on. This Hashiba house had not been built especially for her; she simply inhabited an established annex of the

Silver Flower. Another mistress had probably lived there before her, and she might well find herself sent packing in her turn. She was, so to speak, a drifting reed with a highly uncertain future. What would she do if Shuntai announced that he wanted to marry her? *Could* she leave her patron and become Shuntai's wife? Now that these thoughts were running through her mind, she longed for the chance to take up their conversation again at the next lesson. However, Shuntai never came again. In this he was not alone, either, for Shunpō and Yamato, too, let her know that preparations for their autumn recital prevented them for the time being from coming to give her lessons. None of them ever returned. At first she believed easily enough that the autumn recital was the reason, but they never came even after it was over, and so she naturally practiced the koto less and less. That put an end to her involvement with Shunpō's music. All this had happened years ago—twenty years, as she now recalled. By now the image of Shunpō was cloudy in her mind, and she found that she retained none at all of Shunpō's wife.

Ofune's eyes had conveyed shock and agitation, but Oriku herself hardly reacted at all. By now she had no connection with these people, and it made no difference to her which of them turned up with whom. Ofune knew Shunpō's wife from hearing a concert at the Hagi Garden. This was a garden belonging to a certain Hagiwara, a Koume resident and a wholesaler of the ties used to bind men's topknots. This great merchant, whose product was very famous, had a retreat at Mukōjima where he had built, at vast expense, a beautiful garden that he opened to the public. In it he had planted every variety of hagi, through which he set little brooks flowing, and had dotted the garden with tea pavilions where he had master musicians of all kinds give concerts. Oriku sometimes received invitations, and now and again Ofune went in her mistress's place. On one such occasion Ofune had seen Shunpō's beautiful young wife act as an assistant for her husband, and the woman had made such an impression on Ofune that when she turned up at the Shigure Teahouse with another man, Ofune had been unable to remain calm. Actually, Oriku had wanted to go to that concert herself. She would have liked to see how Shunpō had aged, to hear his koto again after twenty years, and to see Shuntai as well. However, she had preferred in the end not to indulge in stirring up old dreams, and so she had sent Ofune instead. As a result of her forbearance, she had not the faintest idea what Shunpō's new wife was like. She had indeed heard that the mother of Shuntai and Yamato had died, and that Shunpō had taken a second wife, and she would not have minded sneaking a glimpse of the woman; but no, she had renounced the idea. Oriku reprimanded the agitated Ofune, and the day passed without further incident. Surprisingly enough, however, according to Ofune, the woman continued coming thereafter with the same man, a youth with whom she appeared to be in a compromising relationship. Despite not yet having met her, Oriku supposed she must be one of the live-in disciples who had accompanied Shunpō to her Hashiba house all those years ago. At any rate, the idea of meeting her was just too awkward. Oriku contented herself with getting reports from Ofune and pretending to notice nothing. The woman came again several times, with the same young man. Since they stayed in an annex, no one went back there after their meal had been cleared away, and it was impossible to know what they were up to. However, the closet held bedclothes and night-wear, and it was natural to assume the usual things about a couple who stayed there together. There was no reason to make an issue of it to them, but Ofune loudly pursued her solitary campaign.

"If they keep coming like this, Mistress Oriku, there will trouble for you in the end. Once it gets out, and the name of the Shigure Teahouse is involved, it's you who'll regret it."

"It's none of our business, and I keep telling you not to bring it up. Why do you keep talking about it?"

"Are we supposed to simply let it go?"

"We're not *supposed* to do anything, one way or the other. No one's asking any of you for your opinion on the subject, and I don't want to hear it!"

"But if he's her lover, they're committing *adultery*!"

"The regulations governing the operation of an inn forbid the innkeeper to reveal a guest's secrets. Even *you* must know that!"

"That would be fine, if that was all there was to it, but what worries me, Mistress Oriku, is that once upon a time your were Shunpō-sensei's student, weren't you?"

"But that was twenty years ago!"

Oriku refused in the end to pursue the subject, but privately she was concerned. It was highly improper for the wife of Master Shunpō to be indulging in secret love trysts, and the very idea made Oriku seethe inwardly. There was nothing she could do about it, though. Presumably Shuntai and Yamato had both aged. Yamato was six years older than Oriku, and Shuntai must be over fifty by now, since back then he had been about thirty. As for Master Shunpō himself, he had undoubtedly passed seventy. Oriku would not have remembered any of this if Shunpō's faithless wife had not come to the Shigure Teahouse, but with Ofune carrying on about the couple like this, old memories of Hashiba came flooding back.

Just then, as though to make old memories real again, Shuntai turned up for some chazuke, together with a group of other guests. Across from the Mukōjima embankment stood the elegant residence of the painter Kawabata Gyokushō, where Shuntai was apparently a frequent visitor. He came that day with Gyokushō and a group of the artist's young disciples, and as it happened he encountered Oriku, whom his host, Gyokushō, introduced to him as "the mistress of the Shigure Teahouse." Oriku gathered herself to greet him.

"The mistress of the Shigure Teahouse is *you*?" Shuntai paled.

"It has been a very long time. I have been delighted to hear people say you are doing well." Oriku's hands were still to the floor in formal greeting. Shuntai's eyes were popping with astonishment, just as they had done sometimes in the old days. In contrast, Oriku remained perfectly self-possessed.

"I can't believe it! Oriku of Hashiba is now the owner of the Shigure Teahouse? This is absolutely incredible!"

"After my husband died I ran the Yoshiwara business for a while, but the year before last I left there and started up this teahouse. I hope you will favor us again with many visits."

"I must be dreaming! You were still so young and girlish then; but the years will tell, won't they. You're very impressive now, at any rate.

I'm awfully glad to see you!" Oblivious of his host, Shuntai gazed into Oriku's eyes.

"What next? Shuntai and Oriku knew each other when they were young? Why, I hardly know what to think!" Gyokushō teased them merrily, but neither Shuntai nor Oriku said anything further. They confined themselves instead to commonplace remarks and remained silent about the past.

"Is Shunpō-sensei well?" Oriku inquired as Shuntai was leaving.

"Yes, I think I can say he is well. Apart from being blind he has no other infirmity, so he is healthier than the rest of us."

"I am very glad to hear it."

"In the morning he wakes up before anyone else and starts bustling about right away, to the consternation of those who look after him."

"It is a fine thing indeed to be so active in old age. I feel like asking you to greet him from me, but I would rather you didn't let him know you ran into me."

"Oh no, I can't do that!" Shuntai replied with a smile. "I'll tell him as soon as I get back. Our awkward parting at Hashiba, all those years ago, bothered me at the time. I'd forgotten about it since, but seeing you like this has brought it all back. I'll come again." His voiced betrayed emotion, but being with a party prevented him from talking longer.

"I shall look forward to your visit." Oriku's eyes and expression showed she meant it. She wondered what he meant by "awkward parting." The bond between the two of them had snapped then like a broken kite string, and Yamato and Shunpō had stopped coming as well. This had upset her at the time, but all her other lessons took her mind off the matter, and she eventually forgot about it. Now, twenty years later, they had met again. Back then she had felt somewhat attracted to Shuntai, and he had betrayed a degree of feeling for her. Neither had ever said anything, however, and the discrepancy between their respective positions had so complicated the situation that no careless word was possible for either. They had therefore come through it unscathed, although it was hard to say what might have happened if they had been freer to act on their desires.

Oriku's being a kept woman had placed a distance between them, and their thoughts had therefore remained unexpressed, but meeting again after all those years, and exchanging words once more, had set the old wound aching. Now that Oriku was on her own, unencumbered by any constraints, there was no longer any reason to deny the old ache.

"Wasn't that Shunpō-sensei's son?" Ofune's face, as changeable as a chameleon's, had once more gone pale.

"Yes, that was Hagiwara Shuntai," Oriku answered casually. "He used to give me koto lessons."

"Shunpō-sensei's wife is younger than his son, isn't she?" That was what concerned Ofune.

"Never having met her, I really can't say."

"She's much younger, I assure you. Shuntai must be nearly fifty."

"He's not 'nearly'—he's *over* fifty."

"The wife is only in her late thirties, at the most."

"Does it matter? If you keep fussing about it, you'll end up blabbing out something when people are present, and that *would* be a problem."

"Don't worry. You can count on me not to do that."

"I don't know. You certainly talk a lot. In this business you have to get used to seeing what goes on behind the scenes."

"I know that."

"What goes on behind the scenes is always ugly, and if you're going to be shocked by everything you see, then you're in the wrong line of work. Our guests are our lifeline, and we'd be finished without them. We should be grateful to every single one of them and scrupulously avoid gossiping about them in any way. In that respect Shunpō-sensei's wife is no different from anyone who happens by to view the cherry blossoms." Oriku spoke with unusual severity.

"I'm afraid the couple in the annex may be planning to commit double suicide. Neither does anything but cry." A young maid, deathly pale, might turn up now and again with this kind of report. Oriku would then have old Tomé keep a close watch on the place, and when the young couple had safely survived the night and were about to leave, she allowed no one else to go near them. Instead she would say goodbye to them in person, kindly inviting both of them to come again if the Shigure Teahouse had been to their liking. She felt quite motherly at such times and would see the pair off to the foot of the embankment. In this fine tact, the fruit of the years, Oriku hardly recognized her younger self.

Ofune seemed to want to keep speaking of Shunpō's wife and Shuntai in the same breath, but once again Oriku forcefully warned her to keep her mouth shut. Then, a month or so later, Shuntai came again, this time by himself.

"Is Mistress Oriku at home?" he asked gently, standing in the entrance. "I hope she won't mind a guest coming alone."

Oriku rushed out to him and practically took him by the hand to lead him into one of the restaurant's rooms. It was about five in the afternoon, and all were packed, the main one being entirely occupied by a large banquet. All she could do was to take him back to the Paulownia annex.

"I hope you won't mind," she said apologetically. "We have so many people here on Saturdays. This is where *I* live, but when the place is this crowded we sometimes bring guests here too."

"On the contrary, I'm honored that you should bring me to a nice room like this."

He looked around him. "I'm sorry about the other day. I wanted to talk more, but I refrained because I was with Kawabata-sensei." He bowed to her formally, hands to the floor. He seemed different from the Shuntai of old. They exchanged pleasantries, repressing meanwhile the urge to laugh. Then dinner appeared, with saké.

"The menu changes only once a month. It's probably just the same as last time," Oriku observed as she poured him saké.

"Who cares? I'm really here to see *you*." He came right out with it. "By the way, I hope it's all right if I take off my hakama. I just can't relax as long as I have them on—I feel like I'm working." He got to his feet before he had finished speaking and began removing the formal hakama trousers he wore over his kimono. Oriku went around behind him and folded them up. Sure enough, he was just the same. The years had not changed his casual ways.

"The saké's good this evening, isn't it," he remarked, feeling somewhat more at ease now. In fact, he looked thoroughly content. Oriku could only smile. Sitting across from him this way, she felt as if she were back in her Hashiba house, twenty years ago.

"You like the river, don't you," he said. "Your old house was over there on the far bank, wasn't it?"

"Yes, it was. I wasn't consciously thinking of that when I built the place here, but that's how it worked out. It was just across the river."

"Do you still have it?"

"No, I sold it after my husband died. It was up to me to look after the business, since my husband had no children, and the house was no longer needed. It was quite a job." She briefly explained to him how things had worked out. "So I gave my adopted daughter and her husband the business and started this place. Running a Yoshiwara establishment is really too much for a woman."

"I can imagine. Here, though, I gather you're doing extremely well. Gyokushō-sensei was saying wonderful things about your place. Well, let's drink to that. You do drink, don't you?"

"Thank you, I'll have some. This isn't like the old days, after all."

"It certainly isn't!" He shook with laughter. Even now, when he was over fifty, his face when he laughed still looked very much as it had done long ago. He was a better drinker, though, draining cup after cup. Oriku left him alone only to go and greet the guests in the main room. After that, she went nowhere at all. When Ofune came to call her she made excuses and managed to stay with him. The tipsier they became, the more they talked of the past.

"What did you mean the other day, when you spoke of an 'awkward parting'?"

"Didn't *you* find it awkward?"

"I don't remember what I thought. It happened too long ago."

"Ah yes, women *are* fickle, aren't they. *I* haven't forgotten—it still bothers me, and I get an uncomfortable feeling every time I look back on it. But I gather I needn't have worried." His voice resembled a sigh.

"You mean the way you suddenly stopped coming to give me lessons?"

"Yes. That's weighed on me for all these years, but apparently it meant hardly anything to *you*."

"Well, yes, certainly I was hurt at the time. Was there some particular reason?"

"Don't you know?"

"No, I have no idea. All I know is that you stopped coming."

"But you don't know why?"

"No. How could I?"

"The proprietor of the Silver Flower said nothing to you?"

"No, not a thing. He treated me like a child in those days, and never told me anything at all."

"That's terrible. He was the one who stopped me from coming, yet he said nothing to you about it."

"*He* stopped you from coming?"

"That's right. I think he felt I was a threat and kept me away from you to make sure no one slipped up. My father was so angry that he stopped coming too. That's what happened."

Oriku felt herself sobering up fast. The idea that her own patron had stopped Shuntai from coming to see her was a revelation. Had the messenger from Hashiba told tales about them? Had her patron separated them because he was suspicious about what might be going on?

"Really? This is all completely new to me. So that's what happened, is it?"

"I was furious. There I'd been teaching you so carefully, and suddenly I was told not to come anymore. I really felt bad about it."

"I'm sure you did. Knowing nothing at all, I just wondered resentfully why you wouldn't come back."

"You had it backward, didn't you. The resentment was all mine."

"That's a bit much, Shuntai-sensei!" Oriku's thoughts flew back to the past. "Perhaps something in me kept me from objecting to what my husband did. On reflection, I have an idea that I just didn't feel right about things." She watched Shuntai's face intently as she spoke.

Shuntai nodded vigorous assent, then crossed his arms and lifted his gaze to the ceiling, in an attitude of summoning up the past. It seemed to Oriku that they understood each other without any need to resort to words.

Shuntai, however, replied, "Surely there was nothing improper about the degree of feeling we shared. Or am I wrong?"

"It may have been that way for you, but no, I didn't feel right about it. If at the time you'd had the courage to take me in your arms, we might well have gotten into something we couldn't back away from. I'm quite sure of that, at least."

"Oh. What a shame!"

"You really think it's a shame?"

"Yes, I do. I was such a coward in those days!"

"It's still not too late, though!" Oriku laughed, but from the way she said it you could tell she was not joking.

"Really? It's not too late, even now?" Shuntai smiled back and leaned toward her. Both were pretending to make a joke of it, but in fact they were telling each other exactly what they felt.

"If it's not too late, then perhaps I'll pluck up my courage after all." He was beginning to sound more composed.

The conversation then turned elsewhere. Once the old difficulty between them had been smoothed out, and they felt at ease with each other, they had no need to give themselves a great deal more time, nor were they of an age to waste their words. The saké had them both intoxicated.

"You don't have to leave, do you?"

"No, certainly not. Will it be all right if I stay?"

"Of course. You're welcome. This *is* an inn, after all."

"This time there's no one to object, is there?"

"Not a soul. But surely you have a wife?"

"Unfortunately no, I don't."

"Have you remained single all these years?"

"I got married once, but it didn't go well. I learned my lesson, and I've been single ever since."

"You must get lonely."

"I'm used to it by now, and I'm more comfortable on my own. I can always go and amuse myself somewhere, when I feel lonely. That takes care of it."

"You certainly have changed, haven't you?"

"Yes, I have, now that I'm over fifty. You're completely different, too, wouldn't you agree?"

"No doubt. I'm thicker-skinned now. I'm more comfortable on my own, too."

"You're sure you don't indulge yourself and misbehave all the time?"

"No, no, nothing like that. Being single doesn't mean I can just do whatever I please, and sometimes I do make mistakes. They don't amount to anything, though."

"It sounds like a nice life. What with running an inn and restaurant at Mukōjima, you've really hit the jackpot, being single and able to please yourself."

"I employ nearly thirty people, though—it isn't as easy as it looks."

"That's the way it always goes. It's the same for us, with our music. You can forget everything when you're alone with your koto, but all your worldly troubles come crowding in on you as soon as you put it away it again. In my case, I have to take responsibility for all the odd jobs the school requires. My father's in good health, it's true, but he's over seventy, and we can't neglect looking after him, to be sure he's able to live a long life."

"What happened to your sister?"

"She's an odd one—about as odd as they get. Once she turned forty, she shaved her head and became a nun. She's in Kyoto now."

"Really? She's entered a convent?"

"No, she can't manage being a real nun. She looks like a nun, but actually she's hung out her shingle as the Kyoto representative of the Shunpō school of koto, and she has students. She's serious about that, at least."

"Is she as innocent as ever of any relationships with men?"

"I assume so, but I don't really know. Some say she became a nun after some man abandoned her."

"She's so beautiful, she must have had men after her."

"Well, never mind about other people. What matters is here and now. Let's have a good time, then, a really good time."

"Absolutely. Let's have a good time and think about nothing at all."

"Right. I've been doing too much thinking lately. It's strange, the way people put a koto teacher on a pedestal. You have to watch yourself so carefully, when you're giving lessons to some fancy young lady—it's just exhausting. Koto or samisen, the mastery required is the same, but people pay much too much attention to those of us who teach the koto. Running into you again has brought me back to life, or so I feel."

He was quite drunk by now, and if he drank any more he would have to lie down. Oriku tactfully brought their conversation to a close and put him to bed in the next room. Eleven o'clock had come and gone, all was quiet in the main building, and the crickets were beginning to sing. It was early September, and they sang sooner when there were no other houses nearby. Oriku collected the soiled cups and dishes into a corner, tidied up the room, and slipped into bed behind him.

He woke up in the middle of the night and asked for water. After a drink of cold water he put his arms around Oriku. "I've dreamed of this all my life," he said fervently. They slept no more after that till nearly dawn.

Shuntai awoke for the second time past nine in the morning. It was raining outside. Somewhat embarrassed, he got up and went for a bath. He found beer waiting for him on his return. There is nothing like the mild bitterness of beer to quench the thirst of a hangover.

"It doesn't want me to go, does it, this rain," he remarked, leaning against a pillar. "What a wonderful feeling! I feel as though I've turned into the greatest lover in Japan."

Oriku did not reply. Shuntai was completely swept away, but she held to the principle one man, one night, and was doing her best to keep herself in check.

"May I stay on for a while? I'll leave, though, if I'd be in the way."

"Well, but what about your lessons?"

"I really shouldn't, but that's the way it goes. I'm taking the day off."

"What am I going to do with you?"

Still, she was in no mood to send him away. Shuntai was a serious man, entirely different from those artists who enjoy advertising their affairs. Besides, she understood how he felt. They drank beer together and spent an idle day watching the rain. Sometimes they talked about art, more often about life and love. Unlike other, ordinary men he had his own well-considered opinions on everything.

"What is Shunpō-sensei's present wife like?" That topic, too, came up during their day in that little room. Oriku knew she should stay away from it, but it came out anyway.

"You know her. She must have acted as my father's guide on his way to your Hashiba house."

"So she was with him then, was she?"

"Yes. In fact, it's made things quite difficult. Absolutely no one will treat her as his wife."

"There must be a huge age difference between them."

"It's a problem, yes—perhaps my father isn't quite the man he used to be. It makes a mess of the whole household, from one end of the year to the other."

"Actually..." Oriku cut herself off. "His present wife has been here too, you know." It just slipped out. She should never have let it, but her professional discretion had melted away in the casual intimacy of this long, rainy day, spent in the company of a lover whose presence encouraged her to relax.

"With my father, I suppose."

"No. That wouldn't have been a problem. She came with a young man."

She had felt a need to come out with it bravely, but to her surprise Shuntai hardly reacted. It was almost as though he knew already.

"I don't doubt it. She's that kind of woman. I have a pretty good idea who she must have been with."

"But surely she's his wedded wife!"

"Heavens no! Even my father wouldn't actually enter her on the family register! Could I possibly address as 'Mother' a woman who's younger than me—a live-in disciple whom up to now I've just been used to calling Eiko?"

"I see what you mean."

"It's not that I don't understand his feelings, though. He's old, he's blind, and he'd be unbearably lonely without someone to stand beside him. For him, it hardly matters who it is. He can't see her face, after all. She's been a live-in disciple for ages, and I expect he had his hands on her even before my mother died. Considering what little strength my father has left, though, I can't imagine there's anything sexual between them."

"I don't know about that. Some old men could surprise you."

"Well, if anything like that *is* going on, it still can hardly amount to much. It couldn't possibly satisfy a young woman like Eiko."

"That doesn't excuse her finding herself another man, though."

"It's hard to say. This sort of thing certainly isn't right for the wife of a man like my father, if that's the way you want to see her, but if you take her as just any woman, there's undoubtedly a human problem involved. I mean, the business of being married without having sexual relations with her husband."

"You must be about the most understanding son in the entire world."

"I probably am. That's what makes it so difficult. But things would be a lot *more* difficult if my father didn't have Eiko. That's why I believe the only thing to do is to look the other way."

"Ah, I don't like it!" Oriku said, shuddering. She felt that the ugliness of which women were capable had been suddenly exposed.

"Perhaps you don't, but we all get old. The same is true of you or me: your life is a failure if you're overcome by loneliness in old age. It's not too late, though. You should think about it."

"True enough, I have no wish to be a failure."

"We could get married, if you felt like it."

"What? I could marry you?"

"Yes, we could put a sound lid on a cracked pot. I'd say it's too soon for us just to sit around drinking tea together as friends."

"You're joking!" Oriku dismissed the subject with a thin smile, whereupon Shuntai smiled wryly in turn and rose to go. Their long conversation had reached its natural end.

The rain seemed to be letting up. Shuntai called a rickshaw and set off, while Oriku climbed to the top of the embankment and watched him go till his rickshaw was lost to view. She heard no more from him for some time. A gentlemanly disposition mingled in him with a touch of the yakuza boss—a combination Oriku always liked in a man—but marriage was out of the question.

The autumn recital of the Shunpō school of koto was scheduled for two months later, in November, and Shuntai sent Oriku a ticket and a program. Three days after they arrived she had a telephone call from him. "I know how busy you are," he said, "but I do hope you'll come. There's a new song I very much want you to hear." The recital was to start at noon and end at four, thus occupying almost all of a short November day. It was to take place in the Yūraku-za in Marunouchi. According to the program, the song was entitled "Bitter Spring," and it was be performed on a grand scale by Shunpō, Shuntai, Yamato, and all the artists associated with Shunpō's school. Shunpō normally presented one new song each at the spring and autumn recitals.

Newly composed songs are common enough in our time, but for a man who had not performed the established repertoire in about twenty years, it had taken extraordinary efforts to build an entire school of his own upon them. Shunpō's long persistence had borne fruit, and his school had spread across the country. By now it was said to have five thousand students.

"Will Yamato really be there too?" Oriku wondered as she examined the program. Behind Yamato's printed name she imagined a nun sitting onstage with her blue-shaven head and her handsomely colored robes, and a pang went through her. She felt sorrow and pity for Yamato—a woman like herself, but who, far from enjoying Oriku's freedom to do as she pleased, had renounced all profane thoughts without ever having even touched a man. Moreover, the title "Bitter Spring" was something of a worry. When the day of the recital finally arrived, she headed eagerly for Marunouchi and the Yūraku-za.

The Yūraku-za was a small theater, recently built in the latest Western style on vacant ground at Sukiyagashi. Its neat, pretty interior, with its six or seven hundred seats, lacked the kabuki hanamichi passageway that allowed characters to make dramatic entrances onto the stage. There was nothing glamorous about going there, the surrounding area being so dreary, but the clean, convenient theater itself was a pleasant place. It certainly looked unfamiliar to eyes accustomed to the Kabuki-za or the Shintomi-za, but the Shunpō school's great recital had filled it with light, and comely young ladies, dressed in their best, filled all the seats. Their finery had none of the gaudiness now in vogue, the patterns being refined and the color combinations discreet, so that the gathering conveyed a quiet beauty. Oriku had meant to arrive just in time for the piece that interested her, but it was still early in the program, and she soon tired of the endless student performances. None was actually painful to listen to, but two or three were more than enough. Shunpō's new song did not begin until after four o'clock.

Sure enough, the theater was full by then, and some spectators were even standing. Tremendous applause greeted the raising of the curtain. Meanwhile, onstage the performance had already begun. The assemblage of over forty musicians fairly overwhelmed the audience with sound.

Three levels divided the stage, front to back. On the lowest were fifteen male disciples, with their koto slantwise before them. Front and center on the middle level sat Shunpō, in all the gold brocade of his exalted rank, with Shuntai on his right in light gray with the family crest, and on his left Yamato in a purple religious robes, round-backed and no longer haughty as of yore, but simply a handsome, middle-aged nun. On the highest level, at the back, thirty female disciples sat in two rows, wearing crested dark blue-purple, each with her instrument before her, forming an imposing chorus. All these performers, well over forty in number, seemed completely to dominate the small theater, until Shunpō's koto rose above their orchestral harmony. When Shunpō began to play, the chorus fell silent, and for a time he pursued his solo. Then Yamato joined in, and in plaintive tones her lovely voice began the first verse of the song.

> *Cradle, well-cradle,*
> *love of mine from long ago,*
> *darling, oh tell me,*
> *those vows you and I exchanged:*
> *do they mean nothing?*

So year after endless year
there at her old home
below the steep mountainside
laments the forsaken wife.

Shuntai then took up the second verse, his rich voice sounding exactly like his father's.

Ah, it was all too cruel,
the day when we met!
Where dappled rays of sunlight
filter through the cypress grove,
I stand, calling back to mind
the way we once were,
in a past forever lost,
and upon the leaves
dewdrops spill, a fleeting shower
scattered on the evening wind.

Next, Yamato again:

For your great offense
repeated time after time,
often I have tried to leave you,
yet have always failed,
for the fire alive in me
burns on forever,
and the road stretching ahead
never, never ends.

And, once more, Shuntai:

Trembling, I contemplate
the depth of my crime.
This is all I ask of life!
as the nights went by

I thought as I held you close,
yet love in the end
dwindles and soon fades away,
vanishing beyond recall.

The audience listened with bated breath. A love story was unprecedented in this type of koto song, normally composed of a series of somewhat disconnected verses. Yamato took the woman's voice in this tale of wifely longing, and Shuntai the man's, while Shunpō gave them a discreet accompaniment. Once the story was over all three played together, and only then did Shunpō's rich voice ring out:

Now it has fallen to me
to suffer this fate,
how could I cry injustice,
how could I complain?
To a single night in spring
I gave everything,
and although for ten long years
tears have soaked these sleeves,
threatening them with ruin,
I regret nothing at all,
threatening them with ruin,
I regret nothing at all.

Deep feeling pervaded Shunpō's rendition of this closing verse, and the song's achingly sad melody played on as the curtain quietly descended once more.

The audience exploded in applause, but Oriku, entranced, forgot to clap. The long, half-hour piece had carried her beyond herself, and she was, so to speak, savoring its lingering essence. What a marvelous song! It was undoubtedly Shunpō's crowning masterpiece, evoking a wife's love in a manner both noble and brimming with genuine emotion. Most koto songs treat sentiment or scenery in ornate language, but none conveys deep human feeling. The audience had found this one's bold break with tradition overwhelming.

Oriku made no effort to rise even once the curtain was down. She did not even notice the press of people at the exit, not yet having awoken from the spell of "Bitter Spring."

All at once she noticed Shuntai standing before her. The performance over, he had apparently come out into the theater.

"It's raining," he said. "I was concerned about you." He glanced back toward the exit. It had suddenly started raining, and those unequipped for rain had gathered there at the door, chattering noisily.

"It's Shunpō-sensei's masterpiece, isn't it." Oriku had no interest in the rain. The spell of the new composition was with her still. "I was very, very impressed, and I still am, even now that the curtain is down. I've never heard a koto song convey such powerful emotion."

"I'm astonished, too. Obviously it's his great masterpiece. It feels as though he put into it absolutely everything he had."

Shuntai sat down beside her and spoke low in her ear. "As far as I can see, it magnificently evokes his wife's love—the love that bothers you so much—for another man."

Oriku was horrified. "My father overlooks his wife's infidelities," Shuntai continued. "However, it's from them that he took the material for 'Bitter Spring,' which in a sense constitutes his revenge. In this work he has taken revenge on her. It's vengeance truly worthy of an artist, don't you think?"

Oriku shivered, and likewise the blood had drained from Shuntai's face. "'Bitter Spring' is a great work," Shuntai said, "there's no doubt about that. It won't escape criticism, though. It can too easily be charged with leading koto music down the path of excessive grandeur."

"Shunpō-sensei himself must know that, I suppose."

"Of course he does. He founded the work on his wife's infidelity and let the koto express his loneliness."

"In that sense it's positively frightening. Surely it's a far harsher rebuke than one directly delivered in words."

"Does she feel it, though? I pray she doesn't." He closed his eyes and turned his face to the ceiling.

"Shuntai-sensei, your rickshaws are here." The speaker was a young disciple.

"I'm taking you home," Shuntai said. "You can't go by yourself in this rain."

He stood up. The knot of people at the door had thinned out somewhat. Two rickshaws awaited them in the evening downpour. Under a sheltering umbrella a woman was just then stepping into another, immediately behind them. They could not help noticing her.

The woman was Shunpō's wife, Eiko. Shuntai and Oriku exchanged glances as her rickshaw started away. Where was she off to all by herself, without him? Did she really mean to leave him behind even now, after his great autumn recital? They watched the rickshaw disappear into the pouring rain, then turned to exchange glances once more.

CHAPTER EIGHT

"Bitter Spring" (Part 2)

It was pouring when Oriku and Shuntai left Marunouchi, but the rain eased at the Kokuchō corner, and it had stopped entirely by the time they got to Asakusa Bridge. Although it had been torrential, once they had passed Kuramae and reached the Kaminari Gate, the downpour vanished like a dream, leaving only broken clouds floating in the sky. Such an evening shower was unusual in late autumn, and around Hirokōji there was no sign that it had ever rained; the road was dry. This was as far as the rickshaws went, and to go on from Azuma Bridge they changed to new ones. Rickshaw men have their territories too.

"The sky's so clear, you can hardly believe it ever rained at all!" Shuntai stepped from his rickshaw and looked up in amazement at the heavens.

"It happens, you know. The very idea of a downpour at Marunouchi sounds preposterous." Oriku stood beside him, looking up too.

"Aren't you hungry?" she asked.

"Yes, I am. We should eat something, then, if you like."

"By all means. It's still early—where would you like to go?"

"How about chicken? We could go to Daikin or Kaneda."

"At Daikin there are geisha with their samisen—they're a bore. Let's go to Kaneda."

Daikin, which specialized in grilled chicken, was not a good place to talk because the customers often had geisha join them there. Kaneda, near the Denpō-in intersection, favored chicken stew. On the outside it looked old and worn, but the rooms inside were neat and pretty, and the place was quite popular. The second floor was given over to a common dining room, but the smaller rooms in the annex, at the end of a stone path, were done in teahouse style, and the carefully tended garden, with its polished flagstones, made an elegant attraction.

"It's always so nice here, isn't it?"

"Yes, this is the size you need for a proper garden. The one at home is too big to look after this way."

"The gardener here really enjoys his work. You can tell from the way he's laid out the straw guards against frost and snow."

"Even so, though, the work doesn't cost that much in a garden this size."

Chatting idly, they ate their chicken stew and savored their saké. Once they had drunk a little, the conversation returned to the recital. The spectacle of Shunpō's wife setting off in the rain had caught their attention.

"I wonder where your father's wife was going."

"So do I. It doesn't make much sense for her to go off somewhere on a day like today."

"Won't your father be angry?"

"Perhaps, but I suppose he knows it's no use."

"At a time like this, though! A major annual recital! I wonder whether 'Bitter Spring' angered her."

"She'd be smart if it did, but she's just not like that. My father seems not to have much confidence in her lately, either—if he did, he wouldn't let her go off on her own like this."

"Won't it be hard for him, though, getting home without his wife? There won't be anyone to look after him."

"No, there are plenty of people to do that—all the live-in disciples were there. That's no problem. Still, I just don't understand Eiko."

"Not many people could do that."

"I've always known she was a bit different, but her lover's an idiot as well."

"Is he one of the disciples?"

"We'd better talk about something else, especially this once when I have the pleasure of being alone with you."

They dropped the subject and simply drank their saké. The sun went down, and the place seemed even quieter for being right in the middle of Asakusa. Shuntai started talking again about wanting to marry her, once the saké had taken effect. As always, Oriku just smiled and made no reply. Her Shigure Teahouse had been going for only three years, and she could not bear the thought of giving it up when it was finally beginning to do well.

"You could still keep your business going," Shuntai added. Oriku's main worry, however, had to do with the matter of koto music. She had once had a good go at it, but the refined manners associated with it just did not suit her. No, what appealed to her in the end was undoubtedly something more popular, like itchū-bushi or kiyomoto, and while she felt she definitely would not mind pursuing these further, the years had put a greater and greater distance between her and the koto.

It was past seven o'clock by the time they finished eating and left the restaurant, and their steps turned naturally toward Nakamise Avenue and Kannon's great temple itself. After paying their respects there, and at the nearby Asakusa Shrine, they followed Umamichi street to Saruwakachō, where the roof of a large storehouse nearby loomed against the night sky. From there it was only a step further to the Takeya ferry crossing. At Imado Bridge the salt air borne up by the rising tide tingled in their nostrils. The ferryman, with his familiar face, was drinking saké in his hut as he waited for passengers, but he stood up immediately when he saw Oriku and seized his pole, since her generous tips made him glad to take her across at any time. A wintry cold clung to the water's surface, and Shuntai removed his coat and draped it over Oriku's shoulders. "Won't *you* be cold?" she wanted to ask him, but she could not get the words out right. She felt a little awkward, having lived alone all this time, and when they disembarked she gave the ferryman even more than usual.

"Thank you very much indeed," the ferryman said. "Please take good care of yourself!"

Oriku ignored his pleasantries and stepped up onto the embankment. It was a clear, late autumn night. The rows of lights on the opposite bank stood out sharply, with a beauty that never grew old for Oriku. This was the view she saw from morning to night, but it looked quite different to her now that she was with a man she liked. A tall, dark wood loomed beyond Imado Bridge, with the lights of the Shōden Shrine twinkling through the trees, and the red glow in the sky to the left came from the electric lights of the Rokku entertainment district.

"Hiroshige often drew this scene," Shuntai observed, "but none of the prints he made of it is especially outstanding. Since all the beauty has to do with the view across the river, he had no choice but to place people in the foreground, and it's strange the way human figures debase a landscape. That's how it is with the koto songs we write too. A landscape you're trying to convey in music turns into something else when humans enter it, and all the beauty is gone. People muddy up a landscape scene, even when the scene itself is pure. Now, what do you think of *that* idea?" Shuntai was getting quite worked up.

"All that's too difficult for *me*." Oriku began taking off the coat.

"Don't, there's no need! Just keep it on! It's cold on the embankment."

"But are *you* all right?"

"I'm a man. It helps to sober me up."

It was not that late yet, and there were still a few passersby. Next to Chōmeiji Temple a brilliantly lit sign advertised the HOT-SPRING BATHS available at a newly built inn and restaurant.

"Good heavens, when did *that* suddenly go up?" Oriku was shocked.

"Talk about bad taste!"

"Even bad taste has its limits! What can they possibly be thinking of, to let someone put up something like that? A hot-spring inn is all very well, but a hot-spring inn surely doesn't put up *that* kind of sign!"

"I don't know. This sort of thing is going to be going on more and more. It's what happens when people abuse the invention of electric lighting. They say something invented means something destroyed, and it's true. I daresay electric lighting will destroy the beauty of Mukōjima."

"You're very argumentative this evening!"

"I'm like this sometimes—argumentative, I mean. I don't much care for it either. The mood comes over me when I feel especially good or especially bad."

"So which is it this evening—good or bad?"

"I can't imagine feeling bad when I'm out walking with you, Oriku. In a way, you know, you're my first lover."

"What kind of first lover is that? Your first lover after your wife, you mean?"

"She was just a duty. I neither liked nor disliked her. My marrying her had nothing to do with love or desire. That's too bad, I suppose, but at any rate, it didn't last long. It was a big mistake," Shuntai said. After a pause he continued ruefully, "I wish I'd met *you* first."

"You did, though, at Hashiba."

"Yes, but you were spoken for at the time."

"Not permanently, though. You're still drunk, aren't you."

"Not on saké anymore, though, Oriku. I'm drunk on *you*. I feel so good when I'm with you! You're just amazing!"

Absorbed in such banter, they reached the front of the Shigure Teahouse. In close conversation with Shuntai, Oriku enjoyed him more than ever, and he felt the same way about her. Being with her gave his heart wings. No one had ever made him feel so comfortable and so free. Oriku shared his feeling, and both entered the kitchen in high spirits.

"What happened to you? It got so late, we were worried, and we've been telephoning everywhere, trying to find you." Ofune looked grumpy. "Six couples turned up unannounced, and we've had to use the Paulownia annex."

"Dear me!" Oriku turned to look at Shuntai, who was standing in the doorway.

"It seems even my room has guests in it. What are we to do?"

"Well, business is booming, isn't it?"

"Business is all very well, but we have nowhere to go!"

"It's all right, it's all right. I'll just sit down over there by the hearth. I've always wanted to see what it's like to sit there." He sauntered up onto the wooden floor and plumped himself down by the hearth.

"We wouldn't have let anyone use the Paulownia if only we'd known you'd be with Shuntai-sensei!" Ofune still looked out of sorts. There were no secrets between her and her mistress. "I had no idea you'd be here together!"

"It's all right, I tell you! I'm glad for once to sit by the hearth, and while I'm here I'll just have a beer. I'm dying of thirst!"

Behind the hearth stood a huge, black pillar, and next to it a cupboard held eating utensils like teacups, glasses, and small dishes, so as to put them within easy reach for someone making clam chazuke sitting down. Shuntai helped himself to a glass and a little dish.

"You're certainly making yourself at home, aren't you!"

"When you live by yourself as I do, in a single room, you feel like pretending to the master of an entire house. Can't I play man of the house for a day?"

"Certainly not! We couldn't have the master of the house sitting in the kitchen! The Shigure Teahouse would never recover from it!"

"What? Is this business of yours that feeble? You're just flogging the flavor of chazuke, right? Isn't the view half of what you sell?"

"You'd better watch what you're saying, or I'll stick your head in the hearth fire!"

"Aha! Now we're getting to the rough stuff! If my sitting here makes me that much of a nuisance, then I'll be going. I can hardly do anything else, can I, if there's no room for me anywhere. I never thought I'd come all the way to Mukōjima to be turned out!"

"Who's turning you out? Who's telling you to leave?"

"You, just a minute ago! You told me you'd stick my head in the hearth!"

"Right, I'll do it, then! Let's have your head!"

It was a model lovers' quarrel. The ever-cautious Shuntai and the unfailingly respectable Oriku were letting themselves go. Beer came to them there, beside the hearth, and no one seemed much to mind them both drinking together. After all, Shuntai at his relatively young age was an acknowledged koto master, and the Shigure Teahouse staff admired him so greatly that some even felt he was too good for their mistress. Oriku drained her beer in one swallow and then took a turn around the various rooms to greet the guests. Age had not dimmed her fame, and a guest who failed to meet her went away disappointed.

The greetings over, she was on her way back to the kitchen when Ofune whispered to her, "I've arranged a room for you. Please go there!"

"A room for us? Where? There isn't a single one available."

"It's on the upper floor. It's not a proper room, I know, but I've tidied it up for you."

"The upper floor? You mean *your* room?" Annoyed, Oriku felt like asking Ofune whether she could really take Shuntai up to a maid's room.

"But it's awkward, having Shuntai-sensei where he is now."

"Awkward? Why?"

"Well, you see . . ." As she so often did, Ofune put her lips to Oriku's ear. "Shunpō-sensei's wife is here."

"She *is*?" Oriku was astonished. Having watched the woman leave the Yūraku-za in the rain, she had never for a moment imagined her actually coming *here*. What nerve!

"I don't suppose she's alone."

"No, she's with the same young man as always, and I don't like the idea of her coming face-to-face with Shuntai-sensei. That's why I tidied up a place for you on the upper floor. Please go there for the time being. A room is bound to open up somewhere, sometime soon. Not all the guests are planning to spend the night."

"I trust you didn't actually give the two of them *my* room."

"Yes, I'm afraid I gave them the Paulownia. There wasn't anywhere else."

"Why didn't you just turn them away, if there wasn't anywhere else? Why, the very idea!" Oriku unconsciously raised her voice.

"I apologize for having taken them to your room, but it's no use telling me I should have turned them away. You just can't do that kind of thing when you're running a business."

"Well, I don't want there to be anything shady about the business *I'm* running. She's shameless. What is she thinking, coming here? What gall!" Oriku's cries of rage were plainly audible in the kitchen.

"What are you so angry about?" Shuntai was in the best of spirits. "You shouldn't be ranting like that. The maids are so frantically busy, I feel like helping them myself."

"Stop spouting nonsense and just come along with me. There's a room ready for us."

"Did they find one?"

"Ofune took care of it. I don't even know what it's like myself."

Ofune's upper-floor room was at the top of a staircase leading up from in front of the bath. Eight mats in size, with a low ceiling, it also served as a storeroom for various pottery utensils used in the restaurant. Ofune had pushed all those to one side; hidden her own bits and pieces behind a six-panel folding screen; brought in a brazier, meal trays, and an open box for personal effects; and in one way and another had made the place tidy enough to have a drink in.

"What *is* this place?" Shuntai put his hand up to the ceiling. "You'd bump your head in here if you were tall."

"True enough. Actually, it's Ofune's room."

"Ah, yes, she's so tiny, I can see it's just right for her."

"I really didn't mean to bring you anywhere like this."

"Oh, *I* don't mind! It's very quiet and private."

"I'm sorry. Please be patient, just for tonight. After that I won't trouble you with this sort of thing any more."

"Just for tonight? I hope you won't mind if I keep coming."

Oriku was startled. Her great principle—no second night—was going awry. It had happened with Tetsunosuke, and this was Shuntai's second night too. Her promise to herself on the subject was clearly becoming a thing of the past. She had kept it strictly at first, in the early days of her business, but little by little things had gotten out of hand. Could it be that she was getting old?

Drunk once more, Shuntai began talking again about wanting to marry her. "I've never felt so perfectly at home with any woman I've met," he kept saying.

"We don't have to live together, you know. It doesn't have to be right away. What I want is someone who understands me. I want someone I *could* marry some day." He sounded very young.

"Everything would go wrong, as I know all too well, if someone like me got together with some nice young lady studying the koto; and the better I understand that, the less I feel like ever marrying one.

What I need is someone like you, Oriku, with a really rich experience of life."

"You overrate me. All I've ever known is the Silver Flower and the Shigure Teahouse. So much, then, for this broad experience of mine. I don't have any."

"I'm serious, though. Look at me—I'm fifty already! I have no wish to find myself playing house with some pampered young lady."

"That doesn't mean you could make do with a woman like me."

"Oh, I can make do, all right—I'll show you!"

"No, it's not the likes of me you need. Find yourself someone more elegant and respectable. I say this not just for your sake, but for the sake of your whole school."

Their wrangling went on hour after hour, but it never got anywhere. They were too different.

"I'm not the right woman for you," Oriku finally declared, "but, fine, you're the right man for me. If you want us to be together, leave Banchō and come and live with me here."

Shunpō had built himself a mansion in the Banchō section of Kōjimachi. He had a big practice hall where he trained a large number of students, and Shuntai lived in a separate pavilion within the same compound. There was no one else to run the school's affairs when Shuntai was away, now that Yamato had moved to Kyoto.

"I can't leave while my father is alive. That's just my fate." Lacking the courage to escape his cruel destiny, he could only sigh.

Ofune's arrival interrupted their conversation. "We'll be putting the fire out soon," she said. "Would you like anything to eat?"

"It's that late already?"

"Yes, it's past eleven."

"I see. Yes, it *is* late. I had no idea."

Shuntai said he did not want anything, so Oriku told Ofune to go ahead and put it out. "Is there a room available now, somewhere?"

"I'm afraid not. I'm awfully sorry. I'll get things ready for you here."

"The Paulownia is still taken?"

"Yes, it is."

"So they're staying?"

"It seems so."

"She's impossible!" Oriku turned to Shuntai. "Your father's wife is here," she said. It just slipped out, like last time.

"Who with?"

"I don't know. She must have come straight here from the Yūraku-za."

"And she's in *your* room?"

"We always put guests in the Paulownia when the rest of the place is full."

"All right, but to put *her* in *there*!"

He had gone pale, but he cut himself short because of Ofune. Ofune hurried back down the stairs.

"That was a bad idea, putting Eiko in that room."

"Yes, it was. It happened while I was gone. That's why I was so annoyed with Ofune a while ago. I can't turn her out now, though. It makes me so angry to think that because of her I've had to bring *you* to a room like this!"

Dead sober now, and white as a sheet, Shuntai crossed his arms and absorbed himself in thought. "I want to talk to her," he said. "Will you call her, please?"

"I can't do that. An innkeeper must ignore a guest's identity, whoever the guest may be."

"I know that, but the problem is Eiko herself. The situation as it stands is bad for both her and me. The right thing to do, I think, is to point out to her where she is wrong and to ask her to reconsider."

"But not here, please! You'll have to do it somewhere else."

"I see." Arms crossed as before, Shuntai lapsed into silence. Properly speaking, the woman was his mother-in-law, but ever since her days as a live-in disciple he had always referred to her, with familiar simplicity, as Eiko. On marrying his father she changed her name in all seriousness to Takako, but absolutely no one called her that. To Shuntai, she was still Eiko.

While Ofune brought in the bedding and tidied up the brazier and the trays, Shuntai went to wash his hands, and Oriku stopped by the restaurant office, one of her jobs being to look over the day's earnings. After inspecting the old-fashioned account book she washed her face at the bath, rinsed her mouth, and returned to the upper floor. Shuntai was not there. "He wouldn't!" she told herself, but she was worried enough to go back to the office.

"Shuntai-sensei has gone into the Paulownia!" Ofune reported, pale and distraught.

"That's what I was afraid of."

"It happened while you were in the office just now." Ofune remained seated, as though her legs had failed her.

It was no surprise, but the situation was grave—not that by now anything could be done about it. Shuntai, being Shuntai, would no doubt confront Eiko with every last word he had to say on the matter.

"Shouldn't we intervene, Mistress Oriku?" Ofune was trembling.

"No, just let it go. Our fussing would only make it worse."

"You told him she was here, didn't you?"

"It slipped out during the conversation."

"Despite your own warning against talking about guests."

"I realized immediately what I'd done, but it was too late. I want you and the others to pretend you know nothing about it, and you're not to go near the Paulownia."

Oriku could do no more. Although she was able to remain calm and collected on the outside for Ofune's benefit, she was far from tranquil within. What had happened after Shuntai reached the Paulownia? Oriku was worried sick, but she heard no sound of voices.

A paulownia tree stood between the annex and the main house, in lieu of a hedge, and the room was so quiet, you felt as if you were in a mountain village. Eiko and her lover must have trembled when Shuntai burst in on them, quite unannounced.

Naturally, Shuntai never actually threatened them. Though pale, he fully intended to control himself and to resolve the situation.

"Do you not find your conduct as my father's wife somewhat frivolous?" he began evenly. "My father is an old man, and I understand well enough why you should do this sort of thing. Still, you might have found another way to go about it. I shall speak to my father, and I would like you to leave him. If you find it too difficult to tell him yourself, I will do so for you." Shuntai spoke perfectly calmly.

"You mean you don't know, Shuntai-sensei? Your father has taken another lover. Apparently you don't know about it." Her lips trembled as she turned the tables on him, and Shuntai bit his own, as though rocked by her counterattack. He felt like an excited pursuer whose prey had rapped him smartly across the nose.

"His lover is another live-in disciple, of course. You're the only one who doesn't know about it, Shuntai-sensei. The whole household is in on it."

"That doesn't excuse your own behavior."

"I wonder."

"You disagree?"

"After all, I'm not on his family register yet."

"That's irrelevant. What matters is whether or not you love him."

"Love has nothing to do with it. It's a matter of respect. Not that I have any respect for him left, though."

"Then get out of the house and go elsewhere. You'll be better off that way."

"I'll gladly go anytime if you want me to, but you see, I have leave from Shunpō-sensei to do as I please. I therefore believe I am acting within the bounds of the latitude he has given me."

"You have his permission to spend the night at an inn with a man?"

Shuntai was becoming agitated, but Eiko, in contrast, remained unperturbed. Nothing he said could ruffle her calm. The lover was hiding in the next room, and Shuntai could have discovered who he was by opening the sliding panel, but he did not go that far. Beaten, he said little more before he left and returned to the upper floor. After expecting to pillory the woman, he had instead been vanquished himself, and had withdrawn with his tail between his legs.

All was neat and tidy in the upper floor room. The bedding was laid out, and a kettle was boiling on the brazier. He lay down on the quilt and closed his eyes, furious with himself for his own stupidity. For all his determination to keep calm, it was Eiko herself who had succeeded in doing so. He had lost, no question about that. She had been ready for him, almost as though she had been expecting what happened. Whatever agreement she may have reached with his father, it was clear she did not plan to stay with him long.

Whereas *she* knew exactly what she was doing, *he* had foolishly burst in on her in a fit of anger. It was infuriating. Still unmarried at his age, he had at last found a partner who suited him, only to have her turn him down. The self-loathing to which he was often prey overwhelmed him, and he found his own existence intolerable. He was just about to leap noisily to his feet when Oriku entered the room.

"You're wishing you hadn't done it, aren't you?" Oriku had caught something of his mood.

"She wouldn't budge. I never imagined she would be so cool and resolved."

"Your bursting in like that probably didn't surprise her in the least."

"No indeed. She seemed fully prepared for it. She beat me. I'm going home."

"You needn't do that. Besides, there aren't any more rickshaws."

"I'll walk to Azuma Bridge."

"You will not. I won't let you go. I'm me, and Eiko is Eiko."

"That's not what I mean. I've just had a look at how dismal humans can be, and I'm disgusted. I'm a fool."

"But what did Eiko have to say?"

"She says my father has taken a new lover."

"Really!"

"I don't care whether it's true or not. The problem is that he and Eiko don't trust each other anymore—it's so dreary. There's no love between them, yet there they are, using each other for all they're worth. I've finally understood what my father is up to. He's embarrassed to get rid of Eiko openly, before the whole school, and replace her with a younger woman; and Eiko, who knows perfectly well what's going on, is using him to put on a big show of doing whatever she likes. They're despicable."

"You yourself thought your father gave Eiko her freedom because he was losing his powers, didn't you? Far from losing his powers, he's now taken up with someone even younger!"

"I have no wish to despise my father to that degree."

"There's nothing far-fetched about it, though. I think it's quite likely."

"Never mind. I don't want to talk about it anymore." Shuntai fell silent, looking completely out of sorts. The whole thing was a swamp, and it was stupid of him even to think about it.

"Let's talk about something closer to hand," he said. "Let's not talk about my father. Let's talk about *me*."

"What about you?"

"What I should do. That's what I want to think about."

"Could you possibly be a bit clearer?"

"To make myself quite clear: should I marry you, or should I give up on you? Which is it to be? It's no use asking you to be my wife while you go on running this restaurant. What's good for you and what's good for me cancel each other out. We're a pair who just can't get together."

"You're probably right. Both of us have something we can't possibly drop. There's no way around that. I can't give up my business, and you can't do anything about being who you are. That's where this half-baked idea of being married while I go on with the restaurant comes from."

"You've got it. Eiko is horrible, but she has conviction. Me, I'm hopeless. I'm just too wishy-washy. Let's give it up."

It was Oriku's turn to be silent. His unexpectedly stubborn, child-like seriousness made him just like an artist. Oriku would have been glad to let the whole thing pass, but Shuntai was too caught up in it to do that.

Oriku roused Shuntai when she awoke the following morning, and they went to the bath together. While they bathed, she washed his back. The parting that was to come made her feel like pampering him a little. Afterward they ate breakfast in the main room—the Shigure Teahouse's usual breakfast, consisting of rolled egg, miso soup with shijimi clams, boiled spinach leaves, and nori seaweed, and individual lidded bowls of funa carp in the sweet kanro style. They had rice with the meal, but no saké. The rice contained cracked barley, which gave it a rustic character and felt good in the mouth. It was a fine morning, and from the main room they could watch the boats sailing by on the river.

"I'll have to say goodbye to this view too." He looked sad.

"It'll be better for you that way, I think." Oriku was deliberately being hard. She knew the old feelings would return otherwise.

"I'll do my best not to come, but I *will* if I really can't help it. Please don't turn me away."

"Don't talk like a baby. Oriku is always Oriku. I don't change."

"I'm letting go of you because I'm so ashamed of my own weakness. You understand that, don't you?"

"Of course I do. As I keep telling you, you should find yourself a perfectly normal wife. That's the best thing for you to do."

Shuntai sipped his tea without answering. He left at about ten o'clock, without complaint, and without ever asking whether Eiko and her friend had gone. Oriku saw him off to the embankment and watched him get into a rickshaw.

She had broken her strict rule of one man, one night with just two men. She did not yet actually feel parted from Tetsunosuke, and she meant no final parting with Shuntai, either. The men who had a genuine bond with her simply turned up from time to time, as though struck by a sudden memory. Monju would bring his kabuki friends for chazuke and leave again with fond looks. The storyteller Shinkyō would take the ferry over on his way home from the Yoshiwara, to stop by for a morning drink. Bandō Shūsaku, now bearing the new name Hidenojō, never forgot to call politely when duty required. Uzaemon, with whom the bond had not taken, used to say, roaring with laughter, every time he saw her, "You owe me one, Oriku, you owe me one!" Her resolve to hold to this principle had to do with her love for her business, and her fear that any deep romantic entanglement of hers might discourage the customers from coming. That, at least, had been her reasoning, but there was no need for such caution now that the Shigure Teahouse was one of Mukōjima's major attractions. The restaurant was going so well that it was hardly likely to suffer just because Oriku fell in love.

Still, the prudish Ofune censured the lightness of Oriku's ways. "Don't you think you'd do better to decide on someone once and for all," she kept saying, "so everyone here could know who you're with?"

"I don't want to have a single man tying me down. I'm nearly fifty, you know, and I won't feel romantically inclined forever. Don't worry!"

"But, they keep on falling for *you*, Mistress Oriku! You look much younger than your age, and I'm sure you will for a good long while." Ofune did not trust Oriku a bit.

Oriku's experiences with men had left her feeling empty. Looking back over her whole life, she saw that none had brought her deep satisfaction. Each had been pleasurable at the time, but that feeling had passed with the moment, and emptiness was what remained. Her lover in this case was being somewhat irresponsible, and she herself was trying to look the other way.

"I'll be more careful for a while," she replied, not with any undertone of irony, but simply to put an end to the matter.

She did indeed mind herself more carefully once Shuntai was gone. She went out rarely, instead devoting even the dark days of winter to sprucing up her establishment. The return of spring brought all the commotion surrounding Cherry Blossom Bentō, and the pressure of work distracted her from the dreariness of sleeping alone. There were far more blossom-viewers than last year, and sales of the bentō doubled. Oriku had even to put some customers out in the garden, on a round bench. Then the blossoms were gone, and the lively summer season, too, passed without incident. Late autumn brought markedly fewer guests. This was the season of restless melancholy. As work tapered off, Oriku felt like having a good time again and went on repeated outings to plays, music halls, and concerts.

"Look after yourself, Mistress Oriku," Ofune casually warned her. "You can easily catch something in winter."

"It's funny, isn't it," Oriku replied. "I forget about feeling lonely when we're so busy, but it comes back to me when business falls off in winter."

"So you should take hold of yourself now and begin practicing music or something."

"You're right, you're right!" Oriku answered with a wry smile; and there were days when she really did take her samisen out of its bag. Samisen or koto, though, it made no difference. When studying either one absorbed her deeply she could hardly bear to put the instrument aside, but any lapse made it feel foreign to her. She dredged up the half-forgotten itchū-bushi song "Koharu Puts Up Her Hair" and wielded the old, familiar plectrum better than her mediocre teacher had ever done. Her voice, too, had lost nothing of its former quality. "Goodness, Mistress Oriku is practicing singing for once!" Shigezō and Ofune thought, out in the corridor. Old Tomé and all the kitchen maids gathered outside the Paulownia to listen. Oriku's plectrum yielded a clear tone, her voice was as beautifully fresh as ever, and her delivery had all the emotional depth of a master's. She was glad to be back at her instrument after such a long time, and her lovely voice moved everyone there. Near the end, though, the third string snapped.

"Confound it! Luck is against me!" She clicked her tongue in annoyance. Not having the heart to change the string, she put the samisen down.

"Mistress Oriku! Telephone!" A girl came just then to tell her.

Oriku casually picked up the receiver. A woman's voice said, "I am calling on behalf of Mr. Hagiwara." Hagiwara? There was only one possibility.

"Shuntai-sensei has passed away, and Shunpō-sensei would be grateful if you would come to his house." The perfectly composed voice sounded strangely loud. Oriku felt a sharp pang. She wanted to ask whether Shuntai had been ill, but the chilly voice seemed intent on forestalling any such question.

"I shall be there immediately," Oriku replied, trembling. The samisen with the broken string lay before her like an evil omen. She had Ofune lay out suitable clothes for her and went to the bath. Once she was in the tub tears sprang to her eyes. She had no idea what had caused his death, whether illness or something else, but they had parted less than a year ago, and she had been looking forward to seeing him again. Instead, however, his life had suddenly ended. At first this was hard to believe, but she felt as though a happy goal had vanished from before her eyes. The memory of his voice, asking her over and over again to marry him, began to make her wonder whether she had played some part in his death.

"Where are you going?" Ofune had asked anxiously when her mistress paled and put down the receiver. Oriku said nothing, however. Speech was beyond her. "I'll tell you when I get back," she said and set off.

The main gate of the Hagiwara residence was closed. Only the side door stood open. The lattice door at the end of the flagstone walk was wide open, too, but within all was silent. No written message had yet been displayed. A male disciple materialized when she reached the entrance, as though he had been awaiting her arrival. "Please come in," he said, and led her down a long, winding passageway to a separate pavilion facing a garden. A similar passageway linked the pavilion also to the main house. Apparently this was where Shuntai had lived. Oriku caught the fragrance of incense as soon as she stepped into the ten-mat-sized room, and for the first time she understood it was really true. Shuntai's body lay in the center of the room, head to the north, and with a white cloth covering his face. Oriku noticed Yamato, sitting beside him. With her low, stooped posture and shaven head she looked small and somewhat aged.

"Do come in. Look at his face. He seems to have wanted to see you especially." Yamato made room for her. Her kindly, tactful tone had nothing of the sharpness of old.

Oriku put both hands to the floor in greeting to the deceased. Repressing her desire to ask how he had died, she wept as she called the name of the Buddha Amida. Meanwhile Yamato removed the cloth. Oriku was afraid to look, but she nonetheless did so with streaming eyes, her hands still to the floor. The face revealed no trace of suffering; it was as peaceful as though in sleep. Clean-shaven and with neatly smoothed hair, Shuntai seemed to have only just drawn his last breath.

"What happened?" Oriku finally asked. "What made him go so suddenly?" Tears kept her from saying more.

"It was an attack of angina pectoris. We knew nothing whatsoever about it." Yamato's calm speech had a touch of a Kyoto accent. "None of us had even heard of such an illness. He was so patient, I assume he never said anything to anyone even when he was in pain. The doctor came as fast as he could, but it was too late. A camphor injection had no effect."

"Who was with him at the time?"

"A disciple and an old woman who had been looking after him for years."

"Were *you* in Tokyo then?"

"Yes. The autumn recital is approaching, and my father asked me to come. Unfortunately, I ended up being here to give the last attentions to my brother."

"It was fortunate for *him*, though, to have a relative here with him." Oriku's tears spilled over once more. But why? She felt annoyed.

"The old woman came to get me as soon as the attack began, and I rushed to his side. He was still conscious, and so obviously in pain that I tried rubbing his back for him. 'Tell Mukōjima, tell Mukōjima,' he said, twice, but that was all. He didn't go on. 'Mukōjima' meant you."

"You think so?"

"You're the only possibility. My brother was even more eccentric than I am. One try at marriage was enough for him, and he remained single forever after. No amount of urging could convince him to take a wife. When I suggested to him that there must be *someone* he loved, he said he loved Oriku of the Shigure Teahouse." The Yamato of long ago was unrecognizable in this new person, so warm and so saddened by her brother's passing. "He confessed to me that as far as marriage was concerned, he'd happily marry *you*."

"Yes, he told me so himself."

"I know it would have been difficult, though. The Shigure Teahouse is one of the great attractions of Mukōjima, and I understand that you really couldn't have let it go. My brother told me sadly that he gave up when he understood that. I'm the only person he really confided in, poor man." She looked down sorrowfully at his body, as though enveloping him in her love.

Their conversation had just ended when Eiko came in to burn incense for the departed. Not that the accessories for doing so were all they could have been—just a sutra-reading desk and an incense burner that happened to be at hand—but the very modesty of the offering actually gave it greater poignancy. Eiko made hers, then pressed her palms together with a chilly air, saluted Yamato curtly, and left again without even a glance at Oriku.

"Is Eiko still here, then?" Oriku whispered.

Yamato smiled broadly. "It's quite a story," she answered. She said no more, but Oriku had a good idea what she meant. For Shunpō it hardly mattered who his wife was or what she was doing, as long as he could keep up appearances. He therefore kept Eiko with him, despite knowing she was unfaithful, and she calmly went on with her own life.

"My father says his condition will not allow him to attend the wake or the funeral. He told me he wants to pray for my brother alone, and he entrusted me with looking after everything else. So I would like to have the two of us—you and me—act as chief mourners."

"Chief mourners?"

"Yes. I don't propose to suggest anyone else, and the style of the observances hardly matters. I think it would make my brother happy to have the whole thing done in your name and mine."

"Of course I'll gladly do whatever I can, but are you sure it's all right to use my name?"

"Would it bother you?"

"No, on the contrary, I would be honored."

"My brother shied away from formality, and I expect going to his grave with you alone would please him best of all. That's not really possible, though, because there are the disciples to consider; so to make things look right I want to put our names forward together."

"Won't everyone in the school be surprised?"

"Let's surprise them, then. Let's show everyone the lover my brother had."

"But won't Shunpō-sensei be angry?"

"Leave that to me. You need only sit there beside me and say nothing."

"Surely the disciples will complain, though."

"I wouldn't be surprised. Like my father, they care exclusively for appearances. But in this house built on lies, isn't it just as well that one man, at least, lived like a normal human being and acted on his feelings?"

Oriku wept afresh. How had Yamato reached this degree of maturity? Oriku saw in her eyes, as they rested on her brother's body, a beauty like that of the Buddha's own compassion.

The wake that night was only for the immediate family. The next morning an altar was erected, and priests came from Zōjōji Temple in the Shiba district of Tokyo. The house was buried in flowers. Oriku and Yamato sat side by side to greet the mourners, who all looked at Oriku askance. Oriku, however, ignored them. Instead she took advantage of Yamato's quiet strength to devote herself to bidding a heartfelt farewell to Shuntai's spirit. This might never have happened if she had married him, as he had so hoped she would. Perhaps her refusal to do so had driven him to his death. At least, Oriku felt that way. His civil name had been Hagiwara Haruyasu, the characters of which, when given another reading, sounded the same as those in his professional name.

The funeral proper was held in the Zōjōji main hall. Well over three thousand people came. On that day, too, Oriku sat beside Yamato as a chief mourner, reflecting meanwhile that she would never meet a man like Shuntai again.

Everything went smoothly. Once the people were gone, Oriku and Yamato bowed side by side, one last time, to the coffin as it stood there before the altar in the main hall.

"Dear brother," Yamato said, very low, "Oriku is beside you— Oriku, your only love."

Oriku's knees almost gave way under her, but Yamato held her up, took her hand, and placed it on the coffin. Both their hands were cold. All the misdeeds of the past melted away, and Oriku felt she was offering herself, purified, to the departed.

CHAPTER NINE

Kinosuke's Stellar Performance

Oriku and Shigezō often quarreled. Every time a guest complained about the food, Oriku rushed to the kitchen. "What kind of seasoning is *this*?" she would loudly demand to know. "Is *this* what you expect to please a guest with?" Then they would have at it.

"Go ahead, taste it! It has no flavor at all! This is what you call cooking, is it?" Glaring at Shigezō, she would go on, "I don't mind so much if a guest actually complains. What really frightens me is the guest who says nothing and never comes back. You made this, and you still call yourself a chef?"

"All right, all right. Everybody makes mistakes. Give me a break. I'm only human."

"Everybody may make mistakes, but for a restaurant that's not good enough. Once the lot of you start making mistakes, it's all downhill from there."

"I've got it, I tell you. That's enough! I'll make another right away."

"'That's enough,' he says. What do you mean, 'that's enough'? No wonder I'm letting you have it! This restaurant is my life, and I'm not keeping my mouth shut while you shorten it for me."

"I'm only human, I make mistakes. That's why I'm asking you nicely to forgive me."

"Ask me to forgive you, if you like, but spare me this chatter about being only human! I won't have it!"

"If you won't have it, you can please yourself."

With this, Shigezō turned on his heel and left. Oriku remained unruffled, but not Ofune.

"Wait, Shigezō, wait!" Ofune rushed out barefoot into the service entrance after him, but he was already gone. She paled. The chef's disappearance would bring the restaurant to a standstill.

"What are we going to do?" she wailed. "We'll be completely stuck if Shigezō leaves!"

"What nonsense! We've been going for three years, and by now I have a pretty good hang of what goes on in the kitchen. Don't worry about a thing. I'll step in for him."

"So you say, but you won't be cooking for just us, you'll be cooking for the restaurant guests."

"Quiet! We have Yūzō and Jūkichi, and I know I can cook, even if I don't make a big production of it." Oriku refused to budge an inch.

She went down personally to the kitchen, to find the dashi broth all prepared and the boiled vegetables done. There remained only the things that had to be made fresh for each guest—the funa carp sashimi, the umewan soup with chicken and vegetables, and the salt-broiled sweetfish. Yūzō took care of the sashimi. Anyone could look after the broiled dishes, and Oriku was good at seasoning the soup. In other words, Shigezō's absence caused no trouble at all. It *would* be a problem later on, when the time came to purchase further supplies, but in fact most of those were simply delivered, and Oriku could perfectly well handle the matter herself once she developed a good eye for quality. Ofune maintained that they could not go on without Shigezō, Oriku insisted that they could, and the result was yet another quarrel.

Shigezō had left about one o'clock, during lunchtime, and that night they had to look after three parties with prior reservations. "Never mind what Shigezō said," Oriku assured the cooks as they got to work, "he'll be back, I know he will, so just ignore his absence and make sure it doesn't show." They already knew pretty well what to do, having seen it all done so often, and as for the all-important chazuke, Oriku herself made it in any case. As a result, they managed quite well in the end to serve up the usual fare.

Oriku spent all her time in the kitchen, seeing to the seasoning and the presentation of the dishes. "Let's give Shigezō a real surprise," she kept saying, meanwhile working away like mad. She was not really worried, because she was sure he would return—after all, it seemed that he and Ofune were engaged to be married. Ofune was beside herself, though. Oriku carefully ignored her. By about five o'clock all the basic preparations were finished, but Oriku was very tired, having been on her feet continuously since one. The moment things quieted down and she got a chance to sit herself down by the hearth, Shigezō turned up. He looked surprisingly calm and collected.

"I'm sorry," he said. "I gather you've done all the preparations already." He scratched his head.

"I didn't *want* to, but we wouldn't have been able to open otherwise."

"I shouldn't have gotten so angry back there, should I?"

"You're certainly back soon. You should have taken it easy a bit longer, while you were at it."

"Umm." Shigezō scratched his head again and smiled. "I was in a rage when I stalked off, but I felt bad about it by the time I reached Azuma Bridge."

"If you were going to regret it *that* fast, you would have done better not to go anywhere at all. So where have you been all this time, with your regrets?"

"I didn't like the idea of turning round right away, so I went into the Azumabashi Theater."

"You *did*? You must be joking! So you were listening to a gidayū performance? You *were* taking it easy, weren't you!"

"I thought it might calm me down a little. I didn't mean to stay long, but I was spellbound. There's a fantastic chanter performing there, Mistress Oriku!"

"You were just impressed because you so rarely hear gidayū. So who is this chanter? Ayasedayū? Or that bright young Ayanosuke?"

"No, no, Ayasedayū's name was on the program, but he was apparently too sick to perform. I'm talking about his replacement."

"Who could possibly replace Ayasedayū? Not Harimadayū, surely?" Oriku liked gidayū chanting and knew quite a lot about it. Her late husband's distaste for it had prevented her from actually taking lessons, but she had often stolen off to the Azumabashi Theater, and she had heard most of the famous chanters.

"I mean Tsubamedayū. His voice is a little unusual, but his perform-ance was absolutely flawless."

"Tsubamedayū!" Oriku shook her head in perplexity. "The previ-ous Tsubamedayū is now Kōtsubodayū, and he's at the Bunraku Theater in Osaka. He had a special way of writing the name, with three characters. There can't possibly be any other Tsubamedayū."

"I don't know, but I've never heard anything like it. He was extraor-dinary."

"What did he do?"

"*Gappō*. He has a very dry chanting style, but it was just wonderful."

"If he's that good, I'd like to hear him myself."

"He's only a replacement, though—he won't be there long. Go tomorrow, if you can. He comes on about three o'clock."

"I'm surprised they're doing matinées."

"The place was packed. It looked as if he must be even more pop-ular than Ayasedayū."

"He's a nice-looking man, isn't he, this Tsubamedayū?"

"Yes, he's plump, round-faced—quite nice-looking."

"Then it must be the same one who went to Osaka. I thought he'd taken the name Kōtsubodayū. I wonder what happened."

The Azumabashi Theater on Hirokōji Street specialized in gidayū chanting. It always featured one great artist or another, and all seem to have been proud to appear there. Matinée performances there were rare, but they were occasionally scheduled for top chanters, in which case popular women chanters performed in the evening show. It took a great artist to attract a large audience to a matinée.

Talking about gidayū chanting dispelled all thought of their earlier quarrel. Shigezō went to the kitchen, where the enraptured Ofune greeted him with glee, followed by much merry laughter.

The next day, Oriku went alone to the Azumabashi Theater. Here, too, she was known well enough to rate special treatment. "My, my, it's Mistress Oriku from Mukōjima! Welcome, welcome! The show is sold out, I'm afraid, so I'll have to ask you to come in *this* way." She was shown in through the back entrance and crammed in next to the chanter's dais. It happened to be the intermission, and the theater was abuzz. There were a good many women in the audience. In the evening, when the bright young starlets performed, the audience was almost all men, but the matinée audience was about two-thirds women. Next to Oriku's spot sat, very properly, a young woman Oriku was sure she had seen before, prettily made up and with a beautifully colored coral pin in her hair. She made room for Oriku when Oriku came in, as though to cede Oriku her place.

"It's been ages, Mistress Oriku!" she said in greeting. Oriku then recognized her as the young chanter Takemoto Kinosuke.

"Ah, Kinosuke, is it? Yes, it's been a long time." This was a relief. She did not feel quite right, being there all by herself, and it was good to have so pleasant a companion beside her.

"Do you perform here in the evening?"

"Yes. I do hope you'll come."

"So you're at this matinée to learn from the chanters?"

"Yes. It's a rare chance to hear a chanter from the Bunraku Theater itself."

"Tsubamedayū is from the Bunraku Theater in Osaka?"

"Yes, he is." Kinosuke nodded and glanced around her. "Actually," she added in a low voice, "he's the great master Kōtsubodayū."

"So why is he performing as Tsubamedayū? Did he decide not to use his new name after all?"

"No, he really and truly is Kōtsubodayū, but you see, he happened to be in Tokyo because the Bunraku Theater is closed right now, and the theater owner here got hold of him. At least, that's what I hear." She had lowered her voice even further. Apparently his succession to the name Kōtsubodayū had involved a promise never to perform outside the Bunraku Theater itself, and this had prevented him from agreeing to perform at the Azumabashi. Having studied under Ayasedayū, however, he owed his teacher a debt of gratitude that made it impossible for him to refuse to step in during Ayasedayū's illness. He had therefore suppressed his current name and was performing in his teacher's place under his old name. Kinosuke knew all about it.

"I see. So *that's* what happened!"

"He was wonderful. I just can't get over his *Gappō* yesterday."

"I can imagine. I often heard it when he really was Tsubamedayū, but he's certainly come into his own since then. What's he doing today, I wonder?"

"*Horikawa,* apparently."

"That's even better! *Horikawa* is a particular specialty of his." Oriku inched forward. Tsubamedayū came on immediately after the intermission. The stagehand announced his appearance with such verve that Oriku thought he, too, might well have come with the star from Osaka. At the perfect moment the curtain rose. Kōtsubodayū might as well not have bothered to hide his name. The audience knew perfectly well who he was; in fact, many of his fellow artists were there to listen in on the master.

> *Even in the Capital,*
> *for such is this world,*
> *country scenes can still be seen*
> *veiled by wisps of smoke*
> *all along Horikawa,*
> *my own neighborhood.*

His touchingly restrained rendition of the familiar words brought the Horikawa neighborhood to life before one's eyes.

> *On her tender skin,*
> *a shift of pure white below;*
> *above, a purple robe*
> *wisteria-patterned;*
> *scarlet silk in between,*
> *black satin sash-tied;*
> *and her age just seventeen,*
> *the first bloom of youth:*
> *there she stands for all to see,*
> *languid in the rain.*

He sang even this favorite passage in the niagari samisen tuning with unexpected simplicity, giving it no particular vocal emphasis. This was an understated *Horikawa,* one quite unlike what the audience was used to. From the moment Yojirō called out, "Mother dear, I'm back!" to announce his return, the dialogue between him and his invisible mother conveyed a fineness of feeling and a crisply delineated beauty that marked the performance as characteristic of the one-and-only Bunraku Theater in Osaka. No Tokyo chanter could possibly imitate it.

The full title of *Horikawa* is *Chikagoro Kawara no Tatehiki*. The play concerns the love suicide of Denbei, a Kyoto clothing merchant, and Oshun, a prostitute from Pontochō. It dramatizes a real incident from around 1740, one which was then the talk of the town. *Horikawa* is a particularly fine example of a puppet play on a current theme, being brilliant but also affecting, touching in its evocation of family ties, rich in incident, and absorbingly narrated. In the final scene Yojirō, the monkey trainer, weeps as he sings, "See Mr. Monkey dance for good fortune, good fortune!" while Denbei and Oshun exchange marriage cups of saké, then flee toward their deaths. Tsubamedayū gave a breathtaking performance. No doubt he felt impelled to do his very best when standing in for his teacher, Ayasedayū, but at any rate, every word was fully alive. Oshun's famous speech, "Oh, Denbei, please don't say that . . ." entirely satisfied the audience's eager anticipation. He delivered the passage, "I agree, I really do, but ever since we came together . . ." with calculated simplicity, only to then throw himself with utter conviction into "My husband, my dearest love, now death threatens you, could I abandon you and still remain a woman?" Thus his perfectly controlled mingling of the strong and mild, the plain and brilliant, lifted him to the very pinnacle of his art.

Tears streamed down Oriku's cheeks, while the entranced Kinosuke strained forward as far as she possibly could. For both, fascination had obliterated all consciousness of self, and they hardly breathed until the farewell scene was over. Oriku remained speechless even after the curtain had come down to thunderous applause. Meanwhile Kinosuke, all but struck dumb, seemed to be trying to hold in her mind's eye that fading vision of Tsubamedayū.

At last Oriku noticed that the spectators around her were beginning to rise and leave, amid a buzz of talk. "That was really wonderful," she said.

"It was beyond anything human," Kinosuke answered. "That was a god at work." It was with deep feeling that she said, "I'll never feel like chanting again."

"He really is Kōtsubodayū, isn't he? He truly deserves his name."

"He certainly does. He could never do *Horikawa* like that otherwise."

"After this, I can't wait to meet him. I wonder whether he might share a meal with me."

"You'd better not. He's a famous womanizer. I don't like the idea."

"You're always fussing over everything, aren't you? Or is it perhaps that you're in love with him?"

"Mistress Oriku! What a thing to say!" Kinosuke finally flashed the artist's conspicuous smile. "It's you I'm in love with, Mistress Oriku."

"What are you talking about? A woman has no business being in love with another woman."

"I am, though. I always have been. Even back when you were at the Silver Flower."

"Have you really known me that long?"

"That long . . . Well, actually, it's only been about three years. You used to come to hear me quite often, didn't you?"

"Yes, I suppose I did. The theater's easy to get to, and it's a nice place to be."

When returning to the Yoshiwara from town, Oriku used to take a streetcar to the Kaminari Gate, then change to a rickshaw; when the time happened to be right she frequently dropped into the theater to hear the performers. It was natural for her to stop there, unless she was in a hurry, since the theater stood at the intersection of Hirokōji Street and Umamichi Avenue. Ayanosuke and Kotosa were the performers who actually interested her, but the young Kinosuke had quite a following. The men especially made much of her, less for her chanting than her looks. She certainly showed great promise, and her style of delivery resembled singing more closely than chanting. Guests would sometimes bring her to the Silver Flower, where she would perform for the women of the house; and from that time on she had begun following Oriku around. It was she who had liked to sit down right next to Oriku and say, "Mistress Oriku, I just love forthright people like you!"

"If you come too, then, there should be no problem. I'll send Kōtsubodayū an invitation, and you can join us."

"Where will you go?"

"My place—I can't think of anywhere better. It's homey."

"Is it really all right for me to come too?"

"Of course. You can help by bringing him."

"Fine. I'll do my best, then. I won't like it, though, Mistress Oriku, if you start carrying on with him."

"I have nothing like that in mind. I just want to thank him for a wonderful experience and to get him to talk about his art."

"All right, you can count on me to bring him. In exchange, though, I hope you'll become one of my fans."

Once all this was settled, Oriku went home. Shigezō was waiting for her. "How was it?" he asked anxiously.

"It was wonderful. He did *Horikawa* today, and he got buckets of tears out of me."

"That's because you cry so easily, Mistress Oriku," Ofune interjected.

"No, no, that's not it. Just go and hear him yourself! He's *so* good! His art has distinction, it has charm, and it's never the least bit cheap or facile. I was extremely impressed."

"Look out, then! When Mistress Oriku is impressed, she ends up falling in love."

"That's absolutely right. I'm head over heels already."

"Well, that's the way it goes, then. That's exactly what I thought might happen. Ofune and I were just talking about it."

"I hope you'll forgive me, then. It's my little weakness. Whenever I see or hear something wonderful, I simply can't contain myself the way other people do. I want to see what he's like in bed."

"It's a bit of a problem, this weakness of yours, but I suppose it doesn't really matter. You can't be faulted for choosing a great artist like Kōtsubodayū. He's normally in Osaka, though. You'll have a hard time getting together with him."

"Well, actually, I've invited him here for this evening."

"You *have*?"

"*This* evening?"

Shigezō and Ofune both looked amazed.

"You're not joking?"

"Of course not. Kinosuke, who's been so popular these days, will bring him here, so I hope you'll make something especially good. I'm going to take a bath now, and I'd appreciate it if you'd check to see that the temperature's right."

Oriku went off to her room without giving the astonished pair a chance to say another word. The initiative had been entirely hers, but she had no idea whether Kōtsubodayū would really come. The story would probably end with a telephone call from Kinosuke announcing that he had declined the invitation. With that thought in mind, she took her bath and applied some light makeup.

"Your guests are here." Oei had come to let her know.

"What guests?"

"Kinosuke and the gentleman with her. I took them to the Pine room." Oei knew nothing.

Oriku had never imagined him coming so soon or so readily. She dressed in haste and set off for the Pine room, wiping the perspiration from her brow. The Pine, a ten-mat room back-to-back with the main dining room, faced the Paulownia annex across a hedge. Kōtsubodayū stood on the veranda, looking out over the Sumida River. Behind him sat Kinosuke.

"Welcome, welcome!" Oriku's long years of practice with guests had taught her not to overdo her greetings. "I never thought you would really be kind enough to come," she continued. "Welcome to the Shigure Teahouse. Thank you, Kinosuke."

"Not at all, Mistress Oriku. Actually, Master Kōtsubodayū had another engagement, and he canceled it so that he could accept your invitation."

"Goodness! I hardly know what to say. Master Kōtsubodayū is too kind."

"He had already heard of the Shigure Teahouse, you see, but, never having been here, he said he did not want to miss this opportunity to come. He put the earlier invitation off till tomorrow."

"I am overwhelmed. I so longed to meet you, Master Kōtsubodayū, after your wonderful *Horikawa* today, that I made bold to ask you

here. I should never have done it. Thank you so much for coming!"
Oriku was practically prostrate on the floor as she spoke. She had been
sure he would not come, but on the contrary, he had actually broken
an earlier engagement to do so. She could hardly get over it.

"All I serve is chazuke, you know," she went on. "Do you like
chazuke? Will that be all right for you?"

"Thank you very much. The pleasure is all mine," Kōtsubodayū
replied. "I had already noted the figure of Mistress Oriku, who always
goes to Kuwana near Ise to buy her clams, and I had been hoping to
be able to come here. I was therefore delighted to receive your invitation." Surprisingly, his way of speaking was almost pure Edo, with little trace of an Osaka accent. Apparently he had been born in Tokyo—
in Umamichi, in fact.

"I see. I went to Kuwana just last year."

"Yes, and you and I were staying at the same inn. The maid pointed
you out to me. She told me you owned the Shigure Teahouse at
Mukōjima in Tokyo. I thought you were lovely." His Osaka accent was
coming out a bit more.

"Really? I always stay at the Funatsuya when I go to Kuwana. It's
such a nice place."

"It is indeed. The river is wide, since that's the point of confluence
of the Kiso and Ibi rivers, and all that water is beautiful. Yes, it's a
very peaceful inn." His accent was growing stronger.

They talked about Kuwana for a while. Kōtsubodayū was a far bet-
ter-looking man than he had seemed on the chanter's dais.

"If I may ask a personal question, Master Kōtsubodayū, in what
year were you born?"

"December 1878."

"Oh dear!" Oriku leaned back ostentatiously and inspected him
with care. "You're so young! It's almost unbelievable that you can
chant that well at your age. I thought you must be about the same age
as me."

"And yourself, Mistress Oriku, if I may ask?"

"I can't tell you. It's too embarrassing."

Dinner arrived just then, and Kinosuke poured Kōtsubodayū's saké.
Privately, Oriku was disappointed. Having been born before Meiji, she

was ten years his senior. She had been secretly looking forward to amusing herself with this handsome virtuoso, counting on having no regrets even if she happened to go a bit too far; but now that rosy prospect suddenly vanished, and they talked about gidayū chanting instead.

"You give a particularly restrained rendition of passages that other chanters tend to do ornately," she remarked. "Why is that?"

"Well, in recent years gidayū chanting has fallen away from what it used to be. It's become too florid, too preoccupied with playing to the crowd. I prefer to keep that tendency in check, as much as possible, by carefully considering where to let myself go and where to be more discreet."

"In other words, you restrain the audience from shouting out 'Bravo! Bravo!' in exactly those places where they normally expect to do so."

"That's right. Perhaps you could call it 'dimming the old favorites.' Those shouts are very distracting, and I try as much as I can to discourage them."

"Do they throw you off?"

"It's hard to chant when I hear other voices. In *Horikawa*, for example, I identify myself completely with the feelings of Yojirō, Oshun, or Denbei, and I suddenly lose my breath when one of those shouts comes from the audience. In other words, I'm not yet a complete master of my art. I don't believe a real master even hears other voices. No, I'm not there yet."

His modesty was no pretense; it sounded as though it came from his innermost being. This was the kind of seriousness that appealed to Oriku, and she loved him even more for it. Meanwhile Kinosuke, relegated to the role of silent listener, watched the two of them with a look of endless boredom.

"Whom do you respect most in all the world, Master Kōtsubodayū?"

"I respect a great many people, but above all, I suppose, the teacher from whom I learned most directly: Master Tsudayū of Hōzenji."

They talked on and on about the old days. Kōtsubodayū was a good drinker who never put down his cup, and the more the saké affected him, the more volubly he chatted about this or that master from the past, till there was little either Oriku or Kinosuke could do but provide him with an audience. With his mild eyes and gentle laugh, he hardly resembled a man not long past thirty. Both his art and his speech had a genuineness about them that never lapsed into mere pretense. He also brought his drinking to an end with refreshing frankness.

"You have put yourself out a great deal for me," he said. "Thank you very much. When you go to Ise, please continue on to Osaka. I'll be expecting you at the Bunraku Theater. Kinosuke, thank you, too, for all your trouble."

Having expressed his gratitude to them both, he rose to his feet, every inch a fine figure of a man. So clear and clean were his manners that there was no time to approach him further, not a single opportunity to tease, flatter, or flirt.

"He's remarkably proper for an artist, isn't he?" Oriku felt a little tired once Kōtsubodayū was gone. Their talk had been too serious, and her shoulders were stiff.

"That's the way he is, apparently. Still, there are some racy rumors about him." Kinosuke, too, looked exhausted.

"I wouldn't be surprised. He's an attractive man. I could have gotten into the mood myself, if the talk had turned that way, but there was never a chance to steer it in that direction."

"Don't say such things, Mistress Oriku! I have the greatest respect for you, and I don't want to hear you talking that way."

"Why shouldn't I? You're not going to get anywhere with *me*. I'm on my own, and I intend to amuse myself as much as I like with anyone I please. I've fallen for Kōtsubodayū, that's why I wanted to meet him."

"I'll stop you, you know. Whenever you're with him, I'll always be there too." Kinosuke glared earnestly at Oriku. "If you want to have an affair, pick someone else, I don't care who—just not a gidayū chanter. I won't have you doing it with Kōtsubodayū." She drained a teacup of saké in one swallow.

Kinosuke had put a good deal of herself into the effort of keeping Kōtsubodayū company, and her eyes were drooping with fatigue.

Despite her sweet expression, it was in a voice devoid of seductive appeal that she cried, "Ah, Mistress Oriku, I love you, I love you!" meanwhile throwing her arms around Oriku's knees.

"A woman has no business being in love with another woman."

"But I *am* in love with a woman! It's not men I love, no. What I truly love are forthright, open women like you!"

"I don't want to hear this. I don't like this kind of thing."

"You don't like it?"

"No, I don't. I mean that," Oriku replied as discouragingly as possible. "Call it lesbianism, or homosexuality, or whatever you will, as far as I'm concerned it's dirty."

Kinosuke peered up at her from below. "Ooh, yes! I *love* that look of yours!" She pressed herself still harder against Oriku.

"Stop it! I can't stand this! What do you mean by leering at me this way? Let me go!" She tried to pry Kinosuke's hands loose.

"No, I won't, I won't! Stay with me tonight, keep me beside you, *please*! *Please* keep me with you!" She clung to Oriku with all her might. Though small, she was strong, and now that she had hold of Oriku she refused to let go.

"What a nuisance you are! Let me go, I tell you!"

"Keep saying that, and I'll just hang onto you harder."

"Suit yourself, then. This is the last time I'll ever spend any time with *you*!"

"All right, since you hate me anyway. If this is the last time, fine, but please be kind and keep me with you tonight!" She was almost in tears. Oriku would not have thought it of her, but perhaps she was always like this when drunk. At any rate, she simply would not let go. Oriku had no idea what to do with her.

"Go and lie down in my room," she finally said. "I still have a lot of work to do."

"Will you stay with me when you're done?"

"Yes, yes, I will."

With these soothing words Oriku led Kinosuke to the Paulownia. Despite her brazen talk, Kinosuke fell innocently asleep the moment she collapsed into bed. What a strange day it had been, to have ended by saddling Oriku with a burden like this! The quarrel with Shigezō had resulted in her going to the Azumabashi Theater, which had led to her falling for Kōtsubodayū and inviting him home; and that in turn had resulted in this entanglement with Kinosuke.

Thereafter Kinosuke became a frequent visitor to the Shigure Teahouse. Sometimes she brought people with her, and sometimes she came alone. She generally turned up once every ten days or so. To get there she had only to take a ferry across the river, since she lived at Hanakawado, but she was afraid of annoying Oriku if she came too often, and she always studied Oriku's expression anxiously. When she had had some saké she could be difficult to deal with, but when sober she remained a good, quiet girl.

"I don't mind your coming," Oriku would say to her, "just as long as you don't get drunk and make a nuisance of yourself."

"I'm sorry. I don't know what came over me that one evening. I promise not to do anything like that again." Although full of good intentions, she would forget all about them once she began drinking. Still, she did not repeat her initial behavior. When drunk she would put her hand somewhere on Oriku and assume a tragic expression. At first Oriku did not like it one bit, but after a while she came to take it in stride.

"You're back at it, are you?" she would say, lightly slapping the hand Kinosuke had pressed against her.

"Oh, Mistress Oriku, I so long to have you hold me tight!" Kinosuke would reply, wriggling closer.

"Not again! You're impossible! As soon as I'm nice to you, you start pushing your luck."

"But I love you! Let me, *please*! I can't help it, can I, if I love you! I won't come back anymore if you keep giving me those scary looks. I'll just give up!" Then she would hang her head like a scolded child, looking so forlorn that Oriku would feel sorry for her.

"I'm not telling you not to come anymore, am I? All you have to do is behave yourself!"

"But I'm in *love* with you! I don't see anything wrong with a woman loving another woman."

"I won't have it. I don't like women. If you insist on hanging around with me, I want lessons from you. Teach me gidayū chanting."

"What? You mean it?"

"I'm not sure you're the best possible teacher, but I'll manage. I have in mind to learn *Horikawa*. I want you to teach it to me."

"I can't do that! *Horikawa* is out. I know you wouldn't like the way I do it, now that you've heard Kōtsubodayū. How about the 'Sakaya' or 'Nozaki' scenes instead? Let's pick something romantic."

"All right, then, 'Sakaya.' Let's start from 'Lately my Hanshichi…' I want you to teach me properly. I won't go on with it if you don't."

"Whew! Who ever heard of a student pushing her teacher around?"

"If you don't like it, just say no. You keeping talking about wanting to be with me, and I'm trying to accommodate you. You're welcome to refuse."

"Oh, I'll do it, I'll do it. I don't care what airs you put on. By all means let me give you lessons."

"Fine, I'll take them. Bring your samisen tomorrow."

"I'll do that."

So the lessons began the next day. Kinosuke arrived in high spirits, samisen in hand, sat her herself cheerfully down in a professional manner, and started in chanting "Sakaya." Oriku did not actually practice it with her, but she already knew it fairly well from having heard it so often before; so Kinosuke left out some sections in order to concentrate on the most famous part of the opening passage. Sure enough, Oriku learned faster than any ordinary amateur, and thanks to her training in itchū-bushi and kiyomoto she caught on to the musical phrasing very quickly.

"You must have studied something before, Mistress Oriku—otherwise you couldn't possibly learn this fast."

Kinosuke was amazed. Oriku's voice did not carry that well, since she was a woman, but it was beautiful, and in the key passages her delivery tended more toward song than toward dramatic chanting.

This was Kinosuke's profession, after all, and once the lessons were under way she said nothing further to make Oriku uncomfortable. Instead, she applied herself so zealously to her teaching that she worked up quite a sweat, which she washed off with a quick bath once the lesson was over, before going on to her evening performance. The pleasure for her lay simply in being with Oriku, but the lessons were a pleasure too for Oriku, who came to look forward to Kinosuke's arrival.

"By now, it would be pointless for me to insist on learning a whole piece," Oriku declared. "Let's just do the best bits." So after "Sakaya" they spent half a year on the puppet play *Asagao nikki* and the scene "Benkei jōshi."

Then, one early summer day at the end of the rainy season, Kinosuke said gravely, "Mistress Oriku, there's something I need to discuss with you."

"What is it? I want nothing to do with anything unpleasant."

"No, no, it's nothing like that. I just don't know what to do. I'm afraid you may be angry if I tell you about it, though."

"So what's the problem? I can't say anything at all if *you* won't. Do you need money?"

"No, it's something else." Kinosuke hesitated a moment longer. "The Silver Flower in the Yoshiwara is yours, I believe?"

"Yes, but I've passed it on to a young couple. I don't own it."

"But if I let it be known I wanted to become one of the women there, do you think they'd take me?" Her eyes were utterly serious.

"What *are* you talking about? With all your artistic accomplishment, why in the world would you want to enter an establishment like that?"

"But, Mistress Oriku, you see, I've never yet made love with a man."

Oriku was speechless.

"It's true, I swear it. I'm nearly thirty, and I'm still a virgin. Isn't that pitiful? And I'm an *artist*!"

"And that's why you want to become a prostitute?"

"Yes. If I did, I'd end up knowing men, whether I liked it or not."

"You're out of your mind!" Oriku shouted in amazement. She had known Kinosuke was somehow different, but Kinosuke said she was still a virgin, and she seemed to be telling the truth. There really are women artists like this. The life they lead gives them many opportunities to see all sorts of men, and they end up seeing the faults in all of them and deciding to turn away any who chance to approach them. Meanwhile the years go by, and their repressed desires find an outlet in the urge to caress the bodies of other women, such as Oriku. Kinosuke had apparently become that kind of woman. Unable any longer to tolerate her situation, she had hit on the preposterous idea of acquiring experience with men by becoming a prostitute.

"You'd better give more careful thought to this nonsense of yours. Women sell themselves to places like that only under the pressure of dire financial need, and they take up life there in tears. Who ever heard of a woman becoming a prostitute in order to gain experience? It's ridiculous." Oriku's voice had risen to a shout.

"So I really shouldn't do it?" Kinosuke said in a timid, discouraged voice.

"Of course not! Why, the very idea! There you are, a professional artist, and you're still a virgin? What kind of insanity is that? Haven't you ever had anyone make a play for you?"

"Why, yes, I have, but only the kind of men I wouldn't ever want to have around—the kind who like to chase popular women chanters like me. They're all awful."

"That's not true! Just look at Ishii Kenta, who picked off Ayanosuke and married her. What's wrong with *him*?"

"Well, I must just have bad luck with men, then."

"You're not smart about them, that's all. You've got looks, you're not half-bad at your profession—you must have had plenty of them after you. If you're still a virgin, it's because you've made a mess of the whole thing. If you're thinking of becoming a prostitute, why not just go out and have an affair with someone or other?"

"But I don't know anyone to have an affair *with*!"

"There must be *someone*, though—an actor or some other kind of artist."

"I don't know any actors."

"Don't you ever go to the theater?"

"Certainly I go, but not often—I have my own performance schedule, after all."

Oriku was beginning to lose patience with Kinosuke's predicament. She herself had never even dreamed of an affair until she opened her restaurant, and now, in two or three years, she had had any number of them. Her confusion on the subject had vanished as soon as she found out what the reality was like, but of course she had at least known the basic facts of life all along. In the mood now to find the unfortunate Kinosuke a partner, she first telephoned the kabuki actor Monju. At his young age he already had a following and had lately been displaying considerable prowess. Audiences thought quite well of him.

"What can have brought me the pleasure of a telephone call from you?" he responded, in a thoroughly grown-up manner.

"I have a small request to make of you. What time does your play begin?"

"Actually, the theater is closed this month. July and August attendance are poor, so I'm rehearsing for a tour."

"When are you leaving?"

"On the fifteenth, so in another couple of days."

"Are you doing anything tonight?"

"No. I'm always available if you need me. What is it, though?"

"I'll tell you when we meet. It's nothing unpleasant. Please be here by this evening." Then she revised that thought. "I really shouldn't make you come all this way, though. It's a bit far."

"No, no, I don't mind. It's too long since I was last there, anyway." His replies showed the true actor's affability.

"Another thing: You probably know the Azumabashi Theater, at Azuma Bridge."

"The one where the women gidayū chanters perform?"

"Yes, that's the one. Could we meet there at seven-thirty?"

"What an odd place for a rendezvous! Presumably we won't be there for the performance?"

"Well, we might listen to a scene or two. I'll tell you about it after we get together. Seven-thirty, all right? Don't be late!"

Kinosuke was to mount the dais at eight o'clock that evening, to perform a scene often done by women chanters: Shigenoi's parting from her son in the play *Koi Nyōbō Somewake Tazuna*. As a love partner the kabuki actor Monju was perfect for her since, despite being younger, he undoubtedly had plenty of experience with women. Besides—and this was the most important thing of all—with him there would be no complications later.

Oriku was annoyed to find herself involved in the foolish business of finding someone a man to make love with, but at seven o'clock she nonetheless set off for the Azumabashi Theater. She sent no message to Kinosuke, who had agreed that Oriku should do whatever she thought best. She said nothing, either, as she entered the theater, but she took two seats and left word to expect Monju's arrival. Monju came a little before the appointed time and looked around in wonder as he sat down beside Oriku.

"Are you a fan of gidayū chanting these days?" he asked innocently, in a hushed tone. On the dais a middle-aged woman, finishing up a scene from *Taikōki*, was declaiming at passionate volume, clinging to the chanter's lectern as she did so. Over a kimono of plain omeshi cloth Monju had on a haori jacket embroidered with his crest. He certainly looked more grown-up than before, but there was still a boyish quality to his face as he peered at Oriku, smiling broadly. Soon Kinosuke came onto the stage and began her piece.

"What do you think of her?" Oriku murmured to Monju after he had listened for a while.

"She's nice-looking, I'd say. She has a nice voice too, and she's not at all bad."

"Would you like to make love to her?"

"Don't be such a tease," he whispered in her ear. "What do you mean?"

"She has a crush on you. She asked me to introduce her."

"She *did*? If she likes me, I'd be delighted."

"Then come to Mukōjima tonight, and I'll bring the two of you together."

"To Mukōjima."

"That's all right, isn't it? What's past is past, and if it's anywhere else someone might notice you."

"True enough."

"She's a nice girl. Take good care of her."

Oriku said nothing further and listened to Kinosuke, wearing a look of bland innocence. Kinosuke seemed to have noticed her presence, because she put singular passion into Shigenoi's lament and gave it her best performance ever. Oriku knew the story backward and forward, but Kinosuke put such pathos into the way the horse-driver Sankichi, unable to acknowledge Shigenoi as his mother, wept as he sang his horse-driver's song, that she drew tears from Oriku nonetheless.

"She's really into it, isn't she!" As the curtain came down, Monju's eyes were moist as well. "Good gidayū chanting is even better than kabuki." He was impressed.

Since the rickshaws had been ordered beforehand, they went straight out to wait for Kinosuke. The daytime congestion on Hirokōji Street had cleared somewhat, and people were beginning to disperse in all directions toward home. At the Azumabashi Theater, the star performers—Shōgiku and Shōnosuke—were yet to come on, so most of the audience stayed on for them. Only Oriku and Monju left after Kinosuke. Kinosuke herself quickly followed them out, and their train of three rickshaws set off without further ado for Mukōjima.

There is no need to dwell at length on what followed. They repaired to the Camellia annex, where Oriku announced to Kinosuke, "Here's the partner I've chosen for you: the kabuki actor Ichikawa Monju. I trust you can make do with him."

"Make do? Why, he's so young and handsome, I'm the one who should feel ashamed!"

"He thinks highly of you too, you know," Oriku went on, further to fuel the flames. "Your Shigenoi brought tears to his eyes. He says he was thoroughly impressed."

Oriku saw no more of the pair that night; but the thought of Kinosuke, still a virgin at twenty-nine, put her in no mood to smile at the sorrowful destiny that weighs upon women. Some, like herself, end up married without ever having experienced love in any way, while misfortune leaves others virgins far too long. Would Kinosuke have been happier learning the ways of men long ago, or was she even more fortunate to have learned this late in life? At any rate, Oriku prayed for her happiness, and the next morning she let the pair leave without seeing them again. It was Ofune who told her they had gone.

"They asked me to greet you for them, Mistress Oriku. Have they been together like that long?"

Ofune had noticed nothing, and of course Oriku herself remained silent, worrying that her intervention might only have caused unhappiness.

Kinosuke turned up two days later, late in the evening. She was red-cheeked, apparently from a few drinks.

"I'm so sorry for all the worry I've caused you," she said. "I'm so happy, just so happy, now that I know I'm really a woman!"

"What are you talking about? Wasn't that always obvious?"

"Yes, but until that evening two days ago I wondered whether I might not actually be a woman without an opening."

"I beg your pardon? A woman without an opening?"

"People say that. They call a woman who can't function as one a 'woman without an opening.' Everyone used to say that about me." At the age of twenty-nine she still took this insult very seriously.

"So did you turn out to have an opening after all?"

"Yes, I did."

"And did Monju manage to find it?"

"Yes, he did." She never cracked a smile. Oriku quaked inwardly with mirth, but Kinosuke's utter seriousness kept her from laughing.

"Thank you very, very much! I'm so glad all the fog of all those years is gone, and I'm not defective after all, that these past two days I've been drinking from morning till night."

"You can't possibly perform if you're drinking that much."

"No, so I've told them I'm sick, and I won't be working for a while. I just can't tell you how grateful I am." She had tears in her eyes. Her gratitude for that single night was sufficiently plain. Perhaps this was somewhat foolish of her, but after all those years spent without ever a chance to know a man, she had at last experienced a real one, in the flesh. Constantly frustrated in her desire, the poor thing had come secretly to suspect that she was no longer a fully functioning human being: a plight that actually afflicts many a woman. Oriku had done well to intervene, and with Monju there would be no complications. Her purchase of four or five performance tickets from him closed the affair. Kinosuke had tested herself with a stylish young man, and she had passed with flying colors.

Mightily pleased with this success, Oriku was considering a bit of a party for her when, ten days or so later, Kinosuke arrived, elegantly dressed. Her hair was done as usual in a formal, upswept style, but she was wearing a light purple, crested kimono.

"Thank you again for the other day," she said. "I've been on a little trip to Osaka." She had brought Oriku a gift of hard candies.

"What were you doing in Osaka?"

"Actually, I'm going to be married." Kinosuke gave Oriku her most formal, most humble bow.

"Well, *that* was sudden, wasn't it?"

"No, it wasn't. The negotiations had been under way for quite some time."

"Quite some time? Since when?"

"Since last year."

"Last year? So what in the world gave you the idea of amusing yourself with Monju?" Oriku had gone pale. She felt as if everything she had done so seriously had made her look rather a fool.

"Well, you see. . ." Kinosuke seemed to have trouble going on.

"You see, last month my fiancé committed himself to the marriage, but, as I told you, everyone was calling me a woman without an opening, so I just didn't know whether I could really do it. I didn't think I could face life anymore if I got married and then found out I wasn't a functioning woman. That's what finally made me bring the matter up with you. I'm sorry. Please don't be angry. It was a stupid thing to do, to go with another man before getting married, but I wanted to find out if my own body worked. I shouldn't have done it, but at least I got my confidence back. So today I came to apologize."

She was almost in tears. Her reasoning was certainly unusual, but it made sense.

"I knew a future bride shouldn't do such a thing, but without that confidence I wouldn't have felt like going through with it. You're the only person who knows, Mistress Oriku. It's what gave me the courage. It was the only way I could find out. Please forgive me. Please pretend it never happened." She pressed her forehead to the floor and wept.

"Do you plan to stop performing once you're married?"

"I'll decide that once I've moved to Osaka."

"Is your fiancé an artist too?"

"Yes, he is."

"A gidayū chanter, like you?"

"Yes. He's a disciple of Master Kōtsubodayū."

"So you met him when he performed at the Azumabashi Theater?"

"That's right."

"Confound it! You *are* making a fool of me!"

"I'm sorry. Please don't scold me!"

"I'm not scolding you, but for pity's sake, when you then began making such a pest of yourself, coming onto me the way you did, what kind of act was *that*?"

"What a horrid thing to say! It *wasn't* an act! I love you, Mistress Oriku, and if you could find it in your heart to love me, I'd break off my engagement this minute."

"You're crazy!" This time it was Oriku's turn to be angry. Still, Kinosuke had only been confused because she had lost her self-confidence, and it was natural enough that at twenty-nine she should want to get married.

"I'll say no more," Oriku continued. "I'll gladly celebrate your wedding. See that you become a good wife."

"Thank you. I hesitate to ask for any more favors, but actually I have something else to ask of you."

"Oh no, not again! What is it this time?"

"You see, neither of my parents is alive, and my fiancé has lost his parents too. Master Kōtsubodayū is acting as his father, but on my side, Mistress Oriku, I have absolutely no one but you to act in a counterpart manner for *me*."

"What are you talking about? There you go again, leading me on with your sweet talk."

"It's *true*, though, I have absolutely no one else to act as my mother."

"Have you ever heard of a mother procuring her daughter a man?"

"I'm so sorry. You make me feel very small."

"You'd better not ask me to do it again."

"I won't, ever. I promise." Kinosuke's tone was imploring.

After all this Oriku could not bring herself to say no, and with great reluctance she agreed. At it happened, the Bunraku Theater troupe was just then up from Osaka, doing a major performance run at the Kabuki-za. Kōtsubodayū was therefore in Tokyo, and Kinosuke's

fiancé, Sugitayū, was there with him. Kōtsubodayū's legal name was
Kanesugi Yatarō, and the young man had therefore taken the "sugi"
from his teacher's name to form his own stage name.

A letter came from Kōtsubodayū. Apparently those concerned had
decided that it would be too much trouble to hold the wedding in
Osaka, what with all the niceties of procedure and protocol involved,
and that the thing to do was hold it in Tokyo, instead, during the
troupe's current run. The planning for the event was therefore under
way. The letter, beautifully written in the most formally correct style,
began with the usual apology for having remained so long out of
touch and went on to thank Oriku for the service she was about to
render Sugitayū. On the subject of Oriku acting for Kinosuke *in loco
parentis*, he wrote, "In view of your great kindness, I have in mind
also to engage the Shigure Teahouse for the wedding ceremony itself.
I realize that my desire in this regard may strike you as an unwelcome
imposition, but I hope that you will nonetheless see fit to grant your
consent." No problem there: Oriku had been thinking the same thing.
Only Kinosuke looked a little unhappy.

"I just don't feel right about it," she said, blushing.

"But I can't refuse a request like this from Kōtsubodayū. In the first
place, doing it here will be much cheaper. Renting anywhere else
would cost more."

"That's true, and it's extremely important."

"Here, have a look at his letter! You can see all his affection for his
disciple." She put the letter down before Kinosuke and gazed at it
fondly.

"What beautiful writing!"

"It certainly is. They say handwriting reveals character, and I feel
as though I can just *see* his." Oriku narrowed her eyes. "I've fallen in
love with him all over again, just looking at his letter."

"You're really that keen on him?"

"Yes, I am. I'm glad to do anything I possibly can for him."

"In that case, *I* should play go-between for *you*."

"You'd do that?"

"Well, just look at all the trouble I've caused you! The least I can do is try to make it up to you." Kinosuke's tone was utterly serious. She glanced back and forth between the letter and Oriku's face.

The sight of Kōtsubodayū's beautiful writing reminded Oriku how special and rare was a true master of any art, and she felt as though their paired roles in the marriage of Kinosuke to his favorite disciple bound them together with invisible threads. If the wedding was to be held here, they would surely have time for a long, quiet talk.

"I'll do it, I really will," Kinosuke assured her again. "Master Kōtsubodayū likes to have a good time too."

"And this time," Oriku said to herself, "I won't let him just leave again." In her blood she felt the same fire she had known as a young girl, and a deep joy set her heart pounding. She looked forward to the wedding day.

CHAPTER TEN

A Young Gallant in Love

The twentieth-century writer Andō Tsuruo, who was himself the son of a gidayū chanter, described the Mukōjima of Meiji times this way:

> Until Meiji, the name "Mukōjima" apparently evoked the Yaomatsu restaurant, on the river to the left after you crossed first Makura Bridge and then pretty little Shin-Koume Bridge, as well as the lights of the boats fishing there for whitebait. The rice fields before the Mimeguri Shrine were full of egrets, and flocks of red-footed gulls floated on the water between the Takeya and Imado ferry crossings . . . The path to the Hundred Flowers Garden must then have been a sheer delight.

Thus Andō described nostalgically, in his mellow style, the beauty of the Mukōjima of yore. Mukōjima was just the same in the days of the Shigure Teahouse. The egrets were gone, but the small paddy fields before the Mimeguri Shrine were still filled in autumn with nodding, golden ears of rice. In a nook beyond the paddies lived the haiku poet Kikakudō Kiichi, in a one-floor house just right for an Edo aesthete and almost maddeningly discreet amid its surroundings.

To find such scenery, you had only to cross the Sumida River. The blossoms there were of course beautiful in spring, while in summer there was boating, and fall was for moon-viewing; in winter the snowy landscape was more beautiful than anywhere else in Tokyo. The way the citizens went to Mukōjima back in Meiji to enjoy the pleasures of the four seasons showed plainly how much they loved it. The devout made their pilgrimage to the Seven Gods of Good Fortune; poets held their poetry gatherings there; and Mukōjima smiled equally on drinkers of tea and tipplers of saké. As the people of Tokyo well knew, there was a realm just across the river where you could always go for peace and spiritual refreshment, and they cherished the place accordingly. However, their confident affection could not stand against the vicissitudes of time. All too soon, a gaudy electric sign for a bathhouse and inn went up beside Chōmeiji Temple, wreaking havoc on the view.

"Can't they pass a law or something to stop people doing things like this?" Oriku asked, with a sigh and a frown. But it was too late. The establishment with the gaudy sign flourished, and soon there was talk of it adding an annex.

"Mukōjima is more or less finished, as far as I can see. The right kind of clientele won't come out here anymore, now that they're putting up rubbish like that."

"It's just not like that!" Ofune objected. "The world can't help changing. Why, in Maronouchi they've even built a theater without a hanamichi! Mukōjima can't stay the same forever." Surprisingly in touch with the times, she took it all in stride.

"The Shigure Teahouse needs the beauty of Mukōjima, though. Once the scenery's gone, we're through. At this rate, the good days will soon be over." Oriku was thoroughly pessimistic.

"I just can't see it that way. We have as many guests as ever, don't we? Look at our reservations for tonight—every room is going to be full!"

"Oh, we're still all right for the time being, but people will stop coming if they put up any more of *those* things!"

"People's tastes change with the world. With new things around, we'll get more of a new kind of guest. There's nothing whatever to worry about."

"You're certainly taking this very calmly!"

"Well, I'd feel differently about it if the restaurant was going downhill, but lately, as you know, we often have to turn guests away! Just for tonight we've had to tell three parties we were all booked up."

"That's very nice, I agree, but I wonder how long it can go on."

"What *are* you talking about? If *you*, Mistress Oriku, must be so fainthearted about it, then what are *we* supposed to do? Why don't you take a look around the rooms, instead of indulging in all these gloomy thoughts? For some time the guests in the main room have been asking what's happened to you—all of a sudden, lately, you can't be bothered to go and say hello to them. You can't go on like this!"

Oriku smiled wryly under this barrage, rose to her feet, and went to greet the guests in the main room. She assumed they were new to her, but the chief among them turned out after all to be an old habitué of the teahouse.

"Goodness, Hayashida-sensei!" The astonished Oriku put her hands to the floor in greeting.

"Don't 'sensei' *me*! I've been calling over and over for Mistress Oriku, but no, Mistress Oriku wouldn't condescend to show her face! Perhaps you'd rather have nothing to do with me, seeing I'm just a politician, here today and gone tomorrow, but I *would* appreciate at least a look at you!" He teased her mercilessly.

"Oh dear, oh dear! I had absolutely no idea you were here. No one told me! Please forgive me! I didn't know, I really didn't."

"Some favorite guest of yours here is probably here, and you didn't want to leave him. That's it, isn't it? Own up!"

"That's *not* it, not at all. You're the nicest guest I've had here in a long time, Hayashida-sensei."

"Oh no you don't! It's too late now, too late for your transparent flattery! No pardon for you, not tonight!"

"Very well! Strike me dead, then, or whatever else may please you! It'll be an honor just to have been born a woman, if I'm to die by your hand!"

"Listen to her talk!"

"Oh yes, I can talk, I can indeed, on and on! I was just getting all worked up about the way Mukōjima is changing, what with those horrible businesses opening up here, when I saw your face and felt ever so much better. Anyway, I'll beg a drink from you. You can strike me dead later, if you care to." Virtuoso that she was at the business of entertaining, she inched herself right next to him with perfect timing and urged him to drink up.

"All right, then, I'll let you off, but in exchange I won't have you go anywhere else all evening. You must stay right here with me."

"With pleasure, of course! I'll gladly stay with you, if you don't mind putting up with an old woman like me."

Oriku then sat up formally to introduce herself to Hayashida's assembled guests. "I am Oriku. Welcome to the Shigure Teahouse!"

Cabinet Secretary Hayashida Kametarō was a Seiyūkai Diet member and a writer of books on history. Known as the "Boss About Town," he was celebrated around Shinbashi and Akasaka as a politician of discerning taste. With him he had a dozen or so close associates, as well as a somewhat unusual-looking young man.

"Don't worry about *them*," Hayashida explained. "They're all intimates of mine. As for *you*, your fine for lateness is downing five or six cups of saké."

"Excellent, I'll be delighted! I trust you'll pour for me, however."

"No, that's for someone younger. Rumor has it that Oriku has lately been very keen on young men. They say all the young kabuki actors come to you to test their brush, don't they!"

"That's nonsense, Hayashida-sensei! Who's spreading this rubbish?"

"Where there's smoke, there's fire. Twenty or thirty young men have come of age under Mistress Oriku's guidance, or so I hear."

"Go ahead, then, talk! No, I'm not married, and yes, I enjoy the occasional affair, if I come across someone I like; but what's this business of my making men of children, for pity's sake?"

"Don't be so angry! Actually, those rumors have encouraged me to bring you someone a bit like that myself."

He turned to the young man at the very end of the table. "Yoshijirō," he called, gesturing, "get over here!"

The young man, so unlike all these crude-looking politician types in his becoming Japanese dress, came and sat down beside Hayashida.

"This is the actor Nakamura Yoshijirō. Keep him in mind." Hayashida casually introduced the young man.

"My name is Yoshijirō," the young man announced solemnly, his hands to the floor. "Please be good enough to remember me."

"Pleased to meet you. Let's cut the formalities. Make yourself at home."

As she spoke, Oriku kept a close eye on the young man, whose handsome face she could see only in profile. She felt as though she had heard his name before, and seen his face as well. "Nakamura Yoshijirō," she repeated. "Are you by chance the son of Daimonjiya Yoshisaburō?"

"Yes, I am. Yoshisaburō is my father."

"I knew it! I was sure I'd seen you somewhere before. You're so grown-up now."

"I suppose so."

"Years ago, you were in a youth performance at the Hōrai Theater, weren't you?"

"Yes, I was fortunate enough to be given that opportunity."

"And I'm almost certain I remember you dancing *Ame no Gorō*."

"That's right. We did the Dance of the Seven Changes, and I was Gorō. Did you see it?"

"Yes. Kodenji did Danshichi in *Natsumatsuri*, and he got me to buy a ticket from one of his fans. How old were you then?"

"Sixteen."

"And now?"

"Twenty-five."

"So it was nine years ago. Time certainly flies!"

"It does indeed." Yoshijirō gazed happily at Oriku. Utterly bored with the company of politicians whose alien interests made them impossible to talk to, he experienced meeting Oriku, familiar as she was with his past, as a kind of salvation. The Boss About Town, too, was smilingly broadly.

"Sure enough, Oriku, you *would* remember him, wouldn't you, being as mad as you are about the theater?"

"But I've seen him onstage! After dancing Ame no Gorō, he played Isonojō in *Natsumatsuri*."

"Your memory is amazing!"

"Well, you made a very appealing Isonojō. The audience was all abuzz. They loved you."

"I hardly knew what I was doing, back then!"

"I expect you were at your best as a boy. That's the way it is for all of us."

"Not necessarily. Not many really improve, though. It's been all downhill for me, I'm embarrassed to say." He lowered his eyes. Oriku had heard he was appearing lately in cheap local theaters.

"Is Yoshijirō a good dancer?" Hayashida inquired.

"He certainly is. He did Ame no Gorō beautifully. His movements were supple, his poses were beautiful. It was perfect. And he's so nice-looking, too. He's a pleasure to watch." Oriku intentionally heaped praise on him.

"If he's *that* good, Hayashida-sensei, I want to see him myself!" It was one of the Boss's associates.

"Me too!"

The Boss nodded. "I know you now, as it happens," he said, "but I've never seen you perform. There couldn't be a better time. Dance for me, then! Oriku can provide the accompaniment. Show me a dance!"

"As you wish."

"Now, Oriku, no complaints from you! You're to accompany him."

"I've no intention of complaining! I'm glad to do it, if you want, but I'm not sure I can. I don't know the nagauta music."

"You've probably learned kiyomoto, haven't you. I hear you're studying with Umekichi."

"I haven't had many lessons, though, and it's been ages since I've practiced. Everything's gone out of my head."

"Well, how about *Yasuna?*"

"Hmm, yes, I might more or less manage that. I can't do the whole thing, though."

"Never mind! Just do a little. You could start with his entrance onto the hanamichi, go on to the key bit with Old Raizan, and then skip straight to 'If you know anyone like him.'"

"All right, I can do that."

"Anyway, a dance should be kept short in an informal setting like this. Go ahead, then, with apologies for all your trouble."

"My pleasure."

So Oriku called for her samisen, and Yoshijirō danced a passage of

Yasuna. It was five years since she had done any kiyomoto, and her rendition of the entrance music was rather approximate, but Yoshijirō danced with such helpful precision that she somehow got through the lyric's opening passage:

> *Love, I implore you,*
> *let me keep my head, O love!*

This opening is so tricky that in the kiyomoto version of Yasuna the way the performer does it means success or failure for the entire piece. The Noh-style music is stately and sung in a low voice that must nonetheless carry well. After the final, long drawn-out "lo-o-ve," the song goes straight into:

> *When the winds of love*
> *blow my way they leave these sleeves*
> *all in a tangle,*
> *parting me with cruel breath*
> *from my darling girl*

Oriku sang this with great verve and gusto, while Yoshijirō continued his admirable dancing. At last Yasuna enters the stage proper, whereupon he exclaims, "What? You say my girl is here? I don't believe a word of it! You're leading me on again!" Yoshijirō took this speech himself. Then came:

> *When those jealous feelings go,*
> *they leave me at peace—*
> *ah, how very strange it is,*
> *this being in love!*

Oriku did this, alas, in falsetto; such was her penalty for having failed year after year to maintain the voice that once had come so effortlessly, until at last it would not come at all. On the other hand, during the next passage ("Apparently you've forgotten, but ever since we first met last year, in cherry blossom time, each day without news of you has meant misery for me, and every night sleepless torment") she matched her delivery carefully to the dancer's movements, so that the lines came out at last in the mellow voice developed by her gidayū training:

> *I would gladly fall asleep,*
> *yet sleep always eludes me;*
> *not that I miss sleeping much,*
> *wandering beneath the sky*

Everything went smoothly after that, all the way to the closing:

> *If you know anyone like her,*
> *take me to her, please!*
> *he cries, clutching around him*
> *all his finery,*
> *lapses into frenzied grief*
> *and sinks to the ground.*

Yoshijirō danced with spirit, then made a beautiful picture as he sank to the floor, facing away from his audience. Oriku had thrown herself totally into a performance that had captivated Yoshijirō himself.

Once his dance ended, to deafening applause, Yoshijirō bowed again and again to Oriku alone, his back to Hayashida. "Thank you," he said. "I am very grateful. Your accompaniment was wonderful. Dancing has rarely, if ever, given me such satisfaction. I cannot tell you how much I appreciate it."

"I could say the same thing," Oriku replied. "I knew you danced well, but I had no idea *how* well. I was so impressed, so carried away, that here I am all in a sweat! I'm so sorry I went falsetto in that key passage about being jealous."

"Not at all! Your skill at falsetto amazed me. Only a real professional can do that. You must have practiced a great deal."

"No, my practicing is all in the past. Umekichi was still young then, and he was a keen teacher, so I worked hard. I'm no good anymore, though."

"That's not true. It's a real shame you don't use the voice you have more often. The main thing, anyway, is that you kept your eye on my movements and sustained the rhythm. That's what did such wonders for my dancing."

"Well, there's a big difference between performing alone and performing with a dancer. The rhythm has to hold up, or the dancing loses focus, and you just can't have that."

"You must have worked at this sort of thing a great deal in your time, to know all that. I'm extremely grateful."

There's no telling how long the talk may go on when it turns to art.

"Excuse me, you two!" Hayashida hailed them from behind. "Do you think you can just go on chatting together forever? Come over here! Yes, right here! It's time for another drink."

The startled pair apologized. "I'm terribly sorry," Oriku answered. "Yoshijirō's *Yasuna* was so good, I'm simply lost in admiration."

"No, no, I was amazed by Mistress Oriku's beautiful voice."

"You both did well, yes, both of you. Now, saké! Take your cups!"

On one of the extra-large cups rested something wrapped in paper. "Oriku's rich, she doesn't need it. This is for *you*, Yoshijirō."

"Very well." Suddenly formal, Yoshijirō looked hesitantly at Oriku.

"Go on, take it! Accept Hayashida-sensei's generosity."

"I will, then. Thank you very much indeed."

"*Yasuna*'s a bit solemn, though, all by itself. How about dancing a Dodoitsu love song for us? Come on, one more!"

"By all means. Instead of a Dodoitsu, though, I'd like to do a Sanosa ballad. Excuse me, Mistress Oriku, but would you . . . ?"

"You're doing a Sanosa?"

"Yes, that's what Hayashida-sensei wants. Do you mind?"

"I'm turning into a regular music-hall orchestra!"

She picked up her samisen once more, this time to pluck the strings with her fingers, rather than the plectrum that was usually used in Sanosa. Everyone knew the words:

> *A warrior, this man,*
> *high-spirited, resolute.*
> *Harken to his name:*

Takayama Hikokurō!
There upon the Sanjō Bridge
in old Miyako,
he prostrates himself in awe
to the far-off Palace,
and his falling tears become
the Kamo River.

After dancing all this with heroic grandeur, Yoshijirō then passed straight into the next verse, to which he lent a gracefully seductive mood.

Risking life and limb
for an all-consuming love,
she is a stranger to fear.
No demon, no snake
shakes her, just a single thing:
a fickle lover,
blemished by inconstancy.
Eyes on his sleeping face
she sheds a stricken tear.

Despite his youth, he nicely calculated the space available and cultivated a charming economy of gesture. His audience was delighted.

"Yoshijirō dances beautifully," Hayashida proclaimed, "but Oriku's samisen is quite something, too. A fine performance really lifts the spirits. Who's to blame, I wonder, for not sending an artist of this caliber out into the world? And Oriku, too—for goodness' sake, don't go on wasting this treasure of yours by keeping it all to yourself!"

"I'm afraid I'm in business, though. I'm happy to perform for pleasure, but that's not something Yoshijirō can afford to do. I'm very sorry to hear he's down to dancing in local halls. These are the best years of his life, after all. It's a great shame. Can't you do something, Hayashida-sensei, can't you help him return to the Kabuki-za?"

"Hmm. I agree. His father's a kabuki actor, and he was no doubt destined for the great stage, but there's apparently some reason why he can't go back to kabuki. You know a lot more actors than I do, Oriku, and they like you. You should do something for him yourself. I'm asking you, please."

"No, no I couldn't possibly. It's none of my business, you see. He already has a famous father, Yoshisaburō, and I don't think it would be right for an outsider to intervene."

"It seems he and his father don't get along."

"That's not a reason, I'm afraid. They're father and son, after all, whatever difficulties there may be between them. Yoshijirō need only go home and apologize. That should take care of it. If he prefers to be stubborn and *not* apologize, then it's his problem. You can give him a piece of your mind on the subject, Hayashida-sensei."

"Yes, but all this is out of my field, and I'd rather not get involved. I prefer to leave Yoshijirō to you—that's why I got him to come with me tonight. Won't you take charge of him?"

"I see. So *that's* what brought you here."

"To be perfectly frank, yes. I want to return Yoshijirō to his father and have him realize his real talent. That's what he wants, too. Just have him explain it all to you. Please."

"I *was* surprised to see him among your party tonight."

"In the first place, I wanted to see what he could really do, and then I also wanted to hear you sing. In all the years I've known you, I'd never once heard you play the samisen or sing."

"Of course you hadn't. I'm not a geisha, after all."

"And happily my little plan worked, because in one fell swoop I managed both to see Yoshijirō dance and to hear you sing. Thank you again."

Hayashida sat up straight. "I am grateful for your kiyomoto performance," he said. "I entrust Yoshijirō's fortunes entirely to you. Please do what you can for him."

"Be serious, though, Hayashida-sensei! Even if I take him on, that still doesn't mean I can actually do anything for him."

"Don't say that. Look, I'm begging you most humbly. Please do it, please!"

"It's asking a lot of you, I know," Yoshijirō put in, "but please help me!" Like Hayashida, he had put his hands to the floor in supplication, and he was looking up at Oriku from there. Having both young Yoshijirō and the mighty Cabinet Secretary before her in this posture left Oriku no choice. She had to give in.

"I've no way out then, have I?" she said. Privately, however, she called to mind the face of Yoshisaburō, Yoshijirō's father.

Soon Hayashida's entire company rose to go. "I'm counting on you," he said as he left. It was Oriku he was dealing with, after all—he must have known from the start that she would hardly refuse. As for Oriku, there was no turning back now. She took Yoshijirō to her room, where they sat down face-to-face. His looks and build were both perfect for an actor. Much taller now than when she had seen him do Ame no Gorō at the Hōrai Theater, he resembled a somewhat smaller version of Uzaemon.

"Have you known Hayashida-sensei long?"

"No. I met him at the Momiji in Akasaka. The mistress of the establishment has been helping me out."

"I see. She must be Hayashida-sensei's pet, then." Oriku held up the crooked little finger of her right hand. "What's this about, then, between you and your father? As you are now, isn't it sheer impudence on your part to make an issue of this or that? Surely the proper thing would be for you just to do as he says."

"I'm sure you're right."

"I know your father, and I'd be happy to convey your apology to him. Hayashida-sensei will put in a word for you, too, and I'll go and talk to him myself, though I can't say I much like the idea."

"Thank you. It's been two years since I ran away from home, and I miss it. I'm afraid I'll lose my skill if I keep on this way, and fall into the rut of cheap theaters and provincial tours. That's what frightens me now."

"And with good reason. An artist gradually loses his ability when he no longer associates with real masters. It's the same in go, shōgi, kendō, judō, and everything else. You get better with the best, and with the mediocre you go downhill. There's nothing more frightening than that."

"I've come to understand that since I parted company with my father."

"I'm glad you noticed it sooner rather than later. You're still young, and you can quickly recover what you've lost. The world doesn't have the same regard for a kabuki actor who doesn't perform at the Kabuki-za."

"That's so true. I just can't sit still when I think that friends of mine, the same age as me, are now appearing at the Kabuki-za."

"Don't worry, then. If you mind is made up, then I'll bring your father around. Everything will be fine. Now have a drink." Ofune had meanwhile tactfully brought them saké. Yoshijirō reached for his cup.

"Before I have my drink, there's something else I need to talk to you about," he said.

"Something else?"

"Hayashida-sensei said my father and I don't get along, but that's not the issue. The problem is elsewhere."

"Good. I don't know what the matter *is*, but I won't be able to approach him if you don't tell me about it right away."

"To do that I'll have to make an embarrassing confession, and that's why I've been having trouble coming out with it. You see, I'm actually an adopted son."

"You *are*? You're not Yoshisaburō's own son?"

"No. He only has a daughter. He adopted me when I was seven. I was born in the Kansai, the son of a manager employed by the actor Ōnarikomaya. That's how my present father came to discover me and adopt me. My real parents died long ago."

"Isn't Yoshisaburō just like your real father by now, if you were seven at the time?"

"Yes, he is. My father and mother were both extremely kind to me, and I have them to thank for being here today. I've never forgotten all I owe them."

"And rightly so. It took them a lot of work to bring you up to manhood."

"However, something unfortunate happened when I was twenty-two. Apparently, they meant to marry me to their daughter, Onami, and they had long been looking forward to the wedding."

"That sounds normal enough. They wanted you and their daughter to give them grandchildren. I'd think anyone would feel that way."

"Yes, but you see, I knew nothing about it, and I'm afraid that in the meantime I'd committed myself to another woman."

"Oh dear. *That's* a problem. And your parents didn't know?"

"No. They'd never said a word to me about marrying me to Onami, and I'd grown up with her ever since we were little—we were just a year apart. I loved her as a younger sister, but the idea of marrying her had never occurred to me."

"I suppose your parents assumed they didn't have to say anything—you and Onami would naturally marry anyway."

"Very likely, but at any rate, it was a huge shock. I just couldn't believe it. So right there, to their face, I asked them for permission to marry the woman I was committed to."

"You actually did that?"

"Yes, I tried it." He hung his head dejectedly.

"I think I have the picture now. No wonder you and your father don't get along. I understand his being so angry."

"I should never have done it to him."

"You really feel that way?"

"Yes, I do."

"Well, *if* you do, then go ahead and marry Onami. Then I'm sure even he will forgive you." Oriku spoke plainly, as always, but Yoshijirō only hung his head further and became unable to go on. Difficulties over marrying a natural daughter to an adopted son are common enough in artist households.

"What kind of woman is she, the one you're involved with? She's not from the theater world?"

"No, she's a geisha."

"Still?"

"Yes. Actually she stopped for a while, because of me, but that didn't work out, so I arranged a place for her at the Momiji in Akasaka."

"Hmm. So that's how you happen to know Hayashida-sensei."

"Indeed. You see, I'm the reason she went back to being a geisha. I've made life so difficult for her, I can't just drop her now."

"Still, you can't go back to your father unless you leave her, can you? That's right, isn't it?"

"That's right."

"It's a bit much, I'd say, to think you can keep your geisha, against your father's wishes, and aspire at the same time to return to the great stage."

"I'm very sorry, I really am."

"I'm glad to further your interests, since Hayashida-sensei has asked me to, but as things stand now, I don't see what I can do. It meant a complete loss of face for your father to hear you say you didn't want Onami because you were already committed to another woman."

"Undoubtedly."

"Either you leave her and go home, or you remain loyal to love. It's one or the other: you give her up, or you give up your father. There's nothing more to talk about till you decide. There's no role I can possibly play."

"Even *you* feel that way, then, Mistress Oriku."

"It's not just me. Anyone would." Oriku had spoken with intentional bluntness, although his appealing face made it harder for her to do so.

Yoshijirō looked up again, with a resigned expression. "I understand," he said. "I'd like to think about that a little. In the meantime, may I have a drink?"

"By all means, yes, drink up! Drink and think things over. Take all the time you want. I'll think right along with you."

"I'll be very grateful."

Oriku poured for him. He downed several cups in a row, and she, swept along by his mood, did the same.

Ofune brought them more. "Will it be all right if we put out the fire in the kitchen?" she asked.

"Goodness, is it *that* late?"

"It's almost eleven."

"Really! I somehow had the feeling the evening was still young."

"At eleven o'clock it still *is* at Akasaka, but this area seems very peaceful."

"Well, yes, we're out in the country here. It's no distance to Katsushika, you know. We're at the far edge of the city."

"Still, I can't believe how quiet it is. You can really relax here."

"Have some saké. It's just been heated up."

"Thank you, I will."

"You hold your liquor well, it seems."

"I do now. We put on two new shows a month, without ever a day off, and we never get to rehearse properly, so the first performance is a real circus—out there on stage we hardly know what we're doing. We get so fed up, we drink to forget it."

"That doesn't sound good."

"That's why I'm losing my skill. If this goes on much longer, I'll turn into a down-and-out vaudeville actor."

"That'll make it even harder to do anything for you. Nothing much can be done about it, though, if you're set on being with this other woman."

"But that's not good enough, either."

"You'd better think carefully, then. I'll think with you."

"Please do."

"So have another drink. The kitchen fire has been put out, but we still have all this saké, and I can always heat some more, if you like."

"No, it's fine as it is."

Oriku had her reasons for urging him to drink. She intended to get him good and drunk. After eleven o'clock the silence of the wee hours descended on Mukōjima, and the breeze sighing in the reeds announced the approach of spring. Another month and the cherry blossoms would be out. No more long leisurely chats. The Shigure Teahouse would have to start preparing for the season when it made most of its money, and the commotion that reigned once the cherry blossom lunches went on sale would turn the place into a veritable battlefield. Yoshijirō's tedious little troubles seemed petty in comparison with the demands of running a business.

"It's not that I don't understand how you feel, but to be quite frank, it all comes down to the matter of relations with women."

"I suppose so."

"Life is far less forgiving than I am. You'll end up with nothing to eat if you don't look out. You can't forget to take that into account."

"I may starve, yes."

"So which way do you go, left or right? Isn't it time to decide?"

"Yes, it is time. I know."

"Then have another drink."

"No, thank you. I've had more than enough already."

"Don't say that! This is the time to drink as though there were no tomorrow."

"No, no, really, I've had all I can manage, absolutely all I can manage."

He was weaving back and forth as he spoke. She had succeeded during the evening in getting seven or eight flasks down him. Finally, as if the prop he had been leaning against was suddenly knocked out from under him, he missed an attempt to catch himself with his left hand and collapsed limply on the floor.

"I've had it," he said, "I can't drink any more. No more, no more." Only his lips moved.

The sight of his face as he innocently slept drew from Oriku a smile that contained equal parts irony, cruelty, and pity. Sometimes only mercilessness can resolve a dilemma beyond the reach of love. She dragged the slumbering Yoshijirō to the bedding and undressed him down to his underwear. He noticed nothing. Deeply lost to the world, he never opened his eyes, no matter what she did. Then she lay down beside him in her undergarment patterned with autumn leaves, but she found she could not sleep. The wind picked up as the night wore on, and she heard the waves lapping against the bank of the river.

In the middle of the night Yoshijirō woke up. Turning over in bed, he felt around his pillow.

"You want water?" She poured him some water, then sat him halfway up so he could drink it.

At last he realized where he was. "Ah!" he exclaimed, peering at her through the gloom.

"You thought you were in Akasaka? I'm sorry." She moved close to him and put her left arm round his neck. "Sleep, then," she said. "We can talk as much as you like tomorrow. This is what happens when you're an actor."

Oriku smiled once more. His drunken fog was half-cleared, and he did not have it in him to push her away. The young man of twenty-five and the middle-aged woman in her forties were soon locked in close embrace. Out went the lamp at the head of the bed.

Oriku awoke fairly early the next morning. As usual, she went straight to the bath, then prepared Yoshijirō's breakfast and roused him. Somewhat shamefacedly, he, too, took a bath, after which he put on a padded kimono and sat down to eat. He kept his eyes lowered and could not bring himself to look her in the face.

"Good morning," he said.

"It's not that early. In fact, it's past eleven. Are you all right as far the theater is concerned?"

"Yes, it's closed this month. Next month we're off on another tour."

"So you can't even be seen on an Edo stage in blossom time?"

"I'm sorry."

"Well, take your time, then, if your theater's closed. I thought you might like beer this morning. Aren't you thirsty?"

"Thank you. I'm parched." He sat up very correctly, as though to continue last night's conversation, and drank with evident relish the beer Oriku had poured for him. Breakfast was the Shigure Teahouse standard: Kōya tōfu and shiitake mushrooms simmered together, rolled omelet with a touch of shigure clam, miso soup with wakame seaweed, and pickles. The clean taste of all this felt good on the palate. Yoshijirō ate and drank reverently. After two or three glasses he was red in the face.

"There's nothing like the taste of beer in the morning," he remarked. He put down his empty glass and from the veranda gazed out at a passing sailboat. "I had no idea the river was this close!"

"It is, though. I filled in a bit of riverside marsh to build this place, and the river runs right by it."

"Ah, there are some red-footed gulls flying about."

"They come every day. Old Tomé, the watchman, puts out the guests' leavings for them, so a lot of them turn up at this time. They get whatever the guests don't eat—sashimi, broiled fish, and so on. It's quite a feast."

White wings spread wide, they flew, calling, around the garden, catching the scraps. Tomé was apparently standing out behind the main building, basket in hand, and the gulls were flocking to him.

"They gather immediately when Tomé comes out—they recognize the human who feeds them. It's their life, after all. People are just the same. They can either live off the fat of the land, or put up with living in poverty—that's what makes all the difference." She was using the gulls to tease him.

Yoshijirō returned to his seat with a cloudy expression on his face.

"I thought and thought while you were asleep," Oriku went on, "and all I could come up with was that you just can't go on this way. You must realize that yourself."

"I do." His voice was very low.

"This dilemma of yours over women—whether to choose your geisha or Onami—is only secondary. The one thing you really have to consider is where you want to go as an actor. You needn't even think about anything else." She was pressing him as hard as she possibly could.

"Right now you're in love, and that's skewing your judgment. You simply can't afford that. Your first concern should be to do what you need to do to appear onstage at the Kabuki-za. You'll end up wasting your life if you don't drop every other consideration. Down deep, I'm sure you agree."

"Yes, I do."

"Well then, you must subordinate everything else to that one goal. Understand? Your aim is to perform at the Kabuki-za, and you're going to sweep aside anything that stands in your path. Put it down to callousness, by all means."

"Callousness?"

"You know what I'm talking about. You're going to leave your girl-friend, go home to your father, and join the Kabuki-za. Let her go, and I'm sure your father will forgive you."

"No doubt you're right. I just couldn't do it, though."

"You really *are* thick, aren't you!" Oriku purposely raised her voice. "That's why I keep telling you your goal is the Kabuki-za, and you can put the rest down to callousness. Leave her, put up with your conscience, and marry Onami. That's what you have to do."

"That would be fine, of course, if only I *could*."

"Shall I go to the Momiji and talk to the proprietor there myself, if it's too hard for you?"

"No, please don't do that."

All at once, Yoshijirō's expression changed. "I'm extremely sorry, but no, I will not leave her." His voice was high and tense—that of a man who has reached his final decision.

Oriku just scoffed. "You won't leave her, even if that means your sinking to the dregs of the theater world."

"I will not leave her." By now he was deathly pale.

"I see. You're telling me straight out, to my face, that you refuse to leave her. Is that right?" Oriku's voice, too, was suddenly different. "Then what did you mean by sleeping with me, if you love her that much? No doubt I'm older than you, but I never said a word to seduce you. No, *you're* the one who laid hands on me. I stayed with you because you were so drunk, and I didn't want to leave you to suffer alone. That's what happened, right? So there you are, with a girlfriend you value more than your life, yet you laid hands on another woman. What is *that* supposed to mean? Your life is hers, but your little affairs on the side are something else? And you call yourself an actor? You certainly know how to indulge yourself, don't you?" Oriku's face had changed color as well. She knew no mercy now.

"Talk big if you like," she continued, "but I'll have nothing to do with it. I'll tell Hayashida-sensei the whole story, and the Momiji lady, too. I'll let them know in my way exactly what happened. You'd better remember that." She let him have it full blast and rose to go.

Sure enough, Yoshijirō slipped in panic off his cushion, the more humbly to beg her pardon. "Spare me!" he begged. "Please! I apologize!"

"Spare you what? Apologize for what?"

"Please, please, at least don't tell Hayashida-sensei!"

"What are you saying? Why, the nerve! I offer you an acting career at the Kabuki-za, and you have the cheek to tell me you'll keep your girlfriend instead? I've changed since yesterday evening, you know! Yesterday evening I was a chazuke restaurant owner, but I'm your woman now. No doubt you have a number of them, but as for me, I have no husband or anything like one, and I'm free to do exactly as I please. I'm keeping you here after this. Get this straight: you're going nowhere. Take one step outside, and I go right to Hayashida-sensei."

Quite intentionally, she sounded as harsh as a yakuza boss. Yoshijirō shrank and trembled before her. He kept his hands and face to the floor, and his shoulders shook.

"You don't go out, you hear me? Not one step! You're Oriku's husband now. Your acting days are over."

Next, she summoned Ofune.

"I want you to tidy up the upper floor and make it habitable," she said. "This gentleman will be living there." She spoke loudly on purpose. Ofune's eyes were wide with amazement when she left.

Yoshijirō was as white as a sheet. "Mistress Oriku," he said, "I beg your pardon, I beg your pardon!"

Finally he looked up. "I'll do it," he went on. "Please forgive me! Please, please forgive me!"

"Do it? Do what?"

"I'll leave her and return to Shintomichō." His voice was shaking, and he seemed close to tears. Shintomichō was where Yoshisaburō and Onami lived.

"You mean that?"

"Yes, I mean it. I'll do it, I'll join the Kabuki-za."

"I won't have you sneaking out just to evade my threats!"

"I won't be sneaking out! I'm not saying this because of your threats! My choice between vaudeville and the great kabuki stage has nothing whatsoever to do with you."

"You're right enough about *that*!"

"Talking to me as you've done, you've at last gotten it through to me how much you want to make an actor of me. I'd be no man at all if I still refused to change my mind, when even you, who have little reason to care one way or the other, feel that strongly about it. I'll never go back to Akasaka. I know I'll waver if I ever see her again, so I'll be a brute, yes, and stop it right now. I'm going straight back to Shintomichō. Would you kindly come with me?"

"You're going right now?"

"Yes."

"You're sure?"

"I'm sure. Please come with me." He bowed to her again, hands to the floor, and burst into tears.

◆   ◆   ◆

Oriku had done everything to set Yoshijirō on the right course because she hated to see his ability go to waste. She had wanted save this young actor with a bright future, and she had judged that the only way to do this was to spend a night with him. Behind the wish to keep such talent from going astray, there also lurked a degree of attraction to Yoshijirō's youthful good looks.

Yoshijirō soon turned up on the Kabuki-za stage. His apology to Yoshisaburō, his adoptive father, worked, and a certain industrialist acted as the go-between for his marriage to Onami. At the Kabuki-za, he played the comic tōfu buyer at the palace in the "Goten" scene of *Imoseyama*. This major role, performed in the company of such masters as Utaemon (playing Omiwa) and Uzaemon (playing Fuka-shichi) was offered to him to celebrate his return. As to the Akasaka woman, Hayashida undertook to speak to her, and with many tears she renounced her claim to Yoshijirō.

Oriku saw no one after that. She spoke to Yoshisaburō only on the telephone and never visited him. She had no wish to go there; if she did, she might see Yoshijirō. Of course she had meant to settle the matter once and for all, but she would never have resorted to such forceful tactics with someone she disliked. No, it was true enough that she had a soft spot for him. The clincher had been a trick of hers only in retrospect; at the time, she had really meant it. The same was true of the trap she had laid to get him home. It was also just as well that she had not known what kind of geisha the Akasaka woman really was. She had never needed to become involved in that direction. Hayashida-sensei had taken care of it.

Everything went according to plan, and the wedding reception was held at the Seiyōken restaurant in Tsukiji. Oriku, too, received an invitation. The corner of the printed card bore the small, brush-written message, "Please come if you possibly can. Yoshijirō." Should she go, or not? Her hesitation betrayed the lingering spell of that night with him. She had no wish to see any man she had been fond of, even for a single night, beside his bride at his wedding. Still, she detected deep feeling in Yoshijirō's little note. It *would* be nice to see him again, though perhaps from a distance, so she answered that she would be there. The gift she sent was very like her, and, on the day, she arrived punctually at the Seiyōken. She felt uncomfortable sitting at a table to eat Western food, so she dressed as discreetly as possible and aimed to take a safely obscure seat.

Alas, her designated place was at the main table, right across from the bride and groom. Onami's downcast gaze made her face a little difficult to see properly, but she seemed pretty and thoroughly suitable for Yoshijirō. The go-between introduced the bride and groom in the customary manner, and the meal followed. Then dessert was served, and the guests' speeches began. The master of ceremonies called first on "The Cabinet Secretary, the Honorable Hayashida Kametarō." Looking quite unlike anyone's idea of an "Honorable," Hayashida-sensei rose to his feet with a wry smile and briefly pronounced the usual pleasantries. At the end, however, he added some unexpected remarks.

"Ladies and gentlemen," he said, "as you know, circumstances led the groom, Yoshijirō, to spend some time estranged from his father. However, he has returned with flying colors to the Kabuki-za, and now we have had the privilege of celebrating his wedding with Onami, his bride. All this is due to a hitherto unsung heroine. Distressed to see Yoshijirō languishing on the outer fringes of the theater world, she warned him half as a threat and half as encouragement that, unless he went back to the Kabuki-za, he would spend the rest of his life down among the dregs. The outcome was the ceremony that has brought us together today. This unsung heroine is none other than Mistress Oriku, the proprietor of the Shigure Teahouse at Mukōjima."

The astonished Oriku practically fell off her chair.

"Stand up, Oriku, stand up!" Hayashida-sensei urged her. "Say a few words!"

He sat down, and the gathering burst into loud applause. Oriku *had* to stand up. It was all so sudden that no words came to her, and she blushed scarlet. "My congratulations to you both," she finally managed to say. "Hayashida-sensei called me a heroine, but it's not that way at all. Being a great fan of Yoshijirō's, I thought it would be too bad if he stayed where he was. I just encouraged him to return to the great stage. This is so embarrassing! Please forgive me if I say no more." That was all. With a little bow, she sat down again, her face still fiery red.

Thunderous applause and laughter resounded once more. Hayashida-sensei clapped merrily, and even more so the newlyweds, who meanwhile watched her intently. Amid all the clapping, it seemed to her that the sound of Yoshijirō's applause rang out above the rest.

CHAPTER ELEVEN

A Cloud of Blossoms

The Shigure Teahouse earned much of its annual income while the cherry trees blossomed along the embankment. Looking up into them in the early morning, you would glimpse amid the swelling buds a few blossoms just beginning to open, wet with the morning mist and glittering in the light. The spectacle they offered was truly beautiful. Oriku arose before anyone else when the trees came into flower, at an hour when there was still no one to be seen along the embankment. It gave her an indescribable pleasure to walk alone beneath the silent blossoms, with only a pale light in the eastern sky and no curtains hanging yet in the teashop doorways. To the tunnel of fully opened flowers she preferred, as the most beautiful of all, the time when about a third remained in bud; for cherry blossoms start falling almost the moment they open, and that morning when they first unfold is like a dream. She walked as far as Kototoi, gazing up at the new blossoms heavy with dew. The faint light of dawn glimmered from the water of the river, and mist veiled the far bank. She sat down at a deserted teashop, had a smoke, and tasted the good fortune of living at Mukōjima. People began appearing here and there while she absently contemplated the water and the flowers. She was not the only sensitive soul to cherish cherry blossoms at dawn. Some others came strolling along with their saké in an old-fashioned gourd. These were the kind that would strike up a conversation with Oriku, just as someone did today.

"You're out here on the embankment awfully early—you must prefer the flowers at dawn." He went on, "It's so crowded here once the sun is up, you can hardly even walk, and it's impossible to enjoy the blossoms. Dawn is best. There are no tiresome noises, and the flowers are wet with dew. There's nothing better than looking up at them while you have a drink. What do you say? Won't you have one, too?"

Already pleasantly tipsy, he held out a lacquered cup. Oriku did not actually want a drink, but she was happy to have run into someone who shared her feelings. "Thank you," she said. "I know a woman isn't supposed to drink saké in the morning, but perhaps the flowers are a good enough excuse. Yes, please."

"You'll have one? Wonderful! Any friend of the flowers is a friend of mine. By all means have two, or three, or any number." He happily poured Oriku her drink. This was the sort of pleasure you could enjoy for a moment only, near dawn. People crowded in from everywhere once the sun was up, and soon the place was bedlam. Only at dawn was it paradise on earth.

At the Shigure Teahouse, the Cherry Blossom Bentō was already on sale, and the kitchen was a hive of activity. Oriku worked there too, her sleeves tied up out of the way for work. Dawn was the only time she *could* view the blossoms, and accepting saké from a total stranger was a pleasure the blossoms alone could give her.

"Isn't their color just *perfect*? Don't you think cherry blossoms with the dew still on them at dawn are the most beautiful of all?"

"Of course I do. I can't understand all those people who hardly look at them and come just to join the crowd. Not that I'd wish to speak ill of them, since they buy from me."

"Aha! So you're in business here on the embankment?"

"Yes, it's just a few hundred yards away, below the embankment— a chazuke restaurant."

"A chazuke restaurant? Not the Shigure Teahouse, surely?"

"Yes, that's it. You have to be lucky enough to live at Mukōjima to enjoy the blossoms like this at dawn."

"That's right. And to meet the mistress of the Shigure Teahouse here is even better luck. I've always wanted to meet you, and it's really extraordinary that the dawn blossoms should have brought us together!" He could not get over it. "I'm not going to let you go, now that I know you're Mistress Oriku of the Shigure Teahouse. Here, have another."

"Thank you, with pleasure."

"I've only heard about your place—I've never actually been there. They say you go all the way to Ise to buy your clams."

"Yes, I do. That's my restaurant's specialty, after all. And you— what business are *you* in?"

"Ah, yes, I apologize for not having introduced myself. I have a little drinking spot called Sanshi, next to Azuma Bridge."

"Goodness, so you're Sanshi! I'm delighted to meet you. I've been there a few times."

"Really? I had no idea!"

"It's a nice place. I've never had better shijimi shellfish soup anywhere. I'd already eaten dinner when I tasted it, but I really enjoyed it. It's the best in Japan, no doubt about it."

"Now, now, you're embarrassing me. I've never even tasted your shigure chazuke, and here you are carrying on this way about my soup! I can only blush. Thank you, though, for your kind patronage."

"Don't mention it. I'm hardly enough of a patron that you need to thank me. The name Sanshi, 'Three Strings,' is unusual, though. There's a story behind it, I suppose?"

"Yes. Customers often ask me that too. I used to play the samisen, so I just named my place for the instrument's three strings."

"Sure enough! That name made me wonder whether you might once have been a musician, and I was right. What kind of music did you play?"

"Please don't ask. By now I'm sorry I chose the name—it brings back painful memories. On another subject, though, would you mind if I came to your place and tried your shigure chazuke? Or is it too early in the day for that?"

"No, not at all. I'll be glad to have you. In blossom season we don't offer our regular menu, though. Instead, we make what we call a Cherry Blossom Bentō—a box lunch arranged so as to be nice and easy to eat. It has clams in it, so you can have chazuke afterwards, if you like."

"Better and better! I assume it's made up in advance, if it's a bentō. Isn't that right?"

"I doubt that today's bentō are ready yet, but do come anyway. You can at least have a look around the garden."

Oriku had just dashed some water on her face that morning and set off on an empty stomach, so the saké she had drunk was having a fine effect as she led Sanshi drowsily along beneath the blossoms. Sanshi's place at Azuma Bridge was a sit-down drinking spot and eatery specializing in light, Edo-style seafood dishes. In this it was the opposite of the Shigure Teahouse, which kept to freshwater fish. Sanshi himself, the former samisen musician, had about him the compact sort of elegance one would expect of a former artist. He was fifty or so, and his speech conveyed a certain distinction. He also had something of the artist's flirtatious manner and appeal.

The Shigure Teahouse people had only just arisen and opened the rooms, but the making of bentō in the kitchen went on all night, in shifts, so that the fire there was as high as during the day. More and more Cherry Blossom Bentō sold every year. Some customers even came for it from far away, and it always sold out, no matter how much they made. The Shigure Teahouse's Cherry Blossom Bentō was famous for its exceptional quality, and after eleven o'clock the place was packed with bentō customers. When, this morning, Oriku set down a freshly made bentō before him, Sanshi gazed at it a while before eating.

"Ah, that's just beautiful!" he said. "A bentō as fine as that really isn't a bentō at all anymore. This is simply splendid. There are delicacies to go with the saké, you can have shigure chazuke, and you haven't forgotten to put in something sweet, too. I'm very impressed." He picked up his chopsticks and began tasting the food. He ate slowly, and when he had finished took a tour of the garden.

"You must have spent a lot of money on this garden!" he exclaimed. "Just bringing in all the fill must have cost a lot. Surely you're not making all this back by selling bentō."

"You're right. It's half for my own pleasure, so for me those initial expenses don't count. I'd never get anywhere if they did. No, I've given up on them."

"Now I understand why you have such a fancy place. I'd like to put a little more money into mine, too. With a sit-down bar there's only so far you can go. This place of yours makes me very, very envious." Everything hit the spot with him—the food, the garden, the layout of the rooms, everything.

"Here you've gone and made such a beautiful garden," he said, "but do you know they're planning to put up a horrible factory right next to it?" He pointed to the edge of the garden. To the right was the river, while marshland stretched behind them. The garden to the south of the restaurant also backed onto marsh, which lay abandoned, since it filled with water whenever it rained. Beyond the marsh was a boathouse.

"Where's the factory going to be, exactly?"

"Right in front of you, there. The site is marshy now, but they're already filling in next to the boathouse."

"Really?"

"I can hardly believe you haven't noticed, when you're here right next door. After all, the boat factory's to be extended very close to you."

"What? A boat factory?"

"That's right. And there's to be a shoe factory as well. There's a small one already, but I gather it, too, is going to be enlarged. Right now it's behind the Kototoi dango shop. It's been there for a while, but in the flood the year before last the water came up to its roof, so they're building up the site higher and enlarging it. I imagine it'll be a pretty good size."

"Are you *sure*?"

"A friend of mine works at the boat factory. He comes to drink at my place now and again, and he was talking about how they're going to enlarge the factory, so I think it's true."

"I wonder how far it's going to come?" Oriku strained toward him. Even a simple electric sign put up at beautiful Mukōjima to advertise a bathhouse made her furious, but this business of a shoe factory and a boat factory was something else again. Naturally she found it revolting.

"What do they think Mukōjima is, anyway? There are all kinds of places out there to build a factory. They don't have to come and do it *here*!"

"Yes, but actually there have been factories here for ages. It's a bit late to complain about them now. Trees and shrubbery have grown up around them, so you can't see them from the embankment anymore, but when you go down and have a look at them, they turn out to be surprisingly large."

"Well, all right, they're there already, and that's that. But couldn't people at least give a thought to the real character of Mukōjima?"

"I quite agree. I myself got upset with the man who was telling me, and demanded to know why anyone would put up something so barbarous at Mukōjima, where people come from far and wide to see the cherry blossoms. He said being right on the river is perfect for transportation—they can bring in the raw materials and send off the finished product by boat. They'll be building factories all around here, he said, as though it meant nothing to him. It'll ruin the charm of your garden to have a big factory chimney poking up from right next to it."

"Mukōjima is practically a park! No one builds a factory in a park. Isn't there some way to stop this?" She was all worked up by now; but then the sun rose, the weather was fine for once, and the buds would no doubt be opening today. Besides, after ten o'clock the place would be busy again.

"We ended up straying a long way from cherry blossoms at dawn, but I have to thank you for a wonderful morning. I hope I'll be able to come back soon, though I don't quite know when that will be. Anyway, I'll be praying in the meantime for your continued success."

"Goodness, don't talk so gloomily, now that we've finally met! You *must* come back. I'll come to your place too. Things will be much quieter once the flowers are over."

"No, no, my place hardly deserves a special visit. Please forget about that. Well, I must be going." He took out a blue-dyed deerskin wallet with a floral design to pay for the bentō, and he held out another sum, separately wrapped in paper. "I'm embarrassed to offer so little," he said, "but this is for the maids and the kitchen."

"Oh no, I can't possibly have you doing *that* to me! I really must refuse."

"Don't say that! You *must* let me do this much—we're both in the same business, after all. It's no more than a token."

It was just like a true son of Edo to claim being in the same trade as a reason for sending a little something to the kitchen. Oriku accepted it with thanks and accompanied Sanshi to the foot of the embankment. The buds of a short while ago were now two-thirds open and glowing in the morning sun.

Sanshi looked up at the flowering branches. "Aren't they beautiful?" he murmured as though to himself. "This is the perfect moment, considering they begin to fall as soon as they open. Two-thirds in bloom—for people as well as flowers, that's the best time of all."

He looked back at Oriku, then disappeared as though swallowed by the clouds of blossoms. Oriku stood there a moment after he was gone. They had only just parted, yet she felt as though she had dreamed the whole morning. She could hardly believe this man Sanshi was real. The folded paper he had given her turned out, when she opened it, to contain five one-yen bills. This was quite a tip for a one-yen bentō—far too much, in fact, even for a colleague in the trade. Everything had only just happened—the sight of him drinking saké from a gourd under the cherry trees, his praise for the Cherry Blossom Bentō, his kind warning about the new factory—and already it was fading back into the mists. She was sure she had been dreaming, yet the five yen in her hand were real enough.

She gave the money to Ofune and Shigezō. "There aren't many customers anymore who tip the chef! It's very kind of him," Shigezō said; and Ofune, "It's embarrassing to get this much for a Cherry Blossom Bentō!" Both were at once astonished and delighted.

"He's the owner of Sanshi, that place at Azuma Bridge. When the blossoms are over I'm going over there to thank him." Oriku went to sit by the hearth. The bentō customers were beginning to appear. There were parties of women intent on avoiding the worst of the crowds, and old people who had purposely skipped breakfast, the better to enjoy their cherry blossom lunch.

This was the third year the Shigure Teahouse had been selling its Cherry Blossom Bentō, and the fame of the bentō had spread.

Telephone orders from distant places were now quite common. The kitchen hired temporary help and kept going day and night, in shifts. No one complained, since the profit was divided up among everyone once the blossom season was over.

Each year, Oriku adjusted the contents of the bentō and added new, sophisticated touches. This year's contained grilled miso sweetened with sugar and saké; small river fish simmered in a sweet sauce; and rolled egg dotted with tiny dried shrimp. All in all the new bentō tasted much better than last year's, and the quantity was generous too. At one yen it was very reasonably priced. Tokyo people are remarkably fond of bentō. Talk of an excursion, bentō in hand, always delights children and grown-ups alike. Since people prefer homemade over store-bought, Shigezō put in lots of sugar and made sure the flavors were all rich and full, so that the bentō would not seem commercial.

The customers noted these efforts and appreciated them, and at the height of the blossom season the bentō sold like mad. The price was the same as last year, but without the saké; instead, the box was bigger and held more, since it had turned out that a surprising number of customers did not drink. The blossoms themselves remained the same, of course, but the crowds kept growing, and on Sunday the bentō-buyers had to line up to make their purchase. The restaurant's main room might as well have been on fire, it was in such an uproar. Neither Oriku nor Ofune ever had time to sit down. They had done well to give up including the saké, since the drinkers bought some anyway, and the nondrinkers just kept coming. The parade of customers went on and on.

Quiet suddenly descended as sunset approached, and the exhausted Oriku sat herself down by the hearth.

"How about bringing me a drink? My feet and my back are killing me."

Ofune plopped down beside her. "You're not the only one, Mistress Oriku. My whole body's about to give in. The maids and the kitchen help are dead tired too."

"It was quite a day, it certainly was. Tell me, Ofune—how do *you* feel about having to work this hard? If we go on this way, we'll wreck ourselves just for a bit of profit, and we'll regret it forever after. Let's skip the whole next year." Her aching back and legs made her feel that discouraged.

"How can you say that? That's business, isn't it? You have to be grateful for having plenty to do." Ofune was always upbeat like that. "Making money or not isn't what concerns me. I'm just glad when the place does well. If you don't want to do it anymore, then don't. *I'm* not quitting!"

"But this is going to go on for another *month*!"

"Another month, yes, but there won't be so many people when the flowers are gone. There'll be far fewer once the leaves are out. We really have only two weeks to suffer through. Surely we can bear up for two weeks a year. If you prefer not to continue, Mistress Oriku, then by all means take it easy. We'll do it." Ofune looked distinctly annoyed, so much so that it was hard to tell who was the proprietor and who the employee. For fifteen days the whole place worked itself into a lather, but once the flowers were gone, and they renamed their product Shigure Bentō, temporary help was no longer required.

The name changed, but not the content, and the bentō sold very well. It remained on sale till May. Then there came at last a succession of quiet days, and the rainy season arrived. When it was over the heat came rushing in, and once more the Shigure Teahouse was filled with guests seeking the cool air of the river. However, that single rainy season month provided a welcome respite, for there were hardly any guests, and all the establishments around Mukōjima were deserted. In the meantime Oriku went to theaters and music halls, and discharged various social obligations.

One day before the end of the rainy season, in a side room, Ofune came across a guest she did not know. Once the blossom season was past, almost everyone who turned up was an old habitué, and there were no new faces to speak of.

"Do you know this man?" Ofune asked, showing Oriku his calling card with a puzzled look. It read: "Kosugi Eiji, Permanent Director, Mukōjima Boat Factory."

"Never heard of him. What's the Mukōjima Boat Factory?"

"You're the only one unaware of it, Mistress Oriku. It's always been there. It's just below us on the river, next to the Kototoi boathouse. You can't see it from the embankment, though."

"I hate it, this whole business—whether it be a boat factory or a shoe factory. I don't want to meet any such person."

"But he's a guest here, you know. You have to. It's your job to greet the guests—all of them, not just the ones you like."

"All right, I'll go. That's all I have to do, right?"

She stumped off to the back room, where she found a party of three men already quite jolly with drink. She had assumed, because they were from the boat factory, that they would be in clownish suits, but no, all three were in annoyingly tasteful Japanese dress—two in hakama and one without. Her plan was to greet them perfunctorily and then leave again, but the middle-aged one who identified himself as Kosugi detained her.

"We've never met," he said, "but I look forward every year to your Cherry Blossom Bentō. I've always wanted to come here just once, but I gather your guests are so distinguished that I never dared. Tonight, though, I finally got up the courage. Your place and mine are so close, I hope this won't be the last time." He spoke crisply, like a true son of Edo.

"I'm so out of touch with everything, I'd never heard of your place. So there's a boat factory near here?"

"Why, I'm shocked! You're so near the boat factory, and you've never even heard of it? You're a case of 'pitch-dark at the foot of the lighthouse,' aren't you!"

"It's really too bad," one of his colleagues put in. "We're right next door, after all. There's just a stretch of marshy ground between us. Our factory was there long before your restaurant."

"It *was*?"

"Yes, and Mr. Nishimura's shoe factory has been there since 1870. That's more than forty years ago!"

"It's really that old?"

"It certainly is. It started out making army boots, but general demand has been increasing steadily lately, and the factory's been growing every year. It seems they're about to expand it again."

"So I heard. Expanding it is fine, of course, but Mukōjima will be ruined if there's to be a chimney right at the end of my garden."

"I'm sure we'll do all we can not to spoil the view. The river here offers rare transport convenience, though, and I'm sure there will be more factories in the future. We're about to enlarge our boat factory too. It'll be right next to your place. I hope you can see your way to not giving us a hard time. In exchange, our two hundred workers will be happy to use your place for their meetings and parties. I understand that you object to anything so crude, but this is what goes with the march of civilization, and I hope you can manage to accept it. Well, that wasn't by any means what I meant to talk with you about. Please forgive me, and have at least one drink with us?"

Smiling ingratiatingly, he held out a cup with a practiced gesture. Oriku no longer had the heart to be angry. She had felt a flash of rage when Kosugi had talked of the march of civilization and all but announced the construction of more factories, but she understood as she listened that the world was changing, and she lamented that she herself was growing old.

"Construction on the factory extension will begin soon," Kosugi finally said, sitting up straight, "and I am afraid it will be rather noisy for a while. We will do our best, but I hope you will be good enough to understand."

That *did* cause a shadow to pass across Oriku's face. If that was what he had come to tell her, then the factory would indeed be going up, and there would be hammering and banging every day. All the beauty and charm of the place would be gone.

The next day, Oriku took Ofune and Shigezō with her to look at the boat factory and the shoe factory from the river. So far she had assumed that the whole thing was a part of the nearby university boathouse, but that turned out to have been completely wrong. Three wooden boats under construction rested side by side on a supporting structure. The factory seemed to have been extended little by little, and before Oriku even noticed it, it had gotten quite large.

"So this big factory was here all the time!" she exclaimed.

Shigezō smiled wanly. "It was indeed. All of us knew about it."

"And behind the boat factory you can see the shoe factory. It's been growing too."

From the boat Oriku could see that the marshy ground was being filled in. Barges lay moored there—some still laden with earth—and a crowd of workers was putting the earth into place.

"Is the factory really to cover that whole area?"

"Apparently so. If it's to be that big, it'll come right up to us."

"How awful!"

"It certainly is."

With disappointment on their faces they watched the reedy marsh being filled in, till all three were reduced to silence. They were so angry that they rowed straight home again. Sanshi had been absolutely right. They were rushing the job forward, and dozens of workers were there to make sure it got done fast. With two new factories nearby, the Shigure Teahouse would have no more guests at all.

They disembarked and went to Oriku's room to discuss the situation. However, they could only sit there, staring at each other. Not one of them had anything to suggest. Oriku kept saying it was just too abominable, and she began to wonder aloud whether they couldn't apply to the government to put a stop to it; but of course that was out of the question. Since Sanshi knew someone from the boat factory, Oriku went to his place at Azuma Bridge two or three days later, like a drowning man grasping at a straw.

Sanshi had described the boat factory man as a friend when he and Oriku met under the cherry blossoms at dawn, so he might conceivably come up with a good idea. With this thought in mind Oriku entered the little establishment there on the right, just the other side of Azuma Bridge, down by the water next to the steamboat landing. It was early yet. The entrance consisted merely of a noren shop curtain and oiled paper shōji, but the place inside was all clean and neat, with plain wooden tables and long benches. At the back, behind a screen, was a small, private space. Somewhat embarrassed to be by herself, Oriku asked the young waitress whether the owner was there.

The girl said he was and went straight to the kitchen to fetch him, but the man who came out was a stout, bald fellow of about forty.

"I'm the owner," he said. "And who might you be?" His sloppy way of speaking sounded just like a cook.

Oriku's eyes widened in astonishment. "Um, *you're* the owner here?"

"The owner, yes, that's me." Then something seemed to occur to him. "Could you by any chance be a friend of the last owner—Sanshi, the samisen player?"

"That's right. This isn't his place anymore?"

"No, he sold it to me a couple of months ago."

"But why? I thought he was so keen on it."

"He's a musician, you know. It was just a sideline for him, and in the end it didn't do too well. Amateurs tend not to make much of a go of it in the restaurant trade." There was a touch of a sneer in his voice.

"Then where has Sanshi gone?"

"I couldn't say, I'm afraid. Since he's a musician, I suppose he's back at his old profession. Er, excuse me, I'm a bit short-handed." With this abrupt remark the fellow rushed back to his kitchen.

Discouraged as she had been when she reached Azuma Bridge, Oriku had no wish to go directly home now, with an even worse taste in her mouth. It hurt to think of Sanshi failing in business and going back to the samisen. Where could he be, and what kind of musical employment could he have found? He couldn't possibly be happy. Perhaps he had set himself up as a music teacher in some dismal backwater, where hardly anyone came to learn the now half-forgotten shinnai samisen traditions. The present owner had sounded scornful of him.

Oriku walked as far as the Kaminari Gate and, having glimpsed the lantern advertising Shinkyō's name, turned aimlessly into the alley leading to the Namiki Theater. She had not seen him since that time years ago, and she wondered whether he had ever started eating tempura soba again; certainly *she* had forgotten and ordered it several times. So much for the promises between men and women—not that they even matter.

It was still early, and a young warm-up performer was making a dreary job of the comic monologue "Mom and Dad." There were few people in the audience. Oriku groped her way through the dark to lean against a black pillar. The face of Sanshi, now once more a shinnai musician, floated into her mind.

She, too, had been an amateur when she opened her chazuke restaurant, and several people, including her adopted daughter Oito and her husband's sister Otsune, had been dead against it, but she had persevered nonetheless. That had been five years ago, and the memory only made Sanshi's plight more poignant. She had met him just once, but he had touched her somehow. The thought of him forlornly performing shinnai robbed her of any desire to listen to Shinkyō. Emerging into the now-dark alley she took a rickshaw back to Mukōjima. On the way she became aware of a growing feeling that Sanshi's fate distinctly concerned her as well. If they were going to build a factory on the land next to hers, then it was all over for the Shigure Teahouse. The place had no future.

The construction work progressed rapidly from that point. The fill was all in place, and mountains of building materials began arriving by boat. The pounding to firm up the earth of the site went on and on. Oriku frowned whenever she heard it, but the factory ignored her. At first Ofune complained volubly, but then as the days went by she gave in to resignation. She just watched forlornly as gloom engulfed the Shigure Teahouse.

When summer came the noise increased, and distinctly fewer guests came to enjoy the cool air of the river. The construction was obviously taking its toll.

As summer advanced, a big roof began poking up into view, and they got to work on a launching dock. The neighborhood was going downhill fast.

"You seem to be taking all this very calmly, Mistress Oriku!" Such was Ofune's response to Oriku's silence.

"What else can I do? Apparently the company that's building the boat factory is semiprivate and semipublic, and the government is behind the work. It wouldn't do any good to complain."

"If the government's behind it, then why not bring the matter up with Hayashida-sensei? He's such a good friend of our place, he might be able to do something if you asked him. I don't suppose he could make them stop, but perhaps he could get them to build a little further from our boundary, or something."

"Asking him to do that would just put him on the spot."

"Of course it would, but you might as well go ahead. There's nothing to lose, after all. He might be able to put in a word to make them a bit more careful. Maybe they could fix it so we couldn't see the roof, say, or the chimney." Now Ofune was excited. "I'm going to telephone his secretary," she said. "You've got to talk to him."

Oriku had given up, but not Ofune. She rang the Cabinet Secretary's residence. "Cabinet Secretary Hayashida is attending an important conference at the moment," the secretary replied, "and unfortunately it is likely to go on for some time, but he will give you ten minutes, if that will do. Please come to his residence."

"You see? He's willing to meet you. This is no time to be faint-hearted. This place is our life as well as yours, Mistress Oriku, and he says to be there tomorrow at three, so let's go. I'll come with you."

The following day at the appointed time they arrived at the Cabinet Secretary's Nagatachō residence, which dated from early Meiji. The drawing room was furnished with splendid chairs, but the two preferred to stand as they waited. In five minutes Hayashida-sensei entered the room. The usual smile was gone from his face, his mouth was set in a grim line, and, to Oriku he looked pale.

"We apologize for disturbing you this way." Ofune spoke first.

Hayashida neither nodded nor even looked them in the face. "I don't know what you want," he said, "but I'm not up to discussing it today. I must make an announcement of grave importance to the entire nation, and it's impossible for me to hear you out. I'm extremely sorry, but you'll have to come another day." His tone was severe, and his lips were trembling. He was so upset that he seemed an entirely different man from the one they knew.

"By all means. We had no idea this was so critical a moment. We can only apologize for having so thoughtlessly imposed upon you."

"Please forgive us. We will leave immediately."

Oriku and Ofune were thoroughly intimidated. Some momentous change was coming, and he had said he would have to announce it to the nation.

"For the time being I can tell no one anything. I expect the announcement to be in the papers tomorrow, so you can read about it then. I'm sorry, but that will have to be all for today."

He hurried away, and the two dejected women left again through the front door. The late July heat was stifling, and the perspiration began pouring from them as soon as they stepped onto the stone walk.

"He spoke of an important announcement to the nation," Ofune said as they descended the slope toward Toranomon. "What could it possibly be?"

"A new cabinet, perhaps?"

"But Prince Saionji's cabinet came in just last year!"

"Who knows what goes on in the world of politics, though? Cabinets often last only a year or so."

"But would he have looked like *that* if it was just a change of cabinet?"

"True enough. He certainly didn't look himself today, did he?"

They reached Toranomon and boarded a streetcar. To reach the Kaminari Gate they had only to change at Shinbashi. The July sun blazed unbearably while they waited.

"The streetcar just isn't coming, is it?"

"I wonder what the matter is. It certainly isn't coming."

"It's so hot standing here, perhaps we should have a beer somewhere nearby."

"Won't that make us sweat even more?"

"It's almost four o'clock, though. It's much cooler after four, and besides, I'm hungry."

"That's right, we never had time to eat lunch."

"Hashizen's just over there. Let's have a beer."

"You want tempura in this heat?"

"What's wrong with that? You lose your oil when it's hot, so it's good to eat oily things."

They stepped into Hashizen. Tempura, eel, or anything else would be fine as far they were concerned. What they really wanted when they plopped themselves down at the long table was cold beer.

Hashizen, right next to the bridge at Shinbashi, was a popular tempura restaurant. On either side of the narrow room were long planks that served as the dining tables. The menu was posted at the back, on a board that went all the way up to the ceiling. The two women ordered beer and shrimp tempura, and at last began to feel human again.

"Mm, it's so good!"

"Ah yes, cold beer! It's the only thing to drink at a time like this!"

They downed the deliciously cold, bitter brew.

"You know, Ofune. . ." The tone of Oriku's beginning seemed to bode no good. "I'm fed up with the business," she said.

"There you go again, being fainthearted."

"I'm not being fainthearted. I just don't have a good feeling about the future. To me, a factory going up at the end of my garden proves I'm out of luck. I go to Azuma Bridge to see Sanshi, and a new owner has taken over his place. We go to see Hayashida-sensei, and he can't even talk to us. Everything's going wrong. Not a single thing is coming out right. I can't help feeling the end has come for the Shigure Teahouse."

"You must be joking! Whatever may be going wrong has absolutely nothing to do with the restaurant! Why in the world must you sound so discouraged?"

"Well, I *am* discouraged. We haven't been making money lately, and I assume you know about the final accounting for the Cherry Blossom Bentō."

"That's Shigezō's fault. He upgraded the food without considering that the price of the ingredients had gone up."

"It's not just the bentō. I've had enough of the whole business. Last month we operated at a loss."

"What do you expect? Last month was the rainy season."

"We didn't lose money during *last* year's rainy season." Oriku finished her second glass of beer. She was becoming fed up with accurate accounts that showed a deficit.

"All we have to do is be more careful. And with costs going up, we'll just have to raise our prices."

"Confound it, I don't want to! If that's what it takes, I've a good mind to quit!"

"All right, Mistress Oriku, but you still won't find *me* quitting. I'll sort it out with Shigezō, and we'll take care of everything. All you need do is watch."

"Won't we have fewer guests, with a factory next door?"

"Our guests come to enjoy chazuke. What do *they* care if there's a factory, a prison, or whatnot, nearby? You'll only have to collect the profit. Just leave the rest to us. Everything will be fine."

Oriku said nothing. She had just begun to pour herself another glass of beer when a man sitting with his back against the wall on the other side of the room looked her way. His unlined robe of fine, white hemp was tied with a dark blue summer sash of Hakata-weave cloth. He had one knee up, and there was a bottle of beer on the plank table in front of him.

"Goodness me!" Oriku stared at him in amazement.

The man acknowledged her with an air of embarrassment, then lowered his eyes and said nothing.

"You're Sanshi, aren't you?" She moved immediately to get up.

Hearing her call his name, he murmured resignedly, "I apologize for imposing on you that time." Oriku could hardly hear him. Prevented by the presence of everyone else in the restaurant from addressing him loudly, she took her glass over to the other side and sat down across the table from him.

"Have you been here the whole time?"

"Yes."

"And you knew it when we came in?"

"Please don't reproach me. I was too embarrassed to hold my head up."

"You're so cold, Sanshi!"

"Well, I expect you know by now. I let someone else have my place at Azuma Bridge."

"Yes, I know. I went looking for you once the blossoms were over, and this entirely different man came out."

"He's a real cook. He hijacked me, in a manner of speaking. Such are the misfortunes of the amateur."

Bit by bit, Sanshi told her the story. Having lost confidence in his ability as a musician, he started up his little establishment. So far, so good. However, in his inexperience he left all the arrangements and the menu to a cook who began making a fool of him almost as soon as the place opened. As a result, he had failed almost immediately and had had to go back to playing the samisen. The long, sad tale corresponded more or less to what Oriku had imagined, but she keenly felt his misery at having his dream of spending the rest of his life at his little business broken, and at having to go back to the samisen.

"I'll go on ahead of you, Mistress Oriku, if you don't mind," Ofune said tactfully, rising to go. "I'd like to check on things at home." She nodded to Sanshi and left.

The pair quickly relaxed once she was gone. "Actually," Oriku began, "I'm thinking of giving up the Shigure Teahouse."

"But why? Aren't you doing extremely well?"

"I'm afraid not. They've begun building a factory at the end of the garden, just as you said they were going to."

"Sure enough!"

"I went to such trouble to make a pretty garden, and now the factory's going to ruin it. I'm so furious at the heartless way they're wrecking beautiful Mukōjima, I feel like escaping somewhere into the depths of the mountains."

"I don't blame you, but surely the new factory is no reason to quit."

"No, I just can't stand it. I refuse to live in a place with a view of factory chimneys. By the way, I see you have your samisen with you. Where are you headed from here?"

"Don't ask. It's just too embarrassing, being a hand-to-mouth shinnai musician."

"To give a lesson, perhaps?"

"No, I don't want to talk about it. Don't ask." He picked up his samisen case. "I'm working at a local music hall out there somewhere, twanging away and trying to get something out of this hopeless voice of mine."

"But that's *good*! You're doing fine if you can perform at a music hall! Where is it?"

"The July show is over, and next month I'm on tour. No one comes in the summer heat. The star of the tour will be Master Enshi, and there'll be shinnai, magic, and a comic Funny Faces show as well."

"I'll come with you and do the singing, as long as you play the samisen."

"Do you do shinnai, then, Mistress Oriku?"

"A little. Years ago I studied with Miyakodayū."

"Really? Miyakodayū? Then you're the real thing. It would be absolutely wonderful if you'd come with me, but I'm afraid I couldn't pay you a thing." He smiled wryly.

"All right, then how about coming to Mukōjima? You have your samisen. Give me some lessons! It'll come back to me when I actually do it."

"How many pieces did you learn?"

"Just a few. I used to be a brothel keeper's wife, so I studied all sorts of things. When I studied shinnai, I just learned the usual *Ranchō* and *Idahachi*—mainstays like that."

"If you feel like joining me, let's start rehearsing. The tour begins on the second of next month."

"Wonderful! Shinnai is perfect for when you're feeling down, like now."

It was settled. They left Hashizen and boarded the streetcar, carrying a box of tempura. Through the window they could see newsboys running about selling special-edition newspapers. Oriku hardly heard the little bells they were ringing, such was her pleasure at the thought of singing shinnai to Sanshi's samisen accompaniment. When they alighted at the Kaminari Gate and changed to rickshaws, however, they found more newsboys ringing more bells. It occurred to Oriku that the special editions might be about the grave announcement Hayashida-sensei had spoken of having to make to the nation. Meanwhile she reached Mukōjima just as the sun was setting, with Sanshi right behind her.

"Welcome back, Mistress Oriku! Did you see the special-edition news?" Ofune stood there with an extra in her hand.

"It's about the Cabinet, I suppose. It has nothing to do with us."

"No, you don't understand. Just read it."

Ofune handed her the flimsy sheet of paper. The big, black characters fairly leapt off the page: HIS MAJESTY CRITICALLY ILL. The Emperor

Meiji was all-powerful in those days, and the Imperial Household Ministry had published a bulletin describing his condition.

"This is what Hayashida-sensei meant, isn't it, when he spoke of a very grave development."

"That's right. The Emperor must really be very ill if the newspapers are putting out special editions."

They showed the paper to Sanshi. "Oh no, this is bad. This is no time for shinnai. I'll be going, then. I can't possibly play the samisen." He looked ready to leave on the spot.

"No, no, we're out in the country here, it's all right. You can't hear a thing outside. Anyway, please come in."

Oriku urged the reluctant Sanshi along to her own Paulownia annex. It was time for the evening guests to start arriving, but the whole place was silent. No doubt people would be more restrained now, what with the sudden news, and existing reservations would probably be canceled.

Oriku gave Ofune the box of tempura and had her bring them saké with the usual menu.

"I feel awful just thinking about it," she said, pouring him saké. "First I hear your place at Azuma Bridge belongs to someone else, and I start feeling more and more discouraged about the future of the Shigure Teahouse, and now it seems His Majesty the Emperor is ill. It's enough to make you feel the whole world's going wrong."

"I feel the same way. Everything I see, everything I hear offends me."

"Perhaps it's a warning that I should give up the Shigure Teahouse while I'm still ahead."

"No, there's no connection whatever. I'm so depressed, though, I'm ready for a few cups." He gulped them down one after another, meanwhile keeping his samisen case safely behind him.

Oriku drank with him. "No one outside will hear if you play the samisen in here," she said. "Please teach me *Ranchō*, at least."

"Personally, I'd love to, but we'll be arrested for disrespect if anyone out there hears us."

"There's no prohibition against music yet, though, and besides, I want to learn to sing it professionally. It's not as though we were just having a good time. I don't see why it should be disrespectful."

Oriku refused to give up. It seemed to her that art might save her from her misery, now that she no longer felt like keeping the restaurant going. If she could live off shinnai, or kiyomoto, or itchū, then she wanted to give them a serious try. She had taken plenty of lessons during her seven or eight years at Hashiba, thanks to the proprietor of the Silver Flower, and she was proud of her voice. She had studied everything except gidayū and nagauta, and since her husband had liked shinnai, she had received her introduction to it from Miyako-dayū. For herself she preferred the less elaborate itchū, but it had no appeal under the present circumstances. Shinnai struck her as just the thing, with everything going downhill this way. Sanshi reluctantly took out his samisen, and Oriku managed to find her old Shinnai scores in the chest where she kept such things. She wanted to start with *Ranchō* because it was familiar to everyone, even in the remotest village, and would therefore serve them well if they went traveling together. She was already thinking like an itinerant musician.

"All right, I'll just play with my fingers." Sanshi was still concerned.

"It's all right, I tell you! Shinnai and kiyomoto do nothing for me played that way. Please use the plectrum."

"It's all right?"

"I promise. Don't worry about it."

She spoke loudly enough that Sanshi finally relaxed, tuned his instrument, and began softly playing the prelude. A shinnai prelude is reliably affecting, no matter when you hear it. Oriku put herself in the right frame of mind while she listened. There on her score were the notations she had made in red well over a decade ago. The piece includes long exchanges between Omiya, the wife, and the courtesan Konoito, and the pathos of the two roles is difficult to convey when you have not done it for a long time. Under informal circumstances you can skip the dialogue and sing just the best parts, but not for a real performance. Sanshi's samisen rang out clear and true, as befitted someone trained in the Miyakoji tradition, and his plectrum yielded a brilliant clarity. His musicianship was beyond doubt.

Halfway through the score it became clear to Oriku that her dialogue lacked crispness and conviction. "It's no good!" she exclaimed. "The dialogue just won't go right when you haven't done it for so long."

"Not at all! You did beautifully. That's a well-trained voice you have."

"I've had a go at a lot of bits of this and that, but I spent very little time on shinnai. Tonight just have me do the highlight—just 'Fate meant us for each other.'"

"That's the hardest, though! Still, you'll be all right if we take it easy."

"Anyway, let's go over it properly. Tonight will be just to get my voice warmed up. I'm afraid I've forgotten most of it."

Sanshi retuned his instrument and played the key passage, while Oriku sang for all she was worth. The heart of a shinnai piece must be done with full voice, and *Ranchō* succeeds only if the delivery is kept fine and graceful. The piece as a whole is not that absorbing, but its key moments are lovely and widely appreciated, and it is a popular favorite. "Fate meant us for each other" is familiar to practically everyone around town.

Oriku turned her face to the ceiling, took a deep breath, and launched into a fine, old-style rendition of the song:

> *Fate meant us fo-o-r each other,*
> *for ete-e-ernity*
> *Ah, I am so happy now—*
> *that was how I felt,*
> *for we could fulfill our vows,*
> *stand up in the world,*
> *begin our own family,*
> *settle down at last,*
> *if only there were given us*
> *just a single day!*

It all had to be done without pausing for breath, and once it was over Oriku gasped with relief for air.

"Sorry! It's been so long, I just can't keep my voice going!"

"Don't worry, it was splendid! In the first place, your voice is amazing. A voice like yours is rare. No, I'm really impressed. I never imagined you'd be this good. You'll do fine, you'll do just fine." Samisen in hand, he praised Oriku's voice, insisting she had the perfect vocal equipment for shinnai.

"I'm completely out of practice, though. If there's hope, then let's go through the piece again."

"*Hope*? Nonsense! These days, there aren't even any professionals with a fine voice. Surely your voice is too pretty for itchū-bushi."

"Yes, it is. I used to have to keep it under such tight control, it was hard work."

"I can well imagine. It's a golden voice you have—that's no exaggeration. You're no amateur. You're right up there with the professionals. People would gladly pay money to hear you. If you performed at a music hall, Mistress Oriku, the place would sell out, I promise you that, and my stock as a samisen player would go up."

Sanshi was so carried away, he was sure Oriku would be a major artist. As usual, Ofune, Shigezō, and the maids had all gathered outside the room to listen. They dropped whatever they were doing and came to hear whenever Oriku began singing.

"Won't you go on a bit more?" Sanshi asked. "This is too good for just the two of us. Let's give the maids a chance to enjoy it as well."

"No, no, I want a few days' practice first. We can do it then, if you don't mind."

"You *will* do it, though?"

"Oh yes, certainly. I'll be happy to go on tour with you once I've got it right."

"All right, then I'll buckle down to work too."

He prepared once more to play. They did the highlight passage from *Idahachi*, as well as the "Urazato" scene, and as Oriku went on singing she regained increasing mastery of her voice. Strange to say, the more she did so, the more she became intoxicated by the shinnai ballad she was singing. The samisen accompaniment and the text itself, celebrating as they do the agonies of love, perfectly caught the mood of the two performers, who, as they played and sang, felt drunk as though on saké. Oriku and Sanshi both experienced themselves as the characters in the ballad, and the beautiful music swept them along—for Oriku, perhaps because of her exhilaration over the idea of quitting the restaurant. As for Sanshi, his failure in business and his sinking to the level of an itinerant musician had much in common with the hero's plight. Oriku outdid herself in the passage near the end of the closing "Urazato" scene:

> *At his waist, like any man,*
> *he wears a ready dagger*
> *that he now clamps in his teeth;*
> *then he steels himself*
> *stealthily to make his way,*
> *unseen, across the roofs . . .*

Sanshi's samisen, meanwhile, rang out with passionate clarity. They both had a wonderful time, and they remained drunk with pleasure after it was over.

"I'm so happy! To think my voice managed to do *that* for me!" Sanshi had just put down his instrument, and she leaned with all her weight onto his shoulder. "I love shinnai! I love it, I love it, I love it!" She threw her arms around the diminutive Sanshi's skinny shoulders and burst into tears.

The next day, the papers contained nothing but news of the Emperor's grave condition. There were photographs of people sitting on the gravel of the esplanade before the Imperial Palace, where they had gathered to pray for his recovery. All of Japan was plunged in grief. Guests stopped coming to the Shigure Teahouse, but Oriku went on practicing. She was determined to become a genuine artist, and Sanshi devoted himself enthusiastically to nurturing her talent. Both were already united by a love born of art and growing, thanks to their efforts, toward a fruition nurtured by art.

The second of August was the day appointed for the tour's departure. Sanshi remained ensconced till then in Oriku's room.

"So, are you ready to go on tour?"

"Absolutely. I don't know how I'll do, but I certainly mean to try."

Oriku was full of enthusiasm. Quite apart from whether or not she could really spend the rest of her life as an artist, she fully intended to enjoy traveling with Sanshi and perfecting her skill. She assumed that, if she left for a month, the size of the factory would be obvious by the time she got back, and the future of the Shigure Teahouse would be more or less clear. "I hope you don't mind if I'm away for a month," she said to Ofune. "I'm going to pretend I'm a strolling musician." Ofune saw straight through this story. She did not object, but she did not look pleased, either. Sanshi could leave all the arrangements to the advance party from the troupe, so that he only had to set off, unencumbered, when the time came, but Oriku had elaborate preparations to make. She had Sanshi help her put together the crested robe she would wear on the chanter's dais, and on 30 July she packed everything she needed into a large suitcase.

Then bells began ringing again to announce extra editions of the papers. These were no ordinary extras, however, for they announced Emperor Meiji's passing, and shock hushed the sound of voices all over Japan. The same extras announced a five-day prohibition against music and dance. All theaters and music halls, and all activities associated with the entertainment world, were forbidden. The planned provincial tour was of course out of the question. Even the Shigure Teahouse closed its front door and took down its shop curtain, while silence descended on the factory construction site. Oriku and Sanshi were stunned. Keyed up as they had been, they now felt utterly crushed.

"You mustn't give up the Shigure Teahouse," Sanshi remarked out of the blue. His Majesty's death seemed to have dashed their hopes, and, to him, Oriku's vacant expression hinted that the world had further changes in store.

Oriku had no reply, but Sanshi put his hands to the floor before her in dejected salutation. "I'll be going," he said. "I don't know what the future holds, but you, Oriku, please go on with your business. You have such a fine place, it would be a terrible shame just to let it fall to pieces."

Both looked glum as Sanshi began readying himself to go. No rickshaw would come today, though.

"If you're leaving, then let's have the boat take you down to Imado Bridge. It's no distance at all from there to the streetcar stop."

Oriku made no attempt to detain him. It was too late for that. The

Shigure Teahouse people all kept to their rooms, while Ofune never showed herself at all, apparently because they were angry with Oriku for lodging a shinnai musician. Oriku's plan was to have Old Tomé get the boat out and then see Sanshi off to Imado Bridge. No one accompanied them when they went down to the riverbank. They boarded the boat in acute awareness of the prevailing atmosphere behind them, and Tomé rowed briskly away. A little wind came up, raising ripples on the water, while the roof of the Shigure Teahouse receded into the distance.

"I suppose I'll never see you again," Sanshi said sadly. Oriku did not answer. She had little confidence in the future of the Shigure Teahouse, but the idea of living as a performing artist worried her a great deal.

"It's strange, the way we came together," Sanshi went on, "but I was very happy. I'll never be that happy again. Take good care of your restaurant and enjoy all the artistic skill you have. Business isn't much fun, is it. You've struck the right balance, though. It was perfect."

Oriku, too, felt the same sense of resignation that he was encouraging in himself as a way of overcoming sadness. She knew she would cry if she said anything, and she did not want him to see her tears, so she bit her lips and remained silent. This was even sadder.

The boat passed Kototoi and approached the Imado bank, aiming for the Takeya ferry boatman's hut.

"I won't look back when I'm out of the boat. I'll just walk away. Take care of yourself."

Sanshi lowered his eyes, and Oriku softly took his hand. No words came, but the warmth of their joined hands said everything.

The boat approached the landing stage, and Sanshi leapt lightly ashore. True to his word, he did not look back, but instead turned rapidly round the Hamakin corner of Yamanoyado Street. Oriku did not look back, either. She did not have to. While the boat took her back along the windy river, the image of the departing Sanshi lingered vividly, deep in her eyes.

Epilogue

The Shigure Teahouse survived until 1914. Then it disappeared, the land it stood on swallowed up by the shoe factory. Little is known about what happened to Oriku after that. Rumor had her returning to her birthplace in Kōzuke, but actually she went back to Hashiba, where she bought a house and quietly lived out the rest of her life. Her house escaped the fires of the Great Kanto Earthquake in 1923, and it was there that Shinkichi met her. She told him all her stories about the past, for in old age she was still a wonderful talker. She departed this world in 1935, at age seventy-one. Practically nobody knew her in her last years, and she died a solitary death. All in all, she came to life with the Shigure Teahouse and vanished with it. She was the quintessential Meiji woman.

Glossary

Mistress Oriku is fiction, and the real names mentioned in it only lend it an atmosphere of nostalgic plausibility. The identifications below should not be taken too seriously.

A Tight Game: *Godoro*, a rakugo story originally by the Osaka storyteller Katsura Bungo

Andō Tsuruo: A writer and theater critic, son of a gidayū chanter (1908–69)

Asagao nikki: Full title *Shō-utsushi Asagao-banashi*, a puppet play by Chikamatsu Tokusō, first performed in 1832

Ayasedayū: A name probably invented by the author

Azumabashi Theater: Azumabashi-tei, apparently a theater where gidayū chanting was performed alone, without puppets

Bandō Mitsugorō III: (1775–1831)

[Bandō] Mitsugorō: Mitsugorō VII (1882–1961); he took this name in 1906

Bandō Mitsunojō: Apparently an invented figure

[Bandō] Mitsunojō I: Apparently an invented figure

Bandō school: A line of Nihon buyō (Japanese-style dancing) masters

Benkei jōshi: A scene from the puppet play *Gosho-zakura Horikawa Youchi*, by Bunkōdō and Miyoshi Shōraku, first performed in 1737

Blossom-Viewing Broke: *Nagaya no hanami*, a rakugo story by Yanagiya Kosan IV (1888–1947)

bota-mochi: Balls of sweet azuki bean paste, plain or covered with soybean or sesame flour

Bunji: Katsura Bunji VI (1846–1911)

Bunraku: Katsura Bunraku IV (1838–94) or V (1865–1925); probably the latter, since he took the Bunraku name in 1897

chazuke: A favorite home-style dish, consisting of hot tea poured over a bowl of rice topped with any of a wide variety of foods

"Cradle, well-cradle . . .": This opening line echoes a poignant poem from episode 23 of *Ise monogatari* (tenth century), as translated in Royall Tyler, *Japanese Nō Dramas*, Penguin, 1992

Crane and Tortoise: *Tsurukame*, a nagauta piece by Kineya Rokuzaemon X (1800–1858), derived from the Noh play of the same title

Danjūrō: Ichikawa Danjūrō IX (1838–1903)

Danshirō: Ichikawa Ennosuke (1855–1922), a disciple of Bandō Mitsugorō IV. He assumed the name Ennosuke in 1890 and became Ichikawa Danshirō II in 1910

dodoitsu: A type of ballad in everyday language, usually on the theme of love, that became popular in Edo from about 1840 on

gull, red-footed: *Miyakodori*, literally "capital birds." Black-headed gull with red beak and legs

Enba: Enba II (1854–1918)

Enchō I: San'yūtei Enchō I (1839–1900), a major rakugo star who composed a large number of hit stories

Enkyō: San'yūtei (Tachibanaya) Enkyō (1865–1912)

Ennosuke: Ichikawa Ennosuke II (1888–1963), Danshirō's son; he took this name in 1910

Enshi: Presumably, the rakugo master Ryūtei Enshi II (1869–1935)

Enshō: Enshō IV (1846–1904)

En'u: (1860–1924)

Five in a Night: *Gonin mawashi*, a rakugo story about a courtesan and the five men she entertains in one night

Flattery: *Sejiya*, a rakugo story by Enchō

Fujima Kan'emon: Fujima Kan'emon II (1840–1925)

Funny Faces: *Hyakumensō*, a form of entertainment involving disguise and comic face transformations

Gappō: *Sesshū Gappō ga Tsuji*, a puppet play first performed in 1703

gidayū: A kind of narrative chanting, with samisen accompaniment, for the puppet (jōruri) theater, originated by Takemoto Gidayū

(1651–1714) in Osaka. Gidayū chanting was also widely performed and studied for itself, without puppets

hagi: *Lespedeza bicolor*, sometimes translated "bush clover." In Japan an emblem of autumn, when the plant's long, graceful fronds are covered with small, pink flowers

hanamichi: An elevated passageway leading through the audience from the back of a kabuki theater to the stage, used among other things for especially dramatic entrances and exits

Hayashida Kametarō: A successful Seiyūkai politician, born in Kumamoto. He also wrote books on the history of political parties in Japan (1863–1927)

His Master's Man: *Tomoyakko*, first performed in 1828 and a staple of the nagauta dance repertoire. A servant accompanies his samurai master to the gay quarter; slips away from him, lantern in hand; and puts on a brilliant dance display in the spirit of mimicking his master

Horikawa: From the full title, "Horikawa sarumawashi no dan," of the second act of *Chikagoro Kawara no Tatehiki*, first performed in Edo in 1782 as a dramatization of a double suicide that took place in Kyoto circa 1700. (The information about it in the text is partially wrong.) This second act alone remains popular in the modern repertoire. Oshun (from Gion, not Pontochō) has been sent home from her brothel because her lover, Denbei, has killed a samurai rival. Denbei then arrives to seek refuge with her family. For their mother's sake the monkey trainer Yojirō, her elder brother, tried to persuade Denbei to give his sister up. However, when he understands the depth of Denbei and Oshun's love, he allows the two to flee together, while he sings his monkey-trainer song

Ichikawa Chūsha: Ichikawa Chūsha VIII (1896–1971), Danshirō's third son

Ichikawa Danshirō: Ichikawa Ennosuke (1855–1922), a disciple of Bandō Mitsugorō IV; he took the name Ichikawa Ennosuke in 1890 and became Danshirō II in 1910

Ichikawa Kodayū: Danshirō's fifth son (1902–76)

Ichimura Uzaemon: Ichimura Uzaemon XV (1874–1945); he took the Uzaemon name in 1903

Ichizō: Kataoka Ichizō (1851–1906)

Idahachi: *Onoe Idahachi*, a mainstay of the Shinnai repertoire, first performed by Fujimatsu Tsurugadayū in 1747, and based on a failed love suicide that occurred in the same year

Ijūrō: Presumably Yoshimura Ijūrō V

Imoseyama: *Imoseyama Onna Teikin*, a puppet play by Chikamatsu Hanji and others, first performed in 1771 and subsequently adapted for kabuki. It became a major masterpiece in both repertoires. The perennially popular "Goten" (Palace) scene is from Act IV

itchū-bushi: A style of jōruri chanting originated by Miyakodayū Itchū in the early eighteenth century

Itō Hirobumi (1841–1909): The most distinguished statesman of Meiji Japan. The chief framer of Japan's first constitution (1889), he served four terms as prime minister

Izumi Kyōka: A major writer of the period (1873–1939); many of his plays were adapted for the stage

Kabuki-za: The great kabuki theater in the Ginza area of Tokyo

Kawabata Gyokushō: A nihonga (Japanese-style painting) artist (1842–1913)

Keiō Academy: Keiō Gijuku, which in 1910 became Keiō University

Kikugorō: Onoe Kikugorō V (1844–1903)

Kikugorō V: Onoe Kikugorō V (1844–1903)

kinpira-style burdock root: *Kinpira gobō*, thinly sliced burdock root fried in sesame oil, then boiled in soy sauce with sugar and red pepper

Kisen: A kabuki piece, part of a longer play entitled *Rokkasen sugata no irodori*, featuring both kiyomoto and nagauta music

kiyomoto: A type of kabuki music, including samisen and other instruments, originated in Edo by Kiyomoto Enjudayū (1777–1825)

"Koharu Puts Up Her Hair": *Koharu Kamiyui,* a song derived from the classic play *Shinjū Ten no Amijima;* the courtesan Koharu, about to commit suicide with her lover, Jihei, has her hair dressed

Koi Nyōbō Somewake Tazuna: A puppet play by Yoshida Kanshi and Miyoshi Shōraku, first performed in Osaka in 1751; it is an expansion and revision of the earlier play *Tanba no Yosaku Matsu Yo no Komuro-bushi,* by Chikamatsu Monzaemon

Kototoi: "Kototoi" apparently refers to the location of the landing stage before the Kototoi Dango shop, which still exists. The name alludes to a poignant moment in the Noh play *Sumidagawa*— a moment itself derived from an episode in *Ise monogatari* (tenth century)

Kototoi dango: Round balls consisting mainly of rice flour dough, coated or flavored with various ingredients

kyōgen: The comic theater of medieval times

Matsumoto Komazō: Kōshirō VII (1870–1949), Fujima Kan'emon's adopted son, who took the name Kōshirō in 1911

Meiji: 1868–1912, the years covered by the reign of Emperor Meiji

Mind's Eye: *Shingan*, a rakugo story adapted by Katsura Bunraku from an original by Enchō

Miyako Itchū: Miyakodayū Itchū, the head (iemoto) of itchū-bushi. This one may be Itchū X (1868–1928)

Miyakodayū: A master, probably imaginary, in the lineage of Miyakoji

Miyakoji Bungonojō (? –1740), the founder of a style of jōruri chanting known as Bungo-bushi

mokkoku: *Ternstroemia japonica*, an evergreen tree with small white flowers and red berries

Mom and Dad: *Tarachine*, a rakugo story heavily reliant on Chinese-style puns

Mukōjima: An industrial area of Tokyo, along the Sumida River in Sumida-ku, that offered great natural beauty in Meiji times and before

nagauta: A form of song prominent in kabuki and often performed in concerts. It developed mainly in Edo as kabuki dance music. Apart from the singers, the nagauta orchestra consists of several samisen, as well as various drums and flutes

Natsumatsuri: Natsumatsuri Naniwa Kagami, a puppet play by Namiki Senryū and others, first performed in 1745 and later adapted to kabuki. Its hero is Danshichi

Nozaki: Act 1, Scene 2 of *Shinpan Utazaimon*, a puppet play by Chikamatsu Hanji, first performed in 1780

oden: Konnyaku, daikon radish, pounded fishcake (hanpen), kamaboko fish paste, thick fried tofu, etcetera, boiled for a long time in diluted soy sauce; mainly a winter dish

Old Bones: *Nozarashi*, about a man who pours saké over some old bones, and the ghost of the beauty they belonged to comes to spend the night with him in thanks. His neighbor tries the same thing, with incongruously comic results

Ōnarikomaya: Probably Nakamura Ganjirō I (1860–1935)

Pale Blue Cotton: *Hanairo momen*, a Kamigata rakugo story

[The] Peony Lantern: Botandōrō, a ghost story by Enchō

pipe: *Kiseru*, a long-stemmed tobacco pipe with small, one-puff bowl, enjoyed by men and women alike

rakugo: A form of comic monologue originating in the late seventeenth century and still alive on television today

Ranchō: A mainstay of the Shinnai repertoire, composed by Tsuruga Wakasanojō (1717–86)

rin: old form of currency equivalent to one-tenth of a sen

rolled egg: *Tamago-yaki*, egg cooked in a thin layer, then rolled

Ryūshi: Shunpūtei Ryūshi III (1852–1900)

"Saké Shop Scene," the: From the play *Hadesugata Onna Maiginu*, first presented on the puppet (jōruri) stage in 1772

sakura cake: *Sakuramochi*, flat wheat flour cake, crêpe-shaped, wrapped around sweet bean paste

samisen: A three-stringed instrument that became popular in the seventeenth century and permeated Japanese music thereafter

Sanemori: A medieval warrior who figures in the kabuki play *Genpei Nunobiki no Taki*

sanosa: A type of ballad that became popular in Tokyo in 1897

Seiyūkai: "The Friends of Constitutional Government Party," founded by Itō Hirobumi in 1900 and prominent from then until 1940

sen: old form of currency equivalent to one one-thousandth of a yen

Sen no Rikyū: The creator of the tea ceremony (1522–91)

shigure clams: Clams boiled down in tamari soy sauce and flavored with pepper and ginger

shijimi clams: *Corbicula fluminea*, a small freshwater shellfish

shinnai: A style of dramatically sentimental ballad singing derived from gidayū chanting. Its height of popularity occurred in the late eighteenth century, and it survived into the early twentieth

Shiobara Tasuke: *Shiobara Tasuke Ichidai Ki*, a rakugo story by San'yūtei Enchō. Based on the life of Shiobara Tasuke (1743–1816), from Numata in Kōzuke (Gunma-ken). After being performed in 1891 for Emperor Meiji, the story was adopted into elementary school moral training textbooks. "Ao no wakare" was successfully staged as a kabuki play in 1892 by Onoe Kikugorō V, with a script by Kawatake Shinshichi III

shiso-maki: *Umeboshi* or sweetened *miso* wrapped in salted *shiso* leaves

Showa: 1926–89, the years covered by the reign of Emperor Showa (Hirohito)

suteteko: In 1880 San'yūtei En'yū III (1849–1907) danced this dance at the theater, and it became a fad

Taikōki: Act Ten of *Ehon Taikōki*, a puppet play by Chikamatsu Yanagi and others, first performed in 1799

Taisho: 1912–26, the years covered by the reign of Emperor Taisho

Takanawa school: The Takanawa school of Kiyomoto, associated at the time with Enjudayū IV

Takayama Hikokurō: An eccentrically intense devotee of the emperor (1747–93)

takuan: Dried daikon (giant radish), pickled with salt and rice bran

Tanabe Mitsumasa: Apparently an invented character

tempura soba: Soba noodles in a shoyu-based broth, topped with shrimp and vegetables that have been battered and deep-fried

tokiwazu: *Tokiwazu-bushi*, a type of kabuki music with samisen accompaniment, derived from jōruri chanting. It descends from Miyakoji Bungonojō (?–1740) and his disciple Mojidayū (1709–81)

tonkatsu: Deep-fried pork cutlet

Tsubamedayū: An early name taken by the chanter now formally known as Toyotake Yamashiro no Shōjō (1878–1967). He assumed the name Kotsubodayū in 1909 and his final, imperially conferred title in 1947

Tsudayū: Approximately, Takemoto Tsudayū II (1839–1912)

Tsurionna: In kabuki, a tokiwazu dance piece by Kawatake Mokuami

(1816–1893), derived from the medieval kyōgen play of the same title

Utaemon: Nakamura Utaemon V (1865–1940)

utazawa: A kind of popular song, slow and graceful, suitable for singing at parties

Utsubozaru: In kabuki, a tokiwazu dance drama derived from the medieval kyōgen play of the same title

Uzaemon: Ichimura Uzaemon V (1874–1945)

Yasuna: A kabuki dance piece in the kiyomoto repertoire, first performed in 1818

Yoshiwara: A major entertainment ("red light") district, enclosed by a moat and walls, in what is now the Senzoku area of Taitō-ku, Tokyo

"Yudono Scene," the: The Bathhouse Scene in the play *Kiwametsuki Banzui Chōbei*

About the Author

MATSUTARO KAWAGUCHI (1899–1985), one of Japan's most enduringly popular contemporary writers and filmmakers, began his writing career while working for a literary publishing company. He soon won the Naoki Prize, and his work gained wide popularity; his plays and novels garnered him many literary accolades, including the Yoshikawa Eiji Prize for *Shigurejaya Oriku* (*Mistress Oriku*). Kawaguchi's novels, many of which were adapted to film, often evoke the popular arts and entertainment world of old Tokyo.

About the Translator

ROYALL TYLER has a B.A. in Far Eastern Languages from Harvard, and an M.A. in Japanese History and Ph.D. in Japanese literature from Columbia University. He has taught Japanese language and culture at numerous universities, including Ohio State University, the University of Wisconsin, the University of Oslo, and the Australian National University. His previous works include *Japanese Noh Dramas* (Penguin), *The Miracles of the Kasuga Deity* (Columbia University Press), and *The Tale of Genji* (Penguin).